'Fire!'

Drinkwater felt the rush of a passing ball and gasped involuntarily as it spun him around and drew the air from his lungs. One of the helmsmen took the full impact of a round-shot, his shoulder reduced to a bloody pulp as he too swung round and was thrown against the mizen-rail so that his brains were mercifully dashed out at the same fatal moment.

As Drinkwater recovered his balance, a small calibre shot shattered his left arm. The blow struck him with such violence his teeth shut with a painful, head-jarring snap and a second later he felt the surge of pain, which made him gasp as his head swam. For a moment he stood swaying uncertainly, submitting to an overwhelming desire to lie down and to give up. What the hell did it matter? What the hell did any of it matter . . . ?

Also by Richard Woodman:

THE SHADOW
OF THE EAGLE

Richard Woodman

WARNER BOOKS

A *Warner* Book

First published in Great Britain
in 1997 by John Murray (Publishers) Ltd
This edition published by Warner Books in 1998

A CIP catalogue record for this book
is available from the British Library.

ISBN 0 7515 2051 9

Typeset by Hewer Text Composition Services, Edinburgh
Printed and bound in Great Britain by Clays Ltd, St Ives plc

Warner Books
A Division of
Little, Brown and Company (UK)
Brettenham House
Lancaster Place
London WC2E 7EN

For
Gail Pirkis
with many thanks

Contents

PART THREE: CAGING THE EAGLE

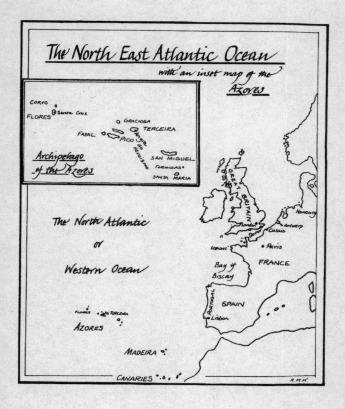

The North East Atlantic Ocean

with an inset map of the *Azores*

Archipelago of the Azores

CORVO
FLORES · Santa Cruz
GRACIOSA
TERCEIRA
FAYAL · PICO
SAN MIGUEL
FORMIGAS
SANTA MARIA

The North Atlantic

or

Western Ocean

FLORES · TERCEIRA
AZORES

MADEIRA

CANARIES

GREAT BRITAIN
Hamburg
London
Antwerp
Dover Calais
Ushant · Paris
FRANCE
Bay of Biscay
PORTUGAL
SPAIN
Lisbon

R.M.H.

PART ONE

A Whisper in the Wind

'Above all, gentlemen, beware of zeal.'
TALLEYRAND, PRINCE OF BENEVENTO

'Where in the name of the devil, is Montholon?'

The tall officer, wearing the jack-boots and undress uniform of the Horse Grenadiers of the Imperial Guard turned from the overmantel and addressed the newcomer, a young captain of hussars whose lank hair hung in old-fashioned plaits about his fierce, moustachioed features.

'Delaborde, where the hell have you been?' added a colonel of hussars in the sky-blue overalls and brown tunic of the 2nd Regiment, staring round the wing of a shabby chair in which he was seated, puffing at a long-stemmed clay pipe.

'Where *is* Montholon?' the horse grenadier repeated.

'Let the poor devil speak.' The fourth occupant of the room commanded. He was dark of feature, his face recessed in the high collar of his plain blue coat, and he had been sitting in the window, quietly reading, while the impatient cavalry officers fussed and fumed.

'Well, Delaborde, you heard what Admiral Lejeune said . . .'

'Colonel Montholon sent me to ask you to wait, gentlemen. He apologizes for keeping you all, but he is not yet free to join us.'

'Why not?' asked the horse grenadier.

'He is waiting upon Talleyrand . . .'

'That pig . . .' A frisson of contempt, mixed with apprehension, seemed to move through the group of officers in the dingy room, enhancing their air of conspiracy.

'It is ironic that it should come to this,' said the colonel of hussars, scratching at the pale weal of a long sabre scar running over the bridge of his nose and down his left cheek. 'Pour yourself a glass Delaborde,' he said, resuming his contemplation of the heavy curls of tobacco smoke that rose from the yellowed bowl of his pipe.

An air of heavy, silent gloom settled on the waiting men, disturbed only by the faint chink of bottle on glass rim and the gurgle of Delaborde's wine. After a few moments Delaborde, prompted by the wine uncoiling in his empty belly, spoke again.

'I am confident Colonel Montholon has the information we want.'

'You mean his sister has the information we want,' sneered the horse grenadier, throwing himself into a spindly chair that stood beside a small, pine table and thrusting out his huge jack-boots so that the rowels of his spurs dug into the meagre square of carpet. The colonel of hussars turned from the wraiths of pipe-smoke and glared at him.

'You may have enjoyed better quarters in the guard,

4

Gaston, but be pleased to respect my landlady's property. This is a palace for a light cavalryman.'

'You aren't thinking of staying,' the horse grenadier remarked sarcastically.

'It looks as though we might have to. Besides it is Paris . . . True I had more princely quarters in Moscow, but they were less congenial . . .'

'For God's sake where the hell *is* Montholon?'

'Delaborde has already told you, Gaston. Now hold your tongue, there's a good man.'

Gaston Duroc expelled his breath in a long and contemptuous exhalation. 'I do not like waiting at the behest of a turd in silk stockings . . .'

'That is no way to refer to the head of the provisional government of France, Gaston,' the colonel of hussars reproved Duroc with a chuckle. 'Talleyrand is not the author of all our misfortunes, merely an agent of destiny. It is we who are going to change that, and if it means waiting until the turd has finished fucking Montholon's sister, then so be it.' Colonel Marbet resumed his pipe.

'Very philosophical, Marbet,' remarked the admiral, looking over his book at Duroc. 'Why don't you join Delaborde in a glass? It seems to have had a good effect upon him.'

They all looked at the young hussar. He had slumped on a carpet-covered chest which stood in a corner of the room, leant his elbow on his shako, and drifted into a doze, the wine glass leaning from his slack fingers.

'Poor devil's hardly had any sleep for a week,' said Marbet, 'he's been escorting Caulaincourt back and forth to Bondy to negotiate with the Tsar. I daresay while

5

Caulaincourt received every courtesy, poor Delaborde was left to sit on his horse.'

Duroc grunted and filled a glass, then the company relapsed again into silence, all of them recalling the tempestuous events of the last few days. Caulaincourt's diplomatic shuttle between the Tsar at the head of the ring of allied armies closing upon Paris, and the beleaguered Emperor of the French at Fontainebleau, had resulted in the allied demand that Napoleon must surrender. A few days earlier, the French senate had cravenly blamed all of France's misfortunes upon the Emperor whom they had formerly fawned upon. Thereafter, Napoleon had abdicated in favour of his young son, but the imperial line was doomed. The British government dug King Louis XVIII out of his comfortable lodgings in Buckinghamshire and prepared to place him on the throne of his fathers. Alone among the crowned heads of Europe who now bayed for the restoration of legitimate monarchy in France, he had never treated with the man they all regarded as a usurper.

To the conspirators in Colonel Marbet's lodgings, the usurper was the elected leader of their country, and the rumours that he had attempted to poison himself gave their intentions a greater urgency.

'Someone's coming!' Duroc's remark galvanized them all. He was on his feet in an instant; Delaborde woke with a start and dropped the glass, caught it on his boot from where it rolled unbroken onto the floor. Colonel Marbet removed the pipe from his mouth and rose slowly, turning in anticipation to the door, while Rear-Admiral Lejeune merely lowered his book.

6

Colonel Montholon threw open the door and was greeted by the stares of the four men.

'Well?' demanded Duroc.

Montholon closed the door behind him.

'Were you followed?' asked Lejeune.

'I don't think so,' said Montholon.

'Well, where is it to be?' Duroc pressed, fuming with impatience.

'Is the Emperor fit to travel?'

'He'll have to travel, whether he likes it or not,' snarled Duroc. 'The point is where to? You do know, don't you?' The tall man turned on Montholon, 'Or have we got to hang about while your sister . . .'

'Hold your tongue, Duroc!' snapped Lejeune, closing his book, standing up and stepping up to Montholon to place a consoling hand upon his shoulder. 'Take no notice of Gaston, Étienne, he's a boor.'

Duroc grunted again and poured another glass. He also filled a second and handed it to Montholon. 'No offence,' he grumbled.

'He's just a big-booted bastard,' Marbet added genially, smiling conciliatorily, his eyes on Montholon. 'Well, Étienne?'

'It's to be the Azores, gentlemen,' Montholon said, then raised the glass to his lips.

There was a sigh of collective relief, then Lejeune, as though finding the news too good, asked Montholon, 'So it is not to be Elba?'

Montholon shook his handsome head. 'No. I am told there has been much debate. The bastards cannot agree . . .'

'What of the Tsar?' Lejeune pressed.

'He consents. Absolutely,' Montholon replied.

But Lejeune's caution had communicated itself to Duroc. 'He's a damned weathercock. Let us hope he doesn't change his mind.'

Montholon shook his head again. 'No; apparently Talleyrand's stratagem was too seductive.'

'He'd be a damned fool not to consent,' remarked Marbet, 'and your sister had this from Talleyrand himself, eh?'

'Yes,' Montholon nodded, 'the source is impeccable.'

Duroc snorted derisively. 'The source is peccant, you mean . . .'

Montholon's eyes flashed and his hand moved to his sword hilt. 'You've no right . . .!'

'Gentlemen, please!' Lejeune snapped and rose smartly, extinguishing the quarrel. 'I will not tolerate such childish behaviour.'

'Well, Montholon's news settles matters,' added Marbet, recalling them to their duty.

The officers sighed, their strained features relaxed and Marbet ordered Delaborde to refill all their glasses, then turned to Lejeune.

'And your ships, my Admiral . . .?'

'Are ready. They can sail the instant they receive word.'

'And the Azores . . .?'

'The Azores?' repeated Lejeune, a gleam of satisfaction lighting his curiously dark eyes, 'They are perfect!'

Marbet snatched up his glass: 'To the new enterprise!'

'Damnation to the English!'

'Long live the Emperor!'

8

The Company of Kings

'A pretty sight, sir.'

Captain Nathaniel Drinkwater lowered the glass and looked at the suave young lieutenant resplendent in the blue, white and gilt of full dress, his left fist hitched affectedly on the hilt of his hanger.

'Indeed, Mr Marlowe, very pretty.' Drinkwater replaced the glass to his eye and steadied the long barrel of the telescope against the after starboard mizen backstay.

'Redolent of the blessings of peace,' Marlowe went on.

'Very redolent,' agreed his commander from the corner of his mouth.

Marlowe regarded the rather quaint figure. They were of a height, but there the resemblance ended. Against his own innate polish, Marlowe thought Captain Drinkwater something of a tarpaulin. True, his uniform glittered in the late April sunshine with as much pomp as Lieutenant Marlowe's own, and Captain Drinkwater did indeed sport the double bullion epaulettes of a

9

senior post-captain, but judging by the way they sat upon his shoulders, he looked a little hunchbacked. As for the old-fashioned queue, well, quaint was not the word for it. It was like an old mare's braided tail, done up for a mid-summer horse fair! The irreverent thought caused him to splutter with a half-suppressed laugh. It sounded like a sneeze.

'God bless you, Mr Marlowe.' The glass remained steadfastly horizontal. ''Tis the sun upon the water and all these gilded folderols I expect.'

Drinkwater swung his glass and raked the accompanying ships. To starboard His Britannic Majesty's ship-rigged yacht *Royal Sovereign* drove along under her topsails and a jib. She was ablaze with gilt gingerbread work and gaudy with silken banners. Aloft she bore the fouled anchor of Admiralty at the fore, the Union flag at her mizen with a huge red ensign at her peak, but at her main truck flew the white oriflamme of the Bourbons, its field resplendent with golden lilies. It denoted the presence on board of King Louis XVIII of France, on passage to his restoration as His Most Christian Majesty. Accompanying the king was a suite which included the Prince de Condé, the Duc de Bourbon and the bitter-featured Duchesse d'Angoulême, the Orphan of the Temple, sole surviving child of the guillotined Louis XVI and Queen Marie Antoinette.

Beyond the *Royal Sovereign*, aboard the huge three-decked, first-rate *Impregnable*, flew the standard of Prince William Henry, Duke of Clarence and third son of King George III. As admiral-of-the-fleet, an appointment the prince had held since 1811, he was carrying out this ceremonial duty of escort as an act of political expediency by the British government. He had been removed from the frigate *Andromeda* in 1789, and had not served at sea since then, despite constant petitioning to the Admiralty. Notwithstanding the elevation of his birth, Their Lordships were deaf to his pleading, for he had commanded *Andromeda* with such unnecessary severity that he had earned the Admiralty's disapproval.

As a sop to His Royal Highness's vanity for this short, but auspicious command, His Majesty's Frigate *Andromeda*, lately returned from Norwegian waters with a prize of the Danish frigate *Odin*, was assigned to the Royal Squadron.

Other ships in company were the British frigate *Jason* and the *Polonais*, lately a French 'national frigate', but now sporting the white standard of the restored House of Bourbon, together with a pair of Russian frigates and the cutter-rigged yacht of the Trinity House.

Having scanned this impressive group of allied ships, Drinkwater closed his glass with a snap and turned on his heel, almost knocking Lieutenant Marlowe off his feet.

'God's bones, man . . .!'

'I beg pardon, sir.'

'Have you nothing better to do than hang at my elbow?'

'I was awaiting your orders, sir?'

'Keep an eye on the flagship, then. I imagine the prince will want some evolutions performed before we arrive at Calais.'

The warning was a product of Drinkwater's brief encounter with His Royal Highness and his flag-captain the previous afternoon, when he had joined the squadron off Dover and had reported aboard the *Impregnable*.

11

The ships had been lying at anchor, awaiting the arrival of King Louis and his entourage from London, whither they had been summoned from Hartwell, a seat of the Duke of Buckingham which had been loaned to the exiled French court. The decision to include *Andromeda* had been taken late at the Admiralty, a result of the interest the prince had taken in the frigate's return from Norway with her Danish prize.

Although his ship was about to pay off at Chatham, Drinkwater had been commanded to remain in commission: His Royal Highness had specifically asked for the 'gallant little' *Andromeda* to be assigned to his fleeting command. Their Lordships had graciously acquiesced and a ridiculous sum of money, sufficient to have fitted out two or three frigates during the late war, had been swiftly squandered on refitting and repainting her. Drinkwater, hurrying down to Chatham, had found the preparations in hand aboard his ship to be quite obscene.

'Good God, Mr Birkbeck,' he had said to the master, 'had I had one quarter of this co-operation from this damned dockyard when I was fitting out the *Virago*, or the *Patrician*, I could have saved myself much anxiety and my people great inconvenience. Why in Heaven's name do they make such a fuss of this business now, eh? I mean where's the sense in it?'

'I imagine the Commissioner sees more profit in pleasing a prince than a post-captain, sir,' Birkbeck remarked drily, and Drinkwater recalled Birkbeck's desire for a dockyard post.

Drinkwater had grunted his agreement. 'Well, it's a damned iniquity.'

''Tis victory, sir, victory.'

12

He found himself muttering the word now, and chid himself for the crazy habit which he deplored as a concomitant of age and, who knew, perhaps infirmity? He recalled, too, the pleasure with which the prince greeted his arrival off Dover. True, His Royal Highness had asked nothing about Nathaniel Drinkwater, scarcely acknowledging him as the victor in the action with the *Odin*, but had continually made remarks about the frigate herself, turning to the suite of officers in attendance, as though he sought their good opinion.

'Who are your officers, Captain?'

Drinkwater had named them, starting with his first lieutenant, 'Frederic Marlowe, sir.'

'Ah yes, I know the fella!' The prince had seized chirpily upon the name. 'Son of Sir Quentin who sits for a pocket borough somewhere in the west country.'

'Ixford, sir, in the county of Somerset,' said a lieutenant helpfully, stepping forward with a sycophantic obeisance of his head.

'Indeed, indeed. Somerset, what . . .'

Only Birkbeck the master and the second lieutenant, Frey, had been in the fight in the Vikkenfiord, and the prince had heard of neither. Drinkwater rather formed the impression that His Royal Highness thought both Marlowe and Lieutenant Ashton, who was known to one of the prince's suite, had both covered themselves with glory in the capture of the *Odin*.

Perhaps it had been sour grapes on his, Drinkwater's part, perhaps it had galled him to be so ignored. He had said as much to the *Impregnable*'s flag-captain Henry Blackwood. Years earlier, in September 1805, it

13

had been Blackwood in the frigate *Euryalus*, who had relieved Drinkwater in the *Antigone*, from the inshore post off Cadiz. A letter in Blackwood's own hand had ordered Drinkwater into Gibraltar and led ultimately to his capture and presence aboard the enemy flagship at Trafalgar.*

'He is a harmless enough fellow,' Blackwood said charitably. 'When he was a midshipman, they used to call him "Pineapple Poll" on account of the shape of his head. Sometimes I'm damned if I think he is capable of a sensible thought, but then he'll surprise you with a shrewd remark and you wonder if he ain't fooling you all the time. The trouble is nobody says "boo" to him and he loves the sound of his own voice. He should have been given something useful to do instead of kicking his heels at Bushy Park with La Belle Jordan. He daren't bungle this little adventure, but at the same time regards it as beneath his real dignity.' Blackwood concluded with a chuckle.

'That must make life difficult for you,' Drinkwater had sympathized.

Blackwood shrugged and smiled. 'Oh, it won't last long. The poor devil hasn't been to sea for so long he scarce knows what to do, but when he makes his mind up to do something, he thinks he's a second Nelson.' Blackwood had laughed again, his face a curious mixture of exasperation and amusement.

Next morning, the boats of the squadron, each commanded by a lieutenant, had brought off King Louis and his suite from Dover. The reverberations of the

* See *1805*

14

saluting cannon had bounced off the white cliffs and the ramparts of the grey castle as flame and clouds of smoke broke from the sides of the allied men-of-war. Simultaneously, the ramparts themselves had sparkled with the fire from a battery of huge 42-pounders, so that the thump and echo of their concussion danced in diminuendo between the wooden sides of the assembled ships. Bunting had fluttered gaily in the light breeze, augmented by the huge white standard which rose to the main truck of the *Royal Sovereign* as the king boarded her. Of imperturbable dignity, King Louis was of vast bulk and still suffering from an attack of gout. Too fat to climb the side, he had been hoisted aboard in a canvas sling, followed by the Duchesse d'Angoulême and other ladies. Meanwhile the seamen in the adjacent ships had manned the yards and cheered lustily, though more at the prospect of shortly being paid off, Drinkwater had suspected, than of respect for the royal personage.

That was undoubtedly true of his own men; what of the French aboard the *Polonais*? After a generation of ferment and opportunity, what were their private feelings? Perhaps they would accept the return of the Bourbon tyranny as the price for peace. As for the Russians, well, who knew what the Russians thought?

The thin rattle of snare drums and the braying of trumpets had floated over the water as the echoes of the guns died away. From the quarterdeck of *Andromeda* the impression given at a distance was of a seething, glittering ants' nest, and Drinkwater had sensed a mood of envy suffusing his own young officers, as though their own presence on the distant yacht would have guaranteed their individual ambitions.

As for himself, was it age that made him relieved that

15

he had not had to pander to the king and his court? He had caught the eye of Lieutenant Frey, the only one of his commissioned officers with whom he had formerly served, and who had recently endured a court-martial from which he had been honourably acquitted. Perhaps the rueful look on Frey's face had spoken for all the foiled aspirations of his young peers; the embarkation of the dropsical and gouty monarch marked the end of the war and thus terminated the gruesome opportunities war presented to them; perhaps, on the other hand, the sensitive Frey was regretting his late commander, James Quilhampton, could not share this moment. The thought pricked Drinkwater with so sharp a pang of conscience that something of it must have shown on his face, for Frey had crossed the deck smartly.

'Are you all right, sir?'

'Yes, perfectly, thank you, Mr Frey,' Drinkwater had said as Marlowe and Ashton turned at the sudden movement. Dizzily, Drinkwater waved aside their concern.

'I thought for a moment, sir,' Frey had observed, lowering his voice, 'you were unwell.'

'No, no.' Drinkwater had smiled at Frey. 'I thought of Mr Q, Frey, and wished he were here to share this moment with us.'

Drinkwater had regretted his confidence the instant he had uttered it, for the shadow had passed over Frey too, and he had shivered, as if it had suddenly turned cold. 'Amen to that, sir.'

For a moment both men had thought of the cutter *Kestrel,* the action she had fought off Norway, and the death of Lieutenant James Quilhampton. It had been the abandonment of her battered hulk for which Frey, as senior surviving officer, had stood trial.

16

'Come,' Drinkwater had remarked encouragingly, 'let us not debar ourselves from some pleasure on this momentous occasion.'

'I think we have already survived the momentous occasions,' Frey said quietly, his eyes abstracted. 'This has an air of hollow triumph.'

Drinkwater had been moved by this perceptive remark, but his private emotions were cut short by Marlowe's sudden comment that a signal was being run up the *Impregnable*'s flag halliards and Birkbeck the master had then hove alongside him, muttering presumptuously that it was the signal to weigh.

Now, in the late afternoon of 24 April, they were well within sight of Calais. To the southward the chalk lump of Cap Gris Nez jutted against the sky; closer the gentler, rounder and more pallid Cap Blanc Nez marked the point at which the French coast turned east, becoming flat and, apart from the church steeples and towers, featureless as it stretched away towards Dunquerque and the distant Netherlands. The little fishing village of Sangatte was almost abeam as the squadron breasted the first of the ebb tide and carried the breeze which had freshed during the day. An hour, an hour and a half at the most, would see them bringing up to their anchors in Calais Road. Drinkwater examined the roadstead ahead of them, then lowered his glass; he looked once more at the irregular formation of the squadron. It was, as Marlowe had said, a pretty sight.

'Flag's signalling, sir . . .'

Drinkwater's attention was diverted by the necessity of obeying the signals of His Royal Highness. As they came up towards Calais, the cannon of the squadron boomed out in yet another round of salutes, impressing upon the fishermen and townsfolk that the dangerous days of republican experiment and alternative, bourgeois monarchy, were dead.

'Sir, may I formally present Captain Drinkwater?'

Blackwood's introduction had an ironic content, since he had met the Duke of Clarence the previous afternoon, but the scene in the great cabin was stiff with formality and Drinkwater made his obeisance with a well-footed bow. Apart from the *Jason*'s captain, he was the last of the allied commanders to be presented. The prince appeared to notice him as an individual for the first time. Drinkwater was some four years the prince's senior, his long grey-brown hair clubbed at the nape of his neck, the scarred cheek and faint blue powder burns on the lean face with its high forehead marking him as a seasoned officer.

This seemed to surprise Prince William Henry, whose genial, full-lipped and rubicund, pop-eyed features broke into an affable grin as he studied the taller post-captain.

'Well Drinkwater,' he almost shouted, 'what d'ye think of *Andromeda*?'

'She's a fine ship for her class, sir,' Drinkwater remarked.

'She's good enough to have taken the *Odin*, ain't she, eh what?'

'Indeed, sir . . .'

'Drinkwater . . . Drinkwater . . . Ah-hah! I have it! Ain't you the fellow that took a Russian seventy-four in the Pacific?'

'Captain Drinkwater makes a habit of taking superior

ships, sir,' Blackwood put in, bending to the royal ear and lowering his voice, 'but it might be tactless to mention it this evening sir.'

'Of course, of course,' boomed the prince, 'I recall, 'twas the *Suvorov*, what, what?' Drinkwater caught Blackwood's eye and saw the *Impregnable*'s captain roll his eyes resignedly at the white painted deckbeam over his head. 'Well, well, we're allies now, eh, damn it. And now the war's over, so 'tis all history, eh what?' The prince looked round beaming, as though he had just carried out a major diplomatic coup and Drinkwater was aware of two officers in the dark green full dress of Russian captains, standing stiffly, their bicorne hats tucked beneath their elbows.

'But you didn't do that in *Andromeda*, eh?'

'No sir, the razée *Patrician* . . .'

'So what the devil d'you do in the *Andromeda*, sir? Are you a jobber, or what?'

Despite a supreme effort at self-control, Drinkwater felt himself colouring at the prince's tactless imputation, unaware of the bristling of his fellow officers, manifested by a slight shuffling of feet and a stir as they waited for the presentations to cease and the conversation to become general.

Mercifully, Captain Blackwood was equal to the occasion, 'Captain Drinkwater is a most experienced cruiser commander, sir, he was off Cadiz with me, and Nelson had especially picked him for the *Thunderer*, but he could not get out from Gibraltar before the action.'

'By God, Drinkwater, that was damned bad luck, what? Picked by Nelson, eh? Wish to God I'd been, instead of being left to rot on shore! By Heaven there's no justice in the sea-service, damned if there is, eh, what?'

The moment of embarrassment passed, the insult turned neatly by Blackwood without the need to reveal Drinkwater's long association with special services, by way of an explanation why so senior a post-captain had yet to tread the quarterdeck of a line-of-battle ship, and why he commanded an obsolescent thirty-two gun frigate that should rightfully have been broken up. Drinkwater moved thankfully aside, leaving young Maude of *Jason* to His Royal Highness's mercy. As he moved aside, the bubble broke and conversation rose about him like a tide. Perhaps, he thought, taking a glass from a silver tray borne by a pig-tailed and stripe-shirted steward, it had been simmering all the while.

'We are neighbours at table, Captain Drinkwater,' said an austere, hollow-eyed man in the plain blue coat with the red collar and cuffs of an Elder Brother of the Trinity House. 'May I introduce myself? Captain Joseph Huddart, late of the Honorable Company's service.'

'Nathaniel Drinkwater . . .' The two men shook hands and lapsed into small talk, moving eventually to sit amid the glittering silver and glass of the Duke of Clarence's white-napered table. Drinkwater's other neighbour was a Russian, the captain of the forty-four gun frigate *Gremyashchi*. He spoke a thick English. Try though he might, Drinkwater had difficulty understanding anything beyond three references to the *Suvorov* and these, he deduced, were far from complimentary. After a few moments, the Russian turned to his farther neighbour, the French captain of the *Polonais* who, after a few exchanges, leaned forward and asked Drinkwater in faltering English:

'Capitaine Rakov, he ask if you are English *officier* who capture Russian ship *Suvorov?*'*

Drinkwater looked from the French officer to the Russian. Rakov was watching him closely.

'I am,' he replied, holding the Russian's gaze. Rakov muttered something, then turned pointedly away and settled to natter in French to the Russian on his left. Drinkwater fell into easy conversation with Huddart, whose bald head and wispy side drapes of hair hid an astute and enquiring mind. They talked of many things, discovering mutual acquaintances from Drinkwater's brief period in China, his escort of a convoy of the Company's East Indiamen and from his earlier service aboard Trinity House buoy yachts. In this vein the evening passed very pleasantly until at last, the prince, having called upon Blackwood to propose the first toast to his royal father, initiated a succession of these in which, at least so it seemed, every crowned head in Europe was thus honoured.

Eventually His Royal Highness prevailed and made some general remarks about his sensibility to the honour of commanding an allied squadron at this happy time of peace, alluding to the restoration of legitimate monarchy in France. He related an anecdote of the king, whom he had escorted ashore earlier in the day.

'His Majesty,' said the prince, perspiration and the tears of emotion upon his florid cheek, 'upon landing on the sacred soil of his native land, embraced the Duchess of Angoulême and said, "I hold again the crown of my ancestors; if it were of roses, I would place it upon your

* See *In Distant Waters*

21

head; as it is of thorns",' and here the sweating prince waved his hand above his head, ' "it is for me to wear it." Most moving gentlemen, most moving, what?'

A murmur of loyal assent ran round the table.

'It seems our Billy has learned a thing or two from *La Belle* Jordan,' remarked Huddart drolly, referring to the prince's former mistress who was also a renowned actress.

'Well gentlemen,' resumed their host, 'the merchant and the mariner have now nothing other than the dangers of the elements to encounter, what? And so the prosperity of their pursuits is by consequence more probable, don't you know. What! And therefore I propose a final toast to the sea-services!'

Like the preceding bumpers, they drank this final one sitting down, their faces perspiring from the heat of the candles, the warmth of their conversation and wine. To Drinkwater, chatting amiably to Huddart in the full flush of drunken fellowship, the prospect of peace, of retirement from the demands of active service and all its alarums, risks and hazards, seemed as rosy as the face of Admiral of the Fleet, His Royal Highness, the Prince William Henry, Duke of Clarence and Earl of Munster.

And just as fulsome.

Nicodemus

Drinkwater could not sleep. He had dined too well and drunk too deeply; moreover he was of an age now that precluded enjoying a full night's sleep and sometime late in the middle watch he irritably entered the starboard quarter-gallery and squatted inelegantly on the privy.

The dark shapes of the anchored squadron were pin-pricked by points of light, where the poop lanterns glowed and ashore a pair of glims marked the entrance to Calais port. Beneath him *Andromeda* lifted to a low ground swell and this motion caused her ageing fabric to creak in a mild protest. She was worn out with service. After the pounding she had taken in the action with the *Odin* she would have been better employed as a hulk, or even broken up. It was ironic that now, at the conclusion of hostilities, and in recognition of her last service attending upon kings and princes, she was fully manned. It was a rare experience for Captain Drinkwater to command one of His Britannic Majesty's cruisers which had a full complement, even after twenty years of war!

He sighed, contemplating the passage of time and feeling not only the ache of his tired body, but a morbid apprehension at his own mortality. He thought often now of death, almost daily since the loss of his friend and sometime lieutenant, James Quilhampton. He felt James's passing acutely and had assumed responsibility for the younger man's widow and child, but the impact upon his own spirit had been severe. He held himself wholly to blame for Quilhampton's death; it was an illogical conclusion. Nathaniel Drinkwater had murdered those whom events cast as enemies of his king and country without remorse, seeing in their deaths the workings of providence, but James's death had been attributable to his following orders, orders that had been given by Nathaniel Drinkwater himself.

'Damn the blue-devils,' he muttered, banishing his gloomy thoughts. He was about to duck through the door into the cabin when he noticed the boat. It was a dark shape and attracted attention by the slight gleam of phosphorescence at its bow and the pallid flashes of the oar-strokes. He thought at first it was a guard-boat, but its movement lacked the casual actions of a bored crew. Moreover, it had curved under the stern of their nearest neighbour, the *Jason*, and was heading directly towards *Andromeda*. Something about the purposeful approach disturbed Drinkwater; his apprehension about death was displaced by something more immediate. Was this another of His Royal Highness's ridiculous jokes? He could not imagine any other reason for the night's tranquillity being disturbed now that His Most Christian Majesty had been landed upon his natal shore to claim the crown restored to him by the grace of Almighty God, the bayonets of the Tsar and the Royal Navy of Great Britain.

From the greater vista of the stern window in the cabin, Drinkwater could see the boat holding unwaveringly to its course towards *Andromeda*.

'Bound to be orders, confound it,' he muttered, unaware that talking to himself was becoming habitual. 'Damn and blast the man!' he swore, pulling the night-shirt over his head and reaching for his breeches. Above his head he heard the faint sound of the marine sentry at the taffrail hail the approaching boat. He kicked his stockinged feet into the pumps he had worn aboard the *Impregnable* earlier that night and peered again through the stern windows. He could see the boat clearly now, the faint gleam of her gunwhale crossed by the moving oar looms. The synchronized swaying of her oarsmen chimed its rhythm with the surge of the phosphorescent bow-wave as the boat dipped and rose slightly under their impetus. He sensed as much as saw these resolved dynamics, a perception born of a lifetime at sea, sub-conscious in its impact on his intelligence. His conscious mind, compelled to wait for an explanation, briefly diverted itself by a recollection of his wife Elizabeth, whose wonder at first seeing phosphorescence in the breakers running up on the shingle strand of Hollesley Bay had given him a profound pleasure.

'You must have seen so many wonders, Nathaniel,' she had said, 'while I have seen so very little of life.'

'I wish I could have shared more with you,' he had replied kindly. He tossed the recollection aside as he heard quite clearly the query from the boat.

'*C'est Andromeda?*'

'The devil . . .' He struck flint on steel and had lit a candle when the tap came at the door. Midshipman Paine's disembodied features appeared round the door.

'Captain, sir?'

'I'm awake, Mr Paine, and aware we have a French boat alongside.'

'Aye sir, and a military officer asking to see you, sir.'

Drinkwater frowned. 'To see me? You imply he asked by my name.'

'Asked for Captain Nathaniel Drinkwater, sir, very particularly. Mr Marlowe said I was to emphasize that, sir.'

'Very well, I assume the officer at least was British.'

'Oh no, sir, Mr Marlowe said to tell you he had a lot of plumes on his shako and Mr Marlowe judged him to be either a Russian or a Frenchman.'

Drinkwater was dragging a comb through his hair while this exchange was in progress. It was not in his nature to bait midshipmen, but Drinkwater knew, though the cockpit thought he did not, that Paine had acquired the nickname 'Tom' on account of having the surname of the English revolutionary. He was a solemn but rather prolix lad.

'And what did you make him out to be, Mr Paine?'

'Well, he does have a fantastic shako, sir, but his voice is . . . well, I mean his accent is . . .'

'Is what, Mr Paine?' enquired Drinkwater, pulling on the full dress coat that he had disencumbered himself of when he had returned from the flagship. 'Pray do not keep me in suspense.'

'Well it's English, sir.'

'English?'

'But Mr Marlowe says the shako ain't English, sir . . .'

But Drinkwater was not listening, he was seized by the sudden thought his visitor might be his own brother who had long been a cavalry officer in the Russian service who had now come to pay him a nocturnal visit. He was certain Edward would be serving on the staff of General Vorontzoff who, Drinkwater had heard, was already in Paris. He swallowed the curse that almost escaped his lips and, doubling his queue, ordered the midshipman to bring the stranger down to the cabin. While he waited, Drinkwater lit more candles and washed his mouth out with a half-glass of wine.

Edward's appearance at this time would be damnably embarrassing. A cold and fearful apprehension formed around Drinkwater's heart. Once, long ago, he had helped Edward escape from England and a conviction for murder.* It had been a rash, quixotic act, but Drinkwater had gained the protection of Lord Dungarth and cloaked the affair under the guise of a secret and special service. Now Dungarth was dead, and an untimely resurrection of the usually impecunious Ned would not merely embarrass his older brother. Just when he might retire and enjoy the fruits of his own service, Edward might now ruin him.

Just as this terrible thought brought the sweat out on Drinkwater's brow and caused his blood to run cold, Midshipman Paine's face reappeared.

'Well, bring the fellow in, Mr Paine . . .'

'He won't come, sir. Says he wishes you to wait upon him on the quarterdeck.'

* See *The Bomb Vessel*

27

'The devil he does! Well, Mr Paine, what d'you make of the fellow, eh?' The idea the stranger was Edward was swept aside by the conviction that this was one of His Royal Highness's daft pranks. This thought was given greater credibility by Mr Paine's next remark.

'Begging your pardon, sir, I told you the officer was speaking English, but what I didn't say was that I thought the officer,' Paine paused, then went on, 'might be a woman, sir.'

'*You* thought the . . . Well, well, we had better go and see . . .'

If it were so, then at least the stranger was not his brother Edward! The cool freshness of the night air soothed some of Drinkwater's irritation. He braced himself for some piece of royal stupidity, aware of a figure in a cloak standing by the entry, but Lieutenant Marlowe loomed out of the darkness by the mizen mast and waylaid him.

'Beg pardon sir, but have a care. If this fellow's a Russian he may be dangerous, sir.'

Drinkwater frowned. 'Dangerous? Why so?'

'You have a reputation, sir . . .'

'Reputation?' Drinkwater's tone was edgy. Then he recalled Rakov's hostility.

'You did take the *Suvorov*, sir . . .'

Marlowe's tone was courtly, a touch obsequious, perhaps a trifle admiring. Drinkwater had destroyed a Russian line-of-battle ship in the Pacific, but that had been six years ago, in what? September of the year eight. Good God, the Russians had changed sides since then, when Boney invaded their country and Tsar Alexander had become the French Emperor's most implacable foe.

'Thank you for your concern, Mr Marlowe.' The lieutenant drew back and let his captain past, his head inclined in the merest of acknowledgements. Drinkwater approached the cloaked figure. The bell-topped shako with a tall white plume, a mark of Bourbon sympathy, Drinkwater supposed, stood out against the dark sea beyond.

'Well M'sieur, are you French or Russian?'

'I am French, Captain Drinkwater . . .' The voice seemed oddly familiar, yet artificially deepened. Paine was correct, a clever lad. He knew in the next instant who his visitor was.

'I know you,' Drinkwater said sharply, stifling any further explanation, and raising his voice slightly, so that the eavesdropping Marlowe and any other curious-minded among the listening anchor-watch might hear, added 'and I think I know your business. You are on the staff of the Prince of Condé. Come, we must go below.'

Drinkwater was certain his night-visitor was not on the staff of the Bourbon prince, and with a hammering heart, turned on his heel and led the way, nodding to the marine sentry at his door as the soldier snapped to attention. The French officer had removed the ridiculous shako to pass between decks, but held it in such a way that it masked his face from the marine's inquisitive stare. He was still half hiding his face behind the plume as Drinkwater, closing the door behind them, crossed the cabin and held up the candelabra on his table.

'You come by night like Nicodemus, but you are, if I mistake not, Hortense Santhonax.'

She lowered the shako and shook her head, not in denial of her identity, but to let her hair fall after its constraint beneath the shako. Drinkwater recalled something else about her. In the imperfect illumination, her profusion of hair still reflected auburn lights. She dropped the hat on a chair and unclasped her cloak. For a moment they both stared at one another. She had half-turned her head away from him, though her eyes were focused on his face. Her hair had pulled over her right shoulder, revealing her neck.

It was a quite deliberate ploy and as his eyes wavered towards the disfigurement, Drinkwater saw the twitch of resolution at the corner of her mouth. The scar ran down from under her hair, over the line of her jaw and down her neck. It was not the clean incision of a sword cut, but marked the passage of a gobbet of molten lead.

He took her cloak and without taking his eyes from her, laid it on a chair behind him. It was warm from her body and the scent of her filled the cabin. He reached out his left hand, gently lifting the hair off her right ear. It was missing.

Hortense Santhonax made no protest at this presumption. He let the hair drop back into place. 'I knew of your injury at the Austrian Ambassador's ball, Madame,' Drinkwater said kindly, 'and I am sorry for it.'

'When a woman loses her looks,' she said in her almost faultless English, 'she loses everything. Thereafter she must live on her wits.'

Drinkwater smiled. 'Then it makes them more nearly men's equals.'

'That is sophistry, Captain.'

'It is debatable, Madame, but you are no less lovely.'

She spurned the gallantry, raising her hand to her neck. 'How did you know . . . about this?'

'Lord Dungarth acquainted me of the fact some time before his death.'

'So, him too.' She paused, and then seemed to pull herself together. 'Men may acquire scars, Captain, and it does nothing but add credit to their reputations,' she remarked, and was about to go on when Drinkwater turned aside and lifted the decanter.

'Is that why you have assumed the character of a man, Madame?' he asked, pouring out two glasses.

She looked at him sharply, seeking any hint of malice in his riposte, but the grey eyes merely looked tired. He saw the suspicious contraction of the eye muscles and again the tightening of the mouth. She accepted the glass.

'Pray sit, Madame; you look exhausted.' He took in her dusty hessian boots, the stained riding breeches and the three-quarter length tunic. There was nothing remotely military about her rig. 'I presume you stole the shako,' he remarked, smiling, handing her a glass.

'There is a deal of convivial drinking in Calais tonight, Captain. A lieutenant of the *Garde du Corps* is going to find himself embarrassed tomorrow morning when the king leaves for Paris.' She returned his smile and he drew up a chair and sat opposite her. He felt the slight contraction of his belly muscles that presaged sexual reaction to her presence. By God, she was still ravishing, perhaps more handsome now than ever!

Was it the wound that, in marring her beauty, somehow made her even more desirable? Or had he become old and goatish?

'That is the first time I have seen you smile, Madame.'

'We have not always met under the happiest of circumstances.'

'Is this then, a happy occasion?'

She lifted the wine to her mouth and shook her head. 'No, I wish it were so, but . . .'

Drinkwater left her a moment to her abstraction. He was in no mood for sleep now and there was something of the extraordinary intimacy that he remembered from their last charged meeting, in the house of the Jew Liepmann, on the outskirts of Hamburg.* But there was something different about her now. He sensed a vulnerability about her, a falling off of her old ferocity. Either he was a fool or about to be hood-winked, but he sensed no scheme on her part to entrap him. Even had she sought to suborn him, she would never have allowed him to lift the hair from her scar in an act that, even now, he could scarcely believe he had accomplished.

She sighed and stirred. 'I have ridden a long way today, Captain Drinkwater, and we are no longer young.'

'That is true. Forgive me; you must have something to eat . . .' He rose and brought her a biscuit barrel, placing it upon the table beside her. She hesitated a moment and he watched her carefully. She was tired, that much was clear, and had undoubtedly lost her former confidence. Was that due to exhaustion, or the consequences of her scars? Had she been abandoned by those friends in high places she had once boasted of: Talleyrand for instance? Even now

* See *Under False Colours*

the *ci-devant* Bishop of Autun, foreign minister and Prince of Benevento, was conducting the government of France during the inter-regnum which would shortly end when Louis was restored fully to the throne of his ancestors. In these changed circumstances, a mistress like Hortense Santhonax would be an embarrassment which the calculating Talleyrand would drop like a hot coal.

He watched, fascinated, as she began to eat the biscuits, swallowing the wine with an eagerness that betrayed her hunger. The soft candle-light played on her features and he felt again the urgent twitch in his gut. He recalled the group of fugitives he had rescued off the beach at Carteret years earlier; Hortense and her brother had been among them. Later, at Lord Dungarth's instigation, she had been put back on a French beach once it was known that she had thrown her lot in with a handsome French officer called Edouard Santhonax. Drinkwater remembered, too, the earl's injunction that they should have shot her, not let her go.* Since then she had risen with her husband's star until he was killed, when her name became linked with that of Talleyrand. Such a beauty was not destined for a widowhood of obscurity. Hortense had been present at the Austrian Ambassador's ball, given upon the occasion of the Emperor Napoleon's marriage to the Archduchess Marie-Louise, and this confirmed she was still welcome at the imperial court despite imperial doubts about her husband's loyalty. Now the restoration of the Bourbon monarchy threatened to set her world upside down again, and while the Bourbons

* See *A King's Cutter*

could not avenge themselves upon the whole of France, they would undoubtedly visit retribution upon the vulnerable among Napoleon's followers.

'Do you fear the restoration? Surely as a friend of Monsieur Talleyrand, whose position, I believe, has never been stronger, you are safe enough?' She looked up at him, and he saw the effort of will it cost her to set her thoughts in order. 'Or are you seeking my protection and asylum in England?'

She almost laughed. 'Talleyrand . . . Protection . . .? Ah, Captain Drinkwater, I can count on nothing further from the Prince de Benevento, nor would I presume,' she paused for a moment, appearing briefly confused. Then she drew breath and seemed to steel herself, resuming in a harsher tone. 'M'sieur le Prince prefers the Duchesse de Courland these days, but I have not come here to beg favours, but to warn you. King Louis may have returned, but his presence in France guarantees nothing; France is in turmoil. Three weeks ago the senate which Napoleon had created passed a resolution which blamed the Emperor for all of France's misfortunes. The Prince de Benevento, as head of the provisional government, has himself resolved to have the Emperor exiled. The Iles d'Azores have been suggested, as has your Ile de Sainte Hélène. Caulaincourt has been running back and forth between Talleyrand and the Tsar as an intermediary.'

'And how are you and I involved in this negotiation between the Tsar Alexander and Talleyrand? You did not come here in the middle of the night to tell me what I may read in the newspapers in London? They also mentioned Elba.'

'Pah, d'you think that a likelihood? Why, it is too

close to France and too close to Tuscany. Austria will not wish to have the Emperor so close.'

'Your Emperor is the son-in-law of the Austrian Emperor.'

'That counts for nothing. Elba is but a ruse, though the world thinks the matter will rest there . . .'

'And you think otherwise?'

'Captain, I *know* otherwise.' The vehemence in her tone was a warning of something to follow. Drinkwater struggled to clear his tired brain.

'I can think of nowhere better than a more remote island such as you have mentioned if the late Emperor is to maintain some dignity. Otherwise I imagine it is not beyond the wit of your new Bourbon master to find an *oubliette* for him.'

'But Captain Drinkwater, do you think he will remain long on an island? Have not your English newspapers been saying otherwise?'

'He will be guarded by a navy whom he has compelled to master the techniques of blockade duty. I think your Emperor would find it very hard to escape . . .'

'What will your navy employ, Captain,' she broke in, the wine reviving her spirits as she warmed to her argument, 'a brace of frigates?'

The sarcasm in her tone as she guyed the English sporting term was clear. There was a sparkle in the green eyes that suddenly lit her face with the animated and terrible beauty he both admired and feared.

Drinkwater shrugged. '*Peut-être* . . .'

'*Perhaps*,' Hortense Santhonax scoffed, 'do you think you can cage an eagle, Captain? Come, my friend, you have more imagination than that!'

'Then, Madame,' Drinkwater snapped back, 'speak

plainly. You have not come to warn me in so circum-
locutory a style without there being something you wish
for . . .'

The remark seemed to deflate her. Her shoulders
sagged visibly as though the weight they bore was
unsupportable. She raised the glass and drained it.
'You are right. I have need of your help . . . There,
I acknowledge it!'

Drinkwater leaned over and refilled both their
glasses. 'Hortense,' he said in a low voice, 'much has
lain between us in the past. We have been enemies for
so long, yet you can feel easy addressing me as *friend*.
Do you remember when I dug a musket ball out of
the shoulder of the Comte de Tocqueville aboard the
Kestrel? I can see you now, watching me; I felt the depth of
your hatred then, though I cannot imagine why you felt
thus. Since that time I acknowledge I might have earned
your hate, but I think you have come here because you
trust me. And, in a strange sense, despite past events, I
find myself trusting you.' He reached out and touched
her lightly on her shoulder. 'Please do go on.'

She gave so large a sigh that her whole body heaved
and when she looked up at him her fine eyes were
swimming in tears.

'Yes, I remember the cabin and the wound . . . I
remember you drinking brandy as you bent over De
Tocqueville with a knife, but I do not remember
hating *you*. Perhaps my terror at escaping the mob,
of having abandoned everything . . .' She sighed and
shrugged, sipping at her glass. 'But I know you to
be a man of honour and that you will not abuse
the confidence I bear.' She took a gulp of the wine
and went on. 'When it was known in Paris that the

British ships which would escort the Bourbon back to France included the *Andromeda* commanded by Captain Nathaniel Drinkwater, I knew also that our lives were destined to touch at least once more.' She paused a moment, and then resumed. 'When we last met in Hamburg, I asked you if you believed in providence; do you remember what you said?'

'I imagine I answered in the affirmative.'

'You said the one word, "implicitly".'

'Did I? Pray continue,' he prompted gently.

'I also learned that you had foiled Marshal Murat's plans by stopping the shipping of arms from Hamburg to America . . .'*

'May I ask how?'

'Captain Drinkwater, you are a senior officer in the English navy, yet,' she gestured round her, 'this is only a frigate. And I know it to be an old and ill-used frigate.'

'You are remarkably well informed.'

'It is also known in Paris that you have had much to do with secret and especial services. Is that not so?'

'Yes, it is true. It is also true that I took over from Lord Dungarth, but my present command . . .' It was Drinkwater's turn to shrug; he was too keenly aware of the irony to offer a full explanation, and let the matter rest upon implication.

'Your appearance here off Calais is providential not only for myself and for France, but for the peace of Europe.'

Drinkwater was suddenly weary. What had the woman come for? He sensed some mystery but so preposterous

* See *Beneath the Aurora*

a claim seemed to be verging on the hysterical, just when the abdicated Napoleon Bonaparte was to be mewed up on a remote island.

'I see you are growing tired, Captain . . .'

'No, no . . .' he lied.

'I must perforce beg you, as a man of influence, sir, to grant me a small competence if I reveal what I know.'

'Competence? You mean a pension?' So that was what it was all about! Here before him, one of the most beautiful women in Europe was begging. She was one piece of the human flotsam from the wreckage of Bonaparte's empire. He felt meanly disappointed, as though her presence here on this night should have some nobler motive. 'So, you have come to trade.'

'I have almost nothing, Captain, and I must look to the magnanimity of my enemies and the honour of a man I have always thought of as a true spirit, wherever our respective loyalties have led us in these past years. I should hate you for what you did to my husband, but Edouard would have killed you . . .'

'He tried, several times, Hortense . . .'

Ashamed of his meanness, he felt a great pity for her. She would not be the only casualty in the fall of France. Though he had been a consistent enemy of his sovereign's enemies, he had often, in the privacy of his own thoughts, admired the establishment of a new order. The regal buffoonery of the preceding day had reminded him of the craziness of the world.

'Pray let us terminate the reminiscences, Hortense, they are painful for both of us. Do I understand you wish me to have you a pensioner of the British government?'

'Please . . .' There was no denying the extremity to which the woman was reduced.

'Sadly, you are unlikely to believe me when I say I am of little influence and certainly quite incapable of finding the support which would gain you such a living . . .'

'I don't ask for very much, Nathaniel; fifty pounds per annum, enough to keep me from the gutter . . . forty even.' She saw him shaking his head and a sudden fire kindled in her eyes. She dropped the intimacy they had fallen into. 'Come Captain, you cannot claim to be of no account. I know you are otherwise; why else are you serving in a squadron commanded by a royal prince? Your Prince William could see to it that I was awarded such a pension! Shall I go and petition him . . .?' She was scornful, her eyes ablaze.

'Madame, Madame, you do not know what you say!' Drinkwater had to laugh. 'His Royal Highness and his brothers are so often in debt that I would counsel you to steer clear of that path. You might find yourself reduced to whoring in his bed in expectation of guineas, only to be paid in florins! England is not France; your Prince of Benevento has far more power than Prince William Henry, and probably a more generous purse, whatever other vices he has.'

'But you can do it, Nathaniel, for God's sake, you must! Do I have to beg? I will . . .' She looked round and saw the cot.

'For God's sake get up! This is too melancholy a drama for such behaviour . . .' Drinkwater was keenly aware that, despite his caution, Hortense Santhonax had boxed him into a corner. 'Forty pounds you say? Well, well, I will see what I can do, though don't depend upon it. Come, come,' he floundered, 'it is not seemly to see you so reduced . . .'

'I have your word?' She had at least the grace to plead.

'You have my word.'

'Thank you, Nathaniel. It gives me no pleasure to be beholden to you.'

'It gives me no pleasure that you are,' Drinkwater replied grimly. He would have to find the woman's pension himself, if he could not obtain funds under some pretext or other. 'So, what is this news that will save Europe?'

To her credit, Hortense Santhonax came straight to the point. 'A group of officers in Paris, unwilling to swear the oath of allegiance to the Bourbon or to take advantage of the dissolution of their vows to the Emperor Napoleon, have already plotted to rescue him from exile.'

She paused a moment, satisfied herself that Drinkwater had taken the bait and went on. 'Talleyrand,' she said, eschewing the former French foreign minister's imperial title, 'is arranging matters so that the Emperor will be exiled on the island of Flores in the Azores. Money has already passed into the hands of certain influential Russians to ensure this, so the decision will be supported by Tsar Alexander. I do not think either the Prince Regent or your government will oppose it. But, having consented not to disturb the peace and tranquillity of France, a deposition to which effect the Emperor has already signed, the Emperor will embark in ships which will convey him from the Azores and transport him to North America. Scarcely will your navy have ordered frigates to watch the islands, than

Napoleon will have vanished, as will many of his guard, to join forces with the Americans. Can you not imagine the joy with which Mr Madison will welcome the greatest military genius the world has ever known?'

'I can imagine Mr Madison regretting his eagerness when Mr Madison is no longer Mr President,' Drinkwater remarked drily, but Hortense was quick to dismiss his scepticism.

'Napoleon Bonaparte will have lost Europe, Nathaniel, but he will gain Canada! The Québecois await him eagerly . . .'

Drinkwater thought of the speculations in the English press and Hortense's earlier reference to them. Napoleon's intended destination of America was at least a speculation. It might be a great deal more. 'And you say the Tsar is complicit in this plot?'

'Absolutely, yes. The matter has been settled between Alexander and Napoleon, thanks to Caulaincourt. I do not believe Napoleon will try and usurp the presidency of the United States, nor that he would again overreach himself, for he too is no longer a young man; but Canada will fall to him, and he will have again an empire the size of Europe! Do you think he cannot beat the British out of the country that was once a possession of France?'

The enormity of the implications came as no surprise to Drinkwater. It was as if the possibility seeped into him, giving form to a deep fear, charged with all the inherent horror of something inevitable. The idea was not new, the thing was perfectly possible and not very difficult. But it marked the base ingratitude of the Tsar, into whose coffers the British had poured thousands of pounds to keep his armies in the field.

'If this is true . . .'

'It is true,' she shook her head as if wishing she could dismiss it. Then she looked up at him, 'And it is worth forty pounds a year.'

But Drinkwater was no longer listening, he had turned away and stared through the stern windows. They had swung to the flood now and the eastern sky was already showing the first glimmer of the dawn. What was proposed was nothing less than the ruin of Great Britain hard upon the heels of the ruin of France. The euphoria of peace would be snatched from an exhausted people, the economy would be wrecked by further war, the troops mutinous if they had to be shipped in great numbers across the Atlantic to confront the resurgent Emperor of the French . . .

It did not bear thinking about. But he could not avoid it. When Britain had lost the Thirteen Colonies of North America, she had still had the vast wealth she derived from India and the sugar islands of the West Indies. Once before India had been threatened by Napoleon, now it was all too clear that it would be the Tsar's patiently obedient and savagely efficient legions who would thrust down towards the sub-continent. Drinkwater had few illusions but that they were capable of such a campaign.

He swung round to find Hortense intently watching him.

'This is not bluff, Madame?' His voice was suddenly hard, his brows knitting above his eyes which glittered fiercely. She felt less sure of herself, saw briefly the man who had killed her husband and who had spent his adult life engaged in a war with the elements as much as her fellow countrymen.

'No, no, if you want proof, you can examine the

papers of the port of Antwerp. Three days after the Emperor abdicated, two frigates, new ships just fitted out in that port, sailed for the Atlantic.'

'If true I doubt I have time to examine any papers . . .' Drinkwater's brain was racing. He, more than anyone else, knew the state of affairs at Antwerp. French money had been building ships on the Scheldt for years. As head of the Admiralty's secret Department he had received regular reports of their progress: no doubt two, three, a dozen frigates and perhaps a seventy-four or an eighty might be in a fit state for sea. And the present time, with the blockade everywhere stood easy, was the most propitious for a quiet departure of two frigates. They could look like Indiamen, by God!

'Do you know the names of these ships?' he asked, his voice rasping.

'I almost forgot,' she said. 'One was to have been called *L'Aigle*, but it has very likely been altered to something more like a Dutch East Indiaman. It was given out that they were bound for the Indies. They wear Dutch colours, but are French, of that you may be certain. Off Breskens they took on arms and men additional to their crews, veterans, men of the Old and the Middle Guard, Chasseurs à Cheval and Empress Dragoons, even Poles of the Lanciers . . .'

'D'you know anything of their passage, Hortense, if they left three days after the Emperor abdicated, then they left on . . .'

'The 9th April, and had weighed anchor from Breskens by the 14th . . .'

'Ten days ago, by God!'

'And they were to go north, to the northwards of Scotland.'

'D'you know who commands them?'

'I do not know the names of the officers who command the ships. The committee in Paris consisted of only a few officers, but one of these will command the *escadron*, how do you say . . .?'

'Squadron.'

'Yes, I had forgotten. It is Lejeune, he is a *contre-amiral, pardon,* a rear-admiral.'

It was too pat; suspicion rose again, clouding Drinkwater's tired mind. 'How are you so well informed? Does Talleyrand have a hand in this?'

Hortense nodded. 'Of course. He presides over everything.' She was unable to conceal her distaste. 'He will accomplish what Napoleon failed to achieve, without lifting a finger . . .'

'But,' Drinkwater repeated, 'how do you know all these details? Talleyrand cannot have discussed . . .' Were these secrets from the intimacy of the bedchamber?

She shook her head. 'No, no, Nathaniel. I know because . . .' She paused and took a different tack, capturing him in the jade gaze of her eyes. 'Do you remember the beach at Carteret, when you came in your little boat and took a frightened *émigrée* off the sand?'

'Yes. It was the first time I saw you.'

'What was the name of your commandant? Griffon . . .?'

'Griffiths.'

'Ah, yes. Do you recall who else came with me in the *barouche*?'

Drinkwater cudgelled his brains. There had been a handful of them, then the light dawned: 'The Comte de Tocqueville, a man called Barrallier who afterwards built ships for the navy and, of course, Étienne Montholon, your brother!'

'Of course. He is now a colonel of chasseurs.'

'And he is privy to this plot?'

'Yes. He has been aide de camp to Caulaincourt and commanded his escort.'

Drinkwater frowned; fatigue and the disagreeable consequences of excess had robbed him of the ability to think through this maze of intrigue. He made an effort to clear his mind and focus his tired eyes upon her, mentally repudiating her obvious allure, so spiced as it was by her propinquity. 'But you are betraying him, Hortense? Are your circumstances so reduced that you would play the traitor to,' he floundered, gathering the catalogue of betrayal, 'to your brother, to Bonaparte, to Talleyrand, to France?'

She was weeping now, shaking and sobbing with tears running down her cheeks and revealing the dust that lay upon them.

'If it had not been you, Nathaniel,' she began in a choked voice, 'I should have taken passage in one of these ships and found my way to England. As it is, I may slip back to Paris unnoticed. Talleyrand is no longer interested in me, I was repudiated by the Emperor and the Bourbon will not want women like me to clutter up his court, nor, would I wish to do so.' She lowered her voice. 'I am a drab, Nathaniel, and like most camp followers, my end will not be an easy one. Your help might at least mitigate my fate.'

She swayed and Drinkwater stooped forward and gently held her by her arms. He was unconvinced, but her hands were on his arms too, and her body touched his, light as a feather, and then with more weight.

45

'Do not underestimate the risk I have run to tell you these things,' she breathed, and added as he remained silent, holding her, 'They are like boys, Nathaniel, these conspirators; they would set the world alight again. Is that what you want? Do you not most desire to go home to your wife and children?'

'That is an odd question to ask at a moment like this,' he said, 'or are we two in sudden accord?' He smiled, the twist in his mouth conveying an intense sadness to her, though he spoke to encourage her. 'Come, Hortense, courage. You have lost none of your beauty . . .'

'I have lost an ear!' Her tone was petulant, as though she could betray her world for this disfigurement, and she lowered her face. 'And I am tired of conspiracy and intrigue.'

'Then it makes us the more equal,' Drinkwater said again. It occurred to him that she had received some unbearable humiliation. 'Suppose this plan of Talleyrand's and the Tsar's worked; suppose Napoleon Bonaparte, sent to exile in the Azores, was sprung from his prison and spirited across the Atlantic; suppose your brother commanded a division of trappers and mountain men in the army of New France, eh? Wouldn't you want to be a part of that? A great lady of Quebec, or Montreal, or even Louisbourg if it was rebuilt? Yet you expect me to believe you would hazard all that against a pension of forty pounds per year?'

He was looking down at her hair, the scent of which rose from its auburn profusion. She raised her face and stared up at him. Her yielding body had become rigid.

'I have nothing, nothing!' She hissed, desperation in her tone. 'Why should I come here, tonight, eh?' She pulled away from him, holding him at arm's length as she might have remonstrated with the son she had never had. 'Why should I not sit in Paris and wait for an invitation to become *La Reine de Louisbourg*, eh?' She threw the title at him in French like striking him with a gauntlet. 'I do not owe you anything, and if I come to trade this information it is not to betray France, or my brother . . .'

'What of Talleyrand?' Drinkwater snapped. 'What of Napoleon?'

'Why is it you English men are so *stupid*?' she spat back. 'I am old! It is known what I have been! It is known what I am now! Why is it impossible for men to understand, eh? You never come to terms with the inevitable, do you? Only the clever, men like Napoleon and Talleyrand, can rise above these petty considerations. It is said in Paris that, despite everything, Napoleon could have rallied the army south of the Loire, but he did nothing. Instead he abdicated in the sure and certain knowledge that only a chapter of his life was over, but not the whole history. He is a Corsican, not a Frenchman. And he believes in fate, just like you.' Hortense paused, to let the point sink in. 'Napoleon has abandoned France just as he abandoned her before and set off for India. Then, when he found his grand design more difficult than he thought, he abandoned his army in Egypt and returned to France. When Admiral Villeneuve failed him at Trafalgar, he abandoned the invasion of England; when he was confronted with difficulties in Spain, he abandoned the war to his marshals; when he was foiled by the Russians, he abandoned his army in the snow . . . Why should he change now? Is fate going to give him another opportunity in Europe?'

47

'No,' Drinkwater said slowly.

'Certainly, I am being selfish. Perhaps this is a betrayal; perhaps this is saving many lives, perhaps . . .' she shrugged and moved slightly closer to him again, lowering her voice, 'this is fate, Nathaniel . . .'

And she pushed against him unashamed, her head bowed unexpectantly, their roles reversed, as though she was now the child and he the parent. His arms went instinctively around her and though he felt the soft roundness of her breasts it was pity, not lust, which rose and overwhelmed him.

'I think we are both too old,' he murmured into the darkness of the shadows beyond her shoulders, and gently stroked her hair. She seemed to shudder, like a small and terrified animal. 'Shall you want a passage to England?'

She pulled back and looked up at him. 'Where could I go in England?'

He shrugged. Suddenly the reaction of his wife to the arrival of a strange, mysterious and beautiful woman claiming refuge, seemed unlikely to be sympathetic.

'Perhaps one day . . .'

'*Peut-être*, Nathaniel. We shall see . . . I have told you everything . . .'

'I shall see you leave tonight with some money. There will be a ready market for English gold in Calais. I shall also ensure provision is made for you.'

'Is that possible?'

He thought for a moment and then nodded. 'Yes, I can arrange matters . . .'

Her relief was pathetic. The fear left her and he felt

her whole body transformed. Lust pricked him as she embraced him once more.

'Hortense . . .'

And then he found himself kissing her as he wished he had kissed her twenty years earlier.

A Clear Yard-arm

The eastern sky was lighter by the moment as Drinkwater paced the quarterdeck. The boat had long since vanished in the direction of the Calais breakwater, the Bourbon cockade deceptively jaunty, visible like a rabbit's scut as Hortense bobbed away.

He thought again of the warmth of her body against his and the prickle of lust still galled him. She had been compliant in that moment of mutual weakness, for they both drew back after a moment, almost ashamed, as though their long acquaintance had been supportable only as long as it was above the carnal.

'I am sorry,' he had muttered, even while he still held her, 'but I . . .'

'I am not a drab, Nathaniel.' There were tears in her eyes again, and it was clear she thought his impropriety had been motivated by that presumption.

'Hortense,' he had protested, 'I did not . . . I meant no . . . Damnation I have been bewitched by you for years. Did you not know it? Had I not a wife and children, I should have long ago . . .'

He had broken off, seeing the pathetic declaration make her smile.

'Ah, Nathaniel, how,' she had paused, 'how *damnably* English.'

'Do not taunt me. Upon occasions, you have made my life wretched. You have resided in my soul as a dark angel. Tonight you are dispossessed of all the diabolism with which my imagination had invested you. For that I am grateful.'

They had let each other go.

'They you will see that I am provided for?'

'You know I will.'

'Yes . . . Yes I did. To that extent your superstitions were correct.' She smiled again.

'You are returning to Paris?' Seeing her nod, he had gone on, 'There is a bookseller in the rue de la Seine whose name is Michel. There, in a month, you will find a draft against a London bank. I shall make it out in the name Hortense de Montholon. Should anything go awry, you may send a message through the Jew Liepmann in Hamburg.'

'You are doing this yourself aren't you? This is nothing to do with the British government, is it?'

'Hortense, the British government will not give Nelson's mistress a pension; why should they do anything for you? I know of you and thanks to the fortune of war, I have the means to make a little money available for you.'

'You are very kind, Nathaniel. Had life been different, perhaps . . .'

'Perhaps, perhaps; perhaps in happier times we shall meet again. Let us cage Bonaparte, m'dear, before any of us ordinary mortals think of our own pleasure.'

Hortense had smiled at the remark and, as he held her cloak out for her, she said over her shoulder, 'You and I are no ordinary mortals, Nathaniel.'

He had merely grunted. To so much as acknowledge by the merest acquiescence any agreement with this *braggadocio* seemed to him, filled as he was with apprehension at her news, to be tempting providence most grievously.

Now he was left to his thoughts and they were in a turmoil. He found it difficult to clear his mind of the image of her. On deck, in the chill of the dawn, it was almost possible to believe it had all been a dream, a bilious consequence of dining too well at the royal table. Was that event any more real, he wondered? And then from his breast the faintest, lingering scent of her rose to his nostrils.

Yet the appearance of the curious 'French officer' had far greater importance than the temptation of Nathaniel Drinkwater. He was in little doubt of the truth of her asseveration. Drinkwater had only the sketchiest notions of the military position of the French army at the end of March, but he had gleaned enough in recent days to know that Napoleon's energies seemed little diminished. He had fought a vigorous campaign in the defence of France, only to be overwhelmed by superior numbers against which even his military genius was incapable of resistance. Finally, it was widely rumoured, it had been the defection of members of the marshalate in defence of their own interests which had prompted the Emperor's abdication.

Under the circumstances, Napoleon was an unlikely candidate for a quiescent exile. And across the Atlantic raged a savage war, a repeat of the struggle from which had emerged the independent United States of America. Drinkwater had cause to remember details of that terrible conflict; as a young midshipman he had tramped through the Carolina swamps and pine barrens and had seen atrocities committed on the bodies of the dead.* More recently, he had been involved in the last diplomatic mission intended to prevent a breach between London and Washington, and he knew of the efforts which the young republic was prepared to make to discomfit her old imperial enemy.†

Nor had his foiling of that effort settled the matter. Yankee ambition was like the Hydra; cut one head off and another appeared. Within a few months of destroying a powerful squadron of American privateers, Drinkwater had been made aware of an attempt by the French to supply the Americans with a quantity of arms. The desperate battle fought in the waters of Norway beneath the aurora may have prevented that fateful juncture, but it may not have been the only one; perhaps others, unbeknown to the British Admiralty's Secret Department which Drinkwater had so briefly headed, had taken place successfully. It seemed quite impossible that his individual efforts had entirely eliminated any such conjunction. In short, it seemed entirely likely that some arms had crossed the Atlantic and that Napoleon and devoted members of his Imperial Guard would follow.

In fact, Drinkwater concluded, it was not merely likely, it was a damned certainty! And then the memory

* See *An Eye of the Fleet*
† See *The Flying Squadron*

of Hortense mimicking his English expletive flooded his memory so that he turned growling upon his heel and came face to face with Lieutenant Marlowe.

'What in damnation . . .?'

'Begging your pardon, sir . . .'

'God's bones, what is it?'

'The French officer, sir . . .'

'Well, sir, what of the French officer?'

'Are there any orders consequent upon the French officer's visit, sir?'

'Orders? What orders are you expecting Mr Marlowe, eh?'

'I am about to be relieved, sir, and under the circumstances, in company with the Royal Yacht, sir, and His Royal Highness . . .'

Suddenly, just as Drinkwater was about to silence this locquacious young popinjay, the ludicrous pomposity of Prince William's title struck him. Overtired and overwrought he might be, distracted by the weight of Hortense's intelligence as much as that of her voluptuous body, he found the term 'Highness' so great a fatuity that he burst out laughing. And at the same time, as he thought of the coarse, rubicund and farting Clarence, he discovered the answer to the question that had been lurking insolubly in his semi-conscious.

'Indeed, Mr Marlowe, you do right to be expectant. The truth is I have been mulling over the best course of action to take as a consequence of that officer's visit, and now I'm happy to say you have acted very properly, sir.'

'Well, I'm glad of that, sir.'

'And so am I.'

'And the orders, sir . . .?'

54

Drinkwater looked at the young lieutenant's face. The sun was just rising and the light caught Marlowe's lean features in strong relief. He was a pleasant looking, pale fellow, with a dark beard, and the stubble was almost purple along his jaw. 'What d'you know of, er, His Royal Highness's habits, Mr Marlowe. I saw you hob-nobbin' with a couple of the *Impregnable*'s officers last night. One of them was the Prince's flag-luff, wasn't he? What I mean is, did either of the young blades tell you what o'clock the Prince rises?'

Marlowe was somewhat taken aback by his commander's perception. 'I know Bob Colville, sir, but I don't recall our discussing His Royal Highness's habits beyond the fact that he enjoys a bumper or two.'

'Or three, I daresay, but that don't serve.' Drinkwater mused for a moment, then added expansively, 'What I need to know, Mr Marlowe, is what is the earliest time I might see the Prince?'

'In a good humour I daresay too,' added Marlowe, smiling, extrapolating Drinkwater's intentions.

'To be frank, Mr Marlowe,' Drinkwater added, a tone of asperity creeping into his voice, 'I don't much care in what humour His Royal Highness is, just so long as he is sufficiently awake to understand what I wish to communicate to him.' Marlowe's look of astonishment at this apparent *lèse-majesté* further irritated Drinkwater who was conscious that he had confided too much in his untried subordinate. 'Have my gig ready in an hour, and pass word for my servant.'

As he shaved, Drinkwater turned over the idea he had. It seemed to have formed instantaneously whilst he had been importuned by Marlowe. The young officer had seen little service of an active nature, although his references spoke of several months on blockade duty off Brest. Still, that did not equate with a similar number of weeks in a frigate in a forward position or an independent cruise, though that was not poor Marlowe's fault. Drinkwater wondered if what he was currently meditating would appeal to Marlowe, whose career, at this onset of peace, seemed upon the brink of termination with no opportunity for him to distinguish himself. Perhaps it would not matter to the well-connected Marlowe, but it might to others, for quite different reasons.

And then Drinkwater extinguished the thought with a wince of almost physical pain. How long had he yearned for a cessation of this tedious and debilitating war? How often had he vowed to give it all up? Had he not received with something akin to relief, orders to pay off *Andromeda* and go onshore, to take up half-pay and wait for death or the superannuated status of a yellow-admiral?

God knew he was haunted by the dead, whose shadows waited for his own to join them. The order to pay off had been rescinded and instead, as a mark of respect to Admiral-of-the-Fleet, His Royal Highness, The Prince William Henry, Duke of Clarence and Earl of Munster, *Andromeda* had been ordered to join the Royal Squadron off Dover!

'We're going out with a bang!' Drinkwater had overheard one of the afterguard remark to a mate, and knew the mood of the men was one of willing co-operation in seeing Fat Louis back to France, before finally laying up the frigate and being paid off to go home. And yet despite this imminent end to the ship's commission, Chatham dock-yard had spared no expense and effort to make good the damage *Andromeda* had suffered in the Vikkenfiord.

56

'You would not believe the difficulties I had to fit out the bomb vessel *Virago* in the year one,' Drinkwater had remarked to Lieutenant Frey, repeating the wonder he had expressed to Birkbeck, 'and then we were under orders to join the great secret expedition to the Baltic. Now we are off on a merry jape to Calais with His Most Christian Majesty which will last a week at the most, and we are getting more paint than a first-rate at Spithead before a review!' And the two of them had resumed their pacing, shaking their heads at the perverse logic of the naval service, while the ship's company fell to their pointless task with evident enthusiasm.

Now Drinkwater was meditating destroying that almost covenanted expectation. He finished shaving and, waving aside his neck linen, sat at the table and drew a sheet of paper towards him. He began to write as his servant poured coffee, pausing occasionally to gather his wits and couch his words in the most telling manner.

It was only as he completed the fourth missive that it occurred to him that the perversity permeating the naval service also ran through its officers. He himself was not exempt from this duplicity: on the one hand he had just poured out expressions of regret to his wife, yet on the other there was a sense almost of relief that he did not yet have to go home and take off his gold-laced undress uniform coat for the last time.

Why was that? he wondered, sealing the letter to Elizabeth. Because he could not face the obscurity of domesticity, or because he was not yet ready to meet the shades of the dead who awaited him there?

* * *

His Royal Highness was not yet awake when Drinkwater presented himself upon the quarterdeck of the *Impregnable*, but Blackwood emerged blear-eyed to greet Drinkwater a little coolly.

'My dear fellow, 'tis a trifle early. Can't you sleep?'

'I beg your pardon, Blackwood, but the matter is important, too important to allow me to sleep.'

'I smell intrigue. I thought you had shaken the dust of the Secret Department off your feet . . .'

'So did I, and I wish to God I had, but it dogs me and last night was no exception.' Drinkwater dropped his voice. 'I had a visit from the shore. An agent of long-standing,' Drinkwater lied, 'has given me disturbing intelligence which, under the circumstances, needs to be communicated to His Royal Highness without further delay.' Tiredness and excitement made him light-headed. He almost choked on the prince's title.

A curious look of doubt and indecision crossed Blackwood's face. 'My dear Drinkwater, is this wise? I mean His Royal Highness may be an admiral-of-the-fleet but he is, how shall I put it . . .?'

'But a fleeting one?' In his elevated state, Drinkwater could not resist the pun. 'I have no doubt His Royal Highness will grasp the import of my news, at least sufficient to give me what I want.'

'Which is?'

'*Carte blanche*, Blackwood, *carte blanche*.'

'To do what, in heaven's name?' asked the mystified Blackwood.

'To chase to the westward. Listen, Blackwood, if I take this news back to Dover and post up to town, I shan't be there before Wednesday and by the time the board have cogitated and informed the Prime Minister and given me my orders it will be too late . . .'

'Well what is this news?' an exasperated Blackwood asked.

'Oh, I beg your pardon. I've been so preoccupied . . . They're going to spring Boney; just when we think we've got him in the bag, he'll be spirited away to America . . .'

'Good heavens! D'you mean Boney will then be free to raise Cain in Canada?'

'Exactly so!'

Blackwood looked straight at Drinkwater. 'By God, Drinkwater, you want discretionary orders over Silly Billy's signature.'

'Yes, I want a clear yard-arm, Blackwood. Two ships have already left Antwerp. I don't have much time. None of us have much time. This American business could drag on for years. If Napoleon is involved . . . well, do I have to spell it out? Surely this whole damned war has to be ended one day.'

'Aye, and the sooner the better . . .' But Blackwood was not so easily impressed and his expression clouded, marked by second thoughts. 'But hold hard. 'Twould not be easy to get Boney out of the Med from Elba . . .'

'But it ain't to be Elba, don't you see; 'tis to be the Azores!'

'But the newspapers . . . I mean they've been talking about Elba . . . The other day the *Courier* mentioned it – there's a copy in my cabin.'

'Blackwood, for pity's sake,' Drinkwater's voice was suddenly hardened by exasperation and conviction, 'I have been up all night, mulling the matter in the wake of this news. You must know the degree to which I have dabbled in intelligence.'

Blackwood stared for a moment at his visitor. 'I've heard you're a shrewd cove, Drinkwater . . .'

'Not really, just grasping at straws in the wind, but experience tells me the wind has a direction and a force.' Drinkwater paused and Blackwood smiled.

'Eloquently put.'

'D'you think Silly Billy knows I have had any connections with the Secret Department?'

'I was indiscreet enough to tell him. He was curious to know why you were so long-toothed and still only had a thirty-two. He recollected you when I mentioned the taking of the *Suvorov*, but that only increased his curiosity. I told him you had been involved in secret operations and that your command of *Andromeda* was temporary and in honour of his own connections with your ship.'

'Well, well. That was a flattering fib.'

'Vanity is the one thing he has in common with Nelson.'

'I shall remember that.'

'Come then,' Blackwood said at last, 'you have convinced me. We should hesitate no longer. Let us go and rouse his Royal Highness from his intemperate slumbers.'

Once persuaded, Blackwood turned on his heel, but the alacrity with which he finally led Drinkwater below, proved a damp and fuming squib. Having passed word, couched with respectful deference, by way of His Royal Highness's flag-lieutenant and thence his valet, that a matter of the utmost urgency had to be communicated to His Royal Highness's person, Blackwood led Drinkwater into his own cabin where they took coffee.

It was clear to Blackwood that Drinkwater had much on his mind and found the wait intolerable; he therefore attempted to calm his visitor, remarking that, 'although the Prince is not himself insistent upon any great ceremony, the damned boot-lickers in attendance upon the Royal Personage are confoundedly touchy upon the point. Of course,' Blackwood added, 'in the ordinary circumstances of a ceremonial task of this nature, none of it is of any great moment. Our present prevailing urgency however, is a different matter. But we will carry the day if we do not upset the tranquillity of the Royal Mind.' Blackwood dabbed his mouth with a napkin, as though to purge the sarcasm.

'On last night's showing,' Drinkwater responded, 'I was not aware there was much of the Royal Mind to disturb.'

'La, sir,' Blackwood said, grinning, 'all the more reason for treating it with respect.'

Drinkwater harrumphed and Blackwood forbore to make further small-talk. They were in fact not left kicking their heels for more than an hour. Lieutenant Colville, resplendent in full dress even at the early hour, commanded their presence in the *Impregnable*'s great cabin.

Both officers bowed as the prince stepped from his night cabin, his red cheeks still shining from the ministrations of the razor and his shoulders shaking the heavy bullion epaulettes upon his shoulders.

'So sorry to keep you gentlemen,' the prince greeted them. 'Pray join me to break your fasts,' he added, waving to a table laid with splendidly fresh white linen and a selection of hot dishes. 'The kedgeree is devilish good . . .'

61

Drinkwater caught Blackwood's eye as he swept his coat-tails aside and sat down. Lieutenant Colville sat next to Drinkwater, a small scribbling tablet and pencil neatly laid beside him.

'Now sir,' the Prince boomed across the table as he spooned the kedgeree onto his plate, 'what's all this urgent nonsense about, eh?' He fixed his popping eyes on Drinkwater and began to shovel the fish and rice into his mouth with a mechanical regularity. 'Surely we all did our duty yesterday, eh what?'

'Your Royal Highness, this is a matter of some delicacy . . .' Drinkwater turned and looked pointedly at Lieutenant Colville. 'The matter I have to discuss with you is confidential.'

The Royal Brow contracted and, with a small explosion of rice grains, His Royal Highness enquired bluntly, 'What's the matter with Lieutenant Colville?'

'Well, nothing, Your Royal Highness,' Drinkwater replied, smiling coldly at the flag-lieutenant whose expression was as outraged as he dared in the presence of two senior captains and an admiral who was also the king's son. 'Except that he is only *Lieutenant* Colville, sir, and therefore cannot, I beg your pardon sir, but *must not* be a party to what I have to say.'

There was a moment's stunned silence. The prince bent forward, fork and spoon poised over the partly ravaged though still substantial pile of food, and looked uncertainly from Drinkwater to Blackwood. Drinkwater noticed again the deference he paid to Blackwood, as though the captain's good opinion mattered.

'If I might say, sir,' Blackwood chipped in quickly, 'Captain Drinkwater's news is properly for the ears of Government . . .' The word was encapitalized in a significant emphasis by the flag-captain and Drinkwater stifled a grin.

'Oh . . . Oh, quite! Quite!' Further rice grains were ejaculated from the Royal Mouth. 'Well Colville, off you go! Off you go! Go and take breakfast in the wardroom!'

There was pointed resentment in the scraping of Colville's chair and he bestowed a look of pure contempt upon Captain Drinkwater as he stooped beneath the deck-beams and left the cabin.

'Well Drinkwater, what's all this nonsense about . . .? Oh damn-and-hell-blast-it, Blackwood, be a good fellow and pass a bottle . . .'

As Colville had risen so had Blackwood, crossing the cabin to close the door communicating with the adjacent pantry and waving out the servant who stood discreetly out of sight but within calling. The Prince's command came as he returned and Blackwood lifted an uncorked bottle of claret from the fiddles atop the sideboard.

'Sir, you are aware of my former duties in connection with the Secret Department, are you not?'

'Yes, yes. Barrow told me all about you, so did Sir Joseph Yorke and Blackwood here did the same. Your stock's pretty damned high, so get on with it, eh? There's a good fellow.'

'Very well, sir. Last night I received intelligence directly from a source well known to me . . .'

'D'you mean a spy?'

'No, I do not. From a person who has had intimate connections with Talleyrand and,' Drinkwater paused just long enough to encourage the prince to look up from his emptying plate, 'Napoleon Bonaparte . . .'

Prince William Henry choked violently and snatched up the glass Blackwood had just filled with claret. Calming himself he wiped his mouth and face with a napkin and rumbled, 'Bonaparte, d'ye say? Go on, sir, pray do go on.'

'This person's attachment to Bonaparte has been severed . . .'

'Ah yes! Didn't I tell you, Blackwood, they'd all come crawling on their damned bellies to save what they've made in the Corsican's service! Didn't I say as much, Blackwood? Didn't I, damn it, eh?'

'You did, sir.'

'Aye. And I said as much to King Louis and the Duchesse d'Angoulême. Told 'em not to trust any damned Bonapartist, well, well.'

'The point is, sir,' Drinkwater broke in, seizing the brief pause in His Royal Highness's self-congratulation, 'we shall have to trust what this person said, because if we don't, we shall rue it.'

Drinkwater had expected further interjections by the prince, but he seemed content to listen and commanded Drinkwater impatiently to 'go on, do go on'.

'I have information that a plot has been matured in Paris that, consequent upon the Emperor Napoleon abdicating . . .'

'Emperor? Emperor, sir? The man is no more than a damned general, General Bonaparte!'

'General Bonaparte, Your Royal Highness, was elected Emperor of the French by plebiscite; he is moreover married to an Austrian Arch-duchess and is therefore still related to the Emperor of Austria. Whatever title he held and whatever title we ascribe to him now matters little, but I lay emphasis upon the point now to,' Drinkwater was about to say 'remind,' but the look in the prince's narrowing eyes, made him change his mind. His sleepless night made him over bold and he came quickly to his senses, 'to acquaint Your Royal Highness of the significance of what Bonaparte has relinquished by his instrument of abdication.'

'He was beaten damn it, Drinkwater! Eh, what?'

'Militarily yes, sir, but his ambition is unbeaten, for he abdicated not in favour of King Louis, but his own son. Moreover, his genius is undiminished.'

'Very well, very well, but what is this to us? He is to be exiled, under guard, locked up as nearly as maybe, what. Yet you come here blathering of plots.'

'Would that it were blathering, sir. The fact is a considerable number of his officers are roaming about disaffected and dissatisfied with the turn events have taken. As we sit here a number are already at sea on passage to rescue their Imperial Master in order to spirit him across the Atlantic to Canada.'

'Canada?' The Royal Brow furrowed again.

'To operate with Yankee support, raise the Québecois, and re-establish Napoleon's dynasty in Canada with a second empire in the Americas.'

'It ain't possible . . . is it?' The prince wiped his mouth and threw down his napkin. His eyes swivelled in Blackwood's direction. 'Well Blackwood? What the devil do you think?'

'Well sir,' Blackwood began, 'I must confess I have my doubts.' Drinkwater's heart sank. 'But I'm afraid 'tis not at all impossible, sir, and I share Captain Drinkwater's apprehensions in the strongest manner. An extension of the war in North America under such circumstances with every disaffected Bonapartist taking passage to join the reconstituted eagles on the St Lawrence will cause us no end of havoc. To be candid, sir, we could not withstand a determined onslaught and might lose the whole of the North Americas. I doubt your Royal Father would greet that news with much joy, sir.'

Blackwood's reference to King George III, languishing in Windsor, mentally affected by the ravages of porphyria, was masterly and had the prince nodding agreement.

'There are other factors, sir,' Drinkwater added. 'It is not only the Canadian French in Quebec that should concern us, but the old Acadian families who now live in Nova Scotia would happily revert to a French state, even a Bonapartist one. Moreover, if you consider the matter a stage further, can you not see that it would be no wild conjecture for King Louis to reunite his divided country and wipe out the past five and twenty years by reaching an accommodation with Bonaparte across the Atlantic . . .'

'My God, Drinkwater,' Blackwood muttered, 'that is an appalling prospect . . .'

'I wish it were all; regrettably my information is that Tsar Alexander is not against this scheme and that can mean only that having accepted our gold to keep his armies in the field, he would discomfit us and assume the leadership of Europe.'

'But is all this possible, what?' The prince's pop-eyed face bore the impact of the political possibilities. Drinkwater was reminded of Blackwood's charitable judgement of the previous night and in that moment he could see the prince as a simple and good, if misguided, man. He was clearly having trouble grasping the complexities of the conspiracy.

'The matter can brook no delay, sir,' he said. 'I am asking only for the despatch of my single frigate, and I fear, sir, the future peace of Europe thus rests entirely with you.'

'Me?' Astonishment had transfigured the prince's face a second time. 'Surely the board, Sir Joseph, Melville, Barrow and all the rest of the pack of political jacks . . .'

'Come, sir, with respect, there is no time! These men, these Bonapartists are already at sea and they are desperate. They will wish to spring their Emperor before we have mewed him up too well. I am under your orders and cannot, would not, act without them, but . . .'

'But, thank God, you hold the highest rank, sir!' Blackwood broke in, enthusiastically leaning forward, 'No one would question your probity in instructing Captain Drinkwater here to pursue these two ships in order that we might nip this matter in the bud!'

'D'you think so, gentlemen?'

Blackwood grasped his wine glass and raised it in a half-toast, half-pledge, hissing 'Remember Nelson, sir, remember Nelson!'

The prince looked from one to another, his eyes suddenly alight with enthusiasm. 'Damn-and-hell-blast-it, you are right, what! Drinkwater! Blackwood!' Their names were punctuated by the chink of glass on glass. 'Should we not take the squadron, eh, what?' asked the prince, visibly warming to the idea. 'Why, with the *Impregnable* and *Jason* under my command . . .'

'I think not, sir,' put in Blackwood smoothly, 'we must maintain station to soothe the Russians' suspicions. D'you see?'

'Soothe the Russians? Eh? Oh . . . Quite! Quite!' His Royal Highness erupted in explosions of acquiescence, as though seeing the point a little uncertainly, through powder smoke.

'It would, moreover sir, add some additional glory to *Andromeda*,' Blackwood added.

'Why, damn me yes, it would, wouldn't it, eh?' Prince William Henry beamed pleasantly, thinking of reflected glory. 'To our enterprise then,' he said, raising his glass.

Relieved on more than one count, Drinkwater drained his almost at a gulp.

'Come Drinkwater,' the prince exclaimed, 'I see some of God Almighty's daylight in that glass of yours. Banish it!'

And Drinkwater submitted against his judgement to the refill, while His Royal Highness rattled on about writing Drinkwater's orders and Blackwood leaned back in his chair, a half smile upon his face.

Ten minutes later Drinkwater emerged on to *Impregnable*'s quarterdeck with Blackwood. 'You stuck your neck out a couple of times, Drinkwater. I thought Billy was going to have apoplexy when you insisted on Boney being an Emperor.'

'A sleepless night and a matter of urgency makes one less diplomatic,' Drinkwater said, his eyes gritty in the full glare of daylight.

'Oh, I don't blame you,' Blackwood added dismissively, 'those damned Bourbons have all gone back to France to put the clock back as though nothing has happened there since the outbreak of their damned revolution.' He shook his head. 'D'you think Boney will rest easily anywhere?'

Drinkwater shrugged, 'Who knows? The closer to France the more dangerous he is to the process of restoration; the more distant, then the more amenable to some adventure like this one. Even if I'm wrong and it's Elba, we won't be sleeping that easily in our beds.'

'No, we thought we had peace once before . . .'

'D'you know they've been building ships at Antwerp for the last eight or nine years. These two frigates that have slipped to sea could be just the beginning of a fleet which could get out the minute we lift the blockade. I tell you, Blackwood, just when we think we can go home with our work done, the whole confounded thing could blow up in our faces.'

'Aye, the Russian interference bothers me. The Tsar's interested in Paris and I daresay his bayonets and Cossacks will prop up the Bourbons if there's trouble from the French army.'

'Exactly!' Drinkwater exclaimed. 'And d'you see, the Tsar can't afford to keep an army of occupation in France without our support and while many of Napoleon's satraps will compromise and throw in their lot with the new order, many more of the less privileged French officers and the rank and file will rally to the eagles. Alexander can give equal support to this because it will be in King Louis' interests to be rid of them. Napoleon will lure them with promises of glory, land grants and the hope of a resurrected New France. I know this is possible because, although I do not have the liberty to explain now, it is not new. We have just scotched a transhipment of arms from France to America, resulting from a secret accord between Paris and Washington.'*

'So, with Boney stirring up Canada,' summarized Blackwood gloomily, 'supported by remnants of the Grand Army and a fleet built largely in Antwerp; with France weakened by an exodus of its army and with us rushing about trying to save what we can, Alexander capitalizes on his success at no further exertion to himself because we would be exhausted and bankrupt.'

'Yes. And if you wish to extrapolate further, we know the Americans are building a first-rate. If the ships in Antwerp were made available to them, sold cheaply like Louisiana, with American seamen taking them down the Channel under our noses while we kick our heels here waving bunting at His Most Christian Majesty . . .'

'Pray, Drinkwater, don't go on. Thank heaven you did not extrapolate all this to poor Billy.' The two men laughed grimly and Blackwood added, 'I fully understand, and will make sure there are no problems with Their Lordships.'

'Thank you.'

'Now, is there anything you want? Any way I can help?'

'No, I think if I can work to the westward and lie off the Azores, I might yet prevent this horror.'

'It is as well you were on hand . . . ah, here's Colville.'

The flag-lieutenant was crossing the deck with a sealed packet which he held out for Drinkwater.

'Thank you Mr Colville,' Blackwood said, nodding the

* See *Beneath the Aurora*

70

young officer away, and then in a lower tone, 'I should have a quick look at them, Drinkwater, to ensure they are what you want.'

Drinkwater broke the seal and scanned the single page. For a moment the two captains stood silently, then Drinkwater looked up, folding the paper and thrusting it into his breast pocket. He held out his hand to Blackwood.

'I declare myself perfectly satisfied, Blackwood, and thank you for your help.'

'*Carte blanche*, eh?' Blackwood smiled.

'*Carte blanche* indeed.' They shook hands warmly.

'Good fortune, Drinkwater,' Blackwood said and turned away. 'Mr Colville! Call Captain Drinkwater's gig alongside.'

A few moments later Drinkwater was seated in the boat. Midshipman Dunn stood upright in the stern, anticipating Drinkwater's order to return to *Andromeda*.

'The Trinity Yacht, Mr Dunn,' Drinkwater said, seating himself in the stern-sheets.

'The Trinity Yacht sir,' piped Mr Dunn and turned to Wells the coxswain, and Drinkwater caught the look of incomprehension that he threw at the older man.

'Aye, aye, sir,' Wells responded imperturbably, ordering the bowman to shove the boat's head off, and the vertically wavering oars came down and dipped into the sea. As they came out of the huge flagship's lee, a gust of wind threatened to carry Drinkwater's hat off and he clapped his hand on its crown. A little chop was getting up and the oar-looms, swinging forward before diving into the grey-blue water, sliced the top off the occasional wave. Casting round to orientate himself, Drinkwater realized the wind was from the south-south-west. He was going to have a hard beat to windward.

The Trinity Yacht lay anchored close to the *Royal Sovereign*, the smallest vessel in the squadron, but rivalling the royal yacht in the splendour of her ornamentation. Cutter-rigged, she bore an ornate beak-head beneath her bowsprit, upon which a carved lion bore a short-sword aloft. Her upper wales were a rich blue, decorated with gilded carving, each oval port being surrounded by a wreath of laurel. Her stern windows and tiny quarter galleries were diminutives of a much larger ship. Across the stern these windows were interspersed with pilasters and in the centre were emblazoned the unsupported arms of the Trinity House.

These arms, a red St George's cross quartering four black galleons, were repeated on a large square flag at the cutter's single masthead and in the fly of her large red ensign which fluttered gaily over her elaborately carved taffrail. Drinkwater was familiar with her and the device; many years earlier he had served in several of the Trinity House buoy yachts.

'Boat 'hoy!'

'*Andromeda*!' Dunn's treble rang out, forestalling Wells's response and indicating by the ship's name, the presence of that ship's captain.

The boat ran alongside the yacht's side and a pair of man-ropes covered in green baize and finished with Matthew Walker knots snaked down towards him. Grasping these he scrambled quickly up the side and on to the deck.

'Good morning,' he said dusting his hands and

touching the forecock of his hat as an elderly officer in a plain blue coat responded. 'I am Captain Drinkwater of the *Andromeda* . . .'

'You are only a little changed, Captain Drinkwater . . .'

'Mr Poulter?'

'The same, sir, the same, though a little longer in the tooth and almost exhausting my three score and ten.'

'Are you, by God? Well, you seem to thrive . . .'

'Captains Woolmore and Huddart are aboard, sir, but neither have yet put in an appearance on deck.'

'I met them last night and spoke at length to Captain Huddart, but best let the Elder Brethren sleep, Captain Poulter,' Drinkwater said, giving Poulter his courtesy title. 'They dined exceeding well last night. I was sorry not to see you there. You were the only commander not present last night.'

'You know the Brethren, Captain Drinkwater, you know the Brethren,' Poulter said resignedly, as though age had placed him past any resentment at the affront.

'Well, they ought perhaps to know His Royal Highness is already astir.'

'Are we expecting orders?'

'I think not yet for yourselves or the rest of the squadron, but I have to leave you in some haste and that is why I am here. Not seeing you last night led me to hope you might be still in command here, but whomsoever I found, I guessed would be willing to take home private letters for me.'

'Of course, Captain, happy to oblige . . .'

'The truth is I have no idea when the squadron will return to port. I anticipate His Royal Highness may not wish to haul down his flag until he has stretched

73

his orders to the limit, whereas you will be returning immediately to the Thames.'

'You have the advantage of me there, then.'

'Huddart mentioned it last night . . .' Drinkwater drew two letters from his breast pocket, checked the superscriptions and handed them to Poulter. 'I'm obliged to you Mr Poulter.'

'Glad to be of service, Captain Drinkwater. Will you take a glass before you go?'

'Thank you, but no. I have to get under weigh without further delay.'

'Where are you bound?'

'Down Channel to the westward,' Drinkwater held out his hand.

Poulter shook it warmly then sniffed the wind. 'You'll have a beat of it, then.'

'Unfortunately yes.' Drinkwater was already half over the rail, casting a glance down at the boat bobbing below.

'Well, it's fair for the estuary,' said Poulter leaning over to watch him descend, the letters, one to Drinkwater's prize agent, the other to Elizabeth, fluttering in his hand.

'And I daresay the Brethren will be anxious to be off, eh, Mr Poulter?' and grinning complicitly Drinkwater sat heavily in the gig's stern-sheets and allowed Mr Dunn to ferry him back to his frigate.

Out of Soundings

The wind settled in the south-south-west, a steady breeze which wafted fluffy, lambs-wool clouds off the coast of France. Clear of Cap Blanc Nez, Birkbeck had the people haul the fore-tack down to the larboard bumkin, and the main-tack forward to the fore chains. The sheets of the fore and main courses were led aft and hauled taut. *Andromeda* carried sail to her topgallants and heeled to leeward, driving along with the ebb tide setting her south and west through the Dover Strait, and while her bowsprit lay upon a line of bearing with the South Foreland high lighthouse, the tide would set her clear of the English coast.

Periodically a patter of spray rose in a white cloud over her weather bow, hung an instant, then drove across the forecastle and waist, darkening the white planking. The sea still bore the chill of a cold winter, and set anyone in its path a-shiver, but the sunshine was warm and brought the promise of summer along with the faint scent of the land.

'France *smells* all right,' Drinkwater overheard Midshipman Dunn say, 'but it don't mean it *is* all right.'

This incontrovertible adolescent logic diverted Drinkwater's attention from the frigate's fabric, for she would stand her canvas well, to consider the plight of the muscle and brain that made her function.

Under any other circumstances, so fine a day with so fine a breeze would have had the hands as happy as children playing, but there was a petulance in Dunn's voice that seemed to be evidence of a bickering between the young gentlemen. Further forward, Drinkwater watched the men coiling down the ropes and hanging them on the fife-rails. From time to time one of them would look aft, and Drinkwater would catch the full gaze of the man before, seeing the eyes of the captain upon him, he would look quickly away.

Nearer to him, Birkbeck the sailing master checked the course for the twentieth time, nineteen of which had been unnecessary. Marlowe and Ashton were also on deck, conversing in a discreet tête-a-tête, except that their discretion was indiscreet enough to reveal the subject of their deliberations to be Captain Drinkwater himself, at whom they threw occasional, obvious and expectant glances.

Drinkwater knew very well what was on their minds; his dilemma was the extent to which he could explain where they were bound and why they had left the Royal Squadron. Why in fact they were headed, not for the River Medway to lay up their ship, but down Channel. It was a problem he had faced before, and often caused a lack of trust, particularly between a commander and a first lieutenant, but it was made far worse on this occasion because of the source of the intelligence which had precipitated this wild passage to the westward. How could he explain the rationale upon which his conclusions were based? How could he justify the conviction that had led him to obtain his orders? Moreover, he knew it was his conscience that spurred him to justify himself at all, not some obligation laid upon a post-captain in the Royal Navy based on moral grounds, or consideration for his ship's company. In retrospect it all seemed like deception, and as the hours passed, Blackwood's suspicions appeared more justifiable. But to set against this was the reflection that Blackwood had come round to support Drinkwater in the end, and what was the diversion of one frigate, if it could save the peace?

On the other hand, what was it to Blackwood, when all was said and done? The man was almost at the top of the post-captain's list and was virtually beyond any recriminations if things miscarried. In such a light, even the support of Prince William Henry might prove a fickle thing, for His Royal Highness carried no weight at the Admiralty.

Drinkwater shoved the worrying thought aside. He would have to offer some explanation to the ship's company, for the news that peace was concluded and the ship was to have laid up, was too well known to simply pass over it if he wanted his people to exert themselves. As matters stood, it was already common knowledge he had been aboard *Impregnable* earlier that morning; it was also known that even earlier a French staff-officer had come aboard and been in conversation with Captain Drinkwater for a long time. Most of the night, it was said in some quarters, which added spice to an even more scurrilous rumour that the captain's nocturnal visitor had been a woman!

This was imagined as perfectly possible among the prurient midshipmen, but when it was later postulated in the wardroom, Lieutenant Marlowe pooh-poohed it as ridiculous.

'D'you think I would not know a woman when she came aboard,' Marlowe said dismissively. 'A lot of Frenchmen do not have deep voices.'

This statement divided the wardroom officers into the credulous and the contemptuous, further disturbing the tranquillity of the ship.

'Well, what d'you think, Frey?' Ashton asked as he helped himself to a slice of cold ham. 'You've sailed with the queer old bird before.'

Frey shrugged. 'I really have no idea,' he replied evasively.

'But you must have!'

'Why?' Frey looked up from his own platter.

'Well, I mean does our Drink-water,' Marlowe laboured the name, thinking it witty, 'make a habit of entertaining French whores?'

Frey casually helped himself to coffee. It was painful to hear Drinkwater spoken of in such terms by this crew of johnny-come-latelies, but Frey was too open a character to dissemble. Drinkwater had, he knew, been a party to some odd doings during the late war, but he did not wish to expatiate to his present company. Why should he? These men were not comrades in the true sense of the word; they were merely acquaintances, to be tolerated while the present short commission was got over. Nevertheless he was assailed by a growing sense of anticlimax in all this. Superficially the task of conveying the rightful king of France back to his realm had a comfortably conclusive feeling about it. It was like the end of a fairy story, with the kingdom bisected in favour of the parvenu hero, and the princess given in marriage to cement the plot. Except that that was not what had happened; the parvenu hero had lost, the princess was snatched back by her father and the kingdom was being returned to the ogre.

'Well, Frey? It seems by your silence that you know damned well our Drinkie's a famous libertine, eh?' goaded Ashton.

'What confounded nonsense!' Frey protested. He did not like Ashton, seeing in the third lieutenant a manipulative and unpleasant character, but his introspection had delayed his response and he had left it too late to defend Drinkwater.

'Tut, tut. Now we know why he never hoisted himself up the sides of a two-decker,' said Marlowe pointedly and with such childish delight that a disappointed Frey concluded the man was either superficial, or of limited intelligence.

'You know very well we were only attached to the Royal Squadron in honour of His Royal Highness,' Frey said, trying to recover lost ground.

'I suppose they had to leave Drinkwater in her,' Hyde, the hitherto silent marine officer, put in, looking up briefly from his book. 'After all he has just taken a Danish cruiser . . .'

'I heard he was damned lucky to get away with that,' said Ashton maliciously, 'and I heard he took a fortune in specie.'

'Is that true, Frey?' asked Marlowe, provoking Hyde to abandon his book.

Frey finished his coffee and rose from the table as *Andromeda* hit a wave and shuddered. An explosion of oaths from his brother officers revealed they had yet to acquire their sea-legs while his were perfectly serviceable.

'I expect so, gentlemen. But if you're so damnably curious, why don't you ask him yourself.' And clapping his hat upon his head, Lieutenant Frey left for the quarterdeck.

Later, Lieutenant Marlowe, having plucked up enough courage from the urgings of Lieutenant Ashton, took Frey's advice. He began to cross the deck, colliding with Birkbeck beside the binnacle as he made his way upwards from the lee hance.

'Steady, Mr Marlowe,' Birkbeck growled, 'in more ways than one.'

'What d'you mean by that?' asked Marlowe, reaching a hand out to support himself by the binnacle.

'I mean,' said Birkbeck in as quiet a voice as would carry above the low moan of the wind in the rigging and the surge and rush of the sea alongside, 'I shouldn't go a-bothering the captain just at the moment . . .'

Marlowe looked askance at Birkbeck. The old man had been on deck since *Andromeda* had got under weigh, seeing her clear of the South Sand Head of the Goodwins and the Varne Bank. He had not been party to the speculation in the wardroom, so how did he know what was in Marlowe's mind? Moreover, he was unshaven and his hair, what there was of it, hung down from the rim of his hat in an untidy and, to Marlowe, offensive manner. Marlowe concluded the ruddy faced old man was an insolent fool. Damn-it, the man was not fit for a quarterdeck!

'I'll trouble you to mind your own business, *Mister* Birkbeck, while I mind mine.'

Birkbeck shrugged. 'Have it your own way, young shaver,' he replied as Marlowe, flushed with the insolence, strove to reach Drinkwater.

The captain had lodged himself securely against the larboard mizen pinrail which, although on the windward side of the ship was, from the effect of the frigate's tumblehome, the least windy place on the quarterdeck. He was staring forward, an abstracted look on his weatherbeaten features against which the line of a sword-scar showed livid.

Just as Lieutenant Marlowe reached the captain, *Andromeda's* bow thumped into the advancing breast of a wave. She seemed to falter in mid-stride, kicked a little to starboard as the wave sought to divert her from her chosen track, then found her course again. But the sudden increase in heel caught the unsteady Marlowe offbalance. To preserve his dignity and prevent himself from falling ignominiously, Marlowe's hands reached out and scrabbled for the ropes belayed to the mizen pinrail. Instead they encountered Drinkwater's arm.

'What the . . .?'

Drinkwater turned, feeling the young man's vain attempt to seize him, then quickly reacted and seized Marlowe's outstretched hand.

'Come, sir, steady there! What the devil's the matter?'

Marlowe regained his balance, but lost his aplomb. 'I beg pardon, sir,' he gabbled all in a breath, 'but I wondered if you have any orders, sir.'

Had Drinkwater not been so dog-tired and had he not been almost asleep on his feet, he might have been in a better humour and laughed at the young officer's discomfiture. Reluctant to leave the deck, yet content to abandon matters to Birkbeck's competence, he had been languishing in the comfortable compromise of a reverie. As it was, only the helmsmen laughed surreptitiously, while Drinkwater showed a testy exasperation.

'Mr Birkbeck?' he called sharply.

'Sir?' Birkbeck came up the sloping deck with a practised, almost, Marlowe thought, insulting ease.

'What orders d'you have?'

'Why, sir, to keep her full-and-bye and make the best of our way down Channel.'

Drinkwater turned his gaze on Marlowe. 'There, Mr Marlowe, does that satisfy you?'

'Well, not really sir. I had hoped that you might confide in me, sir.'

'Confide in you, sir? If you sought a confidence, should not you have been on deck earlier, Mr Marlowe, when we were getting under weigh? After all, you knew of our visitor last night.'

'Well, sir, you did not condescend to inform me of anything consequent upon your visitor. As you know, under normal circumstances as first lieutenant I should not keep an anchor watch, but having done so since we were engaged upon a special duty, I had turned in and there was nothing in your night orders to suggest . . .'

'That you had to forgo your breakfast, no, of course not; but you are first lieutenant of a frigate on active service.'

'*Active* service, sir?' Marlowe frowned, looking round

82

at Birkbeck who caught his eye and turned away. 'I do not think I quite understand, sir.'

'I am very certain you do not understand, Mr Marlowe.'

'But sir,' Marlowe's tone was increasingly desperate, 'might I not be privy to . . .?'

'No sir, you may not. Not at this moment. If Lieutenant Colville was sent out of hearing while His Royal Highness,' Drinkwater invoked the pompous title with a degree of pleasure, sure that it would silence his tormentor, 'gave me my orders, I do not think it appropriate that I confide in you, do you?'

Crestfallen and confused, Marlowe mumbled a submissive 'No, sir.'

'Very well, Mr Marlowe, then let's hear no more of the matter until we are out of soundings.'

Marlowe's mouth dropped open in foolish incredulity. 'Out of soundings . . .?'

Astonishment lent volume to Marlowe's exclamation; Ashton caught it, downwind across the deck, and dropped his jaw in imitation of his senior; Birkbeck caught it and sighed an old man's sigh; Midshipman Dunn caught it and his eyes brightened at the prospect of adventure, and the helmsmen caught it silently, mulling it over in their minds until, relieved of their duty, they would release it like a rat to run rumouring about the berth-deck.

As for Drinkwater, he felt ashamed of his peevishness; this was not how he had hoped to let his ship's company know they were outward bound for the Atlantic Ocean, nor was it how he should have treated his first lieutenant. If he had not been so damned tired . . . He sighed and stared to windward. The comfortable mood eluded him.

The little encounter with Marlowe upset him and left his mind a-whirl again.

As soon as *Andromeda* had cleared Dungeness, Drinkwater went below. He was exhausted and, removing his hat, coat and shoes, loosed his stock and tumbled into his swinging cot. He thought for a moment that even now he would be unable to sleep, for his mind was still a confusion of thoughts. The enormity of Hortense's news, the possible consequences of it, the attention to the details of informing Elizabeth and making arrangements for his informant, the influencing of Prince William Henry and now the bother of his ship's company and its officers, all tumbled about in his tired head. Each thought followed hard upon its progenitor, and always at the end of the spiral lay the black abyss of *what if . . .?*

What if they missed the French ships? What if Hortense had lied? What if she told the truth and he miscalculated? What if the Tsar changed his mind? What if . . .? What if . . .? Slowly the thoughts detached themselves, broke up and shrank, slipping away from him so that only the blackness was there, a blackness into which he felt himself fall unresisting, an endless engulfment that seemed to shrink him to nothing, like a trumpet note fading.

Drinkwater woke with a start. Sweat poured from him and his garments were twisted about his body like a torque. He felt bound and breathless. Sweat dried clammily upon him and the latent heat of its evaporation chilled him. There was a dull ache in his jaw. Then he remembered: he had been drowning! He was wet from the sea; gasping from having been dragged beneath something monstrous, but beneath what?

And then the entire dream came back to him: the water, the strange ship, the noise of clanking chains, the white and ghostly figure that had reared above him: Hortense, pallid as a corpse, beautiful and yet ghastly, as though her whole face was riven by scars. Yet the scars were not marks, but the twists of serpents. It was Hortense, but it was also the Medusa which seemed to be borne as a figurehead on the bow of the strange and clattering ship. Then he was under water and fighting for his life as the noise reached a terrifying crescendo from which he knew he must escape, or die.

As he lay mastering his terror, he recognized the old dream. Once, when he was an unhappy midshipman, it had come to him regularly, marking the miserable days of his existence aboard the frigate *Cyclops*. Since then it had visited him occasionally, as a presentient warning of some impending event. But now he felt no such alarm, as though this terror from his youth could only frighten him when he was weak and exhausted. It was just a visitation from the past; a relic. Old men feared death, not the wearying vicissitudes of misfortune. These, experience taught them, were to be confronted and mastered.

In the past, Hortense's image had sometimes occupied the post of what he had come to call the 'white lady'. Perhaps it was because she had again entered his life that the dream had come roaring out of his subconscious. As he lay there, staring up at the deck-head which glowed in the last reflections of daylight coming in through the stern windows, he mastered the lingering fear which was rapidly shrinking to apprehension. His thoughts ordered themselves slowly but surely, returning him to the state of conscious anxiety from which he had escaped in sleep.

Any analysis of his actions must be seen in the light of good faith. The orders the prompted prince had given him cleared his yard-arm as far as the Admiralty were concerned; all his best efforts must now be bent on reaching the Azores and lying in wait for the French ships. If allied warships brought the Emperor Napoleon to the islands before the French ships arrived, so much the better. Drinkwater would be able to persuade their commanders to remain in the vicinity. If, on the other hand, the French ships lay off the islands in waiting for their Emperor, he would attack them and while he could never guarantee success, he was confident he could sufficiently damage them to prevent them rescuing their prize and carrying out their confounded stratagem.

Then an uncomfortable thought struck him. While he had a full crew, most of which had successfully fought in the Vikkenfiord, his officers were largely inexperienced. It would not have mattered if all they had had to do was act as part of Prince William Henry's Royal Squadron. But now, while his elderly frigate was painted to a nicety, she had not refilled her magazines and was woefully short of powder and ball. True, he had a stock of langridge, grape and musket balls, but there was no substitute for good iron shot. And if that were not enough, he was victualled for no more than a month, two at the most, and carried no spare spars. These thoughts brought him from his bed.

The frigate was still close-hauled on the larboard tack, well heeled over to starboard, and the rush of water along her sides added its undertone to the monstrous creaking of the hull, the groan of the rudder stock below him and the faint tremulous shudder through the ship's fabric as she twitched and strained to the whim of wind and sea.

Drinkwater reached the quarter-gallery, eased himself and poured water into a basin. It slopped wildly as he scooped it up into his face and brushed his teeth. His servant Frampton had long-since abandoned the captain to his slumbers, and Drinkwater was glad of the lack of fossicking attention which he sometimes found intolerably vexing. He retied his stock, dragged a comb through his hair and clubbed his queue. Finally he eased his wounded shoulder into the comfortable broadcloth of his old, undress uniform coat, pulled his boat-cloak about his shoulders and, picking his hat from the hook beside the door, went on deck.

It was almost dark when he gained the quarterdeck. Low on the western horizon a dull orange break in the overcast showed the last of the daylight. Overhead the clouds seemed to boil above the mast-heads in inky whorls, yet the wind was not cold, but mild.

Seeing the captain emerge on deck and stare aloft, the officer of the watch crossed the deck. It was Frey. 'Good evening, sir. Mr Birkbeck ordered the t'gallants struck an hour past, sir. He also had the main course clewed up.'

Drinkwater nodded then, realizing Frey could not see him properly, coughed and grunted his acknowledgement. 'Very well, Mr Frey. Thank you.'

Frey was about to withdraw and vacate the weather rail but Drinkwater said, 'A word with you, Mr Frey. There is something I wish to ask you.'

'Sir?'

'Have you any idea what we are up to?'

'No, sir.'

'What about scuttlebutt?' Even in the wind, Drinkwater heard Frey sigh. 'Come on, don't scruple. Tell me.'

'Scuttlebutt has it that we are off somewhere and that it is due to the, er, officer who came on board last night.'

It already seemed an age ago, yet it was not even twenty-four hours. Drinkwater cast aside the distraction. 'And what do they say about this officer then, Mr Frey?'

'Frankly, sir, they say it was a woman, at least, that is, the midshipmen do.'

'Tom Paine is an intelligent imp, Mr Frey,' Drinkwater replied, smiling. 'He noticed straight away.'

'Then it *was* a woman?'

Drinkwater sighed. 'Yes, though you should not attach too much importance to the fact. I'm afraid she brought disturbing intelligence, Mr Frey, not entirely unconnected with that business in the Vikkenfiord.'

Drinkwater could sense Frey's reluctance at coming to terms with this news. 'Then it is not over yet, sir?'

'I fear not, my dear Frey, I fear not.'

A profound silence fell between them, if the deck of a frigate working to windward could provide such an environment. Then Frey said, 'I think you should tell Marlowe, sir. I do not think him a bad fellow, but he feels you do not trust him, and that cannot be good, sir.' Frey hesitated to voice his misgivings about Ashton. 'I don't wish to presume, sir.'

'No, no, you do quite right to presume, Mr Frey, quite right. I fear I used him ill. It was unforgivable.'

'He certainly took it badly, sir, if you'll forgive me for saying so, though I think Ashton made the situation worse.'

'Oh,' said Drinkwater sharply, 'in what way?'

'Well, sir, I think he put Marlowe up to importuning you; made him stand upon his dignity, if you know what I mean.'

'There was a time when a lieutenant had precious little dignity to stand upon.'

'There was much made of it in the wardroom, sir.'

Drinkwater grunted again. 'Well, well, I must put things to rights tomorrow.'

'You don't mind . . .'

'If you speak your mind? No, no. Under the circumstances, not at all.'

'It's just . . .' Frey faltered and Drinkwater saw him look away.

'Go on. Just what?' he prompted.

'Nothing sir,' Frey coughed to clear his throat, adding, 'no, nothing at all.' As Frey moved away, Drinkwater watched him go, wondering what was on his mind.

To Weather of the Wight

'Well gentlemen,' Drinkwater looked up from the chart at the two officers before him, 'I think I must confide in you both.'

'Are we out of soundings then?' Marlowe asked, a supercilious expression on his face. Drinkwater had forgotten his earlier remark, made more for the sake of its effect, than as a matter of absolute accuracy, but Marlowe's tone reminded him. He stared at the younger man for a moment, taken aback at Marlowe's attitude, so taken aback that a quick retort eluded him.

'Soundings?' he muttered. 'No, of course not,' then he looked up and glared at Marlowe, though he forbore from snapping at him. 'We have yet to weather the Wight.' He tapped the chart, pausing for a moment. 'What I have to say I shall shortly make known to the people, but for the time being it shall be between ourselves. Once we have resolved those difficulties which we can foresee, and there are several, then having taken what remedial action lies within our compass, we can inform the ship. Is that clear?'

'Perfectly, sir,' responded Birkbeck quickly, shooting his younger colleague a sideways glance.

'I think so, sir.' If Marlowe was being deliberately and sulkily obtuse, Drinkwater let the matter pass. He was resolved to be conciliatory, then Marlowe added, 'But is that wise, sir?'

'Is what wise?' Drinkwater frowned.

'Why, telling the people. Surely that is dangerous.'

'Dangerous, Mr Marlowe? How so?'

'Well, it seems perfectly clear to me. It could act as an incitement. If you make them privy to our thoughts, it would exceed their expectations and we should be guilty of an impropriety. Sir.'

'You think it an impropriety to ask them to go into action without knowing why, do you?'

It was Marlowe's turn to frown. 'Action? What action do you think we shall be involved in?' The first lieutenant was wearing his arch look again. It was the condescending way one might look at a senile old man, Drinkwater concluded with a mild sense of shock.

'Well, who knows, Mr Marlowe, who knows? Though it occurs to me we might encounter an American cruiser.' It had clearly not occurred to Marlowe. Drinkwater went on. 'Now then, let us be seated in a little comfort. Mr Birkbeck, you have the other chart there, and if you wish to smoke, please do. Mr Marlowe, do be a good fellow and pass the decanter and three glasses . . .'

But Marlowe was not to be so easily pacified. Doing as he was bid, he placed the glasses on the table. 'Look here, sir . . .'

But Drinkwater's fuse had burned through. His voice was suddenly harsh as he turned on the young first lieutenant. 'No sir! Do you look here, and listen too. We are on active service, *very* active service if I ain't mistaken.' Marlowe seemed about to speak, thought better of it and sat in silent resentment. Drinkwater caught Birkbeck's eye and the older man shrugged his shoulders with an almost imperceptible movement, continuing to fill a stained clay pipe.

'Now then, gentlemen, pay attention: what I have to tell you is of the utmost importance. It is a secret of state and I am imparting it to you both because if anything should happen to me, then I am jointly charging you two gentlemen to prosecute this matter to its extremity with the utmost vigour.'

Drinkwater had Marlowe's attention in full now. Birkbeck knew enough of Drinkwater's past to wear an expression of concern. Drinkwater felt he owed Birkbeck more than a mere explanation; as for Marlowe, it would do him no harm to be made aware of the proper preoccupations of experienced sea-officers.

'I am sorry Mr Birkbeck that we have been diverted to this task and I know well that you were promised a dockyard appointment when this commission was over. Well, the promise still stands, it's just that the commission has been extended.' Drinkwater smiled. 'I'm sorry, but there it is . . .'

Birkbeck expelled his breath in a long sigh. Nodding, he said, 'I know sir: a sense of humour is a necessary portion of a sea-officer's character.'

'Just so, Mr Birkbeck,' and Drinkwater smiled his curiously attractive, lopsided grin. 'More wine?'

He waited for them to recharge their glasses. 'We

are bound to the Azores gentlemen, to trap Napoleon Bonaparte . . .'

'We are *what?*' exclaimed an incredulous Marlowe.

'So it *was* a woman!'

Mr Marlowe could scarce contain himself, puffed up as he was with a great state secret and half a bottle of blackstrap. Birkbeck gave him a rueful glance as the two officers paced the quarterdeck whence the master had suggested they go to take the air and discuss the matters that now preoccupied the first lieutenant and sailing master of the frigate *Andromeda*.

'May I presume to plead my grey hair and offer you a word of advice, Mr Marlowe,' Birkbeck offered. 'Of course, I would quite understand if you resented my interfering, but we must, perforce, work in amity.'

'No, no, please Birkbeck . . .'

'Well, Captain Drinkwater is not quite the uninfluential tarpaulin you might mistake him for . . .'

'I knew he had fought a Russian ship, but I have to confess I had not heard of him in the Channel Fleet.'

'Perhaps because he has seen extensive foreign and special service. Did you know, for instance, that Nelson sent him from the Med, round Africa and into the Red Sea. He brought a French national frigate home, she was bought into our service and he subsequently commanded her. The captain also served under Nelson and commanded a bomb at Copenhagen. Oh, yes . . .' Birkbeck nodded. 'I see you are surprised. Talk to Mr Frey, he was in the Arctic on special service with Captain Drinkwater in the sloop *Melusine* and I believe Frey was captured with the captain just before Trafalgar. I understand Drinkwater was aboard the French flagship . . .'

'As a prisoner?' asked Marlowe, clearly reassessing his commander.

'Yes, so I understand. Later Drinkwater made up for this and battered a Russian seventy-four to pieces in the Pacific.'

'In the Pacific? I had heard mention of the action, but assumed it to have been in the Baltic.'

'That, if I may say so, is the danger of assumptions.' Birkbeck smiled at Marlowe. 'Anyway, I first met him aboard this ship last autumn when he took *Andromeda* over from Captain Pardoe: not that Pardoe was aboard very often; he spent most of his time in the House of Commons and left the ship to the first luff . . .'

'Who was killed, I believe,' interrupted Marlowe.

'Yes. We had trouble with some of the men – it's a long story.'

'I gathered they were mutineers,' Marlowe said flatly.

'Ah, you've heard that, have you?' Birkbeck looked at the young officer beside him. 'Now I understand why you made that remark about incitement.'

'Well, the temper of the men is a matter I should properly concern myself with.' Marlowe invoked the superior standing of a commissioned officer, as opposed to the responsibilities of the warranted sailing master.

'Indeed it is, Mr Marlowe. But you might also properly concern yourself with the temper of your commanding officer. I fear you may have fallen victim to a misapprehension in misjudging Captain Drinkwater. Consider his late achievement. Last autumn, as soon as he came aboard this ship, which had been kept on guard duties and as a convoy on the coast where her captain could be called to the House of Commons if the government wished for his vote, we went a-chasing Yankee privateers

94

in the Norwegian fiords. We took a big Danish cruiser, the *Odin*. It was scuttlebutt then that Drinkwater had some influence at the Admiralty and was wrapped up in secret goin's on. You heard what he said about that woman who came aboard the other night and that she was mixed up in some such business. I've no doubt the matter we are presently engaged upon is exactly as he told us.'

'I had no idea,' mused Marlowe for a moment, then added, 'So, you consider we might see some action?'

Birkbeck shrugged. 'Who knows? Captain Drinkwater seems to think so. Perhaps just by cruising off the Azores we will prevent all this happening, but if Boney escapes, God help Canada.'

'We are playing for very high stakes . . .'

'Indeed we are.'

'But she's an old ship and lacks powder and shot . . .'

'What d'you think we can do about that?'

'I, er, I don't know. Put into Plymouth?'

'It's a possibility . . .'

'But?'

'Not one he'll consider.'

'Why not?'

'It would delay us too much; we'd be subject to the usual dockyard prevarications, difficulties with the commissioner, warping in alongside the powder hulk, half the watch running . . . No, no, Drinkwater will avoid that trap.'

'Well Gibraltar's too far out of our way,' said Marlowe with a kind of pettish finality, 'so what will Our Father do?'

'Can't you guess?' Birkbeck grinned at the young man.

Irritated, Marlowe snapped, 'No I damn well can't!'

Birkbeck was offended by Marlowe's change of tone. 'Then you'll have to wait and see!' he replied, and left the first lieutenant staring after him as he made his way below.

Lieutenant Hyde of the marines sat in the wardroom reading a novel. It was said to have been written 'by a lady', but, despite this, it rather appealed to him. He was an easy-going man whose lithe body conveyed the impression of youth and agility. In fact he was past thirty-five and conspicuously idle. But whereas military officers were frequently inert, Lieutenant Hyde was fortunate to be able to persuade his subordinates into doing their own duty and a good bit of his own. Moreover, this was accomplished with an enthusiasm that bespoke a keenly active and intelligent commanding officer.

The secret of Hyde's success was very simple; he possessed a sergeant of unusual ability and energy. Sergeant McCann was something of an enigma, even between decks on a British man-of-war which was said to be a refuge for all the world's bad-hats. Sergeant McCann was as unlike any other sergeant in the sea-service as it was possible to be; he was cultured. In fact the novel Lieutenant Hyde was reading was rightfully Sergeant McCann's; moreover the sergeant was diligent, so diligent that it was unnecessary for Lieutenant Hyde to check up on him, and he was well acquainted with the duties required of both a sergeant and an officer. This was because Sergeant McCann had once held a commission of his own.

A lesser man would have let bitterness corrode his

soul, but Sergeant McCann had nothing left in the world other than his work. He had been born in Massachusetts where his father had been a cobbler. At the age of sixteen his father had been dragged from their house and tarred and feathered by 'patriot' neighbours for the crime of opposing armed rebellion against the British crown. By morning McCann was the head of his family, his mother had lost her reason and his twelve-year-old sister was in a state of shock. Somehow he got his family into Boston and when that city was evacuated they fled to New York along with a host of loyalist refugees. Young McCann volunteered for service in a provincial regiment, fought at the Brandywine and earned a commission at Germantown. In his absence his mother took to drink and his sister became mistress to a British officer. McCann went south and fought with Patrick Ferguson at King's Mountain, where he was wounded and taken prisoner. After a long and humiliating captivity he found his way back to New York, but no sign of his family. After the peace, in company with other loyalists, he crossed the Atlantic in search of compensation from the British government. In this he was disappointed, and found himself driven to all manner of extremities to keep body and soul together. Finally he entered the service of a moderately wealthy family whose country seat was in Kent. He stuck the subservient existence of an under-footman for three years, then joined the marines of the Chatham division. McCann learned to blot out the past by an intense concentration upon the present. Lieutenant Hyde called him 'my meticulous sergeant' and thus he was known as Meticulous McCann.

Owing to severe losses among the marines during the

preceding cruise, Lieutenant Hyde, Sergeant McCann and a dozen additional red-coated lobsters had been sent aboard *Andromeda* at Chatham shortly before the frigate sailed on her escort duties. The combination of the elegantly languid Hyde and the pipeclayed mastery of McCann was thought by the officer commanding the Chatham division to be ideal for such a ceremonial task.

'Is that damned book *so* entertaining, Hyde?' Lieutenant Ashton now asked.

'It is very amusing,' Hyde replied without looking up from the page, adding, 'Shouldn't you be on deck?'

'Frederic has relieved me. He's under the impression I am acting as his clerk. Anyway, old fellow, I hate to disturb you from your intellectual pursuits, but the Meticulous One awaits your attention.'

'Really . . .' Hyde turned a page, chuckled and continued reading.

'Do please come in Sergeant.' Ashton waved the scarlet-clad McCann into the wardroom, then turned to the marine officer. 'Hyde, you infernal layabout, you quite exasperate me! Sergeant McCann is reporting to you.' Ashton rolled his eyes at the deck-head for McCann's benefit.

Skilfully bracing himself against the heel and movement of the ship, McCann crashed his boots and finally attracted the attention of his commanding officer. Hyde affected a startled acknowledgement of his presence.

'What the devil . . .? Ah. McCann, men ready for inspection?'

'Sir!'

'Very well.' Hyde put his book, pages downwards, upon the table and got up. He seemed to the watching

Ashton not to need to adjust his tight-fitting tunic, but rose immaculate, preened like a sleek bird. He winked at Ashton, picked up his billy-cock hat and preceded McCann from the wardroom. Watching the pair leave, Ashton was shaking his head in wonder at the contrived little scene when a door in the adjacent bulkhead opened and a tousle-haired Frey poked his head out.

'What the deuce is all the noise about?'

'Oh, nothing, Frey, nothing, only Hyde and the Meticulous One.'

'Is that all?' said Frey, preparing to retreat into his hutch of a cabin just as the ship heeled farther over. 'Wind's shifting,' he said, yawning. 'Isn't it your watch?'

'I do wish people wouldn't keep asking me that. The first lieutenant has relieved me.'

'What for?'

'He was feeling generous . . . Frey,' Ashton went on, 'you know Our Father, don't you. What's he like, personally, I mean?'

Frey sighed, scratched his head and came out of his cabin in his stockinged feet. Sitting at the table he stretched. 'I'm not sure I can tell you, beyond saying that I have the deepest admiration for him.'

'They say he's an unlucky man to be around,' Ashton remarked. 'Didn't his last first lieutenant get killed, along with that fellow you were with, what was his name?'

'Quilhampton? Yes, James was killed, so was Lieutenant Huke . . .'

'Well?'

'Well what?'

99

'Well 'tis said we're bound out to the westward in chase of two French ships that have escaped from Antwerp,' expostulated Ashton.

'If that is the scuttlebutt, then it must be true,' said Frey drily, taking a biscuit from the barrel.

'I had it from Marlowe who saw the captain this morning and then heard all about our gallant commander from old Birkbeck.'

'Well then, you know more about it than I do.'

'Oh, Frey, don't be such a confounded dullard . . .'

Andromeda lay down even further to leeward and ran for some moments with her starboard ports awash. Hyde's novel slid across the table and fell on the painted canvas deck covering. Frey bent down, picked it up and gave it a cursory glance.

'Here, put it on the stern settee,' said Ashton. Frey threw it to Ashton who caught it neatly and glanced at the title on the spine. '*Pride and Prejudice*; huh! What a damned apt title for . . .' He looked up quickly at the watching Frey, flushed slightly and pulled the corners of his mouth down. 'Odd cove, Hyde,' he remarked.

Frey stood up; he was about to retire to his cabin and dress for his watch, but paused and said, 'You seem to think most of us are odd, in one way or another.'

Ashton casually spun Miss Austen's novel into a corner of the buttoned settee that ran across the after end of the gloomy wardroom. He stared back at Frey, seemed to consider a moment, then said, 'Do I? Well I never.'

Frey was galled by the evasion. 'What d'you think of Marlowe?'

'Known him for years.' Ashton's tone was dismissive.

'That's not what I asked,' persisted Frey. There was

100

a hardness in his tone which Ashton had not heard before.

'Oh, he's all right.'

'That is what I told the captain,' Frey remarked, watching Ashton, 'though I am not certain I am right.'

'You told the captain?' Ashton frowned, 'and what gives you the right to give him your opinion, or to presume to doubt Mr Marlowe's good name, eh?'

'Something called friendship, Ashton,' Frey retorted.

'Oh yes, old shipmates,' Ashton said sarcastically, 'as if I could forget.'

There was a knock at the wardroom door and Midshipman Dunn's face appeared. 'One bell, Mr Frey,' he said.

'Thank you, Mr Dunn.' Frey shut his cabin door and reached for his neck-linen. There was something indefinably odious about Josiah Ashton and Frey could not put his finger on it. He was too damned thick with Marlowe, Frey concluded, and Marlowe was something of a fool. But it irritated Frey that he could not quite place the source of a profound unease.

As Frey went on deck he passed Hyde's marines parading on the heeling gun deck. They stood like a wavering fence, the instant before it was blown down by a gale. Lieutenant Hyde had almost completed his inspection prior to changing sentries. He caught Frey's eye and winked. For all his intolerable indolence, Frey could not help liking Hyde. One could like a fellow, Frey thought as he grasped the manropes to the upper deck, without either admiring or approving of him.

On deck the watch were shortening sail. The topgallants had already been furled and now the topsails were being reefed. Clapping his hand to his hat and drawing it down hard on his head, Frey stared aloft. The main topsail yard had been clewed down and the slack upper portion of the sail drawn up to the yard-arms by the reefing tackles. The windward topman was astride the extremity of the yard, hauling the second reef earing up as hard as he could, while his fellow yard-men strove to assist by hauling on the reef points as the big sail flogged and billowed.

Lieutenant Marlowe stood forward of the binnacle with a speaking trumpet to his mouth.

'Jump to it, you lubbers!' he was shrieking, though it was clear the men were working as rapidly as was possible. The unnecessary nature of Marlowe's intervention confirmed Frey's revised opinion of the first lieutenant.

Since Frey had last been on deck the weather had taken a turn for the worse. A quick glance over the starboard bow showed the white buttress of the Isle of Wight lying athwart their hawse with a menacing proximity as the backing wind drove them into the bight of Sandown Bay. The reason for Marlowe's anxiety was now clear: he had left the reefing too late, giving insufficient time for the men to complete their task before they must tack the ship. To the north-west, several ships lay at anchor in St Helen's road, while in the distance beyond, a dense clutter of masts and yards showed where the bulk of the Channel Fleet, withdrawn from blockade duties off Ushant, lay once more in the safe anchorage of Spithead. It would be a fine thing, Frey thought, for *Andromeda* to pile herself up at the foot of Culver Cliff within sight of such company!

Frey strode aft, took a quick look at the compass,

gauged the wind from the tell-tale streaming above the windward hammock irons, and then stared at the land. Dunnose Head was stretching out on the larboard bow, and Culver Cliff loomed ever closer above the starboard fore chains, its unchanged bearing an ominous and certain precursor of disaster.

Beside Frey the quartermaster and helmsmen were muttering apprehensively and Frey's own pulse began to race. The seamen coming on deck to take over the watch were milling in the waist. The experienced among them quickly sensed something was wrong. The wind note rose suddenly and to windward the sea turned a silver-white as the squall screamed down upon the ship. For a split second Frey's artistic sensibilities compelled him to watch the phenomenon which looked like nothing so much as the devil's claw-marks raking the surface of the sea.

Midshipman Dunn came running up to Marlowe. 'Captain's just coming on deck, sir.'

Marlowe ignored the boy and continued shouting at the men aloft who were now struggling hard to tame the main topsail. Frey could not see the fore-topsail, but presumed the worst. Frey heard Marlowe's next order with disbelief.

'Aloft there! Leggo those pendants! Let fly the reef-tackles! Standby the yard lifts! Haul away those lifts!' The men stationed at the lifts hesitated and Marlowe leaned forward and screamed at them: '*Haul away, you idle buggers! Haul!*' Then the first lieutenant, a curious, pleading expression on his face, turned towards Frey and the men at the wheels, as though explaining his action. 'We'll reef after we've tacked.'

But he received no consoling approval. Aloft they

had no such appreciation of Marlowe's intentions. The men at the lifts jerked the yards and they began to slew in the wind. The men on the footropes rocked and three at the bunt of the sail let their reef points go, while someone else started the weather reef-tackle so that the topsail shivered in the squall.

The violent movement of yard and sail was sufficient to unbalance the man astride the larboard main yard-arm. He lost his grip of the reef pendant, which streamed almost horizontally away to leeward; then he slipped sideways and fell. He made a futile grab at the loose pendant, but the wind snatched it from him. The next man on the yard tried to seize him, but it was too late. With a cry, the unfortunate seaman fell with a sickening thud at the feet of Captain Drinkwater as he came on deck.

Frey saw the whole thing happen: saw the topman slip and fall, saw Marlowe seek justification for his action and saw him fail to realize what was happening until the body fell to the deck. He saw, too, the look of horror that passed over Drinkwater's face as he came on deck, then saw the captain suddenly galvanized into action, cross the deck, swing forward and take in the whole shambles in a second. Without a speaking trumpet, Drinkwater roared his orders and took instant command of the deck.

'*All hands!*'

The horrified inertia of the ship's company was swept aside, as Drinkwater called them all to the greater duty of saving the ship.

'*All hands about ship and reef topsails in one!*'

The pipes of the boatswain and his mates shrilled and the order sent men to their stations; those already aloft crowded back along the footropes and into the tops. Drinkwater moved smartly across the deck as the men rushed to their positions; ropes were turned off pin rails; lines of men backed up the leading hands as they prepared to clew down the topsail yards again and man the larboard braces. While others stood ready to cast off the lifts and starboard braces, Hyde's marines tramped up from the gun-deck and cleared away the mizen gear.

'Mr Dunn,' Frey called as he ran to his post. 'Take two men and get that poor fellow below to the surgeon.'

Frey took one last look at Culver Cliff. It seemed to loom as high as the main yard.

'Down helm.' Drinkwater stood beside the wheel as the quarter-master had the helm put over and *Andromeda* turned slowly into the wind. There was a touch less sea running now as they rapidly closed the shore where they were scraping a lee from Dunnose Head at the far and windward end of the bay. As the frigate came head to wind, the sails began to shiver and then come aback.

'*Mains'l haul!*' Drinkwater roared.

'*Clew down! Haul the reef tackles! Haul buntlines!*'

The main and mizen yards, their sails slack and blanketed by the sails on the foremast, were hauled round by their braces, ready for the new tack.

'*Trice up and lay out!*'

With Drinkwater's bellowing acting as a noisy yet curiously effective tranquilliser imposing order on momentary confusion, the topmen resumed their positions, a new man occupying the larboard main topsail yard-arm. *Andromeda* bucked into the head sea, her rate of turn slowed almost to a stop. Aloft, the frantic

105

activity of the frigate's competent crew paid off. This fruit of hard service off Norway and Their Lordships' solicitude for a foreign king, which had drafted some of Chatham's best seamen into *Andromeda* to replace her losses, had the topsails double reefed in a few minutes. As the ship continued her slow turn, the wind caught the foreyards fully aback, suddenly accelerating the rate of turn. Drinkwater strode along the starboard gangway the better to see the fore-topsail, but Frey had already run forward and pre-empted him, to wave in silent acknowledgement that all was well.

'*Stand by halliards!*' Drinkwater waited for a moment longer, then gave the final command: '*Let go and haul all!*'

Round came the yards on the foremast and the reefed and thundering topsail was trimmed parallel to those already braced on the main and mizen masts. On the forecastle the headsail sheets were shifted, hauled aft and belayed while the braces amidships were turned up and their falls coiled down neatly on the pins.

'*Lay in! Stand by booms! Down booms!*'

Order reasserted itself aloft. The men began to come down.

'*Man the halliards! Tend the braces and hoist away!*'

The yards rose, stretching the canvas and setting the topsails again. 'Belay! That's well!' Drinkwater turned to Birkbeck who had materialized beside the wheel in all the commotion. 'Steady now, Mr Birkbeck. Let's have her full and bye, starboard tack, if you please.'

Andromeda heeled to larboard and a cloud of spray rose above the starboard bow as she shouldered her way through a sea and increased speed. Beyond this brief nebula lay the white rampart of Dunnose Head while

106

on the starboard quarter Culver Cliff drew slowly, but inexorably astern. After the bowlines had been set up and all about the deck made tidy again, the watches changed. Only a small darkening stain of blood on the hallowed white planks marred the organized symmetry of the man-of-war as she stood offshore again.

'We shall work to weather of the Wight now,' said Drinkwater, handing the deck over to Frey.

'Aye, sir.' Both men stared to windward as they emerged from the lee of the headland. The sea was running high and hollow against the strong ebb and the wind again increased in force. Emerging clear of Dunnose Head and some five miles beyond the promontory, St Catherine's Point stood out clear against the horizon. High above the point, on Niton Down where it was already surrounded by wisps of cloud, stood the lighthouse. Forward, eight bells were struck.

'Judging by that cloud and the shift of the wind we're in for a thick night of it.'

'Aye, I fear so, sir,' agreed Frey. For a few moments the two men stood in silence, then Drinkwater asked, 'Did you see what happened?'

'Yes, I did. Marlowe left reefing too late, then feared embayment and lost his nerve.'

'I assumed he countermanded the order and tried to tack the ship first.'

'That is what happened, sir,' said Frey, his voice inexpressive.

'Do you know the name of the man who fell?'

'No sir; Mr Birkbeck will know.' Frey turned and called to the master who hurried across the deck. 'Who was the fellow who fell?'

'Watson. A good topman; been in the ship since he was pressed as a lad.'

'Thank you both,' said Drinkwater turning away. He was deeply affected by the unnecessary loss. 'Another ghost,' he muttered to himself. Moving towards the companionway he left his orders to the officer taking over the watch. 'Keep her full-and-bye, Mr Frey, run our distance out into the Channel. We'll tack again before midnight.'

'Aye, aye, sir.'

It was only when the captain had gone below Frey realized Marlowe had vanished.

Three Cheers for the Ship

Captain Drinkwater looked up at the surgeon. 'Well, Mr Kennedy?'

'He was barely alive when he reached me.' Kennedy's face wore its customary expression of world-weariness. Drinkwater had known the man long enough not to take offence. He invited Kennedy to be seated and offered him a glass of wine.

'Thank you, no, sir.' The surgeon remained standing.

'Then we shall have to bury him.'

'Yes. They're trussing him in his hammock now.' Kennedy paused and appeared to want to say more.

'There is something you wish to say, Mr Kennedy?' Drinkwater asked, half-guessing what was to follow.

'I hear it was Lieutenant Marlowe's fault.'

'Did you now; in what way?'

'That he had begun to reef the topsails while we were running into a bay, that he left it too late, changed his mind and tried to tack with men on the yards.'

'It's not unheard of . . .'

'Don't you care . . . Sir?'

'Sit down, Mr Kennedy.'

'I'd rather . . .'

'Sit down!' Drinkwater moved round the table and Kennedy sat abruptly, as though expecting Drinkwater to shove him into the chair, but the captain lifted a decanter from the fiddles and poured two glasses of dark blackstrap. The drink appeared to live up to its name as twilight descended on the Channel.

'How many men have died while under your knife, Mr Kennedy?'

The surgeon spluttered into his glass. 'That's a damned outrage . . .'

'It's a point of view, Mr Kennedy,' Drinkwater said, his voice level. 'I know you invariably do your utmost, but imagine how matters sometimes seem to others.'

'But Marlowe clearly did not act properly. He should not even have been on deck.'

'Perhaps not, but perhaps he made only an error of judgement, the consequences of which were tragic for Watson. That is not grounds for . . .'

'The people may consider it grounds for . . .' Kennedy baulked at enunciating the fatal word.

'Mutiny?'

'They turned against Pigot when men fell out of the rigging.'

'Things were rather different aboard the *Hermione*, Mr Kennedy. Pigot had been terrorizing his crew and there was no sign of the end of the war. This is an unfortunate accident.'

'You do not seem aware, sir, of the mood of the people. They were anticipating being paid off. As you point out, the war is at an end and their services will no longer be required. Watson might have even now been dandling a nipper on his knees and bussing a fat wife. Instead, he is dead and the rest of the poor devils find themselves beating out of the Channel, bound God knows where . . .'

'I am well aware of the mood of the men, but you are wrong about the war being over. It seems a common misapprehension aboard the ship; in fact we remain at war with the Americans. However, I quite agree with you that Watson's death is a very sad matter; as for the rest, I had intended telling them when the watch changed at eight bells. But for being overtaken by events, they would not have been kept in the dark any longer. That is a pity, but there is nothing I can do now until the morning. We shall have to bury Watson and when I have the company assembled I shall tell them all I can.'

'The ship is already alive with rumour, sir,' said Kennedy, draining his glass.

'I daresay. A ship is always alive with rumour. What do they say?'

'Some nonsense about us stopping Bonaparte from escaping, though why Boney should choose to run off into the Atlantic, I'm damned if I know. I suppose he wants to emigrate to America.' Kennedy rose, holding his glass.

'I should think that a strong possibility, Mr Kennedy.' It was almost dark in the cabin now and the pantry door opened and Drinkwater's servant entered with a lit lantern.

'Oh, I beg pardon, sir . . .'

'Come in, Frampton, come in. Mr Kennedy is just leaving.'

After the surgeon had gone, Drinkwater ate the cold

111

meat and potatoes Frampton set before him. He was far from content with Marlowe's conduct, but at a loss to know what to do about it. He had been preoccupied with considerations of greater moment than the organization of his ship and now berated himself for his folly. He ought to have known Marlowe had precious little between his ears, yet the fellow had seen a fair amount of service. Then it occurred to Drinkwater that his own naval career had been woefully deficient in one important respect; owing to a curious chain of circumstances the only patronage that might have elevated him in the sea-service had actually confined him to frigates. He must, he realized, be one of the most experienced frigate captains in the Royal Navy. The corollary of this was that he had spent no time in a line-of-battle ship. Perhaps the constraints aboard a ship carrying five or six lieutenants and employed on the tedious but regimented duty of blockade gave young officers of a certain disposition no chance to use their initiative or to learn the skills necessary to handle a ship under sail in bad weather. It seemed an odd situation, but if Marlowe, as son of a baronet, was a favoured *élève* of an admiral, he might never have seen true active service, or ever carried out a manoeuvre without an experienced master's mate at his elbow.

It would have been quite possible for Marlowe to have climbed the seniority list without ever hearing a gun fired in anger! Entry on a ship's books at an early age would have him a lieutenant below the proper age of twenty, with or without an examination, if Marlowe's father could pull the right strings. Drinkwater found the thought incredible, but he forgot how much older than his officers he was. And then it occurred to him that his

112

age and appearance might intimidate those who did not know him; indeed he might intimidate those who *did*!

Did he intimidate Frey?

He must have some sort of reputation: it was impossible not to in the hermetic world of the Royal Navy, and God only knew what lurid tales circulated about him. Then he recalled Marlowe himself making some such reference the night Hortense came aboard, warning him against possible Russian reaction to Drinkwater's presence off Calais. Marlowe knew that much about him. The recollection brought him full circle: Marlowe's initial courtliness could have been a generous interpretation of unctuousness, and although not ingratiating, the man's hauteur in objecting to Drinkwater's proposal to acquaint the ship's company with their task, demonstrated either arrogance or a stupid narrow-mindedness. Or perhaps both, Drinkwater mused.

He had little doubt Marlowe, a man of good birth and social pretensions, was infected with an extreme consciousness of rank and position that coloured all his actions and prevented the slightest exercise of logical thought concerning what he would call his 'inferiors'. There was a growing sensibility to it in the navy, an infection clearly caught from the army, or society generally, and something which Drinkwater heartily reprehended. Men stood out clearly in rank, without the need to resort to arrogance.

Drinkwater grunted irritably. Whatever the cause of Marlowe's disagreeableness, the man was a damned lubber! In tune with this conclusion, Frampton came in to clear the table and Drinkwater leaned back in his chair, toying with the stem of his wine glass.

'There's some fine duff, sir.'

'Thank you, no, Frampton.'

'Very well, sir,' Frampton sniffed.

'Oh, damn it, Frampton, did you prepare it yourself?'

'Of course, sir.'

'Very well then, but only a small slice,' Drinkwater compromised.

Frampton vanished, then brought in a golden pudding liberally covered with treacle. 'God's bones, Frampton, would you have me burst my damned breeches, eh?'

'It'll do you no harm, sir. You should keep your nerves well covered.'

'That's a matter of opinion,' Drinkwater commented drily. He picked up fork and spoon and was about to attack the duff when another thought occurred to him. 'Frampton, would you ask the sentry to pass word for Mr Marlowe.'

'Aye, aye, sir.'

'You sent for me, sir?'

Marlowe swayed in the doorway, the flickering light of the bulkhead glim playing on his features, giving them a demonic cast which somehow emphasized the fact that he was drunk.

'Pray sit down.' Drinkwater considered dismissing him, thought better of it and watched his first lieutenant unsteadily cross the cabin and slump in the seat recently vacated by Kennedy. Drinkwater laid fork and spoon down on the plate, shoved it aside and dabbed his mouth with his napkin, dropping it on the table.

114

'Please tell me what happened this afternoon, Mr Marlowe.'

'Happened? Why, nothing happened. A damned fool fell from aloft, that's what happened.'

'The damned fool you speak of,' Drinkwater said in a measured voice, 'was an experienced topman. He had been on the ship since she commissioned, since he was a boy, in fact.'

Marlowe shrugged. 'The ship was standing into danger and carrying too much canvas.'

'What were you doing on deck? I thought it was Ashton's watch.'

'It was, but I wished Lieutenant Ashton to undertake another duty and relieved him.'

'What other duty?' Drinkwater pressed, though there was nothing very remarkable about the change of officers.

'Oh, some modifications to the watch-bill.'

Drinkwater had the fleeting impression Marlowe was lying, but the man was cunning enough, and perhaps sober enough to think up an excuse. 'We had the men in special divisions for the royal escort. In view of what you told me, I thought it best to rearrange matters.'

'So you took over the deck in order for Lieutenant Ashton to act as your clerk.'

'I took over the deck with the ship carrying too much canvas. Lieutenant Ashton was concerned about it.'

'But neither of you thought fit to tell me.'

'We thought you would know.'

'So you think it was my fault?' Drinkwater asked quietly. Marlowe shrugged again but held his tongue. 'The fact is, Mr Marlowe, that if the ship was carrying too much canvas, it *was* my fault. Nevertheless, the fact does

115

not exonerate you from the consequences of your own misjudgement. Why did you not complete the reefing before attempting to tack ship?'

'The ship was standing into danger,' Marlowe repeated.

'It is a matter of opinion whether or not you had sufficient time to finish snugging the reef down. I'm inclined to believe you had left it too late. You could have taken in a reef earlier . . .'

'I wanted some shelter from the land.'

'Very well, but a more prudent officer would have tacked and then reefed while the ship lay in the lee of the Wight.'

'A more prudent officer?' Marlowe, emboldened by the drink, affected an expression of wounded pride. 'It was because of my prudence that I took action.'

Drinkwater watched; the man was a fool and he himself was rapidly losing patience, but he had no wish to push Marlowe beyond propriety. Before the first lieutenant could say more Drinkwater stood up. The sudden movement seemed to curb Marlowe. He flinched and frowned.

'Mr Marlowe,' said Drinkwater moving round the table, 'I do wish you to consider this matter. You are the worse for liquor. If one of those men forward, whom you affect to despise, should come on deck in the condition you are now in, I daresay you would have him flogged. Now, sir, do you retire to your cabin and reconsider the matter when you are sober.'

Marlowe looked up at his commander and shook his head. 'Trouble with you, Captain Drinkwater,' Marlowe began, levering himself to his feet, 'is you think you know everything.' Marlowe stood confronting Drinkwater. He

116

swayed so close that Drinkwater could smell the rum on him.

'Have a care, Mr Marlowe. Do please have a care.'

Marlowe stood unsteadily and for a moment Drinkwater thought he was going to raise his hand, but then he concluded a wave of nausea affected the lieutenant and he merely covered his mouth. Whatever his motive, Marlowe managed to stagger from the cabin, leaving Drinkwater alone. Drinkwater let his breath go in a long sigh. In his present circumstances, this was something he could well have done without.

Late morning found them still on the starboard tack, but their course lay more nearly west-south-west, for the wind had continued to veer and was now north-west by north. The thick weather that Drinkwater had predicted had run through during the night. Now the wind was lighter, no more than a fresh breeze. The topgallants had been set again, and *Andromeda* bowled along under an almost cloudless sky. If the tide did not play them up and they maintained no less than the nine knots they had logged at the last streaming, they would clear the Caskets and be free to stand out into the Atlantic before long.

Fulmars and the slender dark shapes of shearwaters swooped above the wake in long, shallow glides. The solitary fulmars rarely touched down into the sea, but the shearwaters would swim in gregarious rafts, lifting by common consent and skating away over the waves as the frigate drove down upon them, disturbing their tranquillity. Away to starboard, in line ahead, a dozen white gannets flew as though on some aerial patrol, graceful and purposeful, with their narrow, black-tipped wings.

'I remember gannets like them having blue feet down in the South Pacific,' Drinkwater remarked to Birkbeck as the two older men took the morning air on the weather side of the quarterdeck.

'Aye, they call 'em boobies, I believe,' replied Birkbeck, 'talking of which, you heard about young Marlowe last night?'

'That he was drunk? Yes, I happened to send for him.'

'It doesn't help, sir, if you don't mind my saying so.'

'No, it doesn't.'

''Twould be less of a problem if Ashton didn't possess so much influence over him. I can't make Ashton out. He's a clever enough cove, which is something you cannot say for young Marlowe. The two of them shouldn't be on the same ship, but . . .' Birkbeck paused and shrugged, 'oh, damn it, I don't know.'

'Go on, Mr Birkbeck.'

'To be honest, sir, I ain't sure there's anything to add. It's just that when the senior officer in the wardroom is weak, there is usually trouble. Someone tries to take over.'

'Frey doesn't cast himself in that role?'

'Good Lord, no, sir. Poor fellow sensibly keeps himself to himself.'

'And the marine officer, what's his name? Hyde?'

Birkbeck chuckled and shook his head. 'He's impervious to any influence. An idle dog, if ever there was one, but amiable enough. No, I think there's something personal between Ashton and Marlowe, though what it is, the devil alone knows.'

'Do you know what experience Marlowe has had?' Drinkwater asked. 'He was singularly inept yesterday.'

'I don't think there's much to tell, sir. Borne on the books as a servant, then midshipman in the Channel Fleet. Passed for lieutenant under the regulation age, took part in a boat expedition off Brest, his sole taste of action I shouldn't wonder, and the rest of his time on the quarterdeck of a seventy-four, I think. He was invalided ashore for some reason,' Birkbeck paused, 'could have been drink, I suppose, then he came here.'

'Rather as I thought.'

'Well, I couldn't vouch for the details, but the substance is about right.'

'It must be somewhat tiresome for you in the wardroom.'

'Frey and Hyde are pleasant enough, and Ashton and Marlowe are civil when they are separate; 'tis together they begin to smell fishy.'

'Fishy?'

Birkbeck shrugged again. 'Just something I can smell.'

Drinkwater considered the matter as seven bells were struck. 'I think it is time we buried our dead and I spoke to the people. We will pipe up spirits after that, and this afternoon exercise at the guns.'

'Aye, aye, sir.'

By tonight, Birkbeck thought, the ship should have settled down. He felt he could have put money on it if it were not for Mr Marlowe. And Mr Ashton.

They hove-to and buried the dead Watson at noon, when the ship's day changed. The frigate, with her main-topsail and topgallant backed against the mast and her courses up in their bunt and clewlines, dipped to the blue, white-capped seas that rolled down from the west. After Watson's corpse, in its weighted canvas shroud, had slipped from beneath the red ensign and plummeted to the sea-bed, Drinkwater stationed himself at the forward end of the quarterdeck, his officers ranged about him, the red, white and black files of Hyde's marines drawn up in rigid lines on either side, their backs to the hammock nettings. *Andromeda*'s midshipmen stood together in a pimply gaggle. Like his officers, they had all been sent aboard by their patrons, even sent by the captains of other ships, as though brief service in the vicinity of a prince of the House of Hanover would admit them to the company of the most august. It gave Drinkwater some grim amusement to consider what patrons and parents would say when it got out that instead of being returned to their comfortable berths after a cross-Channel jaunt, they were stretching out into the Atlantic. On the orders of His Royal Highness, of course!

Amidships, over the boats on the chocks in the waist, along the gangways and in the lower ratlines of the main and fore shrouds, the ship's company waited to hear what he had to say, for scuttlebutt had been circulating since the previous day to the effect that the mystery which preoccupied them all would shortly be resolved.

At the conclusion of the short burial service Drinkwater closed the prayer book and nodded to Marlowe. The first lieutenant looked like death, his naturally pale and gaunt features now conveyed the impression of a skull, emphasized in its modelling by his dark beard, imperfectly shaved by his shaking hand.

He had nicked himself in two places and still bled. At Drinkwater's nod he ordered the ship's company to don hats. Drinkwater watched carefully, the degree to which this movement achieved near simultaneity was the first indication as to how well his people thought of themselves as a crew. In the prevailing mood immediately following Watson's burial, and in expectation of news from the captain, the result was promising, if not perfect. Drinkwater settled his own hat and stared about him. Every man-jack forward was staring back. He cleared his throat.

'My lads,' he began, using his best masthead-hailing voice, 'the sad loss of Tom Watson is a consequence of the urgency of our situation. We are bound upon a most important service, one that will not, I hope, detain us at sea for more than a month, two at the most . . .' He paused, gauging from the groundswell of the murmured reaction, how optimistically this news was received. 'We are under the direct orders of Admiral-of-the-Fleet, His Royal Highness, Prince William Henry, Duke of Clarence and Earl of Munster . . .' Drinkwater rather despised himself for invoking all His Royal Highness's grandiloquent titles. It was a deception, of course, an attempt to mislead, to shift the blame to the inscrutable powers of Admiralty and to defuse any speculation that their mission was no more than Drinkwater's own reaction to a rumour brought aboard by a mysterious nocturnal visitor. The visitor could not escape mention.

'We have been informed by special courier from Paris that after Bonaparte surrendered he intends to escape apprehension and avoid exile by crossing the Atlantic. Arrangements to accomplish this are already in motion.

Now, it is not the intention of His Britannic Majesty's government to allow the man who has disturbed the peace of Europe these last twenty years to make mischief in America or, for that matter, His Majesty's possessions in Canada . . .'

To what extent all his men understood this, was unclear. But there were enough intelligent and perceptive souls among them to grasp the seriousness and importance of what he was telling them, to allow its weight to permeate the corporate intelligence of the crew in the next few days. He hoped its gravity would divert any doubts as to why the news from Paris arrived aboard *Andromeda*, rather than the *Impregnable* or the *Royal Sovereign*.

'It is our task to run down to a station off the Azores, to where Bonaparte is to be exiled, to guard the islands and to prevent any unauthorized vessels from releasing him. As you know we are only provisioned for a further two months and we shall have to be relieved by the end of that time. If we meet any man-of-war which does not comply with my instructions, we will engage him. If that happens, I shall expect you bold fellows to show the spirit you lately demonstrated in the fiords of Norway. To this end we shall prepare this ship for action. This afternoon we will exercise at the guns. That is all. God save the King!'

There was a moment's silence, then Lieutenant Hyde stepped forward, doffed his hat and swept it above his head: 'Three cheers for the ship, lads: Hip! Hip! Hip . . .!'

Drinkwater went below with the huzzahs ringing improbably in his ears. The last thing he saw, though, was the ghastly expression on the face of Lieutenant

Marlowe. It made him think of Watson's corpse settling on the ooze of the sea-bed, already half-forgotten.

Under normal circumstances, Drinkwater would have invited his officers to dine with him that day. It was a good way to get to know new faces and to create the bond among them that might be required to prove itself in action. But he was as reluctant to appear to condone Marlowe's behaviour as he was to further discomfit the young man. Whatever Lieutenant Marlowe's shortcomings, he could not be ignored. On the other hand, Drinkwater wanted to know more about Lieutenant Ashton, who would be in command of the starboard battery if they ever engaged Admiral Lejeune's squadron. Instinct told him he should capitalize upon the mood of the ship, and this lost opportunity was just one more irritation caused by Lieutenant Marlowe.

The gunnery exercise had gone off well enough and Ashton's divisions had acquitted themselves with proficiency, but this was due to the drilling and experience the majority of the men had acquired in the past. Marlowe had been conspicuously inactive on the quarter-deck, though Drinkwater had made nothing of it; he had to give the man time to pull himself together and was eager to put the encounter of the previous night behind them both. He was more concerned with maintaining the gun crews' skill. Anxious not to halt the westward progress interrupted by the necessity of burying Watson, they had not lowered a target, but practised broadside firing with unshotted guns and half charges, for Drinkwater could not afford to be prodigal with his powder and had to conserve all his shot.

Nevertheless the activity had been worthwhile, and the concussions of the guns had satisfied their baser instincts. Hyde had employed the usual expedient of having his marines shoot wine bottles to shivers from the lee main yard-arm. 'Generous of the first luff to provide us with targets,' Drinkwater overheard Hyde remark to Frey and was pleased to see the quick flash of amusement cross Frey's serious features. At least, Drinkwater concluded, those two seemed to be getting along well, though Frey's protracted introspection worried him, bringing back gloomy thoughts of its cause.

Going below after the guns had fallen silent, Drinkwater fought off an incipient onslaught of the blue-devils by writing up his journal, but his words lacked the intensity of his feelings and he abandoned the attempt. He was racked with a score of doubts now about the wisdom of backing Hortense's intelligence, of his folly and presumption in badgering Prince William Henry, of the whole ridiculous idea of seeking two frigates in the vastness of the Atlantic and of the preposterous nature of the notion of Bonaparte escaping Allied custody.

In fact, sitting alone in his cabin, rubbing his jaw where a tooth was beginning to ache, he stared astern and watched the horizon rise and fall with the pitch of the ship. It was quite possible to doubt he had received a visitor at all. The surge of the wake as the water whorled out from under the stern where the rudder bit into it seemed real enough, but it too was remote, a near silent event beyond the shuttering of the crown-glazed windows. Through the sashes he watched a shearwater sweep across the wake, following the ever-changing contours of the sea in its interminable search for food. Though skimming the water, its wings constantly adjusting to maintain this position, it avoided the contact which would have brought it down.

The confidence and poise of the bird struck him as something almost miraculous. How did it learn such a skill? Was it taught, or did the bird acquire it by instinct, as a human child learned to breathe and talk? The power and mystery of instincts capable of forming the conduct of shearwaters and the human young, moved ineluctably through all forms of life. The shearwater did not resist the urge to skim the waves, or doubt its ability to do so faultlessly: it simply did it.

Drinkwater grunted and considered himself a fool. Was it doubt more than knowledge that set men apart from the beasts; doubt which caused them to falter, to intellectualize and rationalize what would be simple if they followed their instincts? Hortense Santhonax had been in this very cabin, not a week earlier. She had communicated urgent news and he had believed her, believed her because between them something strange and almost palpable existed. He felt the skin crawl along his spine at the recollection. Instinct as much as the nature of her news had made him act as he did, and he felt in that solitary moment a surge of inexplicable but powerful self-confidence.

He was so deep in introspection that the knock at the door made him jump. It was the surgeon.

'I beg your pardon, Captain Drinkwater . . .'

'Mr Kennedy, come in, come in. Is something the matter?'

'In a manner of speaking, yes. It's the first lieutenant;

he's taken to his bed, claims he's unwell, suffering from a quotidian fever.'

'I gather you do not entirely believe him?' Drinkwater asked, smiling despite himself.

Kennedy pulled a face. 'I tend to be suspicious of self-diagnosis; it has a tendency to be subjective.'

'So what do you recommend?'

'In view of all the circumstances, I think it best to humour him for a day or two. He may be attributing his misjudgements to having been unwell.'

'Yes, that is what I was thinking. It might be an advantage to us all if we were to foster that impression. It would certainly be the best course of action for the ship.'

'D'you want me to cosset him then? Keep him, as it were, out of the way? Just for a little while.'

'Laudanum?'

''Tis said to be a very specific febrifuge for some forms of the quotidian ague, Captain Drinkwater,' said Kennedy, rising, his voice dry and a half-smile hovering about the corners of his mouth.

'Don't you have a less drastic paregoric?'

'He has already tried that, sir,' Kennedy flashed back.

Drinkwater sighed. 'Very well, but only a small dose.' Drinkwater had a sudden thought. 'Oh, Mr Kennedy.' The surgeon paused with one hand on the cabin door. 'Would you be so kind as to join me for dinner today?'

'Of course, sir.'

'Then pass my compliments to Mr Hyde and Mr Ashton, oh, and the purser, Birkbeck and two of the midshipmen. Paine and Dunn will do.'

'Of course, sir, with pleasure.'

'Well, well,' Drinkwater muttered to himself, following Kennedy to the door. Opening it, he confronted the marine sentry. 'Pass word for my servant.'

It was only after the surgeon had left, he thought he should have mentioned his incipient toothache.

The Consequences of Toothache

'I am sorry indisposition keeps Marlowe from our company tonight, Mr Ashton,' Drinkwater said, leaning over and filling the third lieutenant's glass. He had been chatting to Ashton for some time, regularly topping his glass up and the lieutenant was already flushed. About them the dinner in Drinkwater's cabin appeared to be cheerfully convivial. As was customary, a small pig had been butchered for the occasion and the rich smell of roast pork filled the cabin.

'Indeed sir, 'tis a pity.'

'I understand you know him well. Have you sailed with him before?'

'Yes. We were midshipmen in the old *Conqueror* and later lieutenants in the *Thunderer.*'

'Really?' remarked Drinkwater, reflecting that had matters turned out differently, Marlowe and Ashton might have served under his command much earlier. He forbore drawing this to Ashton's attention, however, for the wine was working on his tongue.

'As a consequence of our having been shipmates,

Frederic, I mean Marlowe, became acquainted with my sister.'

Drinkwater gave his most engaging smile. 'Do I gather that they are now intimate?'

Ashton nodded. 'They became betrothed shortly before we sailed.' There was a distinct air of satisfaction about Ashton. 'I imagine Sarah will take our diversion amiss . . .'

'It will not be unduly long, I hope,' Drinkwater persisted, maintaining his mood of confidentiality, but returning the conversation to the personal. 'I suppose the match is an advantageous one?'

Ashton swallowed a mouthful of wine. 'Sarah's a very handsome young lady,' Ashton said, 'as for Fred, well, he'll inherit his father's title and . . .' Ashton seemed suddenly aware of what he was saying and hesitated, but it was too late, he had already indicated Marlowe stood to inherit some considerable wealth.

'Well,' remarked Drinkwater smoothly, as though not in the least interested in Marlowe's expectations, 'I hope the poor fellow is soon back on his feet again.'

'I am sure he soon will be . . .'

'Tell me something about yourself, Mr Ashton. Have you ever been under fire?' Drinkwater closely watched his victim's face.

'Well no, not exactly under fire in the sense you mean. I took part in some boat operations off the Breton coast. We cut out a *péniche* . . .'

'That was alongside Mr Marlowe, was it not?' hazarded Drinkwater. Ashton nodded. 'But no yard-arm to yard-arm stuff, eh?'

'Well no, not exactly, sir.'

'Pity. Still, we shall have to see what we can do about that, eh, Mr Ashton?'

'Er, yes, sir.' Ashton was visibly perspiring now, though whether owing to the heat of the candles, the fullness of his belly or apprehension, Drinkwater was quite unable to say.

'Well, Mr Ashton, we never know what lies just over the horizon, do we?'

'I suppose not, sir . . .'

The meal proceeded on its course and when the company rose they were in good heart. Left alone in his cabin while his servant cleared away, Drinkwater mused on his conversation with Ashton until Frampton's fossicking distracted him and drove him on deck.

A gibbous moon hung above a black and silver sea and Drinkwater found Frey, an even blacker figure, wrapped in his cloak. At Drinkwater's appearance Frey detached himself from the weather rigging.

'Good evening, sir.'

'Mr Frey, would you take a turn or two with me?'

The two men fell in step beside one another and exchanged some general remarks about the weather. The wind held steadily from the north-west and the pale moonlight threw their shadows across the planking of the quarterdeck to merge with those of the rigging and sails. These moved back and forth as *Andromeda* worked steadily to windward, pitching easily and giving a comfortable, easy roll to leeward.

'It's a beautiful night, Mr Frey.'

'It is, sir.'

'I am sorry that your duty kept you from joining me for dinner, but,' Drinkwater lowered his voice, 'truth to tell, I wanted to sound Ashton about Marlowe. I understand the first lieutenant is betrothed to Ashton's sister . . .'

'Ah, that is not known in the wardroom,' Frey said, reflectively.

'That is unusual.'

'But not,' said Frey with some emphasis, 'if you had a reason for not wanting the matter known publicly.'

'You mean, if neither party wanted it known?' queried Drinkwater, intrigued and wondering what Frey was driving at.

'Neither party would want it generally gossiped about if, on the one hand, one did not want the matter to progress; and, on the other, one feared that it would not come to the desired conclusion.'

'Oh, I see,' chuckled Drinkwater. 'You mean Ashton disapproves and Marlowe wishes it.'

'Quite the opposite,' replied Frey, and Drinkwater found himself realizing that Ashton's behaviour did not square with his own hypothesis. 'Ashton wants it,' said Frey, 'but Marlowe does not.'

'Now I come to think of it,' Drinkwater replied, aware the wine had made him dull-witted, 'Ashton seemed keen enough, but what exactly are you hinting at?'

'I may be incorrect, sir, but I believe Ashton has his claws into Marlowe and whatever part Miss Ashton has to play in all this, it would ultimately be to Ashton's advantage.'

'There was some allusion to wealth . . .'

'A considerable inheritance from his father, and, if one can believe the shrewd lobster,' it took Drinkwater a moment to realize Frey was referring to Hyde, 'there is money on his mother's side too.'

'Well, well, well,' Drinkwater said, lapsing into silence

for a while as the two men paced between the carronade just abaft the starboard hance, turned and strode back again towards the taffrail and its motionless marine sentry. 'So how has Ashton achieved this ascendancy?'

'According to Hyde, by the normal manner.'

'You mean the lady has anticipated events?'

'I'd say they had both anticipated events, sir,' Frey remarked drily.

'But if Hyde knows of this scandal, how is the matter not known of in the wardroom?'

'I did not say the scandal was not known about, sir,' said Frey, 'I said the betrothal was not common knowledge.'

'So you did, so you did. I should have been more alert to the subtleties of the affair.' Drinkwater was faintly amused by the matter. 'Now I perceive the effect our diversion into the Atlantic has on all parties,' he remarked, 'not least on poor Miss Ashton.' And in the darkness beside him he heard Frey chuckle.

And as if to chide him for their lack of charity, Drinkwater's tooth twinged excruciatingly.

The frigate settled into her night routine. One watch was turning in, another was already in their hammocks, and the so-called idlers, who had laboured throughout the day, were enjoying a brief period of leisure. The cooks, the carpenter and his mates, many of the marines whose duties varied from those of the seamen, chatted and smoked or engaged in the sailor's pastimes of wood-whittling or knotting.

A few read, and although there were not many books on the berth-deck other than the technical works on navigation which were occasionally perused by the midshipmen, Sergeant McCann was known to have a small box of battered volumes which he had picked up from various sources. His most recent acquisition, Miss Austen's novel, purchased new and which Lieutenant Hyde was so enjoying, was just one of those which he had bought before the ship had sailed. McCann himself, though he had admired the work, had found its reminders of domestic life too painful. At the same time that he had bought *Pride and Prejudice,* he had also acquired a second-hand copy of Stedman's monumental history of the first American War, that struggle for independence which had rendered men like McCann homeless. And although McCann had avoided too often reflecting upon the past, Stedman's partiality for the loyalist cause reopened old wounds.

As a consequence of reading Stedman's book, McCann was unable to avoid the workings of memory and take refuge in his hitherto successful ploy of submerging the past in the present. Moreover, such were McCann's circumstances, that the book shook his sense of loyalty. He had nothing against Lieutenant Hyde, in fact he liked his commanding officer and enjoyed the freedom of action Hyde's inertia allowed him. But it had been officers like Hyde, indolent, careless and selfish, who had degraded his mother and debauched his young sister. He now heartily wished he had not picked up the two heavy volumes of Stedman's works, but having done so, his conscience goaded him unmercifully. Could he not have done more for his mother and sister? He had come to London to seek compensation in order to return to America and rehabilitate his unfortunate dependants, but there had been no money to be gained, and in order to survive he had eventually returned to the only profession war had taught him: soldiering. He had joined the marines with some vague idea that by going to sea he would be the more likely to get back to his native land, though this had proved a nonsense. Year had succeeded year and he had had to abandon hope and find a means to live.

He was no longer a young man; his eyesight was failing and he could not read the pernicious book without a glass. The physical infirmity prompted the thought that time was running out, and while he entertained no doubt that his mother had long since died, he often and guiltily wondered about his sister. But a man who has adopted a mode of acting and made of it the foundation of his existence does not abandon it at once. Indeed, he discovers it is extremely difficult to throw off, so subject to habit does he become. Thus Sergeant McCann at first only indulged in an intellectual rebellion, regarding both Lieutenant Hyde and his own position in relation to his superior officer with a newly jaundiced eye. It was a situation which had, as yet, nothing further to motivate it beyond an underlying discontent. Indeed, McCann was subject to the conflicting emotion of self-contempt, regarding himself as author of his own misery and attributing the abandonment of his sister to base cowardice, ignoring his original motives for leaving North America.

In this he was unfair to himself; but he was unable to seek consolation by discussing the matter with anyone else and consequently endured the misery of the lonely and forlorn. For the time being, therefore, there was no apparent change in the behaviour of Sergeant McCann. But to all this personal turmoil,

Drinkwater's explanation of *Andromeda*'s mission came as a providential coincidence. McCann was uncertain as to how this might help him, but the news brought the current war in America much closer, offering his confused and unhappy mind a vague hope upon which he built castles in the air. Some opportunity might present itself by which he might regain his social standing, and perhaps with it his commission. He conveniently forgot he was no longer young; ambition does not necessarily wither with age, particularly under the corrosive if unacknowledged influence of envy and long-suppressed hatred. Nor did it help that in his conclusion to his master-work, Stedman, a British officer who had served from Lexington to the Carolinas, conferred the palm of victory to the Americans because they deserved it; nor that Miss Austen affirmed that lives had satisfactory conclusions.

Drinkwater was interrupted in his shaving the following morning by Mr Paine who brought him the news that the sails of three ships were in sight to the south-west.

'They're coming up hand over fist, sir,' Paine explained enthusiastically, 'running before the wind with everything set to the to'garn stuns'ls!'

'What d'you make of 'em, Mr Paine?'

'Frigates, sir.'

'British frigates, Mr Paine?' Drinkwater asked, stretching his cheek and scraping the razor across the scar a French officer had inflicted upon him when he had been a midshipman just like Paine.

'I should say so, sir!'

'I do so hope you are right, Mr Paine, and if you are not, then they have heard we are at peace.'

'I suppose they could be American . . .' The boy paused reflectively.

'Well, what the deuce does the officer of the watch say about them?'

'N . . . nothing sir; just that I was to tell you that three ships were in sight to the south-west . . .'

'Then do you return to the quarterdeck and present my sincerest compliments to Mr Ashton and inform him I shall be heartily obliged to him if he would condescend to beat to quarters and clear the ship for action.'

Paine's eyes opened wide. 'Beat to quarters and clear for action. Aye, aye, sir!'

It was difficult to resist the boy's enthusiasm, but Drinkwater concluded he could complete dressing properly before the bulkheads to his cabin were torn down. It was quite ten minutes before he appeared on deck, by which time the boatswain and his mates were shrilling their imperious pipes at every companionway and the slap of bare feet competed with the tramp of the marines' boots as *Andromeda*'s thirteen score of officers and men, a few rooted rudely from their slumbers, went to their posts.

On the quarterdeck, Lieutenant Ashton was quizzing the three ships through a long glass. The sun was already climbing the eastern sky, but had yet to acquire sufficient altitude to illuminate indiscriminately. Its rays therefore shone through the breaking wave crests, giving them a translucent beauty, throwing their shadows into the troughs. This interplay of light threw equally long shadows across the deck, but most startling was the effect it had upon the sails of the three approaching ships, lighting them so that their pyramids of straining canvas seemed to glow.

'I have ordered the private signal hoisted, sir,' said Ashton, 'and the ship is clearing for action.' He shut his glass with a snap and offered it to the captain, 'Up from Ushant, I shouldn't wonder,' he added, by way of justifying himself.

Drinkwater ignored the impertinence and declined the loan of the telescope. 'Thank you, no. I have my own,' and he fished in his tail-pocket and drew out his Dollond glass. Steadying it against a stay, he focused it upon the leading ship. She was a frigate of slightly larger class than *Andromeda*, he guessed, but while it was probable that her nationality was British, Drinkwater knew a number of French frigates were at large in the Atlantic, and the matter was by no means certain.

After a few moments scrutiny, Drinkwater lowered his glass. 'Clew up and lay the maintopsail against the mast, Mr Ashton. Let us take the mettle of these fellows.'

'Aye, aye, sir.'

As the order to 'rise tacks and sheets' rang out, the main and fore courses rose in their buntlines and clew garnets while the yards on the main mast were swung so as to bring the breeze on their forward surface and throw them aback. *Andromeda* lay across the wind and sea, almost stopped as she awaited the newcomers, apparently undaunted at their superior numbers.

'Sir,' said Ashton, 'with Lieutenant Marlowe indisposed . . .'

'Do you remain here, Mr Ashton. Frey can handle the gun-deck well enough.'

'Aye, aye, sir.'

Frey's seniority gave him prior claim to the post on the quarter-deck, but Drinkwater was happier if his more experienced lieutenant commanded the batteries, while Ashton would undoubtedly prefer the senior post at his side. Besides, Drinkwater reflected as he raised his glass again, he could keep an eye on Ashton, who was receiving the reports that the ship was cleared for action. He passed them on to Drinkwater.

'Very well,' Drinkwater acknowledged, keeping the glass to his eye. 'Show them our teeth then, Mr Ashton, and run out the guns.'

The dull rumble of the gun trucks made the ship tremble as *Andromeda* bared her iron fangs.

'They're signalling sir,' Paine's voice cracked with excitement, descending into a weird baritone.

'Well, sir, can you read her number?' asked Drinkwater, aware that his own eyesight was not a patch on the lad's, and saying in an aside to Ashton, 'Better hang up our own.'

'In hand, sir.'

'Good . . . Well, Mr Paine?' Drinkwater could see the little squares as flutterings of colour, but needed the midshipman's acuity to differentiate them. The lad fumbled and flustered for a few moments, referring to the code-book, then looked up triumphantly.

'*Menelaus*, sir, Sir Peter Parker commanding.'

'Very well, Mr Paine. Mr Ashton, I shall want a boat . . .'

An hour later, rather damp from a wet transfer, Drinkwater stood in the richly appointed cabin of the thirty-eight gun frigate. Sir Peter Parker was a member of a naval dynasty, an urbane baronet of roughly equal seniority to Drinkwater.

'We've been cruising off the Breton coast,' he said, indicating the other two ships which had followed

Parker's example and hove-to. He handed Drinkwater a glass of wine and explained his presence. 'I have received orders to sail for America once I have recruited the ship. I need wood and water, but can spare some powder and shot if we can get it across to you all right.'

'I'm obliged to you, Sir Peter. I confess to the Prince's orders being specific on the matter and, had I not run into you would have had to take my chance without replenishment.'

'So,' Parker frowned, 'Silly Billy insisted you stood directly for the Azores in anticipation of Boney's incarceration there, eh?'

Drinkwater nodded. 'Yes. There seems to be a general anxiety about Boney and his eventual whereabouts. He'll be conveyed to the Azores by a man-o'-war, but His Royal Highness thought it prudent to have a frigate on station there directly. I gained the impression the Prince and Their Lordships don't see eye to eye . . .'

'I suppose Billy wants to let them know he's quite capable of thinking for himself,' Parker remarked, laughing.

'I daresay he had a point in believing the Admiralty Board would take their time in sending out a guardship,' Drinkwater remarked pointedly.

'Well, maybe Billy ain't so silly, eh?' smiled Parker, draining his glass. 'Nor is it inconceivable that Bonapartists would want to spirit their Emperor across the Atlantic. He could make a deal of trouble for us there.'

'Perish the thought,' agreed Drinkwater, 'though it is my constant concern.'

'Well, we shall do what we can.' Parker paused to

pass word to his officers to get a quantity of powder and ball across to *Andromeda*, a task which would take some time, and invited Drinkwater to remain aboard the *Menelaus* for a while. The two captains therefore sat on the stern settee reminiscing and idly chatting, while the ships' boats bobbed back and forth.

'So you were part of the squadron that saw Fat Louis back to France then?' Parker asked, and Drinkwater did his best to satisfy Sir Peter's curiosity with a description of the event.

'Seems an odd way to end it all,' he remarked.

'Yes. Somehow inappropriate, in a curious way,' added Drinkwater.

'I presume the Bourbon court will try to put the clock back, while we have to turn our attention to America.'

Drinkwater nodded. 'Though if we bring our full weight to bear upon a blockade of the American coast, we should be able to bring the matter to a swift conclusion.'

'Let us hope so, but I must confess the prospect don't please me and if Boney interferes, we may be occupied for years yet,' Parker said, a worried look on his face, but the conversation was interrupted by a knock at the cabin door and a midshipman entered at Parker's command.

'First lieutenant's compliments, sir, but the wind's freshening. He don't think we can risk sending many more boats across.' The midshipman turned to Drinkwater and added, 'He said to tell you, sir, that we've sent twenty-eight small barrels and a quantity of shot.'

Drinkwater stood up. 'Parker, I'm obliged to you . . .'

The two men shook hands and parted with cordial good wishes.

Out of the lee of the *Menelaus*'s side, Drinkwater felt the keen bite of the wind; another gale was on the way, unless he was much mistaken, despite the fact that ashore the blackthorn would be blooming in the hedgerows.

The gale was upon them by nightfall. During the afternoon the sky gradually occluded and the horizon grew indistinct. The air became increasingly damp, the wind backed and a thickening mist transformed the day. The decks darkened imperceptibly with moisture and, although the temperature remained the same, the damp air seemed cooler.

'Backs the winds against the sun, trust it not, for back 'twill run.' Birkbeck recited the old couplet to Mr Midshipman Dunn. 'Remember that, cully, along with the other saws I've already taught you and they'll stand you in good stead.'

'Aye, aye, sir.' Mr Dunn bit his lip; he had failed to learn any of the 'saws' the master had tried to teach him, but dared not admit it and was terrified Birkbeck was about to ask him to recapitulate. Mercifully the cloaked figure of the captain rose up the after companionway, and Dunn took the opportunity to dodge away.

Drinkwater cast a quick glance about. Aloft the second reef was being put into the topsails. The men bent over the yard, their legs splayed on the foot-rope. Drinkwater peered into the binnacle, the boat-cloak billowing around him. From forward, the smoke coiling out of the galley funnel was flattened and drove its fumes along the deck. Above their heads there was a tremulous thundering as the weather leach of the fore-topsail lifted.

'Watch your helm there!' Birkbeck rounded upon the quartermaster, who craned forward and stared aloft, ordering the helmsmen to put the helm up a couple of spokes, allowing *Andromeda* to pay off the wind a little. 'You'll have another man shivered off the yard if you're not more careful,' Birkbeck snapped reprovingly, then turning to Drinkwater he put two fingers to the fore-cock of his hat.

'North of west, sir, I'm afraid,' Birkbeck reported apologetically to Drinkwater.

'It cannot be helped, Mr Birkbeck.'

They would have to endure another miserable night bouncing tiringly up and down, while the grey Atlantic responded to the onslaught of the wind and raised its undulating swells and sharper waves. It would be chilly and damp below decks; the hatches would be closed and the air below become poor and mephitic, a breeding ground for the consumption and an aggravation for the rheumatics, Drinkwater reflected gloomily. He tucked himself into the mizen rigging and sank into a state of misery. His tooth had ceased to equivocate and the infection of its root raged painfully. He had known for days that the thing would only get worse and it chose the deteriorating weather to afflict him fully. He would have to have the tooth drawn and the sooner the better; in fact a man of any sense would go at once to the surgeon and insist the offending tusk was pulled out. But Drinkwater did not feel much like a man of sense; toothache made a man peevishly self-centred; it also made him a coward. Having his lower jaw hauled about by Kennedy who, with a knee on his chest, would wrest the bulk of his pincers around until the tooth submitted, was not a prospect that attracted Drinkwater. As the sun set invisibly behind the now impenetrable barrier of cloud, the fading daylight reflected the captain's lugubrious mood.

He could, of course, insist Kennedy gave him a paregoric. A dose of laudanum would do the trick, at least until the morning. The idea made him think of Marlowe languishing in his bunk and his conscience stung him. Forcing himself to relinquish the clean, if damp, air of the deck, he went reluctantly below.

In the wardroom Lieutenant Hyde had discovered an equilibrium of sorts, having braced his chair so that he might lean back and read with his booted feet on the wardroom table. At the after end of the bare table Lieutenant Ashton sat in a Napoleonic pose, his expression remote, his hands playing with a steel pen, a sheet of paper before him. Neither officer realized who their visitor was until Drinkwater coughed.

'Oh! Beg pardon, sir.' Hyde's boots reached the deck at the same moment as all the legs of his chair, a sudden, noisy movement which snapped Ashton from his abstraction. He too stood up.

'Good evening, gentlemen. Pray pardon the intrusion . . .'

'Lieutenant Frey has turned in, sir,' offered Ashton.

'I came to see Lieutenant Marlowe.'

Hyde indicated the door to the first lieutenant's cabin and Drinkwater nodded his thanks, knocked and ducked inside. Behind him Ashton and Hyde exchanged glances.

The quarters provided for *Andromeda*'s officers were spartan and what embellishments an officer might bring to his hutch of a cabin conferred upon it a personality.

Lieutenant Frederic Marlowe had two small portraits, a shelf of books and an elegant travelling portmanteau which, standing in the corner, held in its top a washing basin and mirror.

Of the portraits, one was a striking young woman whom Drinkwater took to be Sarah Ashton, though there was little resemblance to the officer he had just seen in the wardroom; the other was of a man dressed in the scarlet and blue of a royal regiment, the gold crescent of a gorget at his throat.

These appointments were illuminated by a small lantern, the light of which also fell upon the features of Marlowe himself. Drinkwater was shocked by the young man's appearance. Kennedy had led him to believe Marlowe's trouble to be no more than a malingering idleness, but the gaunt face appeared to be that of a man afflicted with a real illness, or at best in some deep distress. Marlowe's eyes were sunk in dark hollows and regarded Drinkwater with an obvious horror.

'Mr Marlowe,' Drinkwater began, 'how is it with you?'

Marlowe's lower lip trembled and he managed to whisper, 'Well enough, sir.'

'What is the matter?'

'Quotidian fever, sir, or so the sawbones says.'

Drinkwater had a rather different perception. He looked round the cabin. A small glass stood in the wash basin, and Drinkwater picked it up and sniffed it. The faint scent of tincture of opium was just discernible. For a moment Drinkwater stood undecided, then he turned back to the invalid, and sat himself down in the single chair that adorned the cabin.

'Mr Marlowe, I do not believe you have a quotidian

fever. Pray tell me, to what extent do you owe your present indisposition to the influence of Lieutenant Ashton?' Marlowe's eyes widened as Drinkwater's barb struck home. His eyes glanced at the door to the wardroom, confirming, if confirmation were necessary, the accuracy of Drinkwater's assumption. 'I am aware of your situation *vis-à-vis* Ashton; perhaps, if you wished, you could confide in me. I cannot afford to have my first lieutenant incapacitated; I need you on deck, Mr Marlowe, gaining the confidence of the people . . .'

The shadow of recollection passed across Marlowe's haggard features, then he shook his head vigorously and turned his face away. Drinkwater lingered a moment, then rose, the chair scraping violently on the deck, but even this noise evoked no response from the first lieutenant. 'Damnation,' he muttered under his breath, and stepped back into the wardroom.

Hyde had resumed his reading, though his boots were no longer on the table. Ashton had bent to his writing, but looked up sharply as Drinkwater shut the door behind him and stood before the officers. Realizing their manners, both men made to rise to their feet.

'Please do not trouble yourselves, gentlemen. Good night.'

Rather than returning directly to his own cabin or the deck, Drinkwater descended a further deck in search of the surgeon. He found Kennedy playing bezique with the midshipmen. The intrusion of the captain's features in the stygian gloom of the cockpit produced a remarkable reaction: the midshipmen jumped to their feet, the cards were scattered and Kennedy, who had had his back to Drinkwater, turned slowly around.

'Oh, sir, I er . . . Did you want me?'

'Indeed, Mr Kennedy. I would be obliged if you would pull a tooth for me. At your convenience.'

'There's no time like the present, sir. These young devils have a decided advantage.'

Drinkwater, followed by the surgeon, retired to the half-suppressed sound of sniggering midshipmen.

A few moments later Kennedy joined him in the cabin, producing a small bag from the dark and sinister interior of which gleamed the dull metal of instruments. Drinkwater sat down and braced himself, as much against the motion of the ship as in preparation for Kennedy's ministrations. There was a brief exchange between them, then Drinkwater opened his mouth and allowed Kennedy to probe his lower mandible. It took the surgeon only a few seconds to locate the source of the trouble. He withdrew his probe and searched his bag for another implement. His hand emerged with a pair of steel pincers.

'Humour me and rinse those things in some wine, if you please.'

'It is quite unnecessary . . .'

'Oblige me, if you please . . .'

'Very well.'

Kennedy poured a glass of wine from the stoppered decanter lodged in the fiddles and dipped the closed pincers in it. *Andromeda* groaned mournfully about them as he turned and approached his patient. Drinkwater's knuckles were white on the arms of his chair. Kennedy opened the grim steel tool and bent over Drinkwater, who felt the uncompromising bite of the serrated steel clamp over his own, less robust tooth. There was an excruciating pain which shot like

146

a white hot wire through Drinkwater's brain and he felt the tooth wrenched this way and that as Kennedy bore down on him, twisting his powerful wrist. A faint grinding sound transmitted itself through Drinkwater's skull as Kennedy wrestled with the resisting fang; then it gave way, *Andromeda* lurched and Kennedy almost fell backwards. The pincers struck the teeth in Drinkwater's upper jaw, jarring his whole head. The wine glass fell to the deck and smashed.

A stink filled Drinkwater's nostrils as Kennedy waved the rotting tooth under his wrinkling nose. The surgeon dropped the tooth and pincers, took another glass, filled it and handed it to his spluttering patient.

'God damn and blast it!' Drinkwater bellowed, clapping his hand to his mouth.

'I wouldn't recommend you to swallow, sir. Perhaps the quarter-gallery . . .'

Drinkwater did as he was bid, rinsed his mouth with wine and spat it down the closet. His tongue explored the gaping hole in his teeth as he clambered back into the cabin, a little dizzy and in some pain from the blow to his upper jaw.

Kennedy was clearing away and Drinkwater refilled his glass and filled another for the surgeon.

'Damn me, Kennedy, but you're a confounded brute, and no mistake.'

'I'm sorry,' Kennedy said, smiling, accepting the glass. 'The confounded ship . . .'

'Quite so, but a moment . . .'

'There is something else, sir?'

'Yes. I wish you to cease giving Marlowe laudanum. I am not certain it is having anything other than a deleterious effect.'

147

'It generally does,' Kennedy observed with that clinical detachment that sounded so cold, 'though Marlowe will not see it that way.'

'I don't much care what way Marlowe sees it. I just want that young man back on the quarterdeck, preferably tomorrow.'

'Tomorrow, d'you say?' Kennedy blew his cheeks out and shook his head. 'I don't believe the man is really ill . . .'

'Well there I disagree with you. I think he is ill, but I don't think his lying in his cot is improving him. I also don't believe his disease is fatal.'

'Well, sir,' responded Kennedy in his touchiest tone, tossing off the contents of his glass with an air of affront, 'what d'you believe his disease is, then? I should be fascinated by your diagnosis.'

Kennedy's irritation amused Drinkwater. 'Oh, his disease is of the heart, Mr Kennedy,' Drinkwater said smiling.

'You mean the man is in love?'

'I mean the man is affected by love, or perhaps I should say infected by love, or at least what passes for love in all its complications.'

'Well, sir,' said Kennedy, putting his glass back in the fiddles, 'I have to confess I hadn't noticed the pox, so I suppose you refer to the disease in its emotional form and there, I think, I must confess to having a somewhat limited expertise in the matter.'

'But you will stop the laudanum?'

'If that is what you wish, Captain Drinkwater.'

'It is, Mr Kennedy, thank you. Oh, and my thanks also for pulling my tooth.'

148

'Had I not done so you would have been suffering from a quinsy at best and a poisoned gut else, sir.'

'I'm obliged to you.'

'Thank you for the wine.'

''Tis a pleasure,' lisped Drinkwater, withdrawing his tongue from the gap it compulsively sought to explore. And his sibilant farewell seemed echoed as *Andromeda*'s stern sank into the bosom of a wave, then rose as she drove through the swell which seethed, hissing away into the darkness astern.

A Patch of Blue Sky

Captain Drinkwater was not the only visitor received by Lieutenant Marlowe that evening, for once word of the captain's interest had reached the wardroom, Lieutenant Ashton determined on showing similar concern for a brother officer.

'Well Frederic, this is a pretty pass, ain't it?' Ashton began, sitting in the chair beside the first lieutenant's cot. 'I do believe Our Father thinks you unwell, which doesn't say much for his intelligence, does it?'

At the last remark Marlowe, who had turned his face away from his visitor, swung back. 'Why in heaven's name d'you have to torment me? Do you not have what you want that you must treat me like this?'

Ashton put a restraining hand upon Marlowe's shoulder and shook his head. 'Fred, Fred, you misunderstand me, damn it,' he said, reassuringly. 'I don't wish you ill; quite the contrary, no man would be happier than to see you up and about again.'

'Damn you, Ashton. You're in league with the captain . . .'

'What?' Ashton's incredulity was unfeigned. 'Why in God's name should I have anything in common with the captain?'

'Because,' said Marlowe, twisting round and propping himself on one elbow, 'he has just been here, not an hour ago, maybe less, telling me he wants me on the quarterdeck tomorrow!'

'Well then, that's fine, Fred, fine,' Ashton said soothingly, 'we all want you back at your duty, why should we not? Aye, and the sooner the better as far as Frey and I are concerned.'

Marlowe peered at his visitor suspiciously. The single lantern threw Ashton's face into shadow. 'What d'you mean as far as Frey and you are concerned?'

'Why, because we are doing duty for you . . .'

'Yes, of course . . .'

'What the devil did you think I meant?'

'Oh, nothing . . .'

'Come on Fred, what?'

'Nothing . . .'

'Come on . . . Was it something the captain said?' Ashton asked shrewdly.

'He thinks you have some influence over me,' Marlowe said in a low, shamed voice.

'What damnable poppycock!'

'It could be said to be true, could it not?'

Ashton lost some of his aplomb, recalling his indiscreet remarks to Drinkwater regarding Marlowe's intended marriage: surely it could derive from nothing more? 'Perhaps he knows of you and Sarah,' he said dismissively.

'Have you said anything?'

'Come to think of it I recall mentioning it when we dined together, but it was nothing.'

'So you told him?' The hint of a smile played about Marlowe's mouth. 'And at dinner.'

'Well, yes, I believe I did,' Ashton confessed, flushing, 'but where's the harm in that?'

'Did you tell him of your sister's condition?'

'No, of course not.'

'Damn you, Ashton, I may be a fool, but I can at least keep my mouth shut!'

'There's no harm in it being known you intend to marry her.' Ashton's temper was fraying, but Marlowe had swung his legs over the edge of his cot and lowered himself unsteadily to his feet. He stood in his night-shirt staring down at his persecutor.

'Oh yes,' he said, holding on to the deck-beams overhead and leaning over Ashton. 'Of course. Now get out, and remember when I appear on deck tomorrow which of us is the senior.'

Thoroughly discomfited, Ashton stood slowly and forced a smile at the first lieutenant. 'Of course, Mr Marlowe,' he said mockingly, 'of course.'

Outside the wardroom Ashton almost bumped into the surgeon. The berth-deck was already settled, the air heavy with the stink and snuffles of over five score of men swaying together in their hammocks. The occasional glims threw fitful shadows, but for the most part it was dark as death. The ship creaked and groaned as she worked in the seaway and both men were cursing as they struggled on the companionway. The area was lit by a lantern and the marine sentry outside the ward-room door was a silent witness to their encounter.

'Ah, Kennedy, a damnable night.'

'I am not disposed to argue, Mr Ashton.'

Ashton was about to pass on when an idea struck him. 'There is a matter about which I might be disposed to argue with you, though. Would you join me for a moment in the wardroom.'

'I am not looking for an argument, Mr Ashton.'

'No, no, but a moment of your time.'

The wardroom was empty, its off-duty occupants had retired behind the thin bulkheads that partitioned either wing of the after end of the berth-deck and conferred privacy and privilege upon the officers. The long table that ran fore and aft had been cleared, and its worn oak surface betrayed years of abuse with wine stains, scratches, cigar-burns and boot-marks showing clearly through the greasy wiping that passed for a polishing. At the after end of the wardroom, the head of the rudder stock poked up from the steerage below and was covered by a neatly fashioned octagonal drum head table into which were set some tapered drawers. Across the transom a few glasses gleamed dully in their fiddles. Ashton picked two out and splashed some cheap blackstrap out of an adjacent decanter. Kennedy accepted a glass in silence.

'I have just been to see Lieutenant Marlowe,' Ashton said, taking a draught. 'He seems much recovered.'

'I'm glad to hear it,' replied Kennedy. 'Is that what you wished to argue about?'

'Not really to argue over, just to tell you that he is much improved and therefore your diagnosis of quotidian . . .'

'*My* diagnosis,' Kennedy raised an incredulous eyebrow. 'Well, well, so that is how matters stand, eh?'

'Well, you know what I mean.'

'No, Mr Ashton, I'm not sure that I do. Tell me,' Kennedy ran on without giving Ashton an opportunity to protest, 'is it mischief you're after making?'

'Mischief? How so?'

'Well, that's what I cannot quite fathom, but up to this minute, solicitude is not what I'd have called an outstanding virtue of yours, Mr Ashton. Unless of course, you wish the first lieutenant back at his turn of duty.'

'Well that would be a decided advantage, to be sure, Mr Kennedy,' said Ashton coolly, 'and to know that he is not only back on duty, but able to sustain the effort. I'm led to believe we may yet see some action, despite the peace. 'Twould be most unfortunate if he were to miss an opportunity through suffering from a quotidian fever, or any other kind of indisposition for that matter.'

'I had presumed,' said Kennedy looking into his glass and swirling the last of the wine round, 'that with the coming of peace, opportunities are scarce nowadays and the prize laws will have been revoked by now. Unless, of course, we come up with a Yankee.' He looked up and it was clear from Ashton's expression that he had not thought about this. 'Well, good night to you, Mr Ashton, and thank you for the wine. I'm certain Mr Marlowe will be back at his post very soon.'

Drinkwater slept badly and woke in a sour mood. His gum was sore and his head ached from the wrenching Kennedy had given it. He rose and shaved, damning and cursing the frigate as *Andromeda* did her best to cause him to cut his throat with her motion. Finally

154

he struggled out on deck into the windswept May morning.

Ashton had the morning watch and gave every appearance of being asleep at his post, but he moved from the weather mizen rigging as Drinkwater appeared, punctiliously touched his fore-cock and paid his respects.

'Morning sir. Another grey one, I'm afraid.'

'So I see . . .' Drinkwater cast about him, staring at the heaving sea, leaden under the lowering overcast. The wind was less vicious and although the waves were still streaked with the white striations of spume, and where the crests broke the spray streamed downwind, there was less energy in the seas as they humped up and drove at the ship.

'Well, Mr Ashton,' remarked Drinkwater, clapping a hand to his hat and staring aloft. ''Tis time to shake a reef out of the topsails. This wind will die to a breeze by noon.' Drinkwater looked at Ashton. 'Well, do you see to it, Mr Ashton.'

'Aye, aye, sir.'

Ashton moved away and reached for the speaking trumpet, and Drinkwater fell to an erratic pacing of the quarterdeck, bracing himself constantly against the pitch and roll of the frigate. As he reached the taffrail, the marine sentry stiffened.

'Stand easy, Maggs,' he growled.

'Sir.'

Drinkwater stared astern. The wake was being quartered by birds. The ubiquitous fulmar, the little albatross of the north, skimmed with its usual apparently effortless grace, and there, almost below him, a pair of storm petrels dabbled their tiny feet in the marbled water that streamed out from under *Andromeda*'s stern. Where, he wondered, did those minuscule birds live when the weather was less tempestuous? And how was it that they only showed their frail selves when boisterous conditions prevailed? Did they possess some magic property like the swallow which was said, somewhat improbably, to winter in the mud at the bottom of the ponds they spent the summer skimming for flies?

He grunted to himself, and was then aware of the silent Maggs, so he turned about and walked forward again with as much dignity as rank could induce and the heaving deck permit. To windward the scud was breaking up, looking less smoky and lifting from the *Andromeda*'s mastheads. Aloft, members of the watch shook out a reef and above them he saw the swaying main truck describe its curious hyperbolic arc against the sky.

Out of the recesses of memory he recalled the question old Blackmore used to ask the midshipmen aboard His Britannic Majesty's frigate *Cyclops*. The sailing master would often quiz the young gentlemen to see if they were awake, and Drinkwater chuckled at the recollection as a small, blue patch of sky gleamed for a moment in the wind's eye. He felt his spirits rise.

'Mr Paine!'

The midshipman of the watch ran up, surer-footed than his commander. 'Sir?'

'If a ship circumnavigates the globe, Mr Paine, which part of her travels the farthest?'

Paine's brow creased and he raised his right index finger to his head as though this might aid the processes of intelligence. 'Travels farthest . . .?' The lad hesitated a moment and then light dawned. 'Why, sir, the mastheads!'.

'Well done, Mr Paine. Now do you try that out on the other midshipmen.'

'I will, sir,' the boy said brightly, his eyes dancing and his smile wide.

'Carry on then.'

'Aye, aye, sir.' And Paine shifted his finger to his over-large hat and capered off.

'Was I ever like that?' Drinkwater wondered to himself. The *Cyclops* had been a sister-ship of the *Andromeda* and he remembered how Captain Hope had seemed to him all those years ago an old man who had not gained the preferment he deserved. Sadly Drinkwater concluded he must seem the same to his own midshipmen. He resisted allowing the thought to depress him and his stoicism was swiftly reinforced by a sheet of spray leaping over the weather bow and streaming aft to patter about him. He tasted salt on his lips and felt the sting of the sea-water. The little blue patch had vanished and he wondered if he had not been unduly optimistic in his prediction to Ashton. Nothing, he concluded, would please the young lieutenant more than to recount the captain's misjudgement when he went below at eight bells.

'Sir?'

Drinkwater turned to see Birkbeck hauling himself on deck; it was clear the man was worried. 'What is it, Mr Birkbeck?'

'She's making a deal of water, sir. Three feet in the well in the last three hours.'

Drinkwater frowned. 'Yes, I recall, they were pumping at eight bells in the middle watch. I think that was what woke me ... Damn it, d'you have any inkling why?'

'Not really, Captain Drinkwater; though I've a theory or two.'

'Caulking?'

'Most likely, with some sheathing come away. The old lady's overdue for a docking, if not worse.'

Drinkwater grunted. 'I was just thinking of the old *Cyclops*; she was broken up some years ago.'

'That doesn't help us much now, sir, if you don't mind my saying so.

'No,' Drinkwater sighed. 'Well, we shall have to pump every two hours.'

'Aye, sir, and I'll have the carpenter have a good look down below. We have so little stores aboard, it might be possible to locate the problem.'

'Very well, Mr Birkbeck, see to it if you please.'

Drinkwater turned away to conceal his irritation. A serious leak, though not without precedent, was a problem he could have done without. There were enough unknown factors in his present mission, but to have to return to port and perhaps prejudice the peace of Europe seemed like too bitter a pill to swallow under the circumstances, however far-fetched it might at first sound. He considered the matter. If the ship was working, and the trouble stemmed from this, it would probably get worse, even if the weather improved. He swore under his breath, when Birkbeck's voice broke into his thoughts. His mind had run through this train in less time than it takes to tell it and the master was still close to him.

'Troubles never come singly,' Birkbeck had muttered, and Drinkwater turned to see Mr Marlowe ascending the companionway.

'Perhaps,' Drinkwater muttered from the corner of his mouth, trying to recapture his earlier brief moment of optimism, 'this isn't trouble.'

'I hope you're right.' Birkbeck turned aside, stared into the binnacle and up at the windward tell-tale.

Drinkwater watched Marlowe as he settled his hat and stared about himself. The first lieutenant's face was drawn, but Drinkwater observed the way he pulled his shoulders back and walked across the deck towards him.

'Good morning, Mr Marlowe. 'Tis good to see you on deck,' Drinkwater called, then lowered his voice as Marlowe approached. 'How is it with you?'

Marlowe threw him a grateful look and Drinkwater felt suddenly sorry for the young man. 'I am well enough, sir, thank you.'

'Good. Then you shall take a turn with me and after that we shall break our fasts. Birkbeck has just reported a leak and the carpenter is to root about in the hold during the forenoon to see if he can discover the cause.'

Drinkwater hoped such gossip would wrench Marlowe's mind from self-obsession to a more demanding preoccupation, but Marlowe was having some trouble keeping his feet.

'Come, come, a steady pace will see to it. Eyes on the horizon . . .'

It took Marlowe four or five turns of the deck to master his queasiness and imbalance. Drinkwater made inconsequential conversation. 'Damned pumps woke me up, then Birkbeck reported the water rising in the well. 'Tis one confounded thing after another, but no doubt we'll weather matters. Saw two petrels astern of us this morning. Odd little birds; I found myself wondering where the deuce they disappear to during moderate weather.'

'I guess they settle on the surface and feed when they're swimming. They only have to take to the air when the waves begin to break and come up under the stern where the sea is smooth.'

'Good heavens, Mr Marlowe, I think you've a point there.' Drinkwater's astonishment was unfeigned. Perhaps Marlowe was not the dullard he had been taken for!

'Perhaps you can help on the matter of the leak. The problem is that I was new into the ship last autumn and Tom Huke, her regular first luff, was killed, so only old Birkbeck and the standing warrant officers know the ship well.'

'That's only to be expected, sir.'

'True, but it don't help us fathom the reason for the leak.'

'She's an old ship.'

'I agree entirely; indeed I suspect she's lost some copper sheathing and maybe some caulking, she's been working enough.'

'How much has she been leaking.'

'Birkbeck reported three feet in three hours.'

'A foot an hour.' Marlowe fell silent for a moment. Drinkwater's sidelong glance suggested he was calculating something, then he said, 'Although she's been working, if she's lost sheathing and caulking, I'd have reckoned on a greater depth in the well.'

Drinkwater considered the matter. He realized Marlowe's logical approach had produced a more realistic assessment than his own sudden apprehension over the *effect* of the leak on *Andromeda*'s task. This had diverted him from any real consideration of its cause. Unless it worsened considerably, additional pumping would contain it; it was no concern of his, he chid himself ruefully, to what extent that simple but irksome drudgery would occupy his hapless crew.

They had reached the taffrail and turned forward again. 'Go on, Mr Marlowe. I scent an hypothesis.'

'I have two actually, sir. A wasted bolt in one of the futtocks . . .'

'Very possible. And two . . .'

'You were in heavy action against the, er . . . Pardon me, I have forgotten the name of the ship you captured . . .'

'The *Odin*.'

'Ah yes, the *Odin*. Well perhaps . . .'

'Shot damage!' Drinkwater broke in.

'Exactly so, sir. Maybe a loose plug. May I ask which side you were engaged?'

'The starboard side.'

'Then I shall start looking there.'

'Mr Marlowe, I congratulate you. That is famously argued; if you can only match reality to theory . . .' Drinkwater left the sentence unfinished and changed tack. 'But not immediately. First you shall breakfast with me.'

'Thank you, sir.'

They had reached the windward hance and Drinkwater paused. 'Is that a patch of blue sky there?'

161

'Yes, sir. And I think the wind is tending to moderate.'

'D'you know, Mr Marlowe,' Drinkwater said, pleased with the way things had fallen out, 'I believe you are at least right about that.'

As Drinkwater led Marlowe below to eat, he caught Ashton's eye and was quite shocked by the look he saw there.

'I fear we must get used to skillygolee and burgoo if we are to cruise off the Azores for as long as possible,' said Drinkwater, laying his spoon down with a rattle and dabbing his mouth with a napkin.

'I had better take a look at the hold, sir, if you'll excuse me.'

'I will in a moment, Mr Marlowe, but first a moment or two of your time.' Drinkwater waved the hovering Frampton away. 'Mr Marlowe,' he said, fixing the first lieutenant with a steady stare, 'please forgive me, but I was troubled by the accident that occurred off the Isle of Wight . . .'

'Sir, I . . .' Marlowe's face assumed an immediate expression of distress.

'Hear me out.' Drinkwater paused and Marlowe resigned himself to what he anticipated as cross-examination. 'Tell me, have you ever taken a longitude at sea?'

'Of course, sir,' said Marlowe, taken aback. 'Surely you don't think me incapable of that?' he frowned.

'What method do you use?'

'Well I can take lunar observations, but you have a chronometer . . .'

'But you can take lunars?'

162

'Oh yes. I used to amuse myself on blockade duty aboard *Thunderer* by taking them.'

'Some officers would consider that a tedious amusement, even on blockade duty.'

Marlowe shrugged and the ghost of a smile passed across his features. 'Sir, I am not certain why you are asking me these questions, but I have a certain aptitude for navigation.'

'But not for seamanship?'

Marlowe flushed brick red, caught Drinkwater's eye, looked away, then back again. 'Very well, sir, let me explain. It is true, I do not have a natural aptitude to handle a ship. I find . . . I found it difficult to . . . Damn it! I found it difficult to resolve on the right thing to do first when I found myself in the situation I did the other day.'

'Yet by relieving Ashton, you put yourself in an exposed position,' Drinkwater said, puzzled. Marlowe remained silent and Drinkwater nudged him. 'Come, come, I have seen many officers in my time, Mr Marlowe, and many have made mistakes. Some were foolish, some incompetent and some just made simple miscalculations. You are my first lieutenant and I am seeking an explanation as to why such a thing happened. I do not seek to condemn you, merely to understand.'

Marlowe swallowed and moved uncomfortably in his chair. 'I wished to subject myself to a test, sir.' He produced the words with a faltering diffidence, as if they were torn from him, one by one. Drinkwater watched Marlowe struggle with a detached sympathy, and the complexities inherent in any human being struck him once again.

'You see, sir, I hoped that I might vindicate myself;

163

that I might prove to myself that I was quite as capable as any other officer to tack ship.'

'And prove it perhaps to others, other than myself?' asked Drinkwater shrewdly, the light of perception dawning. 'You have been responsible for some accident, perhaps?'

Marlowe nodded.

'Well, we need not go into that now, but I take it the court-martial acquitted you?'

'There was no court-martial, sir. The matter was not that serious.'

'Not that serious?' Drinkwater queried.

'No ship was lost, sir . . .'

'Go on.'

'Two men were lost overboard.' Marlowe expelled a long breath; the unburdening of confession seemed to release him. 'I was ashamed of myself, sir, robbed of my confidence. I wanted to make amends and then . . . Well, I have another man's life to answer for now.'

'And Mr Ashton was a witness to all this, eh? And is consequently your, how do the French say it? *Bête-noire?*'

Marlowe nodded again.

Drinkwater sighed. Poor Marlowe's superciliousness and his apparent lack of wit and subtlety were the consequences of self-deceit, of attempting to live with failure in the presence of someone who knew all about the cause. And was capable of compounding that knowledge, Drinkwater knew from Frey's scuttlebutt. The unborn bastard was another life to lay to the lieutenant's account. Drinkwater now understood that it was not only Marlowe's conduct which was attributable to his problems; so too was his attitude. Frey's original

164

assessment of him not being such a bad fellow had been accurate. All the damage to his character had been self-inflicted.

'Mr Marlowe, I have no wish to increase your burden, but I think I divine the roots of your misfortunes. Forgive me, but your frankness does you credit and I am aware you are affianced to Ashton's sister.'

'Yes. That is unfortunate.'

'How so? Do you not wish to marry the young lady?'

'Most decidedly, sir, but the ceremony will be delayed by our absence.'

'And the lady is expecting . . .'

'You know!'

'I had heard . . .'

'Damn Ashton!'

'It is unfortunate you do not like your intended brother-in-law . . .'

'Damn it, sir,' Marlowe leant forward, his eyes intense, alive again after the emotional moments of self-revelation, 'the man has designs on my fortune. He seeks to gain an ascendancy over me partly through what he knows of me and also through his sister. That would be bad enough, but this delay . . .' The first lieutenant rose to his feet and ran a hand wildly through his hair.

'Sit down, Frederic, for God's sake,' snapped Drinkwater.

Marlowe turned and stared at Drinkwater, his eyes desperate. 'Sir, I . . .'

'Sit down, there's a good fellow. You are no good to me in this state. We have an important duty to attend to. You are perhaps the last officer in this war to be offered an opportunity.'

'Sir, I am not certain that I am capable . . .'

'Of course you are capable, Frederic! And what is more we shall have you home to marry your Sarah in no time at all.'

'Two months would be too long to avoid a scandal, sir.'

'Well, we shall have to ensure it don't take that long,' said Drinkwater.

'Is that possible?'

'I believe so.'

Drinkwater saw Marlowe relax with relief. 'I hope so, sir, but you just mentioned learning to like burgoo.'

Drinkwater shrugged. 'True. I can't be certain, of course, but I don't believe we shall be kept long on station.' Drinkwater smiled and was rewarded with a reciprocating grin.

'I apologize, sir . . . for my conduct the other night.'

'Let us put the matter behind us; do you just deal with our problems on a day-to-day basis.'

Marlowe rose. 'I shall go and have a look in the hold, sir,' he said, 'and thank you.'

''Tis nothing.'

Marlowe nodded over Drinkwater's shoulder and out through the stern windows. 'There's more blue sky showing now, sir.'

'Yes, it may yet prove a fine day.'

Marlowe stood uncertainly, for a moment he strove to speak, then gave up the attempt and made to leave. Drinkwater called him back. 'Mr Marlowe, would you be so kind as to show the midshipmen the method of determining longitude by the chronometer?'

'Yes, of course, sir.'

'And just ignore Ashton.'

Marlowe nodded. 'Yes. Yes, I will.' He paused again, then blurted out, 'what made you come below and see me last night, sir?'

'I'm not sure,' Drinkwater replied. 'Concern for you, concern for the ship, concern for myself.' He paused and smiled. 'Anyway, why did you come on deck this morning?'

'Because you came to see me last night, sir.'

A Sea Change

Drinkwater's forecast proved accurate. By noon the wind had again swung into the north-north-west, dropped to a fresh breeze and swept aside the cloud cover, leaving only the benign white fluffs of fair-weather cumulus. The depression moved away to the north and east, following its predecessor into the chops of the Channel. The sea now reflected this change in the atmosphere, losing the forbidding grey of the true Western Ocean, and wearing the kindly blue mantle of more temperate latitudes. And, indeed, when Birkbeck, emerging from the hold, found Captain Drinkwater ready to observe the culmination of the sun on the ship's meridian, their southing was substantial.

Things were less optimistic below decks. The working party in the hold had failed to locate the source of the ingress of water, though some credence was given to Marlowe's hypothesis by evidence of water entering the well from the starboard side. In the wardroom Lieutenant Ashton sulked, much to the annoyance of Hyde, who, when distracted from his amusements sufficiently to notice, began to conclude that Ashton was far from being the amiable fellow he had first assumed. Indeed Hyde inclined towards Mr Frey who, it began to emerge, was an officer of some talent with a paintbrush.

Having endured a degree of persecution from brother officers in the past, Frey was inclined to conceal his love of drawing and watercolour painting, but Hyde caught sight of a small picture he was working on, which showed the *Royal Sovereign* flying the Bourbon standard, accompanied by *Andromeda, Impregnable, Jason, Polonais, Gremyashchi* and the Trinity Yacht. Artistic achievement impressed Hyde, and he was driven to confess that he regretted his inability to play an instrument or, indeed, even to sing, let alone draw or paint.

This polite exchange with Frey was overheard by Ashton who was driven to make some mean sarcasm about Hyde's success at playing being assured, provided he tried to play no more than the fool. Hyde, who had been oblivious to Ashton's presence until that moment, spun round.

'What's that you say?' he demanded.

'That should you decide upon playing anything, my dear Hyde, confine it to being a fool.'

For a moment Frey, fascinated by this encounter, thought Hyde would take the remark lying down, but it seemed the marine officer's indolence extended even to govern the timing of his outbursts of temper. In fact, his momentary silence appeared to discomfit Ashton, judging by the expression on the sea-officer's face as he regarded Hyde.

'The fool, sir?' asked Hyde. 'Did you suggest I might be a suitable candidate to play the fool?' There was a note of controlled menace in Hyde's voice that Frey found quite unnerving, despite the fact that it was not directed at himself.

Ashton's face paled. 'A joke, Hyde, a joke.'

And then Hyde had closed the distance between the flimsy door to Frey's cabin and the third lieutenant with a single stride and thrust his face into Ashton's. 'A joke, d'you say, sir? Well, well, a joke . . . A joke to make a fellow laugh, eh? Ain't that what a joke's for, eh Josiah? Well ain't it? Say yay or nay. *You* crack 'em: you should know all about 'em.'

'A joke, yes.' Ashton was cornered, wary. He shot an embarrassed glance at Frey.

'To make us laugh, eh? Eh?' Hyde was relentless; he began to move forward, forcing Ashton backwards.

'Yes.' Ashton appealed mutely to Frey who remained silent.

'Good,' persisted Hyde. 'Since we're agreed on the purpose of a joke, perhaps you'd like to share one with me, Josiah. Listen; if there is a fool hereabouts, it is you. What you hope to achieve by your attitude towards poor Marlowe is your own affair, but whatever it is, or was, you were unwise to make it so public. The man has suffered a humiliation and has, by all the signs this morning, reinvigorated himself. I should scarce have believed it possible had I not seen it for myself. If you have any sense, you will throw yourself on another tack.'

Ashton began to rally under this verbal assault. 'Why you damned impertinent bugger . . .'

'Mr Ashton!' Frey broke in, 'Hold your tongue, sir! I'll not countenance any further discord.' Frey looked

170

at Hyde and observed the marine officer had said his piece. He relaxed and turned away, but Ashton was not prepared to accept advice.

'Oh, you won't, won't you? And what will you do, Frey? Toady to the captain?'

'What the devil's the matter with you, Ashton?' Frey asked, but Hyde broke in, sensing a real quarrel in the offing.

'For heaven's sake, Josiah, stow your confounded gab and leave us in peace.'

'Damn you, and don't "Josiah" me. The pair of you . . .'

'Are what?' snapped Frey, suddenly and ferociously intense. The gleam in his eye seemed to restrain Ashton who swung away, muttering, flung open the door of his own cabin and disappeared, slamming it with such force that the entire bulkhead shuddered. Frey and Hyde looked at each other.

'What the devil was that all about?' asked Hyde in a low voice.

'Just a squall,' said Frey, subsiding, 'but he wants to watch that tongue of his, or it'll land him in trouble.'

Both officers, aware that the flimsy partition failed to provide the conditions for private speculation, let the matter drop. Neither wanted the discord to persist and both had served long enough to know the benefits of silent toleration in the confined world of a frigate's wardroom.

For Drinkwater, the remainder of that day was spent quietly. Having observed the improvement in the weather and determined *Andromeda*'s latitude at local

171

noon, he went below to enjoy a nap. Woken by Frampton at eight bells in the afternoon watch, he sat and wrote up his journal, indulging himself further with a little self-congratulation.

It was clear, he wrote, *that Lieutenant Marlowe's indisposition was some form of self-abasement consequent upon his unfortunate experience off the Wight, and it occurred to me that his lack of confidence must spring, not from a general incompetence, but some past event. I have observed poor Frey much affected by the loss of Jas. Quilhampton and the subsequent ordeal of his court-martial.*

Drinkwater stopped for a moment and stared into the middle distance. Poor Frey; the damage to the little cutter *Kestrel* had resulted in her being abandoned in Norwegian waters. As the senior surviving officer, Frey had had to be judged by a court-martial to determine the extent of her damage in action and the justification for her loss to the naval service. That it had been Drinkwater himself, supported by a survey by Birkbeck, who had pronounced the cutter in an unfit state to withstand the rigours of a passage across the North Sea and ordered her to be abandoned, ameliorated Frey's situation. Nevertheless, the experience of reliving the events in the Vikkenfiord, from which he had been striving to distance himself, revived those feelings Frey had hoped to forget. Not normally given to outward displays of passion or temperament, Frey had become even more introspective. Drinkwater had blamed himself for much of this. It pained him greatly both to have lost his oldest friend and to see another in such poor spirits. He, himself, bore a deep guilt for Quilhampton's death and Frey's grief. The consolation of knowing that he, and they, had done their duty, wore thin to an officer who had been doing his duty for a lifetime. Frey was no less wounded than had been James Quilhampton, when he had lost a hand at Kosseir.

And yet it had been this concern for Frey which had given him the clue to Marlowe's lack of spirit, and Drinkwater found himself wondering about the circuitous nature of events. He dipped his pen, wiped off the excess ink, and began writing again.

Marlowe's introspection was not dissimilar, and from this I therefore concluded Marlowe was obsessed by some event, and that if he were not, if he possessed no spirit, my appeal to him would prove this by its failure. In the event, matters fell out otherwise and I discovered him more of a man of parts than I would have superficially judged. This gives me some satisfaction, and whatever may come of this chase, we may see Marlowe a better man at the end of it than at its commencement.

Drinkwater waited a moment while the ink dried, then turned the page and resumed writing.

It is, moreover, incontrovertible evidence of the workings of providence that out of the consequences of James's death, should come salvation to another soul.

For a moment Drinkwater looked at these words then, with a grim, self-deprecating smile he took his penknife from his pocket and neatly excised the page. He had a sailor's horror of tempting providence, especially when it touched him closely. The dream of the white lady had been too vivid for that.

'The Atlantic is a vast ocean which extends from pole to pole,' Birkbeck said, regarding the half-circle of midshipmen about him, 'and is divided into that part of it which lies in the northern hemisphere and is consequently known as the North Atlantic Ocean, and that part of it which lies in the southern hemisphere and is named accordingly. However, to seamen it is further subdivided; the Western Ocean is the name commonly applied to that portion of the North Atlantic which lies west of the British Isles and must needs be crossed when a passage is made to America or Canada. There is also that part which is known as the Sargasso, an area of some vagueness, but set generally about the equator. Now what is the equator, Mr Paine?'

Paine produced a satisfactory definition and Birkbeck nodded. 'Indeed, the parallel of zero latitude from which other parallels are taken to the northward, or the southward. Now, Mr Dunn, is the equator a great circle?'

'Er, yes sir.'

'Good. And are the other parallels of latitude therefore great circles?'

Dunn's forehead creased with the effort of recollection. Birkbeck's proposition seemed a reasonable enough one. 'Yes, sir.'

'Not at all, Mr Dunn. Of all the parallels of latitude *only* the equator is a great circle. And why is that, pray? Mr Paine?'

'Because a great circle is defined as a circle on the surface of the earth having the same radius as that of the earth.'

'Very good, Mr Paine. Do you understand, Mr Dunn? One might equally have said it should have the same diameter, or that its centre was coincident with that of the earth. Now Mr Dunn, of all the parallels of latitude, only the equator is a great circle, what would you conclude of the meridians?' Dunn looked even more perplexed. 'You do know what a meridian is, Mr Dunn, do you not?'

'I am not certain, sir,' said the boy hopelessly, adding as he saw an unsympathetic gleam in the master's eye, 'is it, is it . . .?' But the floundering was to no avail and Paine was only too ready to capitalize on his messmate's humiliation.

'A meridian is a great circle passing through the poles by which longitude is measured . . .'

'Very good, Mr Paine.' The midshipmen turned as a body to see Marlowe standing behind them. 'And how do we determine longitude?'

'By chronometer, sir . . .'

'By your leave, Mr Birkbeck . . .'

'By all means, Mr Marlowe . . .'

Birkbeck, somewhat discomfited, but in no wise seriously affronted by Marlowe's assumption of the instructor's role, took himself off and, having fortified himself with a nip of rum flip in the wardroom, summoned the carpenter and returned to his painstaking and tedious survey of the hold.

Mr Birkbeck's lecture on the different areas of the Atlantic Ocean seemed borne out in the following days. His Britannic Majesty's frigate *Andromeda*, leaking from her exertions, sailed into sunnier climes. The gale, in its abatement, took with it the uncertain weather of high latitudes and, after almost two days of variable airs, ushered in a north-easterly wind, an unexpected but steady breeze. They were too far north for the trade winds, but the favourable direction augured well for their passage and was no less welcome.

Andromeda's yards were squared and she bore away

175

with a fine bone in her teeth, apparently unconcerned with the problems of her antiquity which preoccupied her senior officers. The ship's company turned the berth-deck inside out, washed clothes and bedding and stummed between decks, sweetening the air. Moreover, the warmer nights and drier weather meant the tarpaulins could be rolled back on the booms, ports opened during the daylight and the entire ship made more habitable. The mood of the people changed in proportion, along with the application of a lick of paint and varnish here and there to brighten up their miserable quarters, no thought having been given to this during the frigate's recent embellishment.

As details of Mr Marlowe's recovery permeated the ends of the ship most distant from the wardroom, they were accompanied by the explanation of illness as causing his temporary loss of control. Alongside this intelligence there went a blasphemous joke that he had been raised from the dead. Lieutenant Ashton's nickname for the captain of 'Our Father' was rather apt in this context and as a consequence the first lieutenant had, quite unbeknown to himself, acquired the soubriquet of Lazarus Marlowe. This, partly generating the changed mood of the ship's company, was yet as much a product of it. In this mild euphoria only Lieutenant Ashton and Sergeant McCann remained burdened, the one having lost control of his future, the other increasingly obsessed and preoccupied by his past.

Indeed, in the case of McCann, the improved weather only exacerbated his condition. As is common with many, memories of youth and past happiness were associated with sunny days and blue skies such as now dominated the flying frigate. Moreover, the farther west they ran, the nearer they drew to the United States, and the fact that this diminishing distance did not constitute a closing of the American coast, worked insidiously upon poor McCann.

Although they had seen a few ships in the Channel and in the Western Approaches, the wide blue reaches of the Atlantic yielded nothing beyond a pair of Portuguese schooners crossing for the Grand Banks. Captain Drinkwater, sensitive to the mellowing mood of the ship and encouraged by the transformation of Lieutenant Marlowe, ordered several gunnery practices as they romped steadily south and westwards.

In addition to the fulmars, gulls and gannets, the dark, marauding shapes of hawking skuas were to be seen intimidating even the large solan geese; flying fish now darted from either bow, pursued by albacore and occasionally driven on board where they were quickly tossed into frying pans to make impromptu feasts for lucky messes or the midshipmen's berth.

And with the flying fish and the albacore came the bottle-nosed dolphins, lifting easily from *Andromeda*'s bow waves, racing in with seemingly effortless thrusts of their muscular tails, to ride the pressure wave that advanced unseen yet tangible, ahead of the massive bulk of the frigate's driving hull. Attempts to catch them usually failed, but occasionally one would succumb to a harpoon or a lure, to end up, poached slowly in Madeira, as steaks on the wardroom table.

On one such occasion, heady with their success, the officers invited Drinkwater to dinner, and notwithstanding the absence of Lieutenant Ashton on watch, they all enjoyed a jolly evening during which the discussion ranged from the general conduct of the late war and the difficulties of securing the person of Napoleon Bonaparte on a remote island, to the possible causes of *Andromeda*'s leak and the contribution to literature of the unknown 'lady' who had written *Pride and Prejudice.*

Watching Marlowe preside over this pleasant evening, Drinkwater concluded his first lieutenant had made a supreme effort and overcome his unhappiness. Furthermore, Drinkwater began to entertain hopes of high endeavour from him, if things fell out as he hoped they would.

But as the days passed and the reckoning so assiduously calculated by Birkbeck, Marlowe and their coterie of half-willing midshipmen, showed them rapidly closing the Archipelago of the Azores, renewed doubts assailed Drinkwater. And while the pleasant weather drew smiles from his men, he paced the weather side of the quarterdeck for hour after hour, going over and over the interview with Hortense, wondering if he was not a quixotic fool after all, seduced at the last by a face which had haunted him for almost all his adult life. She had sought him out; she knew the role he had played in her husband's death; they had been enemies for a score or so of years; so why in God's name should he trust her now?

He ignored the importance of her news and processed events through the filter of guessed motives, suspicions, old anxieties and even fears. He recalled, with that peculiar insistence that only the lonely can as they chew on introspection, how she had seemed an almost demonic presence at one time; an embodiment

178

of all the restless energies of imperial France. She had loomed in his imagination larger than any metaphor: for *she* alone had represented the enemy, and her beauty had seemed diabolical in its power. He had felt this influence suffocating him, drowning him as he fell flailing beneath the overwhelming power of Hortense as the white lady, so that in the wake of the dream, when the rational world reasserted itself, there always lurked a hint of his own impending madness. He shied away from this like a frightened horse, clinging at logic to prevent the otherwise inevitable overwhelming by the 'blue-devils' of mental depression.

He forced himself to consider again Hortense's motives. Why should she do this? Had she not simply been beggared by the damnable war, as she claimed? And what advantage could she gain by casting one ageing fool of a British naval officer on some ludicrous quest amid the billows of the North Atlantic, if the reason for it were not true? He discarded the morbid, fanciful and faintly ridiculous assumptions of his private thoughts, calming himself with the more rational figurings-out of the ordinary.

As his mother was once fond of saying with the bitterness of premature bereavement playing around the corners of her mouth, there was no fool like an old fool. But to set against that charge he brought the experience of a lifetime in the sea-service and a familiarity with the machinations of secret diplomacy.

Nevertheless, there was also the forbidding spectre of their Lordships' disapprobation, as the stock phrase had it. His departure on his self-appointed quest may well have had the blessing of His Royal Highness, the Prince William Henry, Duke of Clarence and so on and so forth, but their Lordships would be well aware that he was well aware that the whole Royal Navy of Great Britain was well aware that His Royal Highness, the Prince William Henry, and so on and so forth, was a buffoon, if not an incompetent!

On the other hand, what point would there be in him dashing off into the Atlantic on his own initiative if he had no good motive? Everyone knew that although the war in Europe was over, the war in North America was not, and it remained perfectly possible for Bonaparte to cause mayhem in Canada. While that much was possible, if not probable, there was another factor Drinkwater now had to consider. *Andromeda* was officially unfit for further active service; she should have been laid up preparatory to passing to the breakers' yard, and her crew, drafted especially for the Royal Escort duty to France, would almost certainly be dispersed to man more sea-worthy ships refitting for the augmentation of the blockade of the eastern seaboard of the United States. Indeed, at that very moment some of those ships might be eagerly awaiting their draft, and thus delayed by *Andromeda*'s absence.

Amid all his considerations of grand strategy, it was this doubt that remained the most disturbing. Try how he might, Drinkwater was unable to argue his way out of this almost certain error of judgement!

Up and down he paced; not seeing the work of the ship passing all about him, scarcely hearing the bells striking the half-hour, the watch-words of the lookouts or the occasional order passed along. He was oblivious to the break-up of the daily navigation class, made so convenient while the solution to the problem of *Andromeda*'s day's work was so easily reconciled in the north-east wind by the simple application of a plane traverse; nor did he notice the daily quarterdeck parade of Hyde's lobsters, nor remark upon Sergeant McCann's uncharacteristically less-than-perfect turnout. Nor indeed, did Captain Drinkwater observe either the energy of the first lieutenant, or the complementary disinterest of the third. Instead he revolved his wretched arguments in a tediously endless mental circumambulation, locked into the introversion of isolation and independent command.

But whatever these private anxieties might constitute, and whatever paramountcy they might assume in any commander's thoughts, the cares of his ship will always intrude, and on this occasion they took the form of Mr Midshipman 'Tom' Paine over whom the pre-occupied Drinkwater almost fell as the youngster dodged about in front of him to attract his attention.

'God's bones! What in heaven's name is the matter?' Drinkwater finally acknowledged the jumping jack trying to waylay him. 'Why Mr Paine, what the devil d'you want?'

Paine was not a whit discomfited by the difficulties he had experienced in accomplishing his simple errand. Jokes about Old Nat were legion in the cockpit.

'Begging your pardon, sir, but Mr Marlowe's compliments, and he wishes me to inform you that we shall require an alteration of course to make our landfall.'

Drinkwater looked over the boy's shoulder. Marlowe and Birkbeck were exchanging a word or two on the far side of the binnacle.

'An alteration of course, eh? Well sir, to what?'

'Ten degrees to port, sir.'

'To port, eh?' He was about to say that in his day it would have been 'to larboard' but such pedantry would be laughable to the young imp. 'Very well, Mr Paine, kindly see to it.'

'Aye, aye, sir.' The lad touched his fore-cock and made to be off when Drinkwater called him back.

'And when you have attended to the matter and adjusted the yards, pray show me your reckoning of the day's work.'

Paine's face fell. His 'Aye, aye, sir' was less enthusiastic.

Laughing inwardly, Drinkwater crossed the deck and stood on the weather side of the helm while *Andromeda's* head was swung through ten degrees of arc and settled on her new course. There was a general tweaking of braces, but neither the motion nor the speed of the ship seemed affected and the ageing hull drove forwards through the blue seas with the white wave crests running up almost astern. It seemed quite impossible that this charming scene could ever be otherwise; that the light, straining canvas above their heads could ever turn a rain and spray-sodden grey, as hard on the horniest hands as raw-hide, or that the great bulk of the hurrying ship could be laid over on her beam ends, or tossed about like a cork.

'So, gentlemen,' he said to Marlowe and Birkbeck, who had both been watching the adjusting of the main yards, 'when do you anticipate sighting our landfall?'

'Shortly after first light tomorrow, sir,' Marlowe answered.

Drinkwater looked at Birkbeck. 'Are you two in agreement?'

'Harmoniously so, sir,' Birkbeck replied with a hint of irony.

'Good. I'm decidedly glad to hear it.' Drinkwater smiled at the two men. Marlowe was a transformed figure. 'Well now, we must consider our best course of action when we arrive.'

'Indeed, sir. How far offshore will you cruise?' Marlowe asked.

Drinkwater rubbed his chin and raised an eyebrow. 'Three or four leagues; sufficiently far to be clear of danger, yet not out of sight of the land. According to my reckoning, our friends will come down on the island from the north-north-east.' He waved out on the starboard quarter, as though their sails might appear at any moment.

'D'you think Bonaparte is already there, sir?' asked Birkbeck.

'We shall send a boat in to find out. Do you prepare the launch, stock it for two days and have Frey,' Drinkwater hesitated, 'no, have Ashton command it. Send in half a dozen marines under the sergeant.' Drinkwater paused as Marlowe nodded. 'But to answer your question about Boney, I consider it unlikely, though not impossible, for him to have reached the island yet. I have no knowledge of when he left Paris, nor of his port of embarkation, but he must have been despatched by the time King Louis landed, I'd have thought, and conveyed by express to the west coast; to Brest, or La Rochelle or L'Orient. A fast frigate might, I suppose, have reached the archipelago a little before us.'

'A British frigate?' asked Marlowe.

Drinkwater shrugged. 'I imagine a British frigate or perhaps a small squadron such as we were lately

183

attached to, would accompany him. As for himself, I suppose his dignity as the elected Emperor of the French would be unsupportable in anything but a French man-o'-war.'

'Not if it was the allies' purpose to humiliate him,' put in Marlowe.

'I think a small island humiliation enough after the domination of Europe,' countered Drinkwater. 'Remember what Nelson wrote: "In victory, let the chief characteristic be magnanimity."'

'A very Christian sentiment sir,' responded Birkbeck, 'but not one which I would expect his most serene and culminated, high and God almighty majesty the Tsar of all the Russias to subscribe to where Napoleon Bonaparte is concerned.'

'Perhaps not,' said Drinkwater grinning, 'though you talk like a canting leveller, Mr Birkbeck. I thought your nimble scholar Tom Paine the republican among us.'

And they all laughed companionably, standing in the sunshine enjoying the fellowship of like minds.

PART TWO

A Wild-goose Chase?

'Well, that's the end of it all, though it's throwing the game
away with all the trump cards in one's hand.'
TALLEYRAND, PRINCE OF BENEVENTO

The Rock

Shortly before dawn Drinkwater woke with a start. Lying in the darkness he listened intently, but could discern no noise; not even the clanking of the pumps disturbed the night, silent but for the laboured creaking of the ship and above his head the faint, measured tread of one of the watch-keepers. Then his cabin was suddenly lit up, as though someone shone a powerful light in through the stern windows. The spectral illumination startled him. His heart thumped with alarm and he was on his feet in a trice, to stare out through the stern windows. An instant later he had an explanation as the ship drove through bioluminescence and the pale green gleam again lit up the night.

He was unable to sleep after this weird though natural phenomenon, and drew on breeches, shoes and stockings. Winding his boatcloak about himself he went on deck. The pacing footsteps revealed themselves to be those of Lieutenant Frey. They exchanged courtesies and Drinkwater asked the routine question.

'All well?'

'Aye, sir. I have a good man stationed aloft in the foretop, though I doubt we'll sight anything before daylight.'

''Tis as well to be on our guard.'

'Yes, of course.'

'The wind is holding fair,' Drinkwater observed. 'One might almost believe we had run into the trades, but our latitude is too high so we must be prepared for our run of luck to end.'

There was a brief pause, then Frey said, 'I believe you're sending the launch ashore, sir.'

'Yes, just to establish whether our friend Boney has been delivered yet.'

'And Lieutenant Ashton's to command her.'

'Yes.'

Frey fell silent. Drinkwater wondered whether he felt himself slighted by the appointment of the junior lieutenant to this task, then Frey asked, 'Will you be going ashore yourself, sir?'

'No.'

For a moment neither man said anything, then Drinkwater remarked, 'I gather there has been something of a sea change in the wardroom, Mr Frey. Things are a little more tolerable, I hope.'

'In a manner of speaking, yes, sir. Where formerly Mr Marlowe seemed to be constantly under the weather, we now have Mr Ashton acting like a spoilt brat. I am of the opinion that acquaintances should not serve together; friendship and duty seem incompatible in the circumstances prevailing in a man-o'-war.'

'Dear me, I hope not,' replied Drinkwater, ruefully.

'Oh, I beg pardon, sir, I didn't mean . . .' The

tone of Frey's voice conveyed an embarrassment the darkness hid.

'Think nothing of it,' Drinkwater chuckled, adding more seriously, 'though I have to confess, Marlowe's change of heart seems almost miraculous.'

'That is what they are saying below decks.'

'I don't follow you.'

'That he was raised from the dead. They call him "Lazarus" Marlowe.'

'Lazarus Marlowe . . .?' Drinkwater tested the name and found himself grinning in the gloom.

'I'm afraid you are cast in a more divine role, sir.'

'You mean . . .? Well, 'pon my soul!'

'Seafaring folk have the oddest notions, don't they?'

'Aye, they most certainly do.'

'If I might change the subject, sir . . .'

'Please do, Mr Frey. I am hard-pressed to find anything I can add in support of the Almighty.'

'I'm sure He would be pleased to know that, sir,' Frey added drily, and Drinkwater could just see the smile on his face as the dawn light crept into the eastern sky. 'What I was going to ask, sir, if I might be presumptuous, is what you intend to do? I mean we have no idea of the whereabouts of Napoleon, do we?'

'No, I appreciate that, nor are we likely to learn. My principal, no my *only* concern, is to intercept and if necessary engage the two ships which have been sent from Antwerp to convey Boney and his staff to America. Anything more would be a gross presumption on my part, not something likely to endear me to Lord Castlereagh or any of his cronies.'

'D'you think we shall engage them?'

A horrible thought crossed Drinkwater's mind; was poor Frey a broken man after the terrible encounter with the enemy in the Vikkenfiord? 'Does it worry you, if it should come to that?'

'Not at all,' Frey answered without hesitation, 'in fact, I should welcome the event.'

'Not, I hope, because you entertain any foolish notions of covering yourself with . . .'

'Death or glory,' broke in Frey with a short, dismissive laugh. 'No, no, nothing like that. To tell the truth, sir, I should think my active service career the more fulfilled if I had one more crack at the French; that damned affair in Norway was somehow unfinished business.'

'I understand. That is one of the reasons I will not send you out of the ship in any boat expedition, Frey. I want you aboard. All the time; at least until this business is concluded.'

'Thank you, sir.'

'If and when we do encounter the French ships I anticipate they will keep close company and try and overwhelm us. They may be full of soldiers, men willing to fight hand to hand, against which our people would prove inadequate.'

'You would want to hold off and manoeuvre to cripple them, and thereby induce a surrender?'

'Exactly. And while the sea conditions will be lively in these latitudes, and we may have trouble pointing the guns to good effect, the steady breeze should enable us to be nimble.'

'Providing their two against our single ship don't corner us like a dog.'

'We shall have to see . . .'

'Yes.'

It was getting rapidly lighter and already the details of the deck about them were emerging from the shadows of the night. Drinkwater began to feel the pangs of hunger stirring in his belly. He would welcome coffee and some hot, buttered toast. His teeth no longer pained him and the swollen gum had subsided so that the idea of masticating on a slice made his mouth water.

'Might I ask your advice about something?'

'Yes, of course.' Drinkwater thrust his self-indulgent day-dream aside. 'What is it?'

'I have given the matter much thought, sir, but I accept the fact that on our return we will be paid off and I am likely to be compelled to exist on half-pay.'

'I shall do my best for you, Mr Frey,' Drinkwater said. The consideration of another dependant loomed in his imagination, accompanied by the added thought that while some perverse chivalry prompted him to offer support to Hortense Santhonax, he felt a reprehensible resentment at the thought of doing the same for poor, loyal Frey.

'Oh, I know you will, sir, and please do not think I am asking for charity. On the contrary, I have some hopes of supporting myself if I must. No, I have been thinking of James Quilhampton's widow.'

'Catriona . . .?' Drinkwater suppressed his surprise.

'I, er, think she might not be averse to accepting a proposal from me.'

'Pardon the question, Mr Frey, but are you attached to the lady?'

'I think she is fond of me, sir, and she has little means of support. She also has the child . . .'

'Ah yes.'

'I felt . . .'

191

'Of course. I understand, but a marriage based upon pity may not be for the best, Mr Frey. The lady is a little older than yourself,' Drinkwater said tactfully. 'That may make a difference in time, and while there may be no other person to claim your affections at the moment, should you be cast ashore upon your own resources, then you may meet someone other than Mistress Quilhampton for whom, without being ungallant, you may come to feel a greater attachment.'

'That is true, sir . . .'

But Frey got no further, for the cry came down from the foretop that land was in sight.

An hour later two steep-sided islands were visible from the deck as the low sun struck their basalt cliffs, conferring upon them a warm, pink colour. To the north-west and perhaps two or three leagues nearer, lay the smaller island of Corvo, while farther off, fine on the port bow, rose Flores.

Drinkwater scrutinized the summit of the island, from which a stream of orographic cloud trailed downwind. Patiently he waited for *Andromeda* to draw near enough for them to see the shoreline, as yet still hidden below the horizon.

'A most appropriate place to cage an eagle,' Drinkwater remarked and Frey, catching the observation, aired a recondite fact: 'The archipelago is named Azores from the Portuguese *açor*, meaning a hawk.'

Among the watch on deck, an air of excitement and expectation animated the men. Word of an impending landfall and a proposed boat expedition had percolated through the ship and the sight of the island, even for those who would approach little closer, nor see more than could be discerned from the frigate's waist, was nevertheless sufficient to break the monotony of their arduous yet dull lives.

'You may close Flores, Mr Frey. We will bring-to off Santa Cruz. I shall want the launch ready then,' Drinkwater ordered, closing his glass with an emphatic snap. 'I am going below for an hour.'

'Aye, aye, sir.'

By the time the watch changed the entire island had risen above the rim of the world and the white breakers of the restless Atlantic could be seen fringing the scree-littered foreshore. Larval cliffs predominated, formed by prehistoric volcanic eruptions, no longer rose-red from the dawn, but grey and forbidding with fresh-water streams cascading into the sea in silver streaks. As they drew closer to Flores they could see clouds of wheeling sea-birds, gulls, petrels and auks, though the officers' glasses were focused not on these aerial denizens, but the few white buildings that formed the port of Santa Cruz. It was something of a disappointment.

'Stap me, but it don't amount to much,' remarked Hyde, voicing the opinion of them all.

Below, Drinkwater completed his preparations. Having washed, shaved and dressed his hair, he eased himself into his undress uniform coat and sat at his desk. Drawing a sheet of paper from his folio, he took up his steel pen, opened the inkwell, inscribed the date and began to write.

To the Governor of Flores,
Santa Cruz.
Sir,
I have the Honour to Command His Britannic Majesty's Frigate Andromeda *presently arrived off this Island under the Express Orders of Admiral of the Fleet, His Royal Highness, Prince William Henry, Duke of Clarence and Earl of Munster.*

Being thus engaged upon a Singular, Special and most Urgent Service, I call upon the Ancient Amity which has Subsisted between our Two Nations since time immemorial and has been Crowned with Victory in the Late War by the Exertions of the Anglo-Portuguese Armies Commanded by His Grace the Marquess Wellington and Marshal Beresford.

To this end, Sir, you will have been informed that Napoleon Bonaparte, lately Emperor of the French, is to be Exiled in the Island of Flores, and kept here until the End of the Term of his Earthly Existence.

However, Information has been made known to His Britannic Majesty's Government that an Expedition has lately been fitted out at Antwerp, and that the Purpose of this Force is to Abduct the Person of Napoleon Bonaparte and to Convey him to America or Canada where his Ambition may yet cause more Misery and Extend a War which His Majesty's Government wish to Terminate as Swiftly as Possible.

This letter comes to you by the Hand of an Officer and I desire you, Sir, having Regard for all the above Circumstances, to inform this Officer whether you have yet taken possession of the Person of General Bonaparte, how he is Accommodated, and whether any Inhabitants of the Island who may have been Fishing Offshore, have reported the Presence of any Men-of-War belonging to any Foreign Power.

I also Request that, upon Receipt of this Despatch, should the said General Bonaparte be already Resident on the Island of Flores, you Undertake to keep a Close Watch upon his Person, his Associates, Staff and Servants. This I Charge you with Under the Terms of the Several Treaties of Mutual Help existing between our two Nations.

Drinkwater paused and re-read his epistle with an amused smile. He had invoked every phrase at his command to alert the Governor of the gravity of the reason for *Andromeda*'s presence off Flores. The long alliance of Great Britain and Portugal, which relied upon several treaties, the first of which dated from as far back as 1373, but the most recent of which was that known as the Methuen Treaty of 1707, had been underwritten by the successes of Wellington's Anglo Portuguese army which had been fighting in the Iberian Peninsula for six years.

He decided he could add little more, other than a courtesy or two, and concluded the letter:

I Regret that my Duty prevents my Calling upon you in Person at this Time, but Trust that you will Afford the Bearer of this Despatch, Lieutenant Jos. Ashton, every Confidence with which you would Honour me.

I am, Sir, your Obedient Servant,

Nathan'l Drinkwater, Captain, Royal Navy

Ensuring the ink was dry, Drinkwater folded the letter, sealed it and added the superscription. Then he left the cabin, jamming his hat upon his head as he did so.

'Hoist the new colours, if you please,' he ordered as he reached the deck, casting about him. The ship seethed with people; two watches were on deck, as were many of those who might have been below. Upon the quarterdeck the blue and white of the officers contrasted with Hyde's immaculate scarlet, a pretty enough picture with the blue sea and sky as a backdrop astern. Ahead loomed the island, the northern extremity of which, Punta Delgada, was stark against the horizon, while its summit, the Morro Alto, was lost in its streamer of cloud.

Santa Cruz proved a tiny, rock-girt inlet, its few buildings dominated by the baroque tower of the church of São Pedro. The tiny habitation was surrounded by the brilliant green of vegetation which refreshed eyes tired of the ocean. This verdure was interspersed by the brilliant colours of a profusion of flowers, the red and yellow of canna lilies, the orange of montbretia and the blue of agapanthus. Amid this almost pastoral scene, a flagstaff bore the blue and white standard of the House of Bragança, a gallant complement to the new red ensign of the senior squadron of the Royal Navy of Great Britain which streamed from *Andromeda*'s peak.

'I've the saluting guns ready, sir,' offered Marlowe.

'Very good, Mr Marlowe. We shall give the Governor seventeen guns. You may commence as soon as we lay the main tops'l against the mast.'

'Aye, aye, sir.'

Drinkwater nodded to Birkbeck. 'You have the con, Mr Birkbeck?'

'Aye, sir.'

'Bring her to off the mole, if you please.'

'Aye, aye, sir.'

'Have you seen Ashton?'

'Here, sir.' Drinkwater turned to see the third lieutenant hurriedly pulling a tarpaulin around him. Such was the bustling mood of the morning that even Ashton looked a happier man.

'Ah, Mr Ashton, is the launch ready?'

'Yes sir. We have but to bend on the falls when we heave-to.'

'You are victualled for two days?'

'In accordance with your orders, sir.'

'Very well. Now pay attention. I have here a letter to be passed to the *Alcaid,* or Governor of the island. Do you ensure that the man to whom you pass this is the senior civil authority at Santa Cruz, do you understand?'

'Yes, sir.' Ashton frowned, taking the letter.

'Is something the matter, Mr Ashton?'

'Sir, with respect, the letter, is it in English?'

'Of course. Why do you ask?'

'Well, sir, I don't wish to sound impertinent, but will these dagoes understand it? I mean,' Ashton added hurriedly, 'I mean the matter is of considerable importance.'

'These dagoes, as you call 'em, Mr Ashton, are Portuguese, the oldest allies of our Sovereign. They have traded with us for years and if the Governor himself does not speak and read English, which I am confident he does, there will be a British vice-consul who will command the language as well as you or I.'

Ashton nodded. 'Very well, sir.'

'Now, I have asked if Bonaparte has arrived on the island, and whether any strange ships have been seen lying off the island. You should press this point particularly and bring me the answer.'

'Aye, aye, sir.'

'Very well. I have provisioned the boat for two days in case anything should miscarry. I shall lie-to hereabouts until you return, but if for any reason you are delayed, keep your men in the boat and ensure the marine sergeant understands that. I don't want British tars running loose among the women and producing a crop of Andromedas and Perseuses nine months hence!'

'I understand, sir.'

'Very well. Good fortune.' Ashton touched the fore-cock of his hat and turned away. 'Mr Birkbeck!' Drinkwater called. 'You may heave her to!'

'Aye, aye, sir!'

'Mr Marlowe! You may commence the salute!'

His Britannic Majesty's frigate *Andromeda* turned in a lazy circle, her bowsprit describing an arc of some two hundred degrees against the sky as her compass card spun from a heading of south-west by west, through north, to east, her yards swinging in their parrels, as the fore and mizen yards were braced for the port tack and her main mast spars left to fall aback. On the forecastle the battery of stubby carronades barked at precise, five-second intervals, paying respects to the Governor of Flores who, Drinkwater hoped, had been alerted to the presence of a British man-of-war offshore. Each unshotted discharge emitted a grey smoke-ring from which the quick-eyed caught sight of the fragments of wadding whirled into the sea.

As the last gun fell silent, *Andromeda* lay stopped across the wind and sea. To starboard the sea flattened in the lee thus formed and with the yard and stay tackles hooked on, the falls manned and set tight, the heavy white carvel launch lifted from the chocks. She was already manned and, as the men stamped away with the ropes, she began her slow traverse across the deck with her weight taken on the yard tackles and walked back on the stays.

Drinkwater, having given this operation a swift

appraisal, had his glass focused once more upon the flagstaff. His expectations were disappointed, for no reciprocating spurt of yellow flame with its lingering cloud of powder-smoke responded to the British salute. Well, he thought, pocketing the glass, he should not complain, perhaps the place was undefended; it certainly amounted to very little. Moreover, *Andromeda* was plainly only a private ship and wore nothing at her mastheads but her pendant, and she was a rather old and worn out one, at that!

Echoing his thoughts, the ship trembled as the mass of the laden boat vibrated the stays. This was transmitted to the masts and thus to the keel itself.

'Interesting to sound the well after this,' Drinkwater said to Birkbeck.

'I'm damned if I can find that leak, sir. I've had the linings out, the ceiling lifted and restowed God knows how many tiers of barrels, barricoes and hogsheads. Damn it, you'd think that with the ship more than three-quarters empty of stores the matter would be easy . . .'

'Nothing in life is easy, Mr Birkbeck, nothing at all,' Drinkwater said soulfully.

'Except begetting brats and earning a woman's bad opinion!' grumbled Birkbeck.

''Pon my word, Mr Birkbeck, I thought you more of a philosopher than that,' Drinkwater laughed, thinking of his own orders to Ashton regarding the conduct of the boat's crew.

'After crawling around that confounded hold, I'd challenge Plato himself to philosophize. Hey! Easy there on that main yard tackle, you'll have them all thrown out of the boat! Beg pardon, sir.'

'Not at all. There, they are afloat now.'

Andromeda, which had been listing as the launch reached the outboard extremity of its traverse and hung suspended above the sea, now recoiled from her forsaken burden. The launch had been lowered so that with a resounding smack the sea had embraced its long hull. A moment later her crew had cast off the falls and these had been recovered. Tossing oars, the launch's bowman bore off and the heavy boat was manoeuvred clear of the frigate's tumblehome. Then her oars were being plied energetically, and with Ashton sitting in the stern and Midshipman Paine standing at the tiller, she was headed gallantly for the shore, a red ensign at her stern and the scarlet of Sergeant McCann's marines a bright spot against the velvet blue of the Atlantic.

All hands on deck lingered to watch the launch diminish as it drew off towards the rock-strewn inlet. Beside Drinkwater, Marlowe had come aft and taken up his glass again.

'I can see masts and yards beyond those rocks, sir,' he observed. 'A brig, by the look of her. Certainly no squadron.'

'D'you see an ensign?' asked Drinkwater, fishing for his own glass, extending it and levelling it against a backstay.

'There's some bunting hanging up, but it's blowing away from us. Looks like red and white . . . No, I can't say for sure, sir.'

'Well, no matter, Ashton's almost there now; we'll know soon enough.' Drinkwater closed his glass again. 'Where's Mr Birkbeck?'

'Gone below sir, to check the well,' said Frey. 'I have the ship, sir.'

Drinkwater nodded. 'Very well, Mr Frey. By the bye, have you broken your fast yet?'

Frey shook his head. 'I can wait a little longer.'

'You may have to wait some hours. Here, Mr Marlowe, do you take the deck. Frey, join me for some breakfast.'

Drinkwater looked at the first lieutenant. Marlowe had gone pale. 'Come, come, Mr Marlowe, 'tis nothing. Send for a sextant and subtend the height of the peak and the shore. If the arc grows quickly, you will mark the rate at which the ship drifts inshore. Should you get an increase of say one eighth in an hour, brace up and stand offshore. I shall only be below.'

Marlowe swallowed and nodded. 'Aye, aye, sir,' he acknowledged, glancing anxiously at the white-fringed reefs surrounding Santa Cruz.

Turning, Drinkwater led Frey below. 'How does a man become a first luff with such a nervous disposition?' he asked himself, pitying poor Marlowe and wondering if his confidence might not have been misplaced after all. The last thing he saw of Marlowe was him sending a midshipman below for his sextant.

Breakfast in the cabin was enjoyed in silence. Frey was tired after his long watch and Drinkwater, having relinquished the deck, was now filled with anxiety. However, when the noise of stamping feet and the changed motion of the ship revealed Marlowe had decided to get under weigh, Drinkwater relaxed.

'He'll be all right, sir,' Frey said.

'I hope you are right.'

As Drinkwater poured a second cup of coffee, Marlowe put *Andromeda* on the port tack, standing offshore to the northward.

'There you are, sir. I told you so.'

Drinkwater stared astern out through the stern windows to where Santa Cruz appeared like a picture in a slide show.

'I believe you are right, Mr Frey.'

Frey smiled. 'A pretty sight, don't you think?' he asked, adding 'Flores means the island of flowers.'

Drinkwater smiled. 'You are certainly well informed. I wonder if Bonaparte will find the view so congenial? Will you make a painting of it?'

Frey nodded. 'Perhaps.'

'I admire the skill, but why d'you do it? I mean it's charming and a delight, and something to mark the occasion, but the effort surely out-weighs the advantages.'

Frey grinned. 'To be sure; but it is no rational matter. One is compelled to do it.'

'Compelled? D'you mean to say you are not a rational creature?' Drinkwater asked with a grin.

'If you mean by that question, am I unmoved by reason? No, of course not, but if you mean do I submit upon occasion to some inner prompting? Then yes, I do. We think we are rational beings, attributing our actions to logical thought, but consider sir, we feel first and often act upon our feelings. Our thoughts arise from our feelings . . .'

'You mean our emotions dominate our thinking?'

'Oh, yes, most certainly; but what makes us rational is that we can think about our emotions. It is from this response that the urge to paint or draw comes.'

'Then your artistic achievement is no more than an urge to copy.'

'To record, perhaps to reproduce, but no more. I make no claim to be a great artist.'

Drinkwater felt the conversation touched a raw nerve. Had his own thinking been too much influenced by his emotions? The possibility made him shudder inwardly.

They might have discussed this longer had not a peremptory knock announced the arrival of Midshipman Dunn.

'Yes, Mr Dunn?' asked Drinkwater, wondering what problem Marlowe had conjured up for himself.

'There's a ship, sir, bearing down towards us from the north-east.'

'Colours?'

'Can't see yet, sir.'

Drinkwater shot a quick glance at Frey. 'The Antwerp squadron?'

Frey shrugged. 'No peace for the wicked,' he muttered.

'Very well, Mr Dunn. Have Mr Marlowe clear for action!'

'You fear the worst?' said Frey, hauling himself wearily to his feet.

Drinkwater gave a short laugh. 'I'm just following my feelings, Mr Frey!'

Diplomacy

Mr Ashton lost sight of the ship sooner than those aboard *Andromeda* saw him disappear behind the outer reef of exposed rocks. At sea level, among the tossing wave crests, with his mind cast ahead on the coming hours, apart from a single glance astern to see the frigate's hull behind a rearing sea and only her topsails and upper masts visible, he gave her no thought at all. To say he was puffed up with the importance of his mission would be only a half-truth, for as is common with men of his stamp, it went against the grain to assume even delegated gravity from a man whom one despised. On the other hand, while in the politest society Captain Nathaniel Drinkwater might be regarded as *de trop*, Lieutenant Ashton knew well enough that while at sea, the commander of a British man-of-war possessed a degree of power not given to many. He was, therefore, in something of a quandary, half wishing to inflate himself, yet concerned that since he was not Captain Drinkwater's favourite, he had been sent upon this mission for reasons as yet unclear to him.

However, the effort of the seamen at the oars as they lent forward, then heaved backwards, was testimony enough to the fact that he had been entrusted with an independent task. He cast a quick look at Sergeant McCann and his lobsters, sitting bolt upright, their plumed billycocks foursquare upon their heads and their muskets between their gaitered knees. Then he transferred his attention to Paine. The lad was standing up, leaning on the big tiller as he strove to keep the heavy launch from broaching.

'Take her in beyond the reef, Mr Paine,' Ashton said self-importantly, 'and then we shall find some sort of a landing, I daresay.'

'Aye, aye, sir.'

Ashton felt a little more composed after this brief exchange; he had finally decided that the importance of his mission overrode personal considerations. As if echoing this sentiment, Mr Paine gave a little cough and said, 'May I ask something, sir?'

'What is it?' Ashton responded expansively.

'This island . . .'

'Is Flores, Mr Paine, westernmost of the Azores.'

'I know, sir,' replied Paine, concealing his irritation at being patronized, 'but is it where they are going to keep Boney?'

'Yes,' replied Ashton, looking again at the volcanic mass of the mountainous interior and the vegetation clinging in profusion to its lower slopes. 'Once here, the world will forget him.'

'Wasn't it Prometheus who was chained to a rock, sir?'

Ashton felt this chatty atmosphere was not one to be encouraged, especially as his knowledge of Greek mythology was sketchy. 'I daresay, Mr Paine, it might well have been . . .'

'It was, sir.' The voice was Sergeant McCann's, and he added conversationally, 'And so too was Andromeda, chained to a rock by her mother who was jealous of her beauty – a curious conjunction, seeing as how the ship is so named . . .'

'And it was Perseus who released her,' Paine added enthusiastically, 'then fell in love with her and . . .'

'Hold your damned tongues, the pair of you!' snapped Ashton, aware that matters had got out of hand. The man at stroke oar was grinning. 'And what's the matter with you? Wipe that foolish smile off your face, or I'll see to it with the cat later.' The man's face changed to a dark and sullen anger. 'What's your name?' Ashton asked.

'Shaw,' muttered the stroke oarsman.

'Shaw, eh. Well mind your manners, Shaw.' And Ashton, having established his position, leaned back in the stern of the now silent boat and contemplated the surge of white water about the approaching reef and the little brig beyond it. The hiss and slop of the following sea, the creak of thole pins, the faint grunts of the oarsmen and the splash of the oar-blades were now the only sounds to accompany his contemplation. Fifteen long minutes later, the launch swept inside the reef and into its shelter. The tiny anchorage opened up ahead of them, and beyond a strip of beach, the town, which was no more than a village.

Within the embrace of the rocks lay the brig, moored stem and stern, while some brightly painted fishing craft were drawn up on the beach beyond. Several of these were the slender *canoas* which the Azoreans used to hunt whales offshore. As the launch swept past the brig, a few curious faces stared down at them.

'Look out, boys,' someone aboard the brig shouted, 'the fooking press-gang's here!'

'Damned impertinence,' growled Ashton, while a curious Paine caught the name *Mary Digby* and the port of registry of *Sunderland* upon her stern.

There were a few idlers on the beach, too, some gathered about the fishing boats, others with lines running offshore. They were all watching the launch run in towards the beach. One man shouted something, though their ignorance of Portuguese prevented them from knowing whether it was a greeting or a complaint that Paine had carried away a hook and line.

'We must land on the beach,' Ashton pronounced.

'Aye, aye, sir,' said Paine quickly, leaning on the tiller to head the launch directly for the half-moon of sand.

'Oars.' The men ceased pulling, their oars rising horizontally while they lay on the looms and caught their breath. The momentum of the launch carried it in a final glide towards the beach.

'Toss oars!' The double-banked oars rose unsteadily to the vertical and Paine gave the final order that had them lowered, blades forward, with a dull clatter. A moment later the launch scrunched upon the sharp-smelling volcanic sand. The bowman leaped ashore with the painter. He was followed by the two men at the forward oars and the trio heaved the boat a little higher as a low swell followed her and broke upon the beach.

Lieutenant Ashton looked at them and then at Paine. 'Are you proposing to land me or the boat's crew, Mr Paine?' he asked sarcastically.

'Heave her up a little more,' Paine ordered, blushing.

'No, no, no,' expostulated Ashton, 'there's no need for all that.' The lieutenant rose with the petulant air of a man put out on another's behalf, and stepped up on the aftermost thwart. The two oarsmen seated there drew aside. One of them was Shaw, the sailor whom Ashton had threatened to flog, and he glared up at Ashton, but Ashton did not notice. He clambered forward over successive thwarts, the oarsmen drawing aside for him. Stepping momentarily on the gunwhale, he jumped ashore, but turned and slipped on the bladder-wrack. He half-fell, but caught himself and, while his coat tail dangled in the wet and slithery seaweed that lay on the tideline, he avoided besmirching his white breeches.

'Damnation!' he swore. The boat's crew to a man, looked out across the harbour as though the view was unsurpassable. One or two shoulders shook with what might have been mirth, but Ashton was staring at Paine whose face was almost contorted in the effort of self-control. 'Mr Paine, the boat's crew are to remain aboard. Sergeant McCann, you may land two sentinels.'

Ashton brushed the sand from his hands, turned about and began to ascend the sloping beach. He was met by an officer in the brown tunic of a regiment of *caçadores*.

'Welcome to Flores, sir,' the swarthy officer said pleasantly in good English.

'Er, obliged, I'm sure,' mumbled the astonished Ashton.

The Portuguese officer smiled. 'I am Lieutenant Da Silva. I served in Spain with General Wellesley. At

Talavera,' Da Silva added as Ashton appeared even more perplexed, but the penny dropped and Ashton took the proferred hand, aware that it and his right cuff were mucky from contact with the wet wrack on the sand. Serve the dago right, Ashton thought venomously, but he smiled as he responded to the vigorous shake of the Portuguese officer's hand. 'I have a message for the Governor - the *Alcaid*,' he added pompously.

'Yes, of course,' Da Silva replied, indicating the way. 'Please come with me.'

'Can you make out her colours, Mr Frey?' Drinkwater's voice betrayed his anxiety as he fumbled in his tail-pocket, extended the Dollond glass and clapped it to his right eye. He swore at the difficulty of bringing the strange ship into focus and hoped Frey's sharper eyes would spot the ensign.

'No, sir, hidden behind the tops'ls.'

'Damnation,' Drinkwater hissed under his breath.

'Sir . . .' Frey spoke slowly, 'there's something familiar about her . . .'

For a moment Drinkwater's glass captured the image of the approaching ship which left an impression upon his retina. He instantly agreed with Frey and they simultaneously identified her: 'It's that Russian frigate . . . What's its confounded name?'

'The *Gremyashchi*!'

'What the devil's she doing here?' Drinkwater asked no one in particular, lowering his glass, his heart suddenly hammering in his breast. But he already knew the answer, just as Marlowe ran up, two fingers to the fore-cock of his hat.

'Cleared for action, sir!' he reported, staring over

Drinkwater's shoulder at the approaching ship foaming towards them, running before the persisting north-easter. 'That's that Russian we sailed from Dover with!' he said.

'Aye, it is . . . Nevertheless, it's as well to take no chances,' Drinkwater remarked obscurely, trying to think tactically. It was enough that Captain Rakov was here, off the Azores; the reason why could wait. 'Very well, gentlemen. Mr Birkbeck, do you bring the ship onto the larboard tack, then heave-to athwart her hawse . . .'

'Aye, aye, sir!'

'Mr Frey, you shall run out the starboard battery when I give the word. Load single ball. Mr Marlowe, be so kind as to have the forecastle carronades loaded with powder only. We shall', Drinkwater paused a moment and braced himself as, under Birkbeck's orders, *Andromeda* turned away from her easterly course and swung to the north-north-west, to sail at an approximate right angle to the Russian frigate's course. He turned to Birkbeck: 'Ten minutes should see us close enough . . .'

'Aye, sir,' acknowledged the master.

'We shall', Drinkwater resumed, 'fire the unshotted carronades to bring her to. If she runs down any more I intend to cripple her, Mr Frey, aim high and knock her sticks about.'

'Aye, aye, sir!'

'Sir, I . . .' Marlowe's face wore an expression of grave concern.

'Not now, Mr Marlowe,' Drinkwater said dismissively. 'To your posts, gentlemen, to your posts,' and seeing Marlowe hesitate, Drinkwater rubbed his hands and added, 'Briskly now, briskly!'

Marlowe shrugged, turned on his heel and ran forward along the starboard gangway. Birkbeck caught Drinkwater's eye and the latter raised his eyebrow; Birkbeck smiled and turned back to watch the approaching ship.

Drinkwater raised his glass again. He could see it was the *Gremyashchi* now, the figurehead of Mars the god of war clearly identified her, and her aspect was opening so that he could just see the white flag with its dark blue diagonal cross fluttering beyond the leech of the main topsail. As *Andromeda* gathered speed on her new tack, the fly of the Russian ensign was again occluded behind the bellying sail. He lowered his telescope a fraction and could just make out a dark gaggle of officers on her quarterdeck.

A flurry of activity could be seen on the *Gremyashchi*'s deck and the straining main course seemed to belly even more, losing its driving power as the sheets were slacked off and then the big sail rose to the yard under the tug of the buntlines and the clew garnets.

Was Rakov clewing up in order to give battle, or merely to exchange pleasantries?

'Now sir?' asked an equally anxious Birkbeck.

'Now is as good a time as ever,' Drinkwater said, coolly, feigning indifference, and Birkbeck's voice rang out with the order to 'clew up both courses and heave her to'. A moment later, *Andromeda*'s main yards were braced round and their sails curved back against the mast, bringing the British frigate to a gently pitching standstill. Drinkwater drew in his breath and hailed the forecastle.

'Mr Marlowe! Fire!'

The carronades forward gave their short, imperative

bark. The cloud of powder smoke blew back over the deck, carrying its sharp stench to the quarterdeck. The Russian ship was now some seven or eight cables away, broad on the starboard bow and Drinkwater scrutinized her, eager to see what the Russian commander would do in response.

For several minutes the *Gremyashchi* continued to bear down on them, seemingly contemptuous of the smaller British frigate almost in her track.

'Run out the guns!'

Drinkwater's order was carried to the gun-deck below and he could feel the rumbles of the gun-tracks as their iron-shod wheels carried the black muzzles out through the ports. Drinkwater could imagine the scene below decks with Frey eagerly dancing up and down the line of guns, urging them spiked round on the target; their crews would be straining on tackles, their gun-captains spinning the breech screws to elevate the muzzles. As they completed their exertions, the gasping crews would squat, kneel or crouch beside the monsters they served, the captains kneeling behind the line of guns, squinting along their brute length, the flint-lock lanyards taut in their left hands, their right hands held up so that Frey could see them report their cannon ready.

Less than half a mile now separated the *Gremyashchi* from *Andromeda*. The Russian continued to bear down before the wind under topsails and topgallants, her dark brown sides as yet unbroken by open ports. Then a brief white cloud appeared on her port bow and hung for a moment, running along with the Russian ship and gradually dispersing as the noise of the discharge was blown down towards the waiting *Andromeda*.

The closed gun-ports seemed to signal an acceptance

of *Andromeda*'s right to dictate terms, for a moment later she sheered away to starboard, heeling over as her yards were braced sharply round and she settled on a course to the north-north-west, parallel to *Andromeda*'s heading.

'She's making off,' said a surprised Birkbeck. Drinkwater was raking the Russian ship with his telescope. The *Gremyashchi* was broadside onto them now and he could see her mizen mast clearly, with her blue and white colours at the spanker peak.

'By God, do you look at that!' It was Hyde, whose scarlet nonchalance had graced the quarterdeck since clearing for action. All along the *Gremyashchi*'s port side, the gun ports opened and she too bared her fangs, despite the leeward heel. Then, in a ragged attempt at simultaneity, Rakov, whose figure Drinkwater had located standing hat-in-hand upon her rail, discharged his guns. The shots raised a line of splashes ahead of the hove-to *Andromeda*.

'And what is all that about?' Hyde asked.

In the glass Drinkwater saw Rakov wave his hat flamboyantly above his head and jump back down on to his own quarterdeck. 'That, Mr Hyde, is to let us know we did not intimidate him.' Drinkwater pocketed the telescope and called his messenger. 'Mr Dunn! Be so kind as to tell Mr Frey to run in the starboard battery and secure the guns. He will have to draw all charges.'

'Run in the guns and draw all charges, aye, aye, sir.'

'We cannot afford to waste any powder or shot,' he remarked to Birkbeck as the master came across the deck from the binnacle.

'D'you wish to run back towards Santa Cruz, sir?'

Drinkwater cast another look at the *Gremyashchi*. Her

stern was square onto them now and there was little sign of her manoeuvring again. A nasty suspicion was forming in Drinkwater's mind. He nodded at the master. 'Yes, if you please.'

Marlowe came aft as the rumbling and vibration in their boot soles told where the 12-pounders below were being run in again.

'He's off after other quarry by the look of it, I'd say, sir.'

'My guess exactly, Frederic,' Drinkwater concurred.

'Looking for what you call the Antwerp squadron, d'you think?'

Drinkwater nodded. 'I cannot think of any other reason for his being here.'

'That rather shortens the odds against us, then.'

'Yes,' said Drinkwater, as the main yards were hauled round parallel with those on the fore and mizen masts and *Andromeda* began to gather headway again. 'Yes, it may well do if he has orders to engage us. He certainly wasn't about to hang about and parley.'

For a moment both men stood side by side, watching the exertions of the men at the braces, trimming the yards almost square across the ship as *Andromeda* answered her helm and swung to port, to run downwind again, heading for Flores which loomed five miles away.

'On the other hand,' mused Drinkwater, 'we are supposed to be allies.'

'Those shots across our bow didn't look very friendly,' laughed Marlowe ruefully.

'No, they didn't, but Rakov might have been trying to cow us.'

'Why should he do that, sir?'

'Oh, I don't know,' Drinkwater replied wearily, unwilling to explain to Marlowe the hostility he had felt from the Russian when Rakov discovered he was the British officer responsible for the destruction of the *Suvorov*. 'It's just a feeling I have,' he added conciliatorily, seeing Frey come up from the gun-deck. 'Perhaps another time, Mr Frey.'

'I rather hope not, sir: they were 18-pounders at least.'

The knot of officers laughed a trifle uneasily. 'Poor old Ashton,' remarked Hyde. 'He's missed all the fun.'

Lieutenant Da Silva had conducted Ashton to the Governor's undistinguished residence where the British officer was received with every courtesy including a glass of wine. Da Silva introduced the Governor, Dom Miguel Gaspar Viera Batata, his secretary, whose name appeared to be Soares, and a tall thin man in a black worsted suit, silver buckled shoes and the elegant affectations of an English fop.

The Englishman introduced himself. 'I am Edmund Gilbert, Mr Ashton, British consul at Angra. By good fortune I am visiting Dom Batata at this time.' Ashton had no idea where Angra was, but his bow was elegant enough and it took them all in.

'Your servant, gentlemen. Lieutenant Josiah Ashton of His Britannic Majesty's frigate *Andromeda*, gentlemen, Captain Nathaniel Drinkwater commanding.' He took Drinkwater's letter from his breast and handed it to Batata.

'Thank you, Lieutenant.' Batata took the letter, slit the wafer and began to read while Soares served the wine. When he had finished reading, Batata passed the letter to Gilbert who blew his gaunt cheeks out and expelled his breath slowly, as if this was an essential accompaniment to the process.

'Well, well, well,' he concluded, refolding the letter and returning it to Batata who passed it directly to Soares.

'May I . . .?' Gilbert sought the Governor's permission which was granted by a grave nod of Batata's head. 'Do I gather from this missive, Lieutenant . . . I beg your pardon, sir, I have forgotten . . .'

'Ashton, Mr Gilbert,' Ashton prompted quickly, colouring uncertainly.

'Yes, yes. Well, Mr Ashton, do I infer your commander, Nathaniel What's-his-name, believes Napoleon Bonaparte is to be exiled here, on the island of Flores.'

'Yes, sir,' replied Ashton, slightly mollified by Gilbert's inability to remember Drinkwater's name and accepting a refill of his glass from Soares, 'if he ain't here already.'

'Here? Already? 'Pon my soul, Mr Ashton, this is the first hint we've heard that Napoleon Bonaparte *ain't*, as you say, Emperor of the French!'

'He has abdicated, gentlemen,' Ashton explained, inflated by his assumption of the role of harbinger.

'You are our wingèd Mercury.' Gilbert echoed Ashton's thoughts with a thin smile.

'King Louis has returned to France.'

'Then the war is over?' asked Batata.

'Indeed yes, sir. In Europe, at least.'

'Ah yes, your country is still at war with the Americans. Now these other ships, Lieutenant, we have no knowledge of them, have we?' Gilbert shrugged and a

216

query to his secretary by Batata produced a negative shrug from Soares. Batata turned back to Ashton. 'We have no knowledge of any other ships other than merchantmen . . .'

'And is there no news at all in the archipelago, of preparations for the reception of Bonaparte, gentlemen?' Ashton asked as Soares bent over his glass again.

Batata shrugged and shook his head. Gilbert was more emphatic. 'I have heard nothing on Terceira and am certain we should have done by now, if such a thing was meditated.'

'Very well,' Ashton bowed, 'thank you for your time, gentlemen. I am sorry to have troubled you.'

'It is no trouble, Lieutenant,' Dom Batata said.

Gilbert addressed the Governor in fluent Portuguese and Batata nodded in agreement, then Gilbert turned to Ashton. 'Mr Ashton, I have been here for ten days attending to some business with the master of the brig *Mary Digby* of Sunderland. If your Captain Drinkwater would condescend to convey me back to Angra, we could quickly ascertain if the packet from Lisbon has brought orders relevant to the fate of Bonaparte.'

'Well, sir, I suppose Captain Drinkwater will have no objection . . .'

'Good, then the matter is settled. Give me a quarter of an hour, and I shall be with you.'

Da Silva accompanied Ashton and Gilbert back to the beach, with two servants bearing between them Mr Gilbert's portmanteau. As they approached the boat, Ashton noticed two of the launch's seamen sauntering ahead of them, each carrying a canvas bag.

'If you will excuse me, Mr Gilbert, I will just get on ahead and prepare the boat for you.' Ashton proferred the excuse and, without waiting for a reply, walked briskly on. A moment later he overtook the two seamen, one of whom he recognized as the launch's stroke oarsmen.

'Shaw!' he called and the man turned round as Ashton hurried up. 'Shaw, what the bloody hell d'you think you are doing out of the boat?'

'We was sent up by, er . . .'

'Went to get fresh bread, sir,' the other man said, holding up one of the canvas bags.

'Who the devil said you could leave the boat?'

'Well, sir, we only sent to get bread, sir, had a tarpaulin muster and reckoned we could afford a few loaves . . .'

'Let me see in those bags.'

'It's only bread, sir . . .'

'Let me see, damn you!' Furious, Ashton pulled the loaves out and hurled them into the water.

'Sir! We paid for them!'

'Aye and you paid for these too, I daresay!' Ashton triumphantly drew two bottles from the bottom of the bag and turned to Shaw. 'Empty yours too,' he commanded.

'Sir!' Shaw protested.

'Empty it, damn you and be quick!' Ashton was aware of Gilbert approaching as Shaw upended the bag. Four richly smelling and warm loaves fell out and two green bottles followed. One hit a stone and smashed with a tinkle, staining the sand with wine. Ashton kicked both loaves and broken glass into the water where screaming gulls were already congregating round the floating debris of the first lot of bread. He hurled the two remaining bottles after them while the fishermen tending an adjacent *canoa*, watched in astonished silence.

'Now get back to the boat and be damned quick about it!' Ashton hissed. He turned as nonchalantly as he could as Gilbert came up to him.

'Trouble, Lieutenant?'

'Not really, Mr Gilbert. Not what I'd call trouble . . .'

'And what would you call trouble, Lieutenant Ashton?' asked Gilbert, spurning the broken neck of one of the bottles with his foot, and looking at the ravenous gulls tearing the loaves apart, their wings beating with the fury of their assault on the abandoned bread.

'Oh, I don't know,' Ashton said, utterly discomfited.

'I suppose finding Bonaparte sitting on Terceira would be trouble of a real nature, don't you think?' offered Gilbert.

'I suppose it would, yes.'

They had reached the boat by then, and Shaw and his mate were resuming their places as oarsmen. Midshipman Paine who had obviously been dozing in the stern-sheets with his hat over his eyes, stirred himself at the commotion in the boat, for Shaw was clearly explaining what had happened, and the boat's crew were staring over their shoulders, sullen and resentful.

'Mr Paine, let us have a hand here, to get this gear aboard.' The two marines posted as sentries came forward. One was Sergeant McCann. As two seamen came out of the boat to pass Gilbert's portmanteau along, Ashton drew McCann aside.

'Sergeant, I thought I made it quite clear that the boat's crew were not permitted to leave the launch?' he asked furiously.

McCann looked down at the lieutenant's hand on his arm and remained silent. 'Sergeant, don't you trifle with me, damn you. You heard what I said.' He shook McCann's arm, barely able to control himself.

'You ordered the boat's crew to remain with the boat, sir, but Mr Paine gave permission for two delegates to nip ashore for some food. The men had brought a little money, d'you see, sir.'

'Sergeant,' insisted Ashton, hissing into McCann's face, 'they had purchased liquor . . .'

'They were not alone, then, Mr Ashton,' McCann snarled, his temper fraying to match the sea-officer's, as he caught the whiff of Ashton's breath.

'I shall have you flogged for your impudence, McCann, when I get you back aboard! Now get in the boat, you damned Yankee bugger.'

McCann coloured; for a moment he contemplated responding, thought better of it and shut his mouth. Then he turned on his heel, nodded to the private soldier to precede him and clambered over the gunwhale.

'All sorted out now?' asked Gilbert matter-off-factly, with his thin, supercilious smile.

'Do mind yourself on the thwarts, Mr Gilbert,' Ashton replied equivocally, waving the consul into the boat.

'After you, my dear fellow.'

'Convention demands you go first, Mr Gilbert.'

'Does it now. Well we had better not flout convention then, had we?'

Five minutes later, the launch was pulling clear of the reef, leaving the harbour in comparative peace, for the gulls had destroyed the loaves and only a few continued to quarrel over the last remnants. As for the watching fishermen, they shook their heads in incredulous wonder and resumed their work.

A Matter of Discipline

The recovery of the launch proved a tediously tricky business in the lively sea running off Flores, despite the lee made by the ship. While Marlowe and Birkbeck struggled with the heavy boat, Drinkwater surveyed his unexpected passenger who had scrambled up the ship's side after Ashton. Clearly Mr Gilbert, whatever else he was, was a nimble fellow, not unfamiliar with ships.

'You wish for a passage to Terceira, Mr Gilbert?' Drinkwater asked, after the ritual of introduction.

Gilbert nodded. 'In case word has arrived there concerning Bonaparte,' the British consul tersely replied.

'Yes, yes, I understand, sir, but my orders indicate he will be brought to Flores,' said Drinkwater, stretching the truth to buttress his argument, 'and I fear if I abandon this station,' he paused and shrugged, 'well, who knows?'

Gilbert frowned. 'But you are here to guard him, are you not?' and then Gilbert's quick intellect grasped the import of Ashton's questions about other men-of-war in the offing. 'Ah, you are expecting other ships, ships which might interfere with arrangements for the accommodation of Boney.'

It was said as a statement of fact and Drinkwater nodded. 'There is, I understand,' he replied, 'a conspiracy afoot in France to have him taken to Canada . . .'

Gilbert's eyebrows rose in comprehension. 'Dear God!' he murmured.

'I see you are as apprehensive as I am.'

'Quite so . . .'

Both men remained a moment in silence, then Drinkwater suggested, 'I can have you put ashore again here.'

Gilbert shook his head. 'I should really return to Angra.' He paused, then added, 'May I take your boat? She will make the passage under sail, I daresay?' he looked at the launch somewhat dubiously.

'It must be upwards of forty leagues . . .'

'No matter, your boat is up to it.' Drinkwater looked askance at Gilbert; he was clearly a man of resilience and resolution. In the waist the launch was swinging slowly across the ship to its chocks on the booms. 'Very well,' Drinkwater agreed, 'she is provisioned for two days, perhaps you will be kind enough to replenish her when you arrive; we are precious short of stores. Some fruit would be most welcome,' he said, and raising his voice he called, 'Mr Marlowe! Have the launch put back in the water!' Drinkwater ignored the moment's hesitation and the sudden irritated stares of the labouring seamen who were quickly ordered to reverse their efforts; he summoned Ashton.

'Mr Ashton, run down to my cabin and take a look at the chart on my desk. A course for Terceira;

you may take Mr Gilbert back to Angra in the launch.'

'Sir, if I might suggest something.'

'Well, what is it?'

Ashton edged round to attempt to exclude Gilbert from his remark to the captain. 'I should like to lay a formal charge against Sergeant McCann.'

'Oh, for heaven's sake, Mr Ashton, now is hardly the moment. What has Sergeant McCann done?'

'Disobeyed my orders, sir,' Ashton hissed intensely.

Drinkwater felt a great weariness overcome him; he was tired of these minor problems, tired of Ashton and the whole confounded pack of these contentious and troublesome men. He was tempted to consign Ashton to the devil, but mastered this intemperate and dangerous instinct; instead he caught sight of Lieutenant Hyde and called him over.

'Mr Hyde, Mr Ashton here says that Sergeant McCann disobeyed his orders.' He turned to Ashton. 'Perhaps you would tell us how this occurred.'

'I left orders that no one was to leave the boat while I waited upon the Governor. Upon my return I found two men had defied me and been into the town . . .'

'*Two* men, d'you say?' Drinkwater asked.

'Yes, and . . .'

'To what purpose did these two men go into town?' Drinkwater persisted.

'That is the point, sir, they had been into town and purchased liquor.'

'What liquor?' Hyde asked.

'What does it matter what liquor? They had disobeyed my orders and left the boat . . .'

'Were sentries posted?' Hyde pressed.

'Yes, of course, under your Sergeant McCann . . .'

'But Sergeant McCann was only in charge of the marines. Who commanded the boat?'

'Well, Midshipman Paine.'

'Then why isn't he in the soup?'

'I think we should have a word with Midshipman Paine,' broke in Drinkwater. 'Be so kind as to send for him.'

It took a few moments to fish Paine back out of the launch which was now bobbing alongside again. He reported to the trio of gravefaced officers on the quarterdeck and was asked for an explanation.

'Whilst you lay in Santa Cruz, Mr Paine, were you not aware that Mr Ashton had given orders to the effect that no one should go ashore?' Drinkwater asked.

'Well, sir,' Paine replied, 'yes and no . . .'

'What the devil . . .?' began Ashton, but Drinkwater put out a hand to stop him going further.

'That is too equivocating, sir,' Drinkwater said, his voice hard and level. 'Kindly explain yourself.'

'Well, sir, I understood Mr Ashton to have said that the boat's crew were not to go ashore. When Shaw asked me if, on behalf of the men, he and Ticknell might not run up to the town to buy some fresh bread, I consulted Sergeant McCann and he felt that it would not be contrary to the spirit of your orders if just two men went. The boat's crew had a tarpaulin muster . . .'

'What d'you mean "would not be contrary to the spirit of my orders"?' demanded Ashton, 'you knew damned well I meant no one could go ashore.'

Paine stood his ground. 'I understood you did not want shore-leave granted, sir, but the men could not desert and had taken money on trust from their ship-mates. I did not see the harm . . .'

'Very well, gentlemen.' Drinkwater silenced the midshipman and strove to keep the exasperation out of his voice. 'It is clear this matter cannot be resolved quickly. It is also clear that we cannot hang about here dithering. Have the launch swung inboard again; we will take Mr Gilbert to Angra ourselves, and the sooner the better. Do you pass word to Mr Marlowe, Mr Ashton; Mr Paine, I shall speak to you later. Mr Hyde, thank you.'

Ashton seemed to hesitate a moment, but then the officers broke away and Drinkwater crossed the deck to where Gilbert awaited his departure, masking his curiosity in a thinly veiled attempt at indifference.

'My apologies, Mr Gilbert, I have changed my mind; we shall run you to Terceira in the ship.'

'Thank you, Captain,' Gilbert replied, smiling, 'I cannot pretend that a long passage in an open boat is much to my liking, though I did not wish to inconvenience you.'

'That was most considerate of you.' Drinkwater returned the smile. 'My chief anxiety is that I do not miss any rendezvous of enemy ships by being absent from my station. The whole thing,' he confessed, 'is something of a hazard.'

'Is such a rendezvous likely now the war is over?'

'Is the war over, Mr Gilbert? I wish I was so sure. Anyway, the die is cast.'

Both men watched while the tackles were hooked on to the launch again. Drinkwater intensely disliked giving orders and counter-orders, for nothing created distrust between officers and men more than such obvious uncertainty in the former.

'I beg your pardon, Captain Drinkwater,' said Gilbert, 'but does your change of heart have anything to do with the little incident ashore?'

'What incident?'

'Well, it is none of my affair, but I observed some breach of discipline which gave rise to your Lieutenant Ashton remonstrating with two of your sailors. They appeared to have offended in some way by purchasing bread . . .'

'Bread?'

'Yes, they had a bag apiece, which Lieutenant Ashton kicked into the harbour. He seems a rather headstrong and intemperate young man.'

'Was there no liquor involved?' Drinkwater asked.

'There may have been a few bottles of wine,' Gilbert replied, 'but my chief impression was of a quantity of bread.'

'Thank you, Mr Gilbert. Perhaps you would like to make yourself as comfortable as possible in my cabin.'

'That is most kind of you, Captain. I can assure you that your cabin will be luxurious compared with the bilges of your launch,' Gilbert said, smiling.

The overnight passage east-south-east towards Terceira cost Drinkwater the remains of his equanimity. Already consumed by anxiety and speculation about the sudden appearance of the *Gremyashchi*, this unwanted diversion of almost two hundred miles to the eastward was a sore trial. Had he not so desperately wanted news of the whereabouts of Bonaparte, he would have returned

Gilbert to Santa Cruz, but at least providence had ensured that *Andromeda* had arrived off Flores at the same time that the English consul had been visiting the island, and they had not had to resort to communicating with a Portuguese vice-consul who, whatever assurance Drinkwater had given Ashton, while perfectly reliable, would not have been so capable of supporting an informed, speculative debate.

However, the presence of the *Gremyashchi* confirmed the veracity of Hortense's intelligence, and the action of Rakov had clearly been as intimidatory as his orders allowed him. But while the appearance of the Russian frigate removed a major doubt in Drinkwater's mind, it caused another: Rakov's purposeful withdrawal to the north and west suggested he too was to rendezvous with the 'Antwerp squadron', and while he was doing this, *Andromeda* was waltzing off to the eastwards with a passenger!

As night shrouded the ship, Drinkwater paced the quarterdeck angry and frustrated, feeling the advantage he had so assiduously cultivated being thrown away with every cable *Andromeda* sailed towards the eastern Azores. In his heart he was doubly annoyed with Lieutenant Ashton.

It was, Drinkwater concluded, a mean thought to ascribe his current woes to the young officer, but he was meanly inclined that evening, reluctant to go down to his cabin which he would have to share with Gilbert, yet irritated by his tumbling thoughts which kept him pacing and fidgeting about the quarterdeck. What was he to make of this damnable business at Santa Cruz? It would have been a silly incident, he had no doubt, but on the one hand lay the argument for order and discipline, and upon the other that for toleration and humanity. And he, as commander, amid his other preoccupations, was obliged to reconcile the essentially irreconcilable.

He paced up and down, only vaguely aware that the watch was about to change with a flurry of activity, the flitting of dark shapes about the quarterdeck, a shuffle of figures around the helm partially lit by the dim glow from the binnacle. He sensed, rather than saw Marlowe on deck, engaged in discussing something with the shorter, slightly stooped figure of Birkbeck. It was then that the idea struck Drinkwater.

He stopped pacing, turned to windward and barked a short, monosyllabic laugh. Coming on deck late, just as eight bells struck, Midshipman Dunn caught sight of the captain and heard the odd sound, stored it away to add to the cockpit's fund of stories about the eccentricity of Old Nat. As for Drinkwater, he turned on his heel, crossed the deck and confronted the first lieutenant. It was too dark by now to see the expression of satisfaction upon his face.

'Mr Marlowe, may I have a word with you?'

'Of course, sir. As a matter of fact, I wanted to speak with you.'

'Oh, what about?'

'I have just been telling the master here, I think I have located the leak.'

'That is very satisfactory, at least I hope it is. Is the matter serious?'

'Serious enough: it's a dockyard job, but we may be able to do something to reduce it.'

'Does it compromise our present situation?'

'Not as long as we have men to man pumps, no, sir,

but it is likely to get worse. I'm afraid the leak is caused by devil-bolts.'

'God's bones,' Drinkwater swore quietly. The dock-yard practice of making repairs with short and inadequate screw-bolts had once been common. It was a mark of the corruption of a great public service, the indolence of its overseers who grew fat on the myriad minor economies they practised widely, and their indifference to the fate of the ships of war placed in their hands for refitting. It was widely believed in the sea-service that ships had foundered in heavy weather owing to their working in a seaway, their planking springing because it was not properly secured to the framework of the ribs.

The loss of HMS *Blenheim* in the Indian Ocean, homeward bound from the Hooghly with Admiral Sir Thomas Troubridge on board, was attributed to this cause and the resulting scandal had, it was generally thought, ended this particular dockyard malpractice. Of course, it was impossible to say when the bolts now causing *Andromeda's* leak had been fitted. Probably some time ago. The slow decomposition of the iron and its infection of the surrounding oak progressively weakened any fastening, even when payed and covered with sheets of anti-fouling copper, but a short bolt, with insufficient of its screwed shank penetrating the futtock behind the planking, would deteriorate and spring within a few years, and such bolts were cheaper and more easily fitted substitutes than the effective oak trenails or heavy copper bolts.

The news somewhat dimmed Drinkwater's satisfaction in having resolved his earlier problem, but it was at least satisfactory to know the cause, and neither problem would vanish unless something were to be done about each of them.

'Well gentlemen, better the devil you know, I suppose.' This little witticism was greeted by respectful chuckles. 'Perhaps you will have a look at the area tomorrow, Mr Birkbeck?'

'Aye, aye, sir.'

'There is another matter though, Mr Marlowe,' Drinkwater went on, 'one that I'd be obliged to you for a moment of your time to discuss.'

'Yes, of course, sir.'

'I'll take my leave then, sir,' said Birkbeck.

'Yes. Goodnight, Mr Birkbeck.'

Drinkwater led Marlowe across the deck to the weather rail where they stood staring to windward, out of earshot of the men at the helm.

'I don't know if you are aware of it, but there was some sort of incident at Santa Cruz today. I gather Ashton left orders that no one was to go ashore, then two men went into the town for provisions and Ashton accused Sergeant McCann of disobedience.'

'I had heard something of the matter. Hyde was rather inflamed about it; he had heard McCann's side of things and said Paine was in command of the boat.'

'Yes, I had gathered that too. Ashton seems to have regarded his instruction as explicit and all-embracing, which is undoubtedly what was intended. Nevertheless, McCann seems to be implicated and Ashton is demanding a flogging for him. I expect Mr Paine was prevailed upon to release two men to get some fresh bread on the grounds that two men did not constitute a boat's crew.'

'And the two men brought back some bottles of wine as well as bread,' added Marlowe.

'Yes, I think you have the scene in your mind's eye. Ashton, of course, painted the picture of a foraging expedition intent on acquiring liquor. The fault, of course, lies with Paine, which is unfortunate, and Ashton no doubt put fuel on the flames with his eagerness to punish the defiance to his order. This, I imagine, is where McCann got involved.'

'I heard from Hyde that Ashton called McCann, a "Yankee bugger".'

'A Yankee bugger?'

'McCann's from Loyalist American stock, sir,' Marlowe explained, 'like Admiral Hallowell.'

'Was McCann provoked?' Drinkwater asked quickly.

'I don't know,' Marlowe replied. 'Knowing Ashton,' he paused, 'well, who knows? Probably.'

'That is what I want you to find out, Frederic. I want you to hold an enquiry tomorrow. We can send Frey in with the boat taking Gilbert ashore and you shall gather evidence in the wardroom. Report to me when you have concluded . . . by tomorrow evening at the latest, by which time we shall, I hope, be resuming our station off Flores. Do you understand?'

'Yes,' said Marlowe.

'It's another chance, Frederic, to rid yourself of this man's influence.'

'He may see it as something else.'

'He may see it how he likes; I am instructing you to carry out this duty and you are the first lieutenant of the ship. Whatever complexion Mr Ashton may wish to put upon the case is quite irrelevant, but it will do you no harm either way. Oh, and by the bye, either way I want the matter examined with scrupulous fairness.'

'Of course, sir,' said Marlowe.

'That way any opinion Ashton may have to the contrary will be conscionably groundless.'

The wardroom presented an untypical appearance next morning, for Marlowe had ordered the table cleared completely and all personal items, which in the usual run of events would have cluttered the place, removed into the cabins of the individual officers. The announcement of this requirement was made at breakfast to which all, except for Frey, the officer of the watch, were summoned. The usually degenerately homely room now took on a forbidding appearance.

'What's afoot?' Hyde asked, aware that some sort of effort was required on his part and that his entire day was being set awry at an early moment by this disruption of routine.

'I am charged with examining the circumstances surrounding the incident which occurred on the mole at Santa Cruz yesterday . . .' began Marlowe, only to be interrupted by an incredulous Ashton who rose and asked:

'You are *what?*'

'Oh do sit down Ashton,' said Hyde laconically, 'and pray don't be too tiresome, I have other things to do.'

'The day you actually accomplish them will be witness to a damned miracle,' Ashton snapped unpleasantly. 'I asked a question and I demand an answer.'

'I think, Josiah,' Marlowe cut in quickly, 'you should heed the advice you have just been given. You shall demand nothing, and sit down at once.' Marlowe took no further interest in Ashton and turned to Hyde. 'I wish you to sit with me, Hyde. We will commence our

233

examination at two bells; Mr Birkbeck, I should be obliged if you would relieve Ashton of his watch this forenoon, in order that we can carry out this duty without delay. He may substitute for you after noon.'

'Very well, Mr Marlowe.' Birkbeck drew his watch from his pocket and stared at it a moment, then he rose, went briefly into his cabin, reappeared and went on deck.

As soon as he had gone, Ashton began to expostulate. 'Look here, Freddy, is this some kind of a joke, because if it is . . .'

'It's no joke, Josiah. I'd be obliged if you would clear that boat-cloak and bundle of papers and remain in your cabin until called.'

'By God, I'll . . .!'

Ashton stood up again with such force that he cracked his head on the deck-beams above and ducked in reaction with a further torrent of oaths. Then, seeing he was cornered, he snatched up his cloak and papers, and withdrew into his cabin, shutting the door with a bang.

'Knocked some sense into himself at last,' remarked Hyde with a grin as Frey entered the wardroom, his hair tousled.

'Hullo, I hope you lubbers haven't done with breakfast yet; I'm ravenous. Sam!' The messman having been summoned, Frey was soon spooning up a quantity of burgoo and molasses, drinking coffee and pronouncing himself a new man, whereupon Marlowe opened the proceedings by summoning Ashton from his cabin. The third lieutenant was quizzed as to the exact nature of his orders and Hyde noted down his reply. He was then told to cool his heels in his cabin, to

234

which order he resentfully complied, giving Marlowe a malevolent glare.

Midshipman Paine was then called and permitted to sit at the table. He admitted having been asked by the boat's crew if they could nominate two of their number to obtain some fresh bread.

'Why do you suppose the boat's crew wished to purchase bread, Mr Paine?' Marlowe asked.

'Because they were hungry, sir, and could smell fresh-baked bread from a bakery across the harbour.'

'And how did you think they were going to pay for this bread, the scent of which so fortuitously wafted across the harbour?' queried Hyde.

'Why sir, from money which they had brought with them.'

'Isn't that a little unusual?' asked Marlowe.

'That they had money, sir?'

'Yes.'

Paine shrugged, 'I didn't think so, sir. I believe it was no more than a few pence.'

'Did any of the marines contribute?'

'I'm not sure, sir. I don't think so.'

'Where was Sergeant McCann at this time?'

'He had posted himself on the beach as one of the sentinels, sir.'

'So he was not party to any of the discussion in the boat.'

Paine shook his head. 'No, sir, though it wasn't really a discussion.'

'Did you think there was any ulterior motive in the men's request, Mr Paine?'

'You mean . . .?'

'I mean, did it, or did it not occur to you that the

men might have come ashore with ready money in order to buy liquor?' Marlowe asked.

Paine flushed. 'Well, sir, yes, it did occur to me, but the smell of the bread persuaded me that . . .' The midshipman's voice tailed off into silence.

'How many men contributed money towards this bread?' Marlowe enquired.

'I can't be absolutely certain, sir, but about a dozen.'

There was a brief pause while Hyde made his notes and then he looked up and asked, 'Did you make a contribution towards the bread, Mr Paine?'

Paine coughed with embarrassment and his Adam's apple bobbed uncomfortably. 'Yes,' he murmured.

'Speak up, damn it,' prompted Hyde, dipping his pen.

Paine coughed again and answered in a clearer voice, 'Yes sir.'

'And it *was* bread you were investing in, I take it?'

'Oh yes, sir.'

'Why?'

'I was hungry, sir.' A thought appeared to occur to the midshipman and he added, 'I was jolly hungry, and I thought the men must be, too, since they had had a long hard pull from the ship, sir.'

'So you thought that justified disobeying Mr Ashton's order?'

Paine's mouth twisted with unhappiness. 'No, not exactly, sir . . .'

'Then do enlighten us, Mr Paine,' pressed Marlowe, 'what *exactly* you did think.'

Paine relinquished the role of martyr and confessed:

'I thought if only two men went, they would soon be back.'

'Soon be back . . .?' prompted Marlowe, his face expectant.

'You know . . . before Mr Ashton returned.'

Both officers sat back and exchanged glances. 'So you deliberately disobeyed Mr Ashton's order?'

'In a manner of speaking, yes, sir.'

'Why?'

Having placed himself at the mercy of his interrogators, Paine's attitude hardened and he fought his corner. 'I thought no harm would come of it.'

'But harm has come of it, Mr Paine,' argued Marlowe.

'Yes, sir, and I regret that and I take full responsibility for it. As a matter of fact, sir, I thought Mr Ashton's order unreasonable. The men could not desert, for the place is an island and for two men out of sixteen to run ashore for some bread, seemed, in my opinion, reasonable enough.'

Marlowe pressed his finger tips together before his face, sat back and regarded the midshipman in silence. Hyde pursed his lips and made a soft blowing sound.

'I had no idea Mr Ashton would make an issue of the matter with McCann, sir. I cannot allow the sergeant of marines to be involved. The truth is that having let Shaw and Ticknell go, I confess I made myself comfortable in the stern-sheets and was roused by the kerfuffle when Mr Ashton returned with the passenger.' Paine finally fell silent and looked down at his threadbare knees.

'Well,' began Marlowe, 'it seems Mr Ashton's wrath was misdirected. You realize what this means, Mr Paine?'

'The gunner's daughter, sir?' Paine's face twisted with apprehension.

'At the very least, my lad.'

Paine drew himself up in his seat. 'Very well, sir.'

'You may carry on. The matter will be referred to the Captain with our recommendations.'

Paine got to his feet. 'Aye, aye, sir.'

When he had retired, Marlowe turned to Hyde and said, 'That would seem to wrap the matter up then.'

'No, Mr Marlowe,' said Hyde, stirring himself, 'it won't do at all. Of course Paine must be punished, but Ashton's treatment of McCann remains reprehensible.'

'That's as may be, Hyde, but the crime was disobedience to Ashton's order and it was Paine, not McCann who was culpable. Ashton's intemperate conduct was unfortunate, but McCann is only a non-commissioned officer of marines.'

Hyde drew in his breath sharply. 'Mr Marlowe, that non-commissioned officer of marines once held a commission in a Provincial regiment and fought for King and Country as, I suspect, Lieutenant Ashton has only dreamed of. He was insulted, called a Yankee bugger, neither of which accusations can be substantiated and for which, had they been used to me, I would have demanded satisfaction!'

'I daresay you would,' observed Marlowe drily, 'but they weren't addressed to you. Anyway, what do you suppose we can do about it?'

'Get Ashton to apologize,' said Hyde in a voice loud enough to be heard on the far side of the flimsy bulkhead dividing the dining area of the officers' accommodation from their personal sleeping quarters. It proved too much for the eavesdropping Ashton, who wrenched the door open and made his appearance at this moment.

'Damn you, Hyde!' he snarled, 'You heard my orders and you've found your culprit. What more d'you want?'

'Well, old fellow,' said Hyde leaning back in his chair, 'since you ask, an apology to McCann.'

'I'll be damned first!'

'Very likely, but Ashton am I correct in thinking you flung the bread, not to mention four miserable bottles of wine – four, mark you, about the number you would drink in a good evening at Spithead, to be shared between at least a dozen men – that you flung this bread into the harbour?'

'Of course.'

'Why "of course"?' persisted Hyde.

'Because they had no business buying it.'

'Ashton, have you never drunk French brandy?'

'Why yes, but . . .'

'Which you had no business buying, I daresay . . .' Hyde sneered and Ashton coloured, realizing he had taken the bait. Beside Hyde, Marlowe smiled.

'And which you would have defended as your own, no doubt,' Marlowe added, whereupon Ashton shot the first lieutenant a look of such pure venom that Hyde was certain Marlowe had hit upon some incident in their mutual past.

'So you will not apologize to McCann?' Hyde pressed.

'The devil I will!'

Hyde completed his note. Marlowe sat forward and

closed the proceedings. 'I believe we asked Sergeant McCann to hold himself ready for questioning. I do not think that will be necessary at this juncture.'

'I shall go and tell him so,' said Hyde, rising and fixing his eyes on Ashton. 'You are a lesser man than I had hitherto thought, Josiah. McCann would have forgiven you a momentary loss of temper. By refusing to withdraw your remark, you not only affirm it, you make him an inferior, and I am not persuaded he is. Certainly not now.'

Hyde swept from the wardroom without a backward glance, leaving Marlowe with a fuming and humiliated Ashton. For a moment the two officers sat in silence, then Ashton rose and leaned over Marlowe.

'I wish,' he said menacingly, 'I had words adequate to describe what I feel for you, Frederic, and I wish I could express the pity I feel for Sarah!'

But if Ashton thought the contempt in his voice could intimidate Marlowe, mention of his sister was a sad miscalculation. Marlowe's spirit was no longer cowed, and he stood slowly and with a new-found dignity to confront his future brother-in-law. 'I pity her too, Josiah, but I have at least the consolation Sarah chose me.'

And with this Parthian shot Marlowe left the wardroom to report to Drinkwater. As for Ashton, he turned to find Frey standing in the open doorway to his cabin regarding him with a cold stare.

A Long Wait

'Angra do Heroismo,' observed Birkbeck, staring through his glass at the principal port on the island of Terceira. Once again *Andromeda* was hove-to and awaiting one of her boats, the port quarter-boat commonly called the red cutter, which had been sent in under the command of Lieutenant Frey to convey Mr Gilbert ashore. It was anticipated that it would be absent for some time and in the interim Captain Drinkwater was in his cabin, dining early with Mr Marlowe and discussing the fate of Mr Midshipman Paine, who slouched disconsolately about the quarter-deck, awaiting the captain's verdict.

Although relieved as officer of the watch by Lieutenant Ashton, Birkbeck remained on deck, watching the red cutter as it swooped over the wave crests and vanished in each succeeding trough. Its worn lugsails were only a shade lighter than the grey of the sea, which had forsaken its kindly blue colour after the wind had swung back into the south-west again. Although only a moderate breeze, this had first veiled the sun, then at noon brought in a layer of thickening overcast which presaged rain and turned the sea a sullen hue.

Finally, Birkbeck could see the cutter no more as it passed into Angra. He shut his glass with a decisive snap and made his way below.

In the cabin, Drinkwater toyed with his wine glass as Marlowe concluded his report.

'So, sir, the nub of the matter is that Paine disobeyed Mr Ashton's explicit order and while Ashton may have acted in an intemperate manner, falsely accusing Sergeant McCann of being the culprit, it is Paine who must be punished.'

Drinkwater grunted. 'Yes, I suppose so. What have you in mind?'

Marlowe considered the matter for a moment and said, 'A dozen strokes, sir.'

'A pity. I thought the boy had promise. This will be a humiliation for him.'

'I had thought of that, sir. It doesn't have to be done over a gun. I can turn the midshipmen out of the cockpit . . .'

'Or the officers out of the wardroom. But the purpose of the punishment is as much to deter others as to strike at the guilty.'

'The others will all know, sir.'

'Yes, that is true. Very well then,' Drinkwater concluded with a sigh, 'you must do as you see fit.'

'There remains the problem of Ashton. Hyde thinks he should apologize to McCann for calling him a Yankee bugger.'

'I must say I rather agree. Notwithstanding the fact

that Ashton set this whole thing off by demanding a flogging for McCann.'

'Well, in the light of our findings that would be outrageous.'

'I agree entirely. Ashton's claim is indefensible and I won't have officers abusing the privilege rank gives them, no matter how high and mighty they consider themselves.'

Marlowe held his peace and waited while Drinkwater came to his own verdict. 'Very well; if Ashton will not withdraw his remark to McCann, I shall make my disapproval known by other means.' Drinkwater paused, then went on, 'You may tell Mr Ashton that for his intransigent insistence on misusing his rank, he may enjoy the privilege of standing watch-and-watch until further notice.' Drinkwater looked at Marlowe, 'Well, d'you have something to say?'

'No, sir.'

'Good. Well go and put Paine out of his misery and then inform Ashton of my decision.'

'Aye, aye, sir.'

Lieutenant Hyde had found Sergeant McCann in the gunner's store, making up cartridges as a means of seeking privacy. Hyde thrust his head through the woollen safety curtain and McCann looked up apprehensively.

'You are not to be flogged,' Hyde said with a grin, and the gentle sag of McCann's shoulders told of his relief. 'It would have been unpardonable to have done so,' Hyde expatiated.

'I have very little faith in the equity of British justice, sir,' said McCann, 'particularly in a man-o'-war.'

'Oh ye of little faith,' said Hyde, 'as a matter of fact, you should have.'

'Why so, sir? Is Lieutenant Ashton prepared to retract his insult?'

Hyde pulled a face. 'Regrettably, no. I would not have thought him a man of mean spirit on first acquaintance,' Hyde went on conversationally, 'just as I would not have thought of the first lieutenant as a man with any backbone, but,' Hyde shrugged, 'ship-board life reveals much.'

'Usually more than one bargained for,' observed McCann. 'But in what way should I be grateful?'

The edge of bitterness in McCann's voice did not escape Hyde, who smiled and said, 'Marlowe has just told me old Drinkwater has put Ashton on watch-and-watch.'

'Ah . . .' An incipient smile twitched the corners of McCann's mouth. 'What about the disobedience to Ashton's order, sir?'

'Ah, that. You are exculpated. Poor Mr Paine is likely to live up to his name.'

'It's a pity Ashton didn't look to his own when handing out the insults, sir,' McCann said, ignoring the joke.

'Now hold your tongue, Sergeant,' Hyde advised. 'Your native forthrightness may be a virtue in America, but it don't serve too well in a man-o'-war.'

'It never serves well in England,' McCann said to himself after Lieutenant Hyde had gone.

In the wardroom, Lieutenant Marlowe regarded the errant midshipman. Mr Paine had been brought before the first lieutenant by the boatswain and Mr Kennedy, the surgeon. Birkbeck had returned to the hold to harry

244

the carpenter and his mates, while Hyde was occupied inspecting his marines on the gun-deck.

'Mr Paine, you are to be given a dozen strokes of the cane for wilful neglect of an order given to you by Mr Ashton when you were lately left in charge of the ship's launch in the harbour of Santa Cruz. Do you understand?'

'Yes, sir.' Paine's voice was a dry croak.

'And have you anything to say?'

'Only that I am sorry for it, sir.'

'Very well. Let us proceed. The boatswain will carry the punishment out and the surgeon will ensure you are not abused. Please remove your coat.'

Paine did as he was bid and, looking round for somewhere to lay it, saw Kennedy's outstretched hand.

'Thank you, sir,' he whispered, giving Kennedy his garment.

Then Marlowe resumed. 'I shall not ask you to remove your breeches, but you shall bend over this chair.' Marlowe indicated a chair at the forward end of the wardroom table.

Paine swallowed hard, stepped forward and bent over the chair, his hands holding the back, the knuckles already white with fear.

'Very well.' Marlowe nodded at the boatswain, who moved forward, revealing the long, flexible twisted rattan cane of his office. The polished silver head nestled familiarly inside his powerful right wrist, the end tentatively touched Paine's buttocks as the midshipman screwed up his eyes.

'Do you wish for something to bite on?' Kennedy enquired. Eyes closed and teeth gritted, Paine shook his head emphatically, eager only to get his ordeal over.

'Carry on, Bosun,' Marlowe commanded, and the petty officer drew back the cane until it struck the deck-head above. Had the punishment been administered in the open air over a quarterdeck carronade as was customary, the swipe of the rattan would have had more momentum. Watching, both Marlowe and Kennedy wondered if Drinkwater had knowingly limited the scope of the boatswain's viciousness by ordering the matter carried out between decks. Paine, however, was not in a position to appreciate the captain's clemency, witting, or otherwise. The rattan's descent whistled in a brief and terrible acceleration, then struck him with such violence that the impact provoked a muscular spasm which in turn moved the rickety chair across the wardroom deck with a squeak. Paine himself made no such sound; for a second his whole body seemed impervious to the blow beyond its sharp, physical reaction. The second stroke was already on its way by the time the agony filled his whole being with its sting. To this, the successive strikes felt only as an increase of the first, terrible violation, like the roll of a drumbeat after the first loud percussive beating of the sticks.

Wave after wave of nausea seemed to press up from the pit of his stomach; it seemed the seat of the chair was forcing itself through his chest, that he would break off the legs by the tension in his arms. As the strokes followed, he tasted salt and knew he was sobbing. He knew too that he was not crying; the sobbing was the only way he could breathe, great gasps of air, sucked in by some reflexive action of his jaw as his lungs demanded it to fill his tensed muscles with oxygenated blood. He had no idea at the time that this gasping successively clamped his teeth upon his tongue.

Even to those watching, the dozen strokes seemed to last forever. Marlowe was reminded of lying awake unsleeping in his family home, listening to the long-case clock strike midnight. Kennedy watched in disgust; the evident relish with which the boatswain acquitted himself of his duty revolted him, and the humiliation of the young man bent double before them, compounded this revulsion. Marlowe averted his eyes for fear of passing out.

'That's enough!' snapped Kennedy the instant the last stroke had been laid on, earning himself a glare from the boatswain.

'I know my duty,' the petty officer grumbled.

'Thank you, Mister,' Marlowe muttered dismissively, wiping the back of his hand over his mouth. Kennedy bent over Paine.

'You all right, younker?'

Paine's back rose and fell as the midshipman took short, shallow breaths. He nodded his head, his hair damp with perspiration. Kennedy looked at Paine's buttocks. Blood and plasma oozed through the cotton drill of his trousers. 'I shall have to deal with that,' he remarked accusingly.

'You may attend to it here, if you wish,' said Marlowe.

'Well, now, that's very kind of you, Mr Marlowe,' Kennedy replied sarcastically.

'Pass word for someone to bring a clean pair of pants and breeches from Mr Paine's chest when you leave,' Marlowe instructed the boatswain, ignoring Kennedy.

'Aye, aye, sir,' replied the boatswain as he put

on his hat and, ducking, left the wardroom to the officers.

'Can you move?' Kennedy asked, as Paine slowly pulled and pushed himself upright. Tears streamed down his sweat-sodden face and blood trickled from his mouth. He finally stood, slightly bent, supported by the wardroom table. His eyes remained closed as he mastered the pain, and as though he refused to open them on the scene of his humbling.

'There, Mr Marlowe,' said Kennedy with heavy sarcasm, 'justice has been done!'

'I'll thank you to hold your tongue, Kennedy,' Marlowe snapped, his own face pale as he fought a rising gorge and turned to the decanter. He paused a moment and then filled a glass.

'Here, Mr Paine,' said Marlowe, holding out the bumper of blackstrap, 'drink this up.'

'Beg pardon, sir, but the boat's returning.'

The midshipman's puckish face, appearing disembodied round the door, had more than the usual impish look about it as Drinkwater woke from his nap with a start accompanied by an undignified grunt.

'The boat's returning, sir.' There was a hint of impudence about the young man's repetition which irritated Drinkwater who considered himself taken for a somnolent old fool.

'Very well, damn it, I heard you the first time!'

The querulous tone of the captain's voice sent the lad into full retreat. He had seen poor Paine return to the cockpit. Drinkwater was left alone to gather his wits. He could not imagine why he felt so tired, and rose stiffly, bracing himself against the lurch of the ship. Rinsing his mouth and donning hat and coat, he went on deck.

On the quarterdeck he forced himself to wait with an outward appearance of disinterest as *Andromeda* was hove-to and the red cutter brought in under the swinging davit falls. He forbore staring over the side while the fumbling snatches of the bow and stern-sheetsman captured the wildly oscillating blocks and caught the hooks in the lifting chains, whereupon the two lines of seamen tailing on to the falls ran smartly along the gangway at the boatswain's holloa to 'hoist away!'.

With the boat swinging at the mizen channels and the griping lines being passed, Drinkwater could see Frey attending to the boat, giving no thought to the anxiety of his commander's mind. But as Frey climbed over the rail and jumped to the deck, he could contain himself no longer.

'Well, Mr Frey?' he asked eagerly, consumed with impatience to learn what intelligence Frey had gleaned ashore. Drinkwater had convinced himself that at Angra the Portuguese Captain-General, overlord of the Azores, would have by now received specific instructions to prepare to receive 'General Bonaparte'. He was not to be disappointed; immediately Frey confronted him, Drinkwater felt the flood of relief sweat itself out of his body, betraying the extent of his inner anxiety.

'The Portuguese Governor received me with every courtesy and said that he had received a despatch brought by Captain Count Rakov to the effect that preparations were to be made to receive Boney and to have him held under open arrest at some villa or other in the country outside Santa Cruz. He also protested that he had received no instructions from Lisbon as to whether he was supposed to cede an island, or to regard Boney as a prisoner. There were some other details about the size of Boney's suite and personal staff which I have to confess I didn't hoist in.'

'No matter . . .' Drinkwater ruminated for a moment, then asked Frey, 'And did you learn when Bonaparte was expected?'

Frey shook his head. 'No, sir, not really. Gilbert asked, but His Excellency did not know and could offer no clues himself. He let Gilbert read the despatch, which was in French, and all Gilbert could conclude was the tone of the language suggested the matter was imminent and that no further information would precede the arrival of Napoleon.'

'Well, that is something,' Drinkwater said.

'But is that sufficient, sir? I mean, it was no more than an intimation.'

'By a shrewd man who, I think, knows his business.' Drinkwater smiled and added, 'I think this enough to act upon.'

'Then we did not labour in vain,' Frey said, pleased that Drinkwater regarded the niggardly news with such relish.

'Not at all. Short of actually running into Boney and his entourage, I think we can pronounce ourselves satisfied.'

'May I ask, then, why we don't simply await the arrival of Boney at Santa Cruz?' Frey asked.

'Because, my dear fellow, we have no real business with Boney; our task is to prevent him being spirited to the United States and to intercept those ships sent by his followers to accomplish this. To do otherwise

250

would be to exceed our instructions,' Drinkwater said, concluding, 'We do not want to be the cause of an incident which might rupture the peace.' He suppressed a shudder at the thought. Exceeding an instruction that was largely self-wrought would have his name earn eternal odium by their Lordships if this affair miscarried.

'I see.' Frey nodded, unaware of the turmoil concealed by his commander's apparently worldly wisdom. 'It could be a long wait then.'

'Perhaps,' Drinkwater replied, and, thus dismissed, Frey disappeared below to divest himself of his boat-cloak and wet breeches while his commander fell to a slow pacing of the quarterdeck, nodding permission for Birkbeck to get the ship under weigh again as soon as the quarter-boat was hoisted.

Despite his misgivings, Drinkwater was clearer in his mind now. There seemed to him little doubt Rakov had brought the news to Angra in pursuit of Tsar Alexander's policy. But was finding *Andromeda* on station off Flores a shock to Rakov, particularly as Rakov had last seen her in Calais Road? In order to implement his master's policy, if he knew about it in detail, Rakov must have realized that the Antwerp ships would profit by his escort, and while Drinkwater might commit *Andromeda* to an action with two men-of-war acting illegally under an outlawed flag, the presence of a powerful Russian frigate would dissuade even a zealous British officer from compromising his own country's honour by firing into an ally!

As for the degree to which Captain Count Rakov was privy to Tsar Alexander's secret intentions, Drinkwater could only conclude however Rakov saw the presence of *Andromeda*, that of *Gremyashchi* was more revealing to himself. There seemed a strong possibility that Rakov's task in conveying the despatch to Angra might be subsidiary to that of pursuing and outwitting Captain Nathaniel Drinkwater of His Britannic Majesty's frigate *Andromeda*. Quite apart from anything else, it would be a small but personal revenge for Captain Drinkwater's destruction of the *Suvorov*.

And then it occurred to Drinkwater that something must have happened to Hortense, for how else could Rakov have followed so swiftly in their own wake? It seemed that while the war was over, the old game of cat and mouse would go on, though who was now the cat and who the mouse, remained anyone's guess.

For Sergeant McCann the fact that Lieutenant Ashton was compelled to stand watch-and-watch held no more satisfaction for him than the beating of Mr Paine. Ashton's double insult had wounded him deeply, vulnerable as he was, reinforcing his feelings of inadequacy as well as affronting his sensibility. These feelings were exacerbated by Ashton's unrepentant attitude, manifested by the lieutenant's haughtiness as he nursed his own wounded pride through the tedious extra duties imposed upon him by Captain Drinkwater.

Under such stress, the predominant aspects of the temperaments of both men dominated their behaviour; the sergeant of marines nursed his grievance, the lieutenant cultivated his touchily arrogant sense of honour. And such was the indifference to private woe aboard the frigate, each man in his personal isolation formed dark schemes of revenge. Under the foreseeable circumstances, such imagined and impractical fantasies were no more than simple, cathartic chimeras.

These disaffections were set against the burgeoning of Mr Marlowe who, under Drinkwater's kindly eye and with the tacit support of Frey, seemed to grow in confidence and stature in the following few days. Frey rather liked Marlowe, whose dark visage held a certain attraction, and had engaged to execute a small portrait of the first lieutenant, a departure for Frey, whose subjects were more usually small watercolour paintings or pencil drawings of the ship and the landmarks which she passed in her wanderings. As for Marlowe, his contribution to the relative success of Birkbeck and the carpenter in partially staunching the inflow of water by caulking and doubling the inner ceiling of the hull, had lent substance of a practical nature to his increased stature. It was thus easier for his fellow ship-mates to attribute his former behaviour to indisposition, and for him to gain confidence in proportion.

With these small ups and downs mirrored throughout the ship's company as the men rubbed along from day to day, *Andromeda* lay to, or cruised under easy sail to the north of Corvo, never losing sight of this outpost of the Azores, yet ever questing for the appearance of strange sails approaching from the north.

But all they saw were the cockbilled spoutings of an occasional sperm whale and, at the southern end of their beat, the hardy Azoreans out in their *canoas* in pursuit of their great game, chasing the mighty cetaceans with harpoon and lance, so that the watching Drinkwater was reminded of the corvette *Melusine* and the ice of the distant Arctic.* Along with this reminiscence, came gloomy thoughts of the inexorable passing of time and the tedious waste of war.

For a dismal week, under grey skies alleviated occasionally by promising patches of blue which yielded nothing but disappointment, *Andromeda* haunted the waters north of Corvo and Flores.

'We haul up and down like a worn-out trollop on Portsmouth hard, draggling her shawl in the mud,' Hyde observed laconically, yet with a certain metaphorical aptness, leaning back in his chair, both boots on the table.

'Indeed,' agreed Marlowe, sighing sadly, thinking of Sarah and his child growing inside her, 'my only consolation is that our diminishing stores will compel Our Father to head for Plymouth Sound very soon.'

'I think,' warned Frey, 'that he will hang on until the very last moment.'

'Well, that's as maybe, but the last moment will arrive eventually,' said the flexible Hyde philosophically.

'I do not think,' Frey said with a wry smile, 'you quite understand how Captain Drinkwater's luck has a habit of running.'

'You mean you think we shall encounter these ships?' Marlowe asked.

Frey nodded. 'Oh yes; I have no doubt of it. They cannot long be delayed now and the presence of that Russian almost guarantees it. Why else did she turn up like a bad penny?'

Marlowe shrugged and twisted his mouth in a curious

* See *The Corvette*

grimace of helpless resignation. 'Perhaps you'll prove to be right, perhaps not.'

'Well, if you ask me,' put in Hyde, 'I think it is a wild-goose chase. All right, the Russkie turns up and his appearance ain't coincidence, but neither is ours as far as he is concerned and my money is on his intercepting these so-called Antwerp ships and turning them back.'

'That would mean *they* had had the wild-goose chase,' laughed Marlowe.

'Or that's what we have all been engaged on,' added Frey, pulling out his pencil and sketch block.

'Well, let's drink to the damnation of His Majesty's enemies, damnation to Boney, wherever he is, damnation to the Tsar of all the Russians, damnation to despair and depression and anything else which irks you,' Hyde said, his boots crashing on the deck as he rose to pour three glasses of blackstrap and pass them to his messmates.

'I do wish you would move with a little more grace and a little less noise, Hyde,' complained Marlowe good-naturedly.

'Sudden decisive action, Freddie, is the hallmark of the accomplished military tactician.'

'Or a lazy oaf,' Marlowe riposted, grinning as he accepted the proffered glass.

'Steady, or I'll be demanding satisfaction,' joked Hyde.

Marlowe pulled another face. 'One touchy sense of honour in a wardroom is enough, thank you,' he said.

'Don't forget Sergeant McCann,' prompted Hyde.

'Oh, he don't count . . .'

'Don't be too sure,' warned Hyde. 'He is no ordinary man.' And Frey looked up from his drawing with a shudder, catching Hyde's eye. 'You all right?' Hyde asked.

'Yes. Just a grey goose flying over my grave,' Frey said quietly.

'More likely a wild goose,' Marlowe added with a short laugh.

'Perhaps,' said Frey in a detached tone of voice that made Hyde and Marlowe exchange glances.

PART THREE

Caging the Eagle

'Napoleon in the Isle of Elba has . . . only to be patient, his
enemies will be his best champions.'
GENERAL SIR ROBERT WILSON

St Elmo's Fire

Drinkwater had experienced no such premonition as Lieutenant Frey. The appearance of the *Gremyashchi* had finally laid to rest the vacillating anxieties and uncertainties of the preceding days, replacing them with a firm conviction that Hortense's report was about to be fulfilled. Nor did he consider Captain Count Rakov would divert the Antwerp ships from their purpose, as was the opinion of Lieutenant Hyde in the wardroom below. Drinkwater's assessment was quite otherwise: Rakov was on the scene to guarantee the matter. There would be no bloodshed, no international incident, Bonaparte would simply be removed from the Bourbon French ship bringing him to Flores, transferred to one of the Antwerp squadron and conducted to the United States.

It was quite clear that the only certain rendezvous where this could be accomplished without attracting undue attention was off the Azores, and the fact that no proper arrangements had been concluded with the Portuguese captain-general at Angra do Heroismo, was evidence none was necessary, for there had never been any real intention of landing Bonaparte in the first place. And to guarantee the Tsar's plan, revealing the sly hand of Talleyrand, the Bourbon commander of the French naval ship carrying the former Emperor into exile would not be accosted by a couple of Bonapartist pirates, but a squadron operating under the ensign of Imperial Russia.

It was a cleverly conceived plan, but, concluded Drinkwater, this embellishment made his own task acutely difficult. It was he alone who would have to assume responsibility for thwarting the Tsar's intention. Not that he entertained any personal doubts as to the rightness of this challenge. It was clearly not in British interests to have the foremost soldier in the world free to command troops in the United States. A successful invasion of Canada would be a disaster for Great Britain, and Drinkwater did not need the protection of Prince William Henry's orders to buttress his own moral doubts, only to afford protection from those in the establishment who might regard his action as intolerably high-handed.

What now nagged him was the impossibility of the task. At least two well-armed ships had sailed under the command of this Admiral Lejeune, and while Drinkwater might have had a chance to out-manoeuvre them, they were now reinforced by the *Gremyashchi*, a powerful frigate in her own right, which alone would be more than a match for *Andromeda*. He was conscious that the action his zeal had now made inevitable could end only in defeat. If any premonition disturbed the tranquillity of Nathaniel Drinkwater during those tedious days in late May, it was that death would take him at the moment of his country's hard-won victory.

In the circumstances such a death would not be without dishonour, but he doubted much credit would accrue to his actions to warm his widow's heart. Poor Elizabeth; she did not deserve such a fate. To be left alone to manage his small estate, not to mention the dependants he had foisted upon her, would be a terrible legacy. His death would, moreover, burden her with the promised annuity to Hortense!

The thought appalled him. In his headlong dash into the Atlantic, thoughts of an early death had not really occurred to him, for he had lived with risk for so long, and while he had intimated in the letter he had sent to his wife by the Trinity Yacht that complications had been introduced into their lives by recent events, meaning those at Calais, he had withheld details as being best dealt with face-to-face. Now he could not even leave her a second letter, for the chances of its being discovered after a bloody action were next to nothing.

He slumped at his desk as behind him a pale, watery sun set over a heaving grey sea. All about him *Andromeda* creaked mournfully, echoing his dismal thoughts and ushering in an attack of the blue-devils. As the daylight leached out of the sky and the twilight gloom increased, he fell into a doze. Hortense and Elizabeth were in the cabin with him, both were restored to the beauty they had possessed when he had first set eyes upon them and both improbably held hands like sisters, and smiled at him approvingly. He woke with a start, his heart beating furiously, possessed with a terrible fear of the unknown.

The cabin was completely dark. During his brief sleep and unknown to Drinkwater, Frampton had entered the cabin but seeing his commander asleep had beat a tactful retreat. Waking thus, Drinkwater was overcome with the feeling that the cabin was haunted by ghosts. In an instant, he had rammed his hat on his head and fled to the quarterdeck wrapped in his cloak.

He almost instantly regretted this precipitate action. The quarterdeck was scarcely less congenial than the cabin; in fact it was a good deal less so. Night had fallen under a curtain of rain which knocked the sea down, hissed alongside as it struck the surface of the water and sharply reduced the temperature of the air. Ashton had the watch, his extra duty relieving Birkbeck of the task, and so the emotional air was even chillier than the atmospheric, though Drinkwater himself took little notice of this and, in his own way, only added to it by his presence.

His cloak was soon sodden, but he paced the windward quarter, his stride and balance adjusting to the swoop and roll of the ship as, with her yards braced up sharply, she stood northwards under easy sail, steering full-and-bye with the wind in the west-north-west. It was a dying breeze and about four bells the rain stopped abruptly as the wind veered a point or two. Drinkwater was vaguely aware of Lieutenant Ashton adjusting the course to the north-eastwards, maintaining the trim of the yards in accordance with the provision of Drinkwater's night orders for cruising stations. Within fifteen minutes the sky was clearing rapidly as the overcast rolled away to leeward and the stars shone out in all their glory.

If the air had been chilly before, it was positively cold now, or so it seemed to Drinkwater as the dramatic change woke him from his reverie and he found himself shivering. He was about to go below and seek the warm comfort of his cot, when something stopped him. He stood like a pointing hound, tingling with instinctive premonition. He looked anxiously aloft. The pale parallelograms of the topsails and topgallants were pale against the sky; the main course was loose in its buntlines, but the fore course was braced sharp up, its tack hauled down to the port bumkin. Behind him the quadrilateral spanker curved gracefully under the pressure of the wind. As he watched, it flogged easily, the failing wind easing and then filling it again, causing a fitful ripple to pass across the sail, from throat to clew. The lines of reef points pitter-patted against the tough canvas. Despite this apparently peaceful scene, something struck him as wrong. Something in the air which made his scalp creep.

'Mr Ashton!'

'Sir?' Ashton stirred from the starboard mizen rigging.

'Get the t'gallants off her!'

'The t'gallants, sir?'

'The t'gallants sir! And at once, d'you hear me?'

Drinkwater could almost hear Ashton's brain turning over the captain's lunatic order, but then the word was passed and the watch stirred out of its hiding places, hunkered down about the decks, and the shapes of men moved about the pin rails and prepared to go aloft. There was little urgency in their demeanour, obvious to Drinkwater's acute and experienced eye, even in the dark.

'Look lively there!' he cried, injecting a sharp urgency into the night. Ashton began to cross the deck towards him and Drinkwater turned away in silent rebuff, staring to windward, watching to see what would happen. Then he saw the cloud as it loomed into the night sky, rapidly blotting out the stars to the north-westwards. He could feel its presence as the air suddenly crackled with the dull menace of the thing, revealing the source of his premonition. It was odd, he thought, as he watched the vast boiling mass of it rear up and up into the heavens, how such a gigantic manifestation of energy could almost creep up on one unawares.

The cumulo-nimbus cloud moved towards them like a mythological creature; potent and awe-inspiring. Drinkwater had no idea of its altitude, indeed he was unable to see the distant anvil-shaped thunder head which was torn from its summit by the strong winds of the upper-atmosphere; nor did he know of the movement of air and moisture within it that made of it a cauldron seething at the temperature ice formed. What concerned him was the wind he knew it would generate at sea level, and the hail that might, in the next quarter of an hour, hit them with the force of buckshot.

Then, as if to signal an intelligence of its own, the thundercloud gave notice of its presence to the less observant men on *Andromeda*'s deck. It was riven from top to bottom by a great flash as the differences in electrical charge within the cloud sought resolution. The sudden, instantaneous illumination galvanized the men into sudden, furious action and within minutes *Andromeda*'s topgallants were off her before the first erratic gusts of the squall arrived; then it was upon them in unremitting fury, producing a high-pitched whine in the rigging as the full force of the wind struck them.

'Steady there,' Drinkwater said, striding across the deck to brace himself alongside the helmsmen, 'ease her if you have to, Quartermaster.'

The frigate heeled to the onslaught and began to accelerate rapidly through the water which foamed along her lee rail. The sea was almost flat; the earlier rain had done its work and now hailstones beat its surface with a roar. *Andromeda* raced through the water so that even Ashton was moved to comment.

'My God, sir,' he said, coming up to Drinkwater, 'she's reeling off the knots as if pursued by all the devils in hell!' He laughed wildly, caught up in the excitement of the moment as, with a tremendous thunderclap, lightning darted all about them and the retina was left with a stark impression of wet and drawn faces about the wheel, sodden ropes and the lines of caulking in the blanched planking. Even the streaks of a million hailstones as they drummed a furious tattoo on the deck remained, it seemed, indelibly impressed upon the brain. So vivid was this brief vision that the quarterdeck seemed inhabited by more ghosts, and Drinkwater shivered as much from the supernatural moment as the cold drenching he was undergoing.

Circumstances remained thus for some twenty minutes, with the ship driving to the north-east, her helm having been eased up to let her run off before the wind a little and ease the strain on the gear aloft, for she still carried her full topsails, fore topmast staysail and spanker. Periodically illuminated by lightning and assaulted by thunder, *Andromeda* ran headlong. After the first moments of apprehension, the glee infecting Ashton had spread to the men at the helm and a quiet chuckling madness gripped them all. The excitement of their speed was undeniable and their spirits rose as the hail eased and then stopped.

As the huge cloud passed over them, it took the wind with it. The first sign of this moderation was a slow righting of the ship, so that while she still heeled over, the angle at which the deck canted eased imperceptibly back towards the horizontal. And it was at this moment that the frigate was visited by the corposant.

It began imperceptibly, so that the watchers thought they were imagining it and made no comment lest their mates thought they had taken leave of their senses; then, as it grew brighter they looked at each other, and saw their faces lit by the strange glow. Out along the yards and up the topgallant masts the greenish luminescence grew, stretching down towards the deck along the stays and lying along the iron cranes of the hammock nettings so that *Andromeda* assumed, in the wastes of the North Atlantic Ocean, the appearance of some faery ship.

The weird glow had about it an unearthly quality which was almost numinous in its effect upon those who observed it, silencing the brief outburst of loquacious wonder which it had initially prompted. Here was something no man could explain, though some had seen it before and knew it for St Elmo's fire. Some it touched personally, sending crackling sensations up the napes of their necks, making their hair stand on end and in a few cases glow with the pale fire of embryonic haloes. All smelt the dry, sharp stink of electrical charge, and as the display slowly faded, a babble of comment broke from the watching men, officers and ratings alike, an indiscriminate wonder at what they had all seen.

Ashton seemed to throw off his peevishness and was unable to resist the temptation to discuss the phenomenon with Midshipman Dunn, while the men at the wheel, kept usually silent by the quarter-master in charge of them, chattered like monkeys. The remainder of the watch, settling down again after their exertions, speculated and marvelled amongst themselves in a ground-swell of conversation.

Isolated by rank and precedent, Drinkwater found himself refreshed as though by a long sleep. Afterwards, he attributed this invigoration to the electrical charge in the air which had been palpable. More significant, however, was the effect it had upon his mental processes. Hardly had the wonder passed and the quiet nocturnal routine settled itself again upon the ship, than his racing mind had latched on to something new.

Gone were the morbid preoccupations of earlier; gone were the complex doubts about the propriety of his course of action, of his conniving to get Prince William Henry to sanction it. Gone, too, was the gloomy, fateful conviction of his own impending doom. He shook off the weight of the dead ghosts he had borne with him for so long. James Quilhampton's was not a vengeful spirit, and the earlier manifestations of Elizabeth and Hortense were exhortations to greater endeavours, not the harbingers of doom!

This train of thought passed through his mind in a second. Having settled in his mind the eventual, anticipated arrival of *Gremyashchi* and the Antwerp squadron, he was now stimulated by a strange optimism. He found himself already considering how, when he met Count Rakov and his unholy allies, he might handle *Andromeda* to the best advantage and perhaps inflict sufficient damage before surrendering, to prevent them accomplishing their fell intent.

He was still on deck at dawn, though he had been fast asleep for three hours, caught by a turn of the mizen topgallant clewline around his waist, a dark, bedraggled figure whose hat was tip-tilted down over one shut eye, who yet commanded in this dishevelled state the distant respect of those who came and went upon the quarterdeck of His Britannic Majesty's frigate *Andromeda* as she cruised to the north of the islands of Flores and Corvo.

Nor did he wake when the daylight lit the eastern horizon and the cry went through the ship that three sails were in sight to leeward.

First Blood

Sergeant McCann was woken as *Andromeda* heeled violently under the onslaught of the squall. He had turned in early, eschewing the company of the corporals, increasingly isolated by his obsessions. His messmates and privates, gaming or yarning about him, reacted to the sudden list of the ship by putting up an outcry, taken up by the adjacent midshipmen so that the orlop bore a brief resemblance to a bear-pit until word came down from the upper-deck that the ship had been struck by a heavy gust of wind and the noise gradually subsided. It had, however, been sufficient to wake McCann from the deep sleep into which he had fallen shortly before.

Now he lay wide awake, the edge taken off his tiredness, his heart beating, staring into the stygian gloom. Like Captain Drinkwater's cabin two decks above him, Sergeant McCann's accommodation was inhabited by ghosts, but unlike his commander's visitation, which had been on the edge of consciousness, McCann could summon his mother and sister almost at will; and unlike Captain Drinkwater he could not pace the quarterdeck to escape his delusions. Instead he embraced himself in his hammock and once again let the sensation of waste and failure flood his entire being.

In the days they had lain off the Azores, Sergeant McCann's self-loathing had eclipsed the affront he had felt at Ashton's double insult. Instead he had convinced himself that if he were neither a Yankee nor a bugger, he was something worse: he was a coward. Looking back upon his worthless life, he saw that he had always taken the path of least resistance, a path the politics of his parents had set him on. He realized his loyalism had not been based on any personal conviction but was an inherited condition, and while he had given his oath to the king as a provincial officer, it had been as much to revenge himself upon those who had despoiled him of his natural inheritance, rather than out of any principle towards the crown and parliament on the far side of the Atlantic Ocean. Recalling the homespun battalions confronting the British regular and provincial troops across the Brandywine, he realized he had always had more in common with them than the rough infantrymen and their haughty officers, or the poor benighted Hessian peasants and their red-faced and drunken *junkers*.

In contrast, on the exposed deck above the unhappy McCann, his tormentor, Lieutenant Ashton, was undergoing a transformation. The wild schemes born out of his anger were washed out of him by the squall and the visitation of St Elmo's fire. But Sergeant McCann enjoyed no such liberation. His preoccupations were deeper rooted and the springs of his being were wound tighter and tighter by his misery. Having set it aside for so long he found he was no longer able to forsake his past, unable to detach it from the present, and subconsciously ensured it was to influence the future.

Eventually, in common with all those in the gloomy orlop, Sergeant McCann fell asleep, awaiting the events of the dawn.

Lieutenant Frey woke Drinkwater who was stiff and uncomprehending for a moment or two, until the import of Frey's news struck him.

'Do you lend me your glass,' Drinkwater urged, holding out his hand. Grasping the telescope Drinkwater hauled himself up into the mizen rigging, the mauled muscles of his shoulder aching rheumatically after the exposure of the night. Drinkwater's hands were shaking as he focused the glass, as much from apprehension as from cold and cramp, but there was no denying the three sails that were, as yet, hull-down to the eastward. And while it was too early to distinguish one of them as the *Gremyashchi*, he already knew in his chilled bones that among them was the Russian frigate.

For a long moment Drinkwater hung in the rigging studying the three ships, estimating their course and guessing their speed. He was computing a course for *Andromeda*, by which he might intercept the 'enemy' in conformity with the idea he had hatched during the night. He could not call it a plan, for to lay a plan depended upon some certainties, and there were no certainties in his present situation. He doubted if *Andromeda*, against the darker western sky, had yet been seen by the strangers, but it would not be long before she was, for Rakov would have warned *Contre-Amiral* Lejeune of the presence of the British ship. Drinkwater turned, Frey's face was uplifted in anticipation.

'Wear ship, Mr Frey, and lay her on a course of south-east; set all plain sail and the weather stun' s'ls. Be so kind as to turn up all hands and have them sent to break their fasts. We will clear for action at eight bells, after the ship's company have been fed.'

'Aye, aye, sir!'

Drinkwater was almost ashamed of the gleam his words kindled in Frey's eyes. He jumped down on to the deck and, leaving Frey to handle *Andromeda*, went in search of Frampton, some hot water and his razor. Meanwhile the word of impending action passed rapidly through the ship. Between decks she sizzled with a sudden stirring as the watches below were turned out, to dress, bundle up their hammocks and stow them in the nettings on the upper deck while the complaining cook flashed up the galley range and cauldrons of water went on for burgoo. In the wardroom the officers rummaged in their chests for clean linen, the better to ward off infection if they were wounded; in the cockpit the midshipmen unhooked their toy dirks from the hooks on the deck-beams above their heads, and chattered excitedly. Even Mr Paine, for whom the last few days had been a humiliating ordeal, livened at the prospect of being able to prove himself a man in the changed circumstances of an action. In the marine's mess, the private soldiers quietly donned cross-belts and gaiters, while a corporal checked the musket flints in the arms racks; Sergeant McCann dressed with particular care, and sent the messman forward to the carpenter with his sword and the instruction to hone it to a fine edge. He also carefully checked the pair of pistols which were his private property and the last vestige of his former employment as a provincial officer.

As the watches below assembled at the tables on the gun-deck to receive their hot burgoo, a black, gallows humour was evident, containing less wit than obscenity, more readily endured by those at whom it was aimed than would normally have been the case under ordinary circumstances, for by such means was courage invoked.

'Jemmy,' one wag shouted across the deck, 'you'll get your pox cured today, if you're lucky!'

To which the rotting Jemmy swiftly replied, 'Aye, you cherry, an' you may never get the chance to catch it!' This grim exchange provoked a general mirth, broken only by the order to relieve the watch on deck and the subsequent pipe of 'Up spirits!'

After this necessary ritual, the marine drummer ruffled his snare and beat them all to quarters, at which the bulkheads came down aft, and Drinkwater's insubstantial private quarters metamorphosed into an extension of the gun-deck. All along the deck, the tables had vanished, whisked away like a conjuring trick, giving a prominence to the bulky black guns. The breechings were cast off and the cannon moved inboard from their secure, stowed positions with their muzzles lashed hard up against the lintels of the gun-ports. Their crews ministered to them, clearing the train-tackles, worming the barrels and checking the firing-lanyards and flints of the gun-locks. On the upper deck the carronades and chase guns were cleared away; Hyde held a swift parade of his marines and sent them to their posts. Then Drinkwater called all the officers to the port hance from where he was watching the three strange sails.

They were hull-up by now and one was plainly

identified as the *Gremyashchi*. Although unable to see any name, Drinkwater remembered Hortense had said one of the ships from Antwerp was called *L'Aigle* and had speculatively concluded that she was the nearer of the trio, a frigate of at least equal, and probably superior force to *Andromeda*, if only in the calibre and weight of metal of her guns. On her port quarter lay the second Bonapartist ship, while the Russian was ahead of and slightly more distant than the others. Drinkwater marked this disposition with some satisfaction: Captain Count Rakov had made his first mistake.

Andromeda was running down towards the three ships with the wind almost dead astern. They lay on her port bow and, if both she and her quarry remained on their present courses, they would be in long cannon shot in about an hour. Drinkwater relished the time in hand, though he knew it would play on his nerves, for it would play on the enemy's too. With her studding sails set and the morning light full on her spread of canvas, *Andromeda* would look a resolute sight from the Franco-Russian squadron as she bore down upon them. The morning was bright with promise; the blue sea reflected an almost cloudless sky, washed clean by the passage of the cold-front in the night. A small school of dolphins gambolled innocently between *Andromeda* and her objectives which continued to stand southward, apparently unmoved by the headlong approach of the British frigate. Drinkwater was gambling on Rakov and Lejeune assuming he was running down to quiz them, not to open fire, and this seemed borne out by the lack of colours at the peaks of the strange ships.

Drinkwater was aware of the restless gathering behind him. As *Andromeda* ran with the wind, even the coughs and foot-shufflings of the waiting assembly of officers were audible. He turned around and caught Marlowe's eye.

'You have the weather gauge, sir,' the first lieutenant remarked nervously.

'*We* have the weather gauge, gentlemen,' Drinkwater corrected with a smile, 'and perhaps we shall not have it for long . . .' He looked round the crescent of faces. Marlowe was clearly apprehensive, while Hyde remained as impassively calm as ever; Birkbeck showed resignation and Ashton a new eagerness. As for Frey, well Frey was an enigma; best known of them all and much liked, he had become a more difficult man to read, for there was an eagerness there to match Ashton and yet a wariness comparable with Birkbeck's and perhaps, remembering his friend James Quilhampton, a fear akin to Marlowe's. But there was also a touch of Hyde's veneer, Drinkwater thought in that appraising instant, and yet of them all, Frey's complexity most appealed to him. Frey was a good man to have alongside one in a tight corner. Drinkwater smiled again, as confidently and reassuringly as he could; he was being unfair because he knew Frey of old. They would all acquit themselves well enough when push came to shove.

'Well gentlemen,' he said, indicating the other ships, 'this is what we have been waiting for. Now pay careful attention to what I have to say, for we are grievously outnumbered and outgunned and, if we are to achieve our objective, we have to strike first, fast and very hard, before we are brought to close action and lose any initiative we may be able to gain by engaging on our terms.

'It is my intention that we do all we can to avoid

275

a close-quarters action. If my information is correct, the two Bonapartist ships will not only have sufficient gunners, but they will be full of sharp-shooters and soldiers, enough to make mince-meat of our thirteen score of jacks. I shall therefore be using the ship's ability to manoeuvre and will attempt to disable them first. They will almost certainly attempt the same trick, so I am counting on the accuracy of our shot. Frey and Ashton, your respective batteries must be fought with the utmost energy and economy. We must have no wasted powder or shot; we cannot afford it. I am not so much concerned with the precision of broadsides, rather that every shot tells. Make certain, *certain* mark you, every gun-captain comprehends this. D'you understand? Ashton?'

'Yes, sir.'

'Frey?'

'Aye, sir.'

'Very well. Now mark something else: when I order you to be prepared to stand-to I want everything at maximum readiness except that the guns are to be kept concealed behind closed ports. The order to open ports will be automatic when I order the commencement of fire and I will endeavour to allow enough time for the guns to be laid. D'you follow?'

'I'm not sure I do, sir,' said Ashton.

'I don't want *Andromeda* to be the first to show her teeth, Mr Ashton, though I hope we shall draw first blood.' Drinkwater paused, then added for Ashton's benefit, 'If we are to fire into a Russian ship, I need the pretext of self-defence . . .'

'Ah, I see, I beg pardon . . .'

'Very well. Mr Marlowe,' Drinkwater turned to the first lieutenant, 'I leave the upper deck guns in your hands, but the same procedure is to be followed.'

'I understand, sir.'

'Mr Hyde,' Drinkwater swung round on the marine officer, 'your men are to do their best to pick off anyone foolish enough to show himself, but particularly any officers. Pray do not permit any of your men to anticipate my order to open fire.'

'Very good, sir.'

'Mr Birkbeck, I shall want the ship handled with all your skill. I shall feint several times at their bows and if you can oblige me, bear up and rake, preferably across their sterns.' Drinkwater turned back to the lieutenants, 'So you gentlemen in the gun-deck must be aware that if we ain't standing off and knocking the sticks out of them, I shall want the elevation dropped and shot sent down the length of their decks. Such treatment may demoralize the soldiers among 'em. We shall see.

'As for the Russian, well Rakov is our greatest threat, the more so because we don't know his orders or his intentions. We do know he ain't here on a picnic and I am convinced he followed us from Calais suspecting our intention and determined to stop us. It all depends upon the mettle of the man and when and where he chooses to engage us. My guess is he may try and overwhelm us when we are otherwise occupied, but at least he has to work his way up from the lee station first . . .'

'He appears to be doing that already,' interrupted Ashton, indicating the ships over Drinkwater's shoulder.

'Indeed he does, Mr Ashton,' replied Drinkwater, who had observed the *Gremyashchi*'s converging course some moments earlier, 'but then I should have been surprised if he hadn't, eh?' Drinkwater paused and looked round them all. 'Well now, are there any questions?' He paused as the officers shook their heads. 'No? Good. Well, let us hope providence gives us at least a chance, gentlemen. Good fortune to you all. Now, if you please, be so kind as to take post.'

He turned and levelled his glass as they moved away. He would have liked to say something to Frey, but that would not have been fair on the others. Anyhow, what could he say? That they had a couple of hours before they would be prisoners, and while they might not be prisoners for long, the humiliation of defeat was a risk that lay beyond the greater hurdle of death itself? Such thoughts lay uneasily alongside the affirmations of duty. He sniffed as he strove to focus on the *Gremyashchi*, but had to wipe his eye before he accomplished this simple task. Beside him someone coughed. He kept the telescope firmly clamped to his eye socket and spoke from the corner of his mouth.

'Ah, Mr Marlowe, I did not deliberately keep you out of my orders; yours might be the most difficult task and I would ask you to steel yourself. If I should fall, you are to strike at once, the only proviso being that the ship has endured some enemy shot. I would not have an unnecessary effusion of blood . . .'

'If I do that, sir, and do not prosecute the action with some energy, I may be taken for a coward.'

'You may indeed, Mr Marlowe, but that is preferable to death and will at least legitimize your offspring. Believe me, sir, this damned war has gone on long enough and there are men aboard the ship deserving of a better fate.'

'But, sir, by your own persuasion, if we do not

stop this migration of Boney, the war may drag on.'

'I like "migration", Mr Marlowe; it implies Boney is a sum of greater proportion than one man, but you are to obey my orders, do you hear, sir?'

'I hear you, sir . . .'

Drinkwater suppressed a smile. Marlowe's intention to disobey was as clear as the sunlight now dancing upon the blue waves of the ocean. He was truly steeled and his self-doubt had been banished by his sense of honour. It was a mean trick, Drinkwater concluded, and might yet add a bastard to the Ashton clan! Unconsciously, Drinkwater too resorted to the crude gallows humour of men preparing themselves for the possibility of death or wounding.

'There's a good fellow,' he said, closing the telescope and turning to smile at the first lieutenant. 'Now, will you have a string of bunting run up to the lee fore-tops'l yard-arm. Anything will do, just to confuse them.' He jerked his head at the three ships. 'They're all flying Russian colours. I suspected they might.'

'They're trying to intimidate us,' Marlowe asserted. 'Damned cheek!'

'Well, let's return the compliment. And let us discharge a chase gun to draw attention to the hoist.'

Drinkwater paid little attention to the sequence of flags that was run aloft a few minutes later beyond noting the gay colours were brilliant in the spring morning. Truth to tell, Mr Paine, to whom this duty had fallen, had paid little attention either, but the dull report of the gun gave a spurious authority to the fluttering bunting, investing it with an importance it did not have and perhaps buying *Andromeda* a

279

further few minutes of respite as she bore down upon what must now be conceived as the enemy.

For Drinkwater, patiently watching the range of the three ships decrease, the flaunting of Russian ensigns by all three ships suggested at the very least a malign intent and the connivance of the Tsar's officers. He imagined Count Rakov must have boarded the two French ships at sea and held council with Lejeune. In fact the possibility of French and Russian ships enjoying a rendezvous to the north of the Azores seemed most likely now, accounting for the delay in the Antwerp ships appearing off the archipelago. Such an argument, ominous though it was, was but further confirmation of the factual content of what had once been a mere whisper upon the wind.

Or upon the lips of Hortense Santhonax.

Drinkwater paid particular attention to the *Gremyashchi*. Idly, as he studied the Russian ship working back to windward, he wondered what her name signified. It was no matter, and he was more interested in observing how Rakov handled her and how swiftly she answered his intentions. It was difficult to judge; at the moment she was simply close hauled and sailing harder on the wind than the two Bonapartist ships, losing a little speed by comparison, but closing with them so that if *Andromeda* stood on, the interception would be as near coincidental as human heart could contrive, if human heart wished for it.

While this might be Captain Count Rakov's desire, it was not Nathaniel Drinkwater's, for it would be a trap from which escape would be impossible and he was aware that once he had been engaged by all three ships, or even only two, he would find it impossible to extricate himself. He therefore called the master and, without taking the glass from his eye, said, 'Mr Birkbeck, take the stun's'ls in if you please. After which you may clew up the main course. We will let the fore course draw a little longer.'

'Aye, aye, sir.'

Birkbeck picked up the speaking trumpet and within a minute or two the studding sails bellied, fluttered and then collapsed inwards, drawn into the adjacent tops to be stowed away. After this the booms were struck inboard, running into the round irons above the upper yards on the fore and main masts, until they were next required.

'Main mast there!' bellowed Birkbeck, 'Clew garnets there! Rise tacks and sheets!'

Without the driving power of the studding sails and main course, *Andromeda* slowed perceptibly. While the *Gremyashchi* continued to haul up to windward, closing her consorts, the common bearing of the three ships began to draw ahead.

'Bring her round two points to starboard, Mr Birkbeck.'

'Two points to starboard, sir, aye, aye.'

Remaining to windward, *Andromeda* drew on to a parallel course, slightly increasing her speed as she came on to a reach so that, after a few moments, the relative bearings of the enemy steadied again.

'Mr Marlowe, another gun, I think, to draw attention to our signal.'

The forecastle 9-pounder barked again, but prompted no response. Drinkwater began to feel an elation in his spirits. The squadron was standing on and in this apparent steadfast holding of their course, Drinkwater read a degree of irresolution on their part. Were they waiting for Rakov to act first, perhaps, in the capacity of senior officer? He was, however, acutely aware that pride always preceded a fall and his glass was most often focused on the *Gremyashchi* which was now slightly to windward of the French ships, though still to leeward of *Andromeda*, and a little less than a mile ahead, on her port bow.

'Rakov dare not wear, for it would cast him too far to loo'ard and he dare not tack for fear of missing stays . . .'

'By God, sir! You're wrong! He's going about!' Marlowe's voice cracked with excitement as ahead of them the Russian frigate turned into the wind and prepared to come round to pass closely between the French ships and *Andromeda*. It was a bold move and while it would mask the gunfire of her consorts, a broadside from the *Gremyashchi* could well serve to incapacitate the British frigate and thereby deliver her to the guns of the combined squadron.

'Mr Paine!'

'Sir?'

'Run up a different hoist. Make us look a little desperate.'

'A little desperate, sir. Aye, aye.'

For a brief, distracted moment Drinkwater thought there might have been a hint of sarcastic emphasis on the diminutive adjective, but then he was passing word to the gun deck: 'Larboard battery make ready; langridge and round shot if you please.'

Drinkwater heard the order taken up and passed below. With the angle of heel the elevating screws would need winding down. He would have to lessen the angle of heel to assist the gunners.

'Mr Birkbeck! Clew up the fore-course!'

He levelled his glass on the *Gremyashchi* again. She was passing through the wind now, hauling her main yards. White water streamed from her bow as she plunged into the head sea as she turned. Then she had swung and her sails rippled and filled on the port tack. She began gathering speed towards *Andromeda* on a reciprocal course to leeward. Instantly Drinkwater saw his opportunity. He felt the surge of excitement in his blood, felt his heartbeat increase with the audacity of it. Bold though Rakov had been, Drinkwater might out-Herod Herod.

'Starboard battery make ready!'

'Chain shot ready loaded sir!' It was Frey's voice, Frey at the quarterdeck companionway, ducking below at the same moment.

'Mr Birkbeck, I want the ship taken across his bow . . .'

'Sir?'

'At the last moment, d'you hear?'

'You'll rake from ahead sir?'

'Exactly. Will you do it?'

'Aye, sir!'

'At the last moment . . .'

'We risk taking her bowsprit with us.'

'No time to worry about that, just carry us clear. Man the braces and square the yards as we come round. Mr Hyde, some target practice for you lobsters!'

'Can't wait, sir!' Hyde called gaily back.

No one on the upper deck was unaware of Drinkwater's intentions and, thanks to Frey, most men on the gun-deck understood. Those that did not, knew something was about to happen and both batteries waited tensely for the opportunity to open fire.

Drinkwater cast a quick look at Marlowe. He was so pale that his beard looked blue against his skin. 'Remember what I said, Mr Marlowe,' Drinkwater reminded his first lieutenant in a low voice, 'if I should fall.'

Marlowe looked at him with a blank stare, into which comprehension dawned slowly. 'Oh yes, yes, sir.' Drinkwater smiled reassuringly. Marlowe smiled bravely back. 'I shall not let you down, sir,' he said resolutely.

'I'm sure you won't, Mr Marlowe,' Drinkwater replied, raising his glass again and laying it upon the fast-approaching Russian.

Andromeda remained the windward vessel and Drinkwater knew at once that Rakov intended to use his heel to enable his guns to fire higher, aiming to cripple the British frigate, cross her stern with a raking fire and then take his time destroying her. It was always a weakness of the weather gauge that although one could dominate the manoeuvring, when it came to a duel, the leeward guns were frequently difficult to point.

Rakov was clewing up his courses, confident that *Andromeda* was running into the trap with her futilely flying signals and every gunport tight shut.

'D'you wish me to try another hoist, sir?' asked Paine.

'Good idea, Mr Paine,' responded Drinkwater, adding, 'and a gun to windward, Mr Marlowe, to add to the effect.'

'Aye, aye, sir.'

Details were standing out clearly now on the *Gremyashchi*. Her dark hull with its single, broad buff strake was foreshortened, but the scrollwork about her figurehead, her knightheads and bowsprit were clear, so clear in the Dollond glass that Drinkwater could see an officer forward, studying his own ship through a huge glass.

'Keep the guns' crews' head down, Mr Marlowe, we're being studied with interest.' A moment later the unshotted starboard bow chaser blew its wadding to windward with a thump. In an unfeigned tangle of bunting and halliards which trailed out to leeward in a huge bight, Mr Paine was the very picture of the inept greenhorn struggling to get a flag hoist aloft in blustery weather; the matter could not have been better contrived if it had been deliberate!

Beside Drinkwater, Birkbeck was sucking his teeth, a nervous habit Drinkwater had not noticed before. 'Shall I edge her down to loo'ard, sir?'

'A trifle, if you please . . .'

Drinkwater's heart was thumping painfully in his breast. What he was about to attempt was no ruse, but a huge risk. If *Andromeda* turned too slowly, or the men at the braces did not let the yards swing, the wind in the sails would tend to hold the ship on her original course. If he turned too early, he would give Rakov time to respond and if too late all that might result was a collision, and that would spell the end for Drinkwater and his ship.

'Stand by, Mr Birkbeck!'

Drinkwater's voice was unnaturally loud, but it carried, and Birkbeck was beside the wheel in an instant. If only Rakov would show his intentions . . .

'Make ready on the gun-deck!'

Drinkwater was conscious that in another full minute it would be too late. The two frigates were racing towards each other, larboard to larboard at a combined speed of twenty knots. *Gremyashchi*, having the wind forward of the beam, was heeling a little more than *Andromeda*, exposing her port copper which gleamed dully in the sunshine. *Andromeda*'s heel was less, but sufficient to require almost full elevation in her port guns. Not, Drinkwater thought in those last seconds, that she would be using them first.

The time had come for Drinkwater to commit himself and his ship to a raking swing by passing *Andromeda* across *Gremyashchi*'s bow, come hell or high water. Just as he opened his mouth to shout the order to Birkbeck, the *Gremyashchi*'s larboard ports opened and her black gun muzzles appeared, somewhat jerkily as their crews hauled them uphill against the angle of heel.

'Now Birkbeck! Up helm!' Birkbeck had the helm over in a trice, but Drinkwater's heart thundered in his breast and his skin crawled with apprehension as he watched *Andromeda*'s bowsprit hesitate, then start to move across the rapidly closing *Gremyashchi*, accelerating as the frigate responded to her rudder.

'Braces there!' Birkbeck shouted.

'Starboard battery, open fire when you bear!'

Marlowe was running aft along the starboard gangway and beneath their feet the faint tremble of gun trucks running outboard sent a tremor through the ship. Along the upper deck the warrant and petty officers at the masts and pin rails were tending the trim of the yards, driving *Andromeda* at her maximum speed as she swung to port, right under the bows of the *Gremyashchi*.

286

Drinkwater saw the officer with the long glass lower it and look directly at the British ship, as though unable to believe what he had first observed in detail through his lenses; he saw the man turn and shout aft, but *Gremyashchi* stood on, and even fired a gun in the excitement, a shotted gun, for Hyde cried out he had spotted the plume of water it threw up, yards away on their starboard beam. As *Andromeda* turned to port, the component of her forward speed was removed from the equation. The approach slowed, allowing *Andromeda* time to cover the distance of the offset from her windward station.

Then the forwardmost gun of Frey's starboard battery fired, followed by its neighbours. The concussion rolled aft as each successive gun-captain laid his barrel on the brief sight of the Russian's bow as it flashed past his open port, like a pot shot at a magic lantern show. And on the upper deck, first the chase gun, then the short, ugly barks of the carronades as they recoiled back up their slides, followed the same sequence, the gun crews leaping round with sponges and rammers, to get in a second shot where they were able. As for Hyde's marines, they afterwards called it a pigeon shoot, for they claimed to have picked off every visible Russian in the fleeting moments they were in a position to do so, though whether this amounted to four or seven men remained a matter of dispute for long afterwards.

Andromeda's rolling fire was more impressive than a broadside; there was a deliberation about it that might have been coincidence, or the fruits of twenty years of war, or the sheer bloody love of destruction enjoyed by men kept mewed up in a wooden prison for months at a time, year-in, year-out, denied the things even the meanest, most indigent men ashore enjoyed as their natural rights. And if the liveliness of the sea deprived Drinkwater of the full effect of a slow raking, the destruction wrought seemed bad enough to allow him to coolly pass his ship clear to leeward of the faltering Russian as, obedient to her helm, *Andromeda* swung back on to her original course and swept past the *Gremyashchi*, starboard to starboard. So confident had Rakov been that Drinkwater would hang on to the weather gauge that hardly a starboard gun opposed her.

'Run down towards those French ships, Mr Birkbeck, then we will tack and come up with the *Gremyashchi* again . . .'

'Drive a wedge between 'em, eh sir?' It was Marlowe, darkened by powder smoke and the close supervision of the upper deck carronades, who ranged up alongside Drinkwater and suddenly added, 'By God, you're unarmed, sir!'

Drinkwater looked down at his unencumbered waist. Neither sword nor pistol hung there. 'God's bones, I had quite forgot . . .'

'I'll get 'em for you sir.' And like a willing midshipman, Marlowe was gone.

Drinkwater turned and looked at the *Gremyashchi*, already dropping astern on the starboard quarter. Her starboard ports were open now, and several shots flew at *Andromeda*, but there was no evidence of a concerted effort and it was clear Rakov had been completely outwitted and had had all his men up to windward to assist hauling his cannon quickly out against his ship's heel.

'How far from her were we, sir?' Birkbeck asked conversationally. 'I was rather too busy to notice.'

'I'm not sure,' Drinkwater replied, 'thirty or forty yards, maybe; perhaps less; long pistol shot anyway.'

Both men spared a last look at the *Gremyashchi*. It was impossible to say what damage they had done; none of her spars had gone by the board and only two holes were visible in the foot of her fore-topsail, but they were fast approaching the two French ships, the nearer of which had the appearance of an Indiaman and was clearly frigate built. It was oddly satisfying for Drinkwater to read the name *L'Aigle* on her stern, beneath the stern windows. Hortense and her intelligence seemed a world away from this!

Beyond *L'Aigle*, lay the smaller French ship, a corvette by the look of her, and both had their guns run out.

'Not too close, I don't want to risk them hitting our sticks, but would like a shot at theirs.'

'Aye, aye, sir.' Birkbeck replied, impassive to his commander's paradoxical demand.

'Down helm, my lads, nice and easy.' Birkbeck conned the ship round and Drinkwater walked forward and bellowed down beneath the booms, 'Now's your chance, Mr Ashton; larbowlines make ready and fire at will when you bear!' He turned, 'Ah, Marlowe, you're just in time . . . Thank you.'

Drinkwater took the sword and belt from Marlowe who laid the brace of pistols on the binnacle and hurried off. Drinkwater caught Birkbeck's eye and raised an eyebrow.

Then Ashton's guns fired by division, the forward six first, then the midships group and finally the aftermost cannon, by which time the forward guns were ready again, and for fifteen minutes, as *Andromeda* ran parallel to *L'Aigle*, they kept up this rolling fire. It was returned with vigour by *L'Aigle*, but the corvette scarcely fired a shot, being masked by her consort.

Drinkwater could see the spurts of yellow flame and the puffs of white smoke from which came the spinning projectiles, clearly visible to the quick eye.

'Have a care Birkbeck, they're using bar shot . . .'

A loud rent sounded aloft and the main-topsail was horizontally ripped across three cloths and half the windward topmast shrouds were shot away, but the mast stood. A few innocuous holes appeared in *L'Aigle*'s sails and even the corvette suffered from some wild shot, but there appeared to be little other damage until Hyde called out there was something wrong amidships and that he had seen a cloud of splinters explode from a heavy impact.

Drinkwater was far more concerned with the conduct of *Andromeda* herself. As long as he struck without being hit, he was having at least a moral effect upon his enemy. He raised his glass and could see the blue and white of infantrymen on the deck of *L'Aigle*.

'Password to Mr Frey, I am going to rake to starboard!' he called, turning to Birkbeck, but the master was ahead of his commander.

'Let fly the maintops'l sheet . . . !'

Andromeda began to slow as the driving power of the big sail was lost; *L'Aigle* and the corvette appeared to accelerate as they drew ahead, and then Birkbeck put the helm up and again *Andromeda* swung to port, but instead of passing under the bow of an enemy, she cut across the sterns of *L'Aigle* and then the corvette, whose name was now revealed as *Arbeille*.

They were, however, moving away, and although having achieved his aim in allowing them to pass ahead before turning, Birkbeck's swing to port was a little later than the copybook manoeuvre. Nevertheless, it was clear who was dominating events as *Andromeda* drove across the sterns of both French ships, cutting through their wakes as Frey's guns thundered again. Nor was there any mistaking the damage inflicted, for the shattering of glass and the stoving in of the neatly carved wooden columns, the caryatids and mermaids adorning their sterns, was obvious. Staring through the Dollond glass, Drinkwater could clearly see a flurry of activity within the smashed interior of *L'Aigle*. By a fluke, the Russian ensign worn by the *Arbeille* had been shot away and a replacement was quickly hoisted in the mizen rigging: it was the *tricolore*.

'Shall I wear her now, sir?' Birkbeck was asking, and Drinkwater swung round, snatched a quick look at the *Gremyashchi*, almost two miles away by now, but still holding on to her original course. She had either sustained some damage, or was breaking off the action.

'If you please, Birkbeck, let us give chase to the Russian and see what he does.'

'Now they're discarding pretence and showing their true colours, sir,' remarked Marlowe as he returned to the quarterdeck, gesturing to the French ships. *L'Aigle* had joined her consort in sporting the ensign of the Revolution and Empire and both were also turning in *Andromeda*'s wake.

'Well, sir,' Marlowe remarked cheerfully, 'at least we drew first blood.'

'Indeed we did, Mr Marlowe,' Drinkwater replied, 'indeed we did.'

Rules of Engagement

'Mr Frey, sir!'

'Ah, Mr Paine . . .'

'Message from the captain, sir.' Paine paused to catch his breath and caught Ashton's eye. Smoke still lingered on the gun-deck and the atmosphere was acrid with the stink of burnt powder and the sweat of well over a hundred men. Having reloaded, most of the guns' crews had squatted down and were awaiting events. Some chewed tobacco, others mopped their heads and a low, buzzing chatter filled the close air. Frey, standing upright between the beams of the deck above, stretched. His face was already grimy, but his expression was one of cheerful expectation.

'Well,' he prompted, 'what's the news?'

Ashton joined them. He ran a grubby finger round the inside of his stock. Paine noticed he had yet to shave.

'Captain's compliments, gentlemen,' Paine said diplomatically, 'and to say the gun crews acquitted themselves very well. He don't know how much damage we've done, but we ain't, beg pardon, we haven't suffered anything bar a few holes aloft. We're in chase of the Russian again and Captain Drinkwater says to keep it up. He'll do his utmost to continue manoeuvring and hitting from a distance. He says to be certain sure I tell you not to waste powder and shot and to make every discharge count.'

Frey looked from Paine to Ashton with a smile. 'That seems perfectly explicit, eh Josh?'

'Yes,' said Ashton, yawning. By rights the third lieutenant should have been turned in after standing his watch; he was beginning to feel the cumulative effects of his punitive regime of watch-and-watch.

'So round one's to us, eh young shaver?' Frey said light-heartedly. 'How long before we've caught up with the *Gremyashchi*? We can't see her from down here.'

'About an hour, may be a little more. We've reset the courses.'

'We can see that from the waist,' Ashton said with a cocky air, indicating the open space amidships and the bottoms of the boats on the booms. Sunlight shone obliquely through the interstices, the shafts prominent in the lingering gunsmoke, oscillating gently with the motion of *Andromeda*.

'Very well, Mr Paine,' said Frey, 'pass our respects to Captain Drinkwater . . .'

'And tell him we've suffered no casualties down here and are none the worse for the experience,' added Ashton.

'Except for a crushed foot,' Frey corrected reprovingly. 'Poor little Paddy Burns tried to stop a recoiling 12-pounder.'

Thinking of the bare-legged powder-monkeys, Paine grimaced and Ashton said callously, 'The damned little fool got in the way.' Frey pointedly ignored Ashton and nodded dismissal to the midshipman before he turned to cross the deck and peer out of a gun-port to see if he could catch a glimpse of the pursued *Gremyashchi.* As Paine made off, Ashton called him back.

'Mr Marlowe all right, Mr Paine?'

'Mr Marlowe, sir? Why yes . . .'

'Good, good.' Ashton paused, but Paine waited, puzzled at the question. Ashton realized the need of an explanation was both superfluous and demeaning, especially to a midshipman, and waved Paine away, but Paine's own solicitude had been awakened.

'Sir!' He arrested Ashton's turn forward and Frey looked up from his position crouched by the gun-port.

Ashton swung round and stared at the importunate midshipman.

'What happened to Burns, sir?' Paine asked.

'Kennedy's taking his foot off now,' Ashton said coldly and, turning on his heel, resumed his walk forward.

Paine ran back up to the quarterdeck where he caught Drinkwater's eye. 'Beg pardon, sir, both Mr Frey and Mr Ashton send their respects and perfectly understand your orders.'

'Very well.'

'And they've had one casualty.'

'Oh? Who is it?'

'A powder-boy, sir,' Paine said, recalling just in time Captain Drinkwater's proscription of the term 'powder-monkey', especially by the young gentlemen.

'Which one?' Drinkwater asked.

'Burns, sir.'

'Burns . . .' Drinkwater frowned. 'Oh, yes, I know the lad; dark hair and a squint. Was he killed?'

'No, sir, a recoiling gun-truck crushed his foot. He's in the surgeon's hands at the moment.'

'Thank you, Mr Paine. And you, are you all right?'

'Perfectly, sir, thank you.'

Drinkwater nodded and then resumed his scrutiny of the *Gremyashchi* on their port bow; the Russian frigate was nearer now and Paine was aware he had been absent from the quarterdeck for some time, so much had they shortened the distance. They would be in action again soon and a moment of panic seized him and he blurted out, 'Beg pardon again, sir, but I'm very sorry . . .'

Drinkwater turned and looked at the youngster in some surprise. 'What on earth for, Mr Paine?'

'For making such a mess of getting that flag hoist aloft, sir.'

Drinkwater's smile cracked into a brief laugh and he patted the midshipman on the shoulder. 'My dear Mr Paine, think nothing of it. As far as the enemy was concerned, I think you managed the business most ably. As a *ruse-de-guerre* I imagine it achieved its objective.'

Paine's incomprehension was plain, but he did not question Drinkwater's reply. On any other occasion he would have been dressed down by one of the officers for making so abysmal a hash of the simple task. Action, it seemed, was played to different rules, those of engagement he supposed, so he resumed his station, puzzled but happier. He had survived what Mr Frey had called the first round; perhaps he would be lucky and survive the second.

*　　*　　*

Lieutenant Hyde took advantage of the hiatus to look to his men. Instructing his two corporals to issue more cartridges and ball, he ordered Sergeant McCann to make his rounds of the sentries posted throughout the frigate.

'See the boys are all right, Sergeant, and make sure they don't feel left out of things.'

McCann ignored the deck sentinels at the after end of the quarterdeck. They were always stationed there, action or not, to maintain a guard and to throw the life-preservers over the side if any unfortunate jack fell overboard.

Below, on the gun-deck, there was a sentry at the forward and after companionways to ensure no one ran below without authority. By this means the cowardly or nervously disposed were kept at their stations and prevented from seeking the shelter of the orlop deck. Only stretcher parties, officers or midshipmen carrying messages were permitted to pass the companionways, along with the powder-boys like Paddy Burns, who carried ammunition up from the magazines and shot lockers to satisfy the demands of the gun-captains.

McCann ascertained there had been no problems with either of his men at these posts and went below where, in the berth-deck and the orlop, other solitary marines did their duty despite the mayhem raging on the decks above. Spirit room, outer magazine, the stores and the hatchways to the holds, each had its guard and every man professed all was well, one asking to be relieved for a moment while he in turn eased himself. McCann obliged then left the comforted soldier to his miserable, ill-lit duty in the mephitic air of the hold.

McCann returned up the forward companionway and walked aft along the gun-deck, exchanging the odd remark with several of the gun crews.

'Cheer up, Sergeant,' one man chaffed, 'what've you got to be glum about up there in all that sunshine and iron rain!'

'Mind your manners,' McCann responded morosely and then found himself confronted by Lieutenant Ashton.

'Silence there!' Ashton ordered, obstructing the marine. 'Well, McCann, what the deuce are you doing down here?'

McCann recognized provocation in Ashton's voice. 'Checking the sentries, sir, on the orders of Lieutenant Hyde.'

'Are you, indeed . . .?'

'If you'll excuse me, sir . . .'

Ashton drew aside with deliberate slowness. 'Off you go, Sergeant Yankee.'

McCann paused and confronted the urbane Ashton. With difficulty he mastered his flaring anger, though his eyes betrayed him, allowing Ashton to add insolently, 'Have a care, Yankee, have a care.'

McCann turned and almost ran aft up the companionway, gasping in the sunlight and fresh air, as if he had escaped the contagion of a plague-pit. He had no idea why Ashton had staged the unpleasant little scene, but it crystallized all the pent up venom in McCann's tortured soul. As for Ashton, idling away the time before *Andromeda* resumed the action, he felt little beyond a petty amusement that might have been nothing more than the result of mere high spirits and the elation of a man carried away by the excitement of the morning, if it had not had such fatal consequences.

*   *   *

As *Andromeda* slowly overhauled the *Gremyashchi*, Drinkwater strove to make some sense out of the situation. Astern of the British frigate, *L'Aigle* and *Arbeille* were coming up hand over fist, though they would not reach *Andromeda* before she herself was in range of the Russian. It was clear Rakov, who could have brought Drinkwater to battle within a few moments by reducing sail, was content to trail his coat, drawing the British after him, in the hope that he could pin *Andromeda* long enough for the two French ships to come up and overwhelm her.

In short, it seemed to the anxious Drinkwater that, having won a brief advantage, he was now allowing himself to be drawn into a trap which could have only one consequence. His alternative was to put the wind a point abaft the beam and escape on *Andromeda*'s fastest point of sailing. Within this tactical debate there lurked a small political imperative. Rather than run, Drinkwater considered whether to back his hunch, or not. If he proved right, then he might yet extricate his ship from what otherwise seemed her inevitable humiliation. There was something about Rakov's trailing away to the north that did not quite square with the setting of a trap. Drinkwater could not quite put his finger on his reason for thinking thus, beyond an intuition; perhaps that first raking broadside of *Andromeda*'s had had an effect, and perhaps the damage had been more moral than physical.

Captain Count Rakov had been sent with his ship to prevent Drinkwater from thwarting the Tsar's plan. That much was obvious; but what were Rakov's rules of engagement? It was inconceivable that having chased *Andromeda* out to the Azores, he did not have any! But

298

was Rakov empowered to destroy a British man-of-war? Such an event would at the very least cause a rupture between London and St Petersburg and might be a *casus belli*, touching off a new European war. As matters stood, the exchange of fire between *Gremyashchi* and *Andromeda* could be written off as 'accidental', an unfortunate misunderstanding which both governments regretted profoundly.

Drinkwater lowered his glass, his mind made up. He was lucky, damned lucky. As things stood at that precise moment, he had enough room to call Rakov's bluff.

'Mr Birkbeck!'

'Sir?'

'Wear ship! I want to pass between those two Frenchmen. Mr Marlowe! Mr Hyde! D'you hear?'

'Aye, aye, sir!'

'Mr Paine, be so kind as to let the officers on the gun-deck know my intentions.'

The cries of acknowledgement were followed by a flurry of activity as *Andromeda* gave up her chase and prepared to turn to bite her own pursuers. While his action with *Gremyashchi* could be dressed up as a regrettable incident, *L'Aigle* and *Arbeille* both now flew an outlawed flag. 'Mr Protheroe,' he called to an elderly master's mate who ran up and touched his fore-cock. 'Be so kind as to make a log entry to the effect that the frigate of which we are in pursuit has been determined to be unequivocally Russian, we have broken off the chase and intend to proceed to compel the two privateers formerly in company with her and sheltering under her colours, to strike the former French tricolour which they promptly hoisted when the Russian frigate stood away from them.' Poor Protheroe looked confused and nodded uncomprehendingly. 'Write it down, man, quickly now . . .'

Flustered, Protheroe finally complied and Drinkwater repeated his formal explanation. If he fell in the next two or three hours, posterity would have that much 'fact' to chew upon.

'I have it, sir,' Protheroe acknowledged. Such a veneer of legality would suffice. But if Rakov followed him round to close the trap, Drinkwater would know the worst. Birkbeck was looking at him expectantly.

'Ready, Mr Birkbeck?'

'Aye, sir.'

'Very well. Carry on.'

'Up helm!' Birkbeck sang out, and the shadows of the masts, sails and stays once more waltzed across the white planking as *Andromeda* answered her rudder and turned about.

All four ships were now reaching across the north-westerly wind, the Russian heading north-north-east, with the *Arbeille* and *L'Aigle* on a similar course, but some three miles to the southward of the *Gremyashchi*. Between them *Andromeda* now headed back to the south, her course laid for the gap between the two French ships. At the same moment Drinkwater saw the folly of this move Birkbeck made the suggestion to pass downwind of the leeward ship, the weaker corvette *Arbeille*, a suggestion Drinkwater instantly sanctioned, it having occurred to him simultaneously.

'You know my mind, Mr Birkbeck, but feint at the gap and make them think they have us.' Drinkwater could hardly believe his luck. On a reciprocal course it was not unreasonable for an arrogant British officer to take his ship between two of the enemy and while it exposed her to two broadsides, it allowed the single ship the opportunity to fire into both enemy ships at the same time and thus double her chances of inflicting damage. But by suddenly slipping across the bow of the leeward ship, he would place the *Arbeille* in the field of fire of *L'Aigle* and thus deprive *Contre-Amiral* Lejeune of the heavier guns of the bigger vessel.

Drinkwater ran forward to the waist and bellowed below. Frey's face appeared, then that of Ashton. 'Starboard guns, Mr Frey: double shot 'em and lay them horizontally; zero elevation!'

'Aye, aye, sir!'

Ashton looked crestfallen. 'You'll get your turn in a moment or two, Mr Ashton, don't you worry.'

They were rushing down towards the enemy now and Drinkwater resumed his station, casting a look astern at the *Gremyashchi*; she remained standing northwards. Rakov was detaching himself. At least for the time being. A sudden, sanguine elation seized Drinkwater, the excitement of the gambler whose hunch is that if he stakes everything upon the next throw of the dice, all will be well. It was a flawed, illogical and misplaced confidence, he knew, but he dare not deny himself its comfort in that moment of anxious decision.

But then he felt the unavoidable, reactive visceral gripe of fear and foreboding. There were no certainties in a sea-battle, and providence was not so easily seduced.

Sauce for the Goose

'Fire!'

The French corvette lay to starboard, so close it seemed one could count the froggings on the scarlet dolmans of a dozen hussars standing on the *Arbeille*'s deck with their carbines presented, yet so detached one scarcely noticed the storm of shot which responded to the thunder of *Andromeda*'s broadside.

Drinkwater felt the rush of a passing ball and gasped involuntarily as it spun him around and drew the air from his lungs. Beside him Protheroe fell with a cry, slumping against Drinkwater's legs, causing him to stumble. One of the helmsmen took the full impact of a second round-shot, his shoulder reduced to a bloody pulp as he too swung round and was thrown against the mizen fife-rail so that his brains were mercifully dashed out at the same fatal moment.

As Drinkwater recovered his balance, a small calibre shot shattered his left arm. One of the hussars had hit him with a horse pistol. The blow struck him with such violence his teeth shut with a painful, head-jarring snap and a second later he felt the surge of pain, which made him gasp as his head swam. For a moment he stood swaying uncertainly, submitting to an overwhelming desire to lie down and to give up. What the hell did it matter? What the hell did any of it matter . . .?

'Are you all right, sir?'

What was the point of this action? They were little men whose lives had been lived under the shadow of the eagle. Rakov and Lejeune and Captain Nathaniel Drinkwater were mere pawns in the uncaring games of the men of power and destiny. Why, he could feel the chill in the shadow of the eagle's wings even now, and see the beguiling curve of Hortense's smile seducing him towards his own miserable fate. What would the omnipotent Tsar Alexander care for the fate of Count Rakov and his frigate? Or would the great Napoleon, whose ambition had contributed to the deaths of a million men, concern himself over the fate of a few fanatics who could not settle themselves under a fat, indolent monarch?

'Are you all right, sir?'

The British contented themselves under a fat, indolent monarch; or at least a fat, indolent regent. Why could these troublesome Frenchmen not see the sense of playing the same game . . . God's bones, but it was cold, so confoundedly cold . . .

'Sir! Are you all right?'

He saw Marlowe peering at him as though through a tunnel. He could not quite understand why Marlowe was there, and then his mind began to clear and the nausea and desire to faint receded. He was left with the pain in his arm. 'I fear,' Drinkwater said through clenched teeth, mastering his sweating and fearful body, 'I fear I am hit, Marlowe . . .'

'But, sir . . .'

'Send . . . for . . . laudanum, Marlowe . . . Pass word . . . to Kennedy . . . to send me . . . laudanum.' He breathed in quick and shallow gasps which somehow eased him.

'At once.' Marlowe saw with a look of horror the bloody wound just above Drinkwater's elbow.

Drinkwater's perception of the action was seen through a red mist; it cleared gradually though his being seemed dominated by the roaring throb of his broken arm. He was dimly aware the guns had fallen silent, that the shadows of the masts and sails once again traversed the deck which pitched for a few moments as *Andromeda* was luffed up into the wind. Then the guns thundered out again, adding to the throbbing in his head. Somewhere to starboard, he perceived the shallow curve of the *Arbeille*'s taffrail lined with shakoed infantry-men, and the sight roused him. By an effort of will he commanded himself again.

A fusillade of musketry swept *Andromeda*'s quarter-deck. Drinkwater felt a second ball strike him, like a whiplash across the thigh, then someone was beside him, holding a small glass phial.

'Here sir, quick!'

He swallowed the contents and for a moment more stood confused, trying to focus upon Hyde's marines whose backs were to him as they lined the hammock nettings, returning fire. Then *Arbeille* drew away out of range and *Andromeda*, having raked her, fell back to port, making a stern board.

Drinkwater felt the opiate spread warmth and contentment through him; the pain ebbed, becoming a faint sensation, like the vague memory of something unpleasant that lay just beyond one's precise recollection. He was aware that *Andromeda* had come up into the wind under the stern of the French corvette and he was aware of Kennedy blinking in the sunlight, hovering at his elbow.

'Hold still, sir, while I dress your wound.' Kennedy clucked irritably. 'Hold still, damn it, sir.' Drinkwater stood and supinely allowed the surgeon to cut away his coat and bind his arm. 'You have a compound fracture, sir, and I shall have to see to it later.' Kennedy grunted as a musket ball passed close. 'Luckily the ball must have been near spent; 'tis a mess, but no major blood vessels have been severed. I may save it if it don't mortify.'

'Thank you for your encouraging prognosis, Mr Kennedy,' Drinkwater said, his teeth clenched as Kennedy finished pulling him about with what seemed unnecessary brutality. He turned back to the handling of the ship as Kennedy grabbed his bag of field dressings and scuttled back to the orlop. It must have been the first time the surgeon had been so exposed to fire, he thought idly.

'Who gave orders to rake?' he asked no one in particular.

'You did, sir,' a hatless Birkbeck reassured him.

'What are our casualties?'

'I've no idea, though a good few fellows have fallen, but we knocked that corvette about . . .'

'Where's Marlowe?'

'Here, sir.'

Under the laudanum, Drinkwater's mind finally

cleared. The elation he had felt earlier returned, imbuing him with confidence. The wound in his thigh was no more than a scratch, his broken arm no more than a damnable inconvenience, already accommodated by shoving his left hand into his waistcoat. He strode to the rail. The marines withdrew to make room for him and he stared to starboard. The sterns of both French ships were now eight or nine cables away: the *Arbeille* trailed a tangle of wreckage over her port side and *L'Aigle* had shortened sail to keep pace with her. Their stern chase guns barked and a brace of shot skipped across the water and thudded ineffectually into *Andromeda*'s hull.

'Where's that damned Russian?'

'Somewhere beyond the Frogs, sir,' Marlowe volunteered.

Drinkwater cast his eyes aloft. All the topsails and topgallants were aback. Intact, they were nevertheless peppered with holes, and severed ropes hung in bights. Men were already aloft splicing.

'Throw the helm over, Mr Birkbeck!' Drinkwater ordered, 'Let's have her in pursuit again and bring that lot to book!'

Contre-Amiral Lejeune lay board to board with his wounded consort only as long as it took him to appraise the damage. A moment later *L'Aigle*'s yards were braced sharp up and the frigate detached herself on the port tack, moving away from the corvette preparatory to rounding on the British frigate. As *Andromeda* also gained headway and began to come up with the almost supine *Arbeille*, *L'Aigle* tacked smartly and began to run back towards the British frigate. This

306

time being caught in the cross-fire was inevitable. By using the *Arbeille* to mask *L'Aigle*'s guns, Drinkwater had also ensured the French frigate's preservation and fed her company with the desire to avenge her weaker consort. Undamaged, *L'Aigle* bore down to finish off the perfidious Englishman. Lejeune was staking his own mission on a final gamble.

'We are the bully cornered, I fancy,' Drinkwater remarked lightheartedly. He was aware that he had held the initiative and was now about to surrender it. But he was thinking clearly again; in fact his mind seemed superior to the situation, detached and almost divine in its ability to reason, untrammelled by doubts or uncertainties. He gave his orders coolly, as the first of *Arbeille*'s renewed fire struck *Andromeda*, in passing the corvette to engage her larger and more formidable sister.

Frey's battery fired into the *Arbeille*. Drinkwater could see the boats smashed on her booms and the wreck of her main topgallant and her mizen topmast; he saw men toiling on her deck to free her from the encumbrance while the brilliant tunics of her complement of soldiers fired small arms, augmenting her main armament of 8-pounders. It puzzled Drinkwater that shots from *Andromeda* had flown high enough to knock down so much top-hamper, but they were soon past the *Arbeille* and preparing to engage *L'Aigle*.

'Mr Ashton! Now's your chance! Fire into the frigate, sir!'

'Aye, aye, sir!'

'Stand by to tack ship!'

Then Ashton's port battery crashed out in a concussive broadside, only to be answered by the guns of *L'Aigle*.

Within a few moments, Drinkwater knew he had met an opponent worthy of his steel. Whatever the history of *Contre-Amiral* Lejeune, here was no half-sailor who had spent the greater part of the last decade mewed up in Brest Road, living ashore and only occasionally venturing out beyond the Black Rocks. Nor had his crew found the greatest test of their seamanship to be the hoisting and lowering of topgallant masts while their ship rotted at her moorings. Lejeune and his men had been active in French cruisers, national frigates which had made a nuisance of themselves by harrying British trade.

As they passed each other and exchanged broadsides, both commanders attempted to swing under their opponent's sterns and rake. *L'Aigle*, by wearing, retained the greater speed while *Andromeda*, turning into and through the wind to tack, slowed perceptibly. The guns were now firing at will, leaping eagerly in their trucks as they recoiled, their barrels heated to a nicety, their crews not yet exhausted, but caught up in the manic exertions of men attending a dangerous business upon which they must expend an absolute concentration, or perish.

Aboard both frigates the enemy shot wreaked havoc and although the smoke from the action did not linger, but was wafted away to leeward by the persistent breeze, to shroud the *Arbeille* as she too drifted to the south-eastward, it concealed much of the damage each was inflicting upon the other.

Having tacked, and having not yet lost any spars, Drinkwater temporarily broke off the action by holding his course to the southward in an attempt to draw Lejeune away from Rakov, who still stood northwards but who had, significantly, reduced sail. Lejeune bore round without hesitation.

'He's damned confident,' said Marlowe, studying *L'Aigle* through his telescope.

'Of reinforcement by the Russian?' mooted Drinkwater, levelling his own glass with his single right hand, then giving up the attempt.

'Are we to resume the action, sir?' asked Birkbeck.

'Very definitely, Mr Birkbeck. Now we are going to lay board to board on the same tack. That will decide the issue, and we have at least reduced the opposition to one.'

'For the time being, sir,' Birkbeck said, looking askance at Drinkwater.

'I am not insensible to the facts, Mr Birkbeck,' Drinkwater said brusquely, 'but if we can but cripple *L'Aigle*, she will not be in a fit state to take Bonaparte to the United States, and if we can but take her, well the matter's closed.'

'You are considering isolating and boarding her then, sir?' asked Marlowe.

'I am considering it, Mr Marlowe, yes. Please shorten down, Mr Birkbeck. We will allow this fellow to catch up.'

'Very well, sir.' Birkbeck turned away.

'The master ain't happy, Marlowe,' Drinkwater remarked, raising his glass again.

'I think,' Marlowe said slowly, '*he* is not insensible to the fact that *you* have taken an opiate, sir.'

Drinkwater looked hard at the first lieutenant. 'He thinks I am foolhardy, does he?'

'He wishes to survive to take up that dockyard post you promised him.'

'I had forgotten that. And what of you, Mr Marlowe? Do you think me foolhardy?'

Drinkwater saw the jump of Marlowe's Adam's apple. 'No sir. I think you are merely doing your duty as you see it.'

'Which is not as you see it, eh?'

'I did not say so, sir.'

'No. Thank you, Mr Marlowe.' Then a thought occurred to Drinkwater. 'By the bye, Mr Marlowe, pipe up spirits.'

The helmsmen heard the order and Drinkwater was aware of a shuffling anticipation of pleasure among them. It would do no harm. 'Sauce for the goose,' he muttered to himself, 'is sauce for the gander.'

The respite thus gained lasted for only some twenty minutes. The forenoon was almost over, but the day was unchanged, the sea sparkled in the sunshine and the steady breeze came out of the northwest quarter. The four ships were spread out over a large right-angled triangle upon the ocean. At the northern end of the hypotenuse lay the *Gremyashchi*, now hove-to; at the point of the right-angle, the battered *Arbeille* continued to lick her wounds and drift slowly down to leeward. Both vessels were awaiting the outcome of events at the far end of the hypotenuse, where *Andromeda* lay, and astern of her, swiftly catching her up, *L'Aigle* followed.

Despite the scepticism of his sailing master, Drinkwater was confident of having almost achieved his objective. If the *Arbeille* was commanded by an officer of similar resolution to that of *L'Aigle*, and it seemed impossible that he should not be, the fact the corvette had dropped out of the action suggested she had sustained a disabling proportion of damage. He clung on to these thoughts, arguing them slowly, interspersed with waves of pain from his arm which gradually became more assertive as the effect of the laudanum wore off.

Under her topsails, *Andromeda* stood on and her crew awaited the enemy. As *L'Aigle* approached, Drinkwater skilfully maintained the weather gauge by edging *Andromeda* to starboard every time he observed Lejeune attempt the same manoeuvre with *L'Aigle*. On the upper-deck the marines and the gunners relaxed in the sunshine, going off a pair at a time to receive their rum ration on the gun-deck. This hiatus was soon over.

His head throbbing with the beat of his pulse, Drinkwater strode forward and bellowed down into the waist, 'Stand-to, my lads. The Frenchman is closing us fast; there's hot work yet to do.'

Lieutenant Ashton had not given a second thought to Sergeant McCann after the marine had departed from the gun-deck. His baiting was the vice of a man who habitually used a horse roughly, sawed at the reins and galled his mount with a crop, a man who was given to mindless and petty acts of cruelty simply because fate had placed him in a station which nurtured such weaknesses. Since his schooldays, Ashton had learned that small facts gleaned about others could be put to entertaining use, and McCann had been a trivial source of such amusement. Yet he was not a truly vicious man, merely a thoughtless and unimaginative one. His solicitude for Marlowe, expressed in his question to young Paine, had been out of concern more for his sister and her unborn child than for the actual well-being of the man responsible for impregnating her. Blood-ties, if they were inevitable, should not be reprehensible, and it mattered much to Josiah Ashton that Marlowe acquitted himself well, perhaps more than to Frederic Marlowe himself. It would not have mattered much to Ashton had Marlowe been killed, provided only that his death was honourable, or appeared so, even if some stain upon his sister's good character was then unavoidable.

As he waited in the gun-deck for the action to resume, Ashton, having dispensed with Marlowe, was calculating his chances of advancement if matters fell out to his advantage. Down below he was relatively safe, unless they were boarded, and even then he was confident that his own skill with a small sword and a pistol would keep him out of real trouble. Marlowe, he judged, might attempt some quixotic act and was as likely to get his come-uppance in a fight, assuming he survived the next hour. Word had already come down to the gun-deck that Captain Drinkwater had a shattered arm. If he did not fall it was quite likely that gangrene would carry him off later. On the other hand, perhaps some opportunity for Ashton to distinguish himself would emerge during the forthcoming hours.

Ashton looked across the deck to where Frey, ever diligent, peered out of a gun-port, striving to see the enemy frigate coming up from astern. Frey was senior to him, but who knew? Perhaps he too would stop a ball before the day was over.

'I can't see a damned thing,' Frey complained, crossing the deck and passing close to Ashton as he bent to stare out of one of his own larboard battery gun-ports. 'Ah, here she comes. Looks as though it's your turn for it first.' Frey smiled and patted him on the shoulder. 'Good luck.'

'Good luck,' Ashton replied with more duty than true sincerity.

A moment later one of the gun-captains called out, 'Here she comes, me lads!' and a ripple of expectation ran through the waiting men, like a breeze through dry grass.

'Lay your guns,' Ashton commanded. He waited until, like statues, the crews stood back from their loaded and primed pieces, their captains behind the breeches, lanyards in hand. Eventually, all along the deck the bare arms were raised in readiness.

'Fire!' Ashton yelled, and the gun captains jerked the lanyards and jumped aside as the still-warm guns leaped inboard with their recoil, and their crews fussed round them again.

On the deck above, Sergeant McCann had ensured each marine checked his flint and filled his cartouche box. Worn flints would cause misfires, and most of his men had fired profligately.

'Make every shot count,' McCann warned them, 'and every bullet find its mark.'

His men muttered about grandmamas and the sucking of eggs, but they tolerated Meticulous McCann. He was a thoughtfully provident man and though few knew him enough to like him, for he had too many of the ways of an officer to enjoy popular appeal, they all respected him.

When the captain's warning to stand-to and prepare to receive fire came, Hyde merely nodded to McCann, who repeated the order. It was then, in the idle, fearful moment before action, McCann thought of Ashton, and as he lowered his weapon and lined foresight and backsight on a small cluster of gilt just forward of *L'Aigle*'s mizen mast, it was Josiah Ashton's image that his imagination conjured up beyond the muzzle of his Tower musket.

It was almost three bells when Ashton's guns barked again, beating the enemy by a few seconds. Although the range was short, Drinkwater had Birkbeck edge *Andromeda* away from *L'Aigle*, to prevent Lejeune running up too close and attempting to board and exploit his greater numbers. Even so, the storm of enemy musketry was prodigious, and the rows of hammocks were destroyed by lead shot ripping into them, fraying the barricade they made, so that the shredded canvas fluttered in the breeze. Those balls which passed over the hammocks in their nettings, either buzzed harmlessly overhead, or found a target. Most passed by, but a few struck the masts, or the boats, and a few knocked men down.

As for the enemy's round shot, they thudded into the hull or struck the lighter bulwarks, sending up an explosion of splinters. Occasionally a ball came in through a port, struck a carronade and ricocheted away with a strident whine. Others flew higher, aimed to bring down *Andromeda*'s upper spars, discommode those on the upper deck and rob the British frigate of the ability to manoeuvre which she had thus far so brilliantly exploited to avoid such a fate. The cries of the dying and the wounded filled the air again, and a large pool of blood formed at the base of the mizen

314

mast, pouring in a brief torrent from the shattered body of a topman lying across the trestletree boards of the mizen top high above.

The action had reached its crisis, and Drinkwater, increasingly assailed by the agony of his wounded arm, knew it. He fought the excruciating ache and the desire to capitulate to its demand to lie down and rest; his mouth was dry as dust and his voice was growing hoarse from shouting, though he could not recall much of what he had said in exhorting his men.

He knew too, that whatever the shortcomings of his ship and her company, they could not have fought her with more skill and vigour. From Birkbeck masterfully conning her, to the men who put the master's orders into practice; from the solicitous and grateful Marlowe running about the upper-deck directing the carronades, to the lieutenants and gunners below, he could not have asked for more. Nor should he forget Kennedy and his mates, labouring in the festering stink of the orlop, plying scalpel and saw, curette and pledget to save what was left of the brutalized bodies of the wounded. His own mortality irked him: he would have to submit to the surgeon's ministrations if he survived the next hour, for his bandaged arm oozed blood.

The thunder of their own guns bespoke a furious cannonade; the decks trembled with the almost constant rumblings of recoil and running out of the 12-pounders of the main armament, and it was clear to Drinkwater's experienced ear that Frey's unengaged gunners had crossed the deck to help fight the larboard battery. In fact Frey had assumed command of the forward division, an order Ashton had not liked receiving, though he could not avoid obeying it, for to do so would have been to have transgressed the Articles of War in refusing to do his utmost in battle.

But Ashton could not deny the effectiveness of the reinforcement, and so furious did the gunfire become that not even the brisk breeze could now clear the smoke and the gap between the two ships became obscure. Neither the officers in the gun-deck nor those upon the quarterdeck could now see very much. *L'Aigle* was marked by her lines of flashing muzzles and the tops of her masts above the cloud of powder-smoke. Then they heard a cheer ripple along the upperdeck and watched as, in an almost elegant collapse, *L'Aigle's* main topmast went by the board. Within a quarter of an hour, however, *Andromeda* had lost her own mizen mast and the wreckage brought down her main topgallant. Two carronades on the quarterdeck were also dismounted in the general destruction of her bulwarks adjacent to the mizen channels. A moment later she had lost her wheel and all those who manned it as her upper-deck was swept by a hail of grapeshot.

Marlowe was nowhere to be seen in the confusion as Drinkwater summoned a hatless and dishevelled Birkbeck who seemed otherwise unscathed. 'She'll get alongside us now, by God!' the sailing master bellowed above the din.

'We must have given as good as we've got!' Drinkwater roared back.

For a few moments there was utter confusion, then *L'Aigle* loomed close alongside and through the clearing smoke they could hear cries of *'Vive L'Empereur!'* and *'Mort à l'Anglais!'* as the French soldiers whipped themselves into a frenzy.

'Prepare to repel boarders!' Drinkwater shouted, his

voice cracking with the effort as his head reeled, and then the two ships came together with a sudden lurching thud and a long, tortured grinding. Above their heads on the quarterdeck, *L'Aigle*'s mainyard thrust itself like a fencer's extended and questing *épée*, wavering as the two ships moved in the seaway. Shapes like ghosts appeared over the rail as veterans of Austerlitz and Borodino, of Eylau, Friedland, Jena and Wagram prepared to launch themselves across the gap between the two frigates, on to *Andromeda*'s deck.

Lower down, beneath the pall of smoke that lay in the gulf between the two ships, Frey had seen the approach of *L'Aigle* and heard the excited shouting of the battle-mad troops. The cry to repel boarders came down through the thick air in the gun-deck and passed along the lines of cannon in shouted warnings.

Frey withdrew from his observation post and hurried aft to where Ashton was scurrying up and down his guns, half bent as he squinted along first one and then another as they jumped inboard for reloading. Steam sizzled as the wet sponges went in, adding a warm stickiness to the choking atmosphere. Frey tapped him on the shoulder.

'Josh!' Frey bellowed until he had attracted his colleague's attention. 'Josh! I'm taking my fellows to reinforce the upper-deck.'

'What?' Ashton was almost deaf from the concussion of the cannon and Frey had to shout in his filthy ear before Ashton understood.

'No, let me. You fight the guns.' The words were uttered before Ashton realized the implications: he had given voice to his thoughts and wavered briefly, half-hoping Frey would contradict the suggestion.

'If you want to go fire-eating good luck to you.' Frey nodded assent, straightened up and hastened back up the deck, half bent to avoid collisions with the beams. 'Starbowlines!' he bellowed, 'Small arms from the racks and follow Mr Ashton on deck! D'ye hear there? Starbowlines with Mr Ashton to the upper-deck! We're about to be boarded!' Men came away from the guns and helped themselves to cutlasses, withdrawing across the deck to where Ashton hurriedly mustered them while Frey turned back to invigorate the now flagging port gun-crews.

'Bear up, my boys, we can still blow their bloody ship to Old Harry!'

As Ashton led his men off, Frey's guns continued to engage *L'Aigle*'s cannon muzzle to muzzle.

On the quarterdeck Hyde came into his own. In a few seconds, he had concentrated his lobsters into a double line of men behind which Drinkwater and Birkbeck could gather their wits and attempt to avert disaster. By passing messages to the steering flat, *Andromeda* might yet break free of *L'Aigle*'s deadly embrace, but they had first to clear away the wreckage of fallen masts and throw back the wave of invaders.

Birkbeck's gaze ran aft and he clutched with thoughtless violence at Drinkwater's wounded arm. 'By God, sir! Look! There's the Russian!'

He pointed and Drinkwater, shaking from the pain of Birkbeck's unconscious gesture, turned to see above their stern the taut canvas of the *Gremyashchi* as she bore down into the action.

The Last Candle

Drinkwater felt the chill of foreboding seize him. The game was up.

He was conscious of having fought with all the skill he could muster, of having done his duty, but the end was not now far off. He saw little point in delaying matters further, for it would only result in a further effusion of blood, and he had done everything the honour of his country's flag demanded. Besides, he was wounded and the effect of the laudanum was working off; spent ball or not, it had done for his left arm and he could no longer concentrate on the business in hand. He was overwhelmed with pain and a weariness that went far beyond the urgent promptings of his agonizing wound. He was tired of this eternal business of murder, exhausted by the effort to outmanoeuvre other equally intelligent men in this grim game of action and counter-action. The effort to do more was too much for him and he felt the deck sway beneath his unsteady feet.

'Here the bastards come!'

It was Marlowe waving his sword and roaring a warning beside him. The first lieutenant had lost his hat like Birkbeck, and his sudden appearance seemed magical, like a *djinn* in a story, but it was a Marlowe afire with a fighting madness. Both his amazing presence and his words brought about a transformation in Drinkwater.

To strike at that moment would have resulted in utter confusion: Napoleon's veterans were after a revenge greater than the mere capture of a British frigate and the thought, flashing through Drinkwater's brain in an instant, compelled him to a final effort.

'God's bones! The game is worth a last candle . . .'

But his words were lost as, with a roar, the boarders poured in a flood over the hammock nettings and aboard *Andromeda*. They were answered by a volley from Hyde's rear rank of marines who promptly reloaded their muskets in accordance with their drill. Beside Drinkwater, Birkbeck drew his sword in the brief quiet. The rasp of the blade made Drinkwater turn as the front rank of marines discharged their pieces from their kneeling position.

'Stand fast, Birkbeck! I promised you a dockyard post. Hyde, forward with your bayonets!'

Drinkwater had his own hanger drawn now and advanced through the marines with Marlowe at his side. He distinctly heard Marlowe say 'Excuse me,' as he shouldered his way through the rigid ranks, and then they were shuffling forward over the resultant shambles of the marines' volleys.

Only the officers had been protected by Hyde's men; as the Frenchmen scrambled over the hammock nettings and down upon *Andromeda*, they had encountered the upper-deck gunners, topmen and waisters, the afterguard and those men whose duties required them to be abroad on the quarterdeck, forecastle and the port gangway. At Drinkwater's cry to repel boarders, most of these had seized boarding pikes, or drawn their cutlasses if they bore them.

L'Aigle's party had not been unopposed, but they outnumbered the defenders and while some were killed or remained detained in the hand-to-hand fighting, more swept past and were darting like ferrets in their quest for an enemy to overcome, in order to seize the frigate in the name of their accursed Emperor. Hyde's marines had fired indiscriminately into the mass of men coming aboard, hitting friend and foe alike, aided by discharges of langridge from the swivel guns in the tops that now swept *L'Aigle's* rail and inhibited further reinforcement of the first wave of boarders.

All this had taken less than a minute, and then, after their third volley, Hyde's men were stamping their way across the deck, their bright, gleaming steel bayonets soon bloodied and their ranks wavering as they stabbed, twisted and withdrew, butted and broke the men of the Grand Army who had the audacity to challenge them at sea, on their own deck. They were all slithering in blood and the slime that once constituted the bodies of men; the stink of it was in their nostrils, rousing them to a primitive madness which fed upon itself and was compounded into a frenzied outpouring of violent energy.

White-faced, Drinkwater advanced with them, his left shoulder withdrawn, his right thrown forward. With shortened sword arm, he stabbed and hacked at anything in his way. He was vaguely conscious of the jar of his blade on bone, then the point of a curved and bloody sabre flashed into his field of view and he had parried it and cut savagely at the brown dolman which bore it. A man's face, a thin, lined and handsome face, as weather-beaten as that of any seaman, a face disfigured with a scar and sporting moustachios of opulent proportions and framed by tails of plaited hair, grimaced and opened a red mouth with teeth like a horse. Drinkwater could hear nothing from the hussar whose snarl was lost in the foul cacophony to which, hurt and hurting, they all contributed in their contrived and vicious hate.

The hussar fell and was shoved aside as he slumped across the breech of a carronade. The enemy were checked and thrust back. Men were pinioned to the bulwarks, crucified by bayonets, their guts shot out point-blank by pistol shot, or clubbed with butts or pike-staves, and then with a reinforcing roar Ashton's gun crews came up from the waist, eager to get to closer grips with an enemy they had shortly before been blowing to Kingdom Come with their brutal artillery.

Drinkwater sensed rather than saw them. It was all that was needed to sweep the remaining able-bodied French, soldiers and seamen alike, back over the side of *Andromeda* and across the grinding gap between the two heaving ships. Drinkwater was up on the carronade slide himself, trying to get over the rail one-handed. Frustrated, he put the *forte* of his hanger in his mouth, afterwards recalling a brief glimpse of dark water swirling between the tumble-home of *L'Aigle* and *Andromeda*. He leaned outwards and seized an iron crane of *L'Aigle*'s hammock nettings as Ashton's men joined Hyde's marines and their combined momentum bore the counter-attack onward.

*　　*　　*

Sergeant McCann had been the right-hand marker as Lieutenant Hyde ordered the marines to advance. They had only to move a matter of feet; less than half the frigate's beam, but every foot-shuffling step had been fiercely contested, and McCann felt his boots crunch unmercifully down upon the writhings of the wounded and dying. The pistols in his belt felt uncomfortable as he twisted and thrust, edging forward all the time, but they reminded him of his resolve.

Suddenly he was aware of movement on his extreme right. As the flanker, he turned instinctively and saw Lieutenant Ashton lead the gunners up out of the gun-deck. He grinned as his heart-beat quickened and Ashton, casting about him to establish his bearings and the tactical situation, caught sight of Sergeant McCann appearing in the smoke to his left.

'Forward Sergeant!' he cried exuberantly, engaging the first Frenchman he came across, a dragoon officer who had shed his cumbersome helmet and fought in a forage cap and a short stable coat. The dragoon slashed wildly, but Ashton was supported by two sailors and the three of them cut the man to his knees in a second. The dragoon fell, bleeding copiously. Lieutenant Ashton felt a surge of confidence as he swept his men forward.

Smoke enveloped them and Ashton half turned, again shouting 'Come on, Sergeant!' his voice full of exasperation. Unable to see the full fury of the action on the quarterdeck, Ashton hacked a path forward and then, as the pressure eased, McCann advanced at a quickening pace. The line of marines began to gain momentum as the column of gunners continued to emerge from the gloom of the gun-deck.

Below, their remaining colleagues carried on adding their remorseless thunder to the air as they fired indiscriminately without aiming, into the wooden wall that heaved and surged alongside.

Sergeant McCann followed Lieutenant Ashton as he clambered over the bulwark amidships, and stretched out for the fore chains of *L'Aigle*. He could have killed Ashton at that moment, stabbed him ignominiously in the arse as he had sworn to do, but he faltered and then Ashton had gone, and with him the opportunity.

Further aft Lieutenant Marlowe had reached *L'Aigle*'s mizen chains and was hacking his way down upon the quarterdeck of the French frigate. Between the two British officers, the line of defenders bowed back, but it had already transformed itself as the French attack was repulsed and the tide turned. As Marlowe struck a French aspirant's extended arm and deflected the pistol ball so that it merely grazed his cheek, the whole line began to scramble aboard *L'Aigle*.

Carried forward by this madness, Drinkwater felt his ankle twist as he landed on the enemy deck, and he fell full length, cushioned by the corpse of a half-naked French gunner who lay headless beside his gun. The stink of blood, dried sweat and garlic struck him and he dragged himself to his feet as a fellow boarder knocked him over again. The seaman paused, saw whom he had hit and gave Drinkwater a hand to rise.

'Beg pardon, sir, but 'ere, let me . . .'

'Obliged . . .'

It seemed quieter now and Drinkwater took stock. There were fewer of the enemy, which seemed strange since they were now aboard *L'Aigle*. The wave of men he had led aboard dissipated, like a real wave upon a beach, running faster and faster as it shallowed, until, extended to its limit, it stopped and ran back. Bloody little fights took place everywhere, but the numbers of men already slaughtered had robbed *L'Aigle* of all her advantage, and it now became apparent to what extent *Andromeda*'s cannon-fire had damaged the French ship.

About the helm lay a heap of bodies and Drinkwater caught the gleam of sunlight on bullion lace. Was one of the ungainly dead *Contre-Amiral* Lejeune? The boats on *L'Aigle*'s booms were filled with holes, her main fife-rails were smashed to matchwood, releasing halliards and lifts. Parted ropes lay like inert serpents about the decks, drawing lines over and about the corpses, like some delineation of the expiring lives which had left an indelible impression upon the carnage.

About the broken boats on the booms amidships and at the opening of the after hatchway, Hyde's marines were clustered, firing down into the gun-deck below, thus preventing any reinforcement of the upper-deck such as Ashton had managed, and which had turned the tide of the battle. Elsewhere a handful of British jacks chased solitary Frenchmen to their deaths, and it seemed in that short, contemplative moment that they had achieved the impossible and seized *L'Aigle*. Drinkwater thought he ought perhaps to order his own guns to cease fire, but when he stopped to think about anything the pain of his broken arm came back to him and he wanted to give in to it. Surely providence was satisfied: surely he had done enough. Then, as if from a great distance, Drinkwater heard a cry.

'Look to your front, sir!' There was something urgent and familiar about the voice. Slowly he turned about and saw through the smoke, the hazy figure of Birkbeck standing above *Andromeda*'s rail and gesturing. 'Look to your front!'

'What the deuce are you talking about?' Drinkwater called, unaware that the terrible noise of battle had partially deafened him and he had been shouting his head off so that his voice was a feeble croak.

'The Russian! The *Gremyashchi*!' Birkbeck waved over Drinkwater's head, gesturing at something and Drinkwater turned again. Looming above the port bulwark of *L'Aigle*, unscathed and perhaps a foot higher in her freeboard, the big Russian frigate appeared. Drinkwater could see her bulwarks lined with men, many of them fiercely bearded, like the Russians he had seen on the coast of California many, many years ago . . .

And then he suddenly felt the naked exposure of his person.

'Take your men below, Sergeant!'

Ashton shoved a marine aside and pointed down into *L'Aigle*'s gundeck.

'Sir?'

'You heard me! Lead your men below and clear the gun-deck.'

McCann hesitated; Ashton was ordering him to a certain death.

'Are you a coward?'

'The hell I am . . .'

'Then do as you are ordered! I'll take my men down from forward.'

326

Furious, McCann ported his musket and began to descend into the smoke-filled hell. 'Catten,' he instructed one marine, 'run back aboard and let the master know we're going below before that stupid bastard has us all shot by our own gunners. The rest of you, follow me!' he cried.

Ashton was right: he, McCann, *was* a coward. Only a coward would have submitted to the thrall of soldiering; only a coward would have passively acquiesced to this madness and only a coward would have let slip the opportunity to rid the world of Josiah Ashton. Almost weeping with rage, McCann charged below.

What confronted the invaders when they spread out across *L'Aigle*'s gun-deck was horrifying. The planking was ploughed up by shot. In places, splinters stood like petrified grass. Stanchions were broken and guns were dismounted. Sunlight slanted into the fume-filled gloom through the frigate's gun-ports. *Andromeda*'s 12-pound shot at short range had beaten in the ship's side in one place, while the grape and langridge she had poured into *L'Aigle* had piled the dead about their guns in heaps.

On *Andromeda*'s gun-deck, Lieutenant Frey received the message to cease fire from Mr Paine who also added the request for the larboard guns to be withdrawn and the ports shut.

'What's amiss?' asked Frey, unable to do more than shout to hear his own voice.

'We need your men on deck, sir. Most of our fellows are aboard the Frenchman and that bloody Russian's just coming up on her disengaged side!'

'Where's the captain?' Frey asked.

'I last saw him going over the side with his hanger in his teeth.'

'Good God!'

Frey turned and began bellowing at his men.

As McCann shuffled forward in the oppressive gloom of *L'Aigle*'s gun-deck, resistance became increasingly fierce. It was clear that some of the soldiers had either retreated to the shelter of the guns amidships, or had been held in reserve there. A volley met the marines and several men fell. McCann took shelter behind the round bulk of the main capstan and prepared to return fire as if in his native woods, sheltering behind the bole of a hickory tree.

As his eyes became accustomed to the semi-darkness McCann began to select targets and fire with more precision. A small group of marines took cover either with him or behind adjacent guns. He was conscious of an exchange of fire at the far end of the deck where Ashton was attacking down through a pale shaft of sunlight lancing in by way of the forward companionway. It was clear that there, too, resistance was disciplined and effective. Then above the shots and yells, McCann heard Ashton's voice.

'McCann! Where the devil are you? Come and support me you damned Yankee blackguard!'

Ashton's intemperate and ill-considered plea took no account of McCann's own predicament, but was a reaction to the situation Ashton's headstrong action had landed him in. But its insulting unreasonableness struck a chord in McCann's psyche, and his spirit, loosened by the heat of battle, broke in hatred, remorse and the final bitter explosion of his reason.

And then McCann saw Ashton standing halfway down the forward companionway, illuminated by the shaft of light that lanced down from the clear blue sky above. He presented even an indifferent marksman a perfect target, and the fact that no Frenchman amidships had yet hit him confirmed McCann in his belief that Ashton had been providentially delivered to his own prowess. He knew the moment was fleeting and his Tower musket was discharged: McCann drew a pistol from his belt, laid it on Ashton's silhouetted head, and fired. As the smoke from the frizzen and muzzle cleared Ashton had vanished. McCann's triumph was short-lived; a second later he heard Ashton's voice: 'McCann, give fire, damn you!'

Alone, his bayonet fixed and his musket horizontal, Sergeant McCann forsook the shelter of the capstan and, with a crash of boots and an Indian yell, ran forward. Four balls hit him before he had advanced five paces, but his momentum carried him along the deck and he could see, kneeling and levelling a carbine at him, a big man whose bulk seemed to fill the low space.

'Sergeant McCann . . .!' Ashton's plaintive cry was lost in the noise of further musketry. McCann saw the yellow flash of the big horse-grenadier's carbine. The blow of the ball stopped him in his tracks, but it had missed his heart and such was his speed that it failed to knock him over. He shuffled forward again and in his last, despairing act as he fell to his knees, he thrust with his bayonet. Gaston Duroc of the Imperial Horse Grenadiers parried the feeble lunge of the British marine with his bare hand.

'Sergeant McCann, damn you to hell!' cried Lieutenant Ashton, retreating back up the forward companionway and calling his men to prevent the counter-attacking French from following and regaining the upper-deck.

Captain Drinkwater was aware of men about him, though there were few enough of them.

'My lads . . .' he began, but he was quite out of breath and, besides, could think of nothing to say. It would be only a moment or two before the Russians stormed into *L'Aigle* and wrested the French ship back from his exhausted men. He closed his eyes to stop the world swaying about him.

'Are you all right sir?'

He had no idea who was asking. 'Perfectly fine,' he answered, thanking the unknown man for his concern. And it was true; he felt quite well now, the pain had gone completely and someone seemed to be taking his sword from his hand. Well, if it meant surrender, at least it did not mean dishonour. If they survived, Marlowe and Birkbeck would manage matters, and Frey . . .

The bed was wondrously comfortable; he could sleep and sleep and sleep . . .

He could hear Charlotte Amelia in the next room. She was playing the harpsichord; something by Mozart, he thought, though he was never certain where music was concerned. And there was Elizabeth's voice. It was not Mozart any more, but a song of which Elizabeth was inordinately fond. He wished he could remember its name . . .

'Congratulations, Lieutenant.'

Frey bowed. 'Thank you, sir, but here is our first

330

lieutenant, Mr Marlowe.' Frey gestured as an officer almost as dishevelled and grubby as himself came up. A broken hanger dangled by its martingale from his right wrist. In his hands he bore the lowered colours of *L'Aigle.*

'What's all this?' Marlowe demanded, his face drawn and a wild look in his eye. His cheek was gouged by a black, scabbing clot. The appearance of the Russian had surprised him too, for he had been occupied with the business of securing the French frigate upon whose deck the three men now met.

'Captain Count Rakov, Marlowe,' Frey muttered and, lowering his voice, added 'executing a smart *volte-face* in the circumstances, I think.'

'I don't understand . . .'

'For God's sake bow and pretend you do.' Frey bowed again and repeated the introduction. 'Captain Count Rakov . . . Lieutenant Marlowe.'

'Where is Captain Drinkwater?' asked the Russian in a thick, faltering accent. 'I see him on the quarterdeck and then he go. You,' Rakov looked at Marlowe, 'strike ensign.'

'I, er, I don't know where Captain Drinkwater is . . .' Marlowe looked at Frey.

'He is dead?' Rakov asked.

'Frey?'

'Captain Drinkwater has been wounded, sir,' Frey advised.

'And die?'

'I do not believe the wound to be mortal, sir.' Frey was by no means certain of this, but the Russian's predatory interest and the circumstances of his intervention made Frey cautious. Rakov's motives were as murky as ditchwater and they were a long way from home in a half-wrecked ship. Frey was not about to surrender the initiative to a man who had apparently changed sides and might yet reverse the procedure if he thought Captain Drinkwater's wound was serious.

'In fact, Mr Marlowe,' Frey lied boldly, 'he left orders to proceed to Angra without delay.' Frey turned to Rakov and decided to bluff the Russian and hoist him with his own petard. 'And he asked that you, Count Rakov, would assist us to bring our joint prizes to an anchorage there. He regretted the misunderstanding that occasioned us to fire into each other. I believe there was some confusion about which ensigns these ships were flying.'

Rakov regarded Frey with a calculating and shrewd eye, then turned to Marlowe. 'You command, yes?' he broke the sentence off expectantly.

'Yes, yes, of course,' Marlowe temporized. 'If that is what Captain Drinkwater said . . .'

'He was quite specific about the matter, gentlemen,' said Frey with a growing confidence.

'You British . . .' said the Russian and turned on his heel, leaving the *non sequitur* hanging in the air.

'Whew,' exhaled Frey when Rakov was out of earshot.

'D'you mind telling me what all that was about, damn it?' Marlowe asked.

'I think we won the action, Frederic, in every sense. Now, you had better see whether we have enough men to get this bloody ship to Terceira.'

'Have you seen Ashton?'

'Ashton? No, I haven't, but I suspect the worst.'

'Oh God . . .' Marlowe stood uncertainly shaking his

head. Then he looked up at Frey, a frown on his face. 'I've a curious ringing in my ears, Frey . . .'

'Count yourself lucky that's all you've got,' said Frey. 'Now let us take stock of matters, shall we.' It was a gentle hint more than a question, and Marlowe dumbly nodded his agreement.

A Burying of Hatchets

'Mr Gilbert, please forgive me for not coming ashore . . .'

'My dear Captain Drinkwater, pray do not concern yourself. It is you who have been put to the greater exertion, I do assure you.' Gilbert smiled urbanely. 'As for the Captain-General, why, he perfectly understands your situation and joins me in wishing you a speedy recovery.'

'Please convey my thanks to His Excellency and, pray, do take a seat.'

Gilbert sat in the cabin chair opposite Drinkwater whose left arm was doubled in a splint and sling. He observed the sea-officer's pallid complexion as Drinkwater moved uneasily in his chair, evidence of the pain he was in.

'Frampton, a glass for Mr Gilbert.'

'Thank you.'

Frampton offered a glass from a small silver tray and Gilbert raised it in a toast. 'To the squadron that never was,' he said, indicating the view from the stern windows of the cabin. Lying at anchor between the commanding guns of His Britannic Majesty's frigate *Andromeda* and His Imperial Majesty's frigate *Gremyashchi*, lay the *Arbeille* and *L'Aigle*.

'Your fellow Marlowe gave a vivid account of the action,' Gilbert said, sipping his wine. 'It seems a pity it will go unrecorded, but . . .' he shrugged, *'c'est la guerre.'*

Drinkwater raised his own glass and half-turned to contemplate the view. The sheltered anchorage of Angra lay between low, *maquis*-covered slopes, and the subtle, poignant scent of the land permeated the open sash. The ships presented a curious appearance, the regularity of their masts cut down by the action and now undergoing repair. The shortfall of spare spars occasioned by *Andromeda*'s hurried departure for escort duties was being made good from the stock aboard the French ships, so that it was estimated that within three or four days all would be sufficiently sea-worthy to attempt the passage to a home port. And therein lay complications.

'That is where you are wrong,' Drinkwater said, swinging round to Gilbert. 'Unfortunately it is not war; unfortunately it is a mess, though you are correct it will go unrecorded. Poor Marlowe will be disappointed if he expects to get a step in rank or even to take a prize home. We have taken no prizes . . .'

'I entirely agree, Captain, and the situation is the more complicated since we received news from Lisbon only yesterday that Napoleon Bonaparte has for some time been installed as King of Elba . . .'

'Elba?' Drinkwater frowned. 'I know only of one island of Elba and it is off the Tuscan coast, a dog's watch distance from France, not far from Naples . . .'

'Your incredulity is unsurprising, but it is the same Elba.'

'Good God!'

'I have no idea why the place was selected; it seems the height of stupidity to me.'

'So all the endeavours of these poor benighted devils would have been wasted, which consideration begs the question of my own . . .'

'And Rakov's,' added Gilbert.

'I suppose that is some consolation.'

'I understand from young Marlowe that Rakov played a double-game.'

Drinkwater nodded. 'It would seem that having offered the Bonapartists his protection, he abandoned them when it became obvious that to do so meant a full-scale engagement with a British frigate. I don't know how much discretion Rakov was permitted in the interpretation of his own orders, but he can scarcely have been sleeping easily since our confrontation.'

'It was just as well that he did have a change of heart,' said Gilbert. 'According to Marlowe, he was in a position to retake *L'Aigle* . . .'

'Ah, yes, but he came alongside the French ship on the opposite side to ourselves; had he meant mischief to the last, he would have ranged alongside our unengaged, starboard side.' Drinkwater paused a moment, then added, 'We were a sitting duck.'

'I see,' said Gilbert contemplatively, adding, 'Well, the interpretation of your own orders cannot have been easy.'

The remark brought a rueful smile to Drinkwater's

face. 'I enjoyed far greater latitude than Count Rakov,' he said, then cutting off any further comment which might have been indiscreet and let too much slip to a stranger, Drinkwater said, 'As matters stand now, Rakov's action has fortuitously compromised no one.'

'Indeed not. In fact, quite the contrary, for if the Lisbon papers are to be believed, and I have one here,' Gilbert put down his wine glass and fished in a large black-leather wallet, ''twas the Tsar himself who approved Elba.'

'The Tsar?' queried Drinkwater, 'But that makes no sense.'

'Unless His Imperial Majesty had second thoughts.' Gilbert held out the newspaper.

'I don't read Portuguese,' said Drinkwater drily.

'Of course not, I do beg your pardon . . .'

'It occurs to me that if you were able to read that to Rakov, we might defuse any further problems.'

'Why not read it to them all? Boney's partisans should know this too. It diverts their attention from America back to Europe . . .'

'And will ensure we can send both ships in to a French port,' added Drinkwater enthusiastically.

'Who commands the French?'

'As far as I can determine, their original leader was a Rear-Admiral Lejeune but he was mortally wounded and it would seem that a military officer is now the senior.'

Gilbert uncrossed his legs and sat up, placing his half-empty glass on the table. 'Captain, may I presume to make a suggestion to which I am also able to make a modest contribution?'

'By all means.'

'Would you be prepared to host a dinner here, this afternoon? I shall send off a porker and some fresh vegetables, together with some tolerable wine. If you invited, say, three French officers, Rakov and two of his own men together with some of your own, we might stop any further unpleasantness and thereby offer all the other poor devils an explanation.'

'Would you act as interpreter of the newspaper?'

'Yes, why? Oh, you are thinking the French or the Russians might not trust us?'

''Tis a possibility.'

'You are quite right; I will bring one of the Portuguese customs officers.'

Drinkwater nodded and Gilbert, pulling out a gold hunter, said, 'At three of the clock?'

'What time have you now . . .?' Drinkwater confirmed Gilbert's Azorean time coincided with *Andromeda*'s own ship's time and nodded. 'We shall expect you then. I will arrange to have invitations delivered.'

Gilbert rose, his manner suddenly brisk. 'We both have work to do, Captain, so I shall take my leave for the nonce and look forward to seeing you later.' He smiled. 'An event like this certainly livens up a dull, if pleasant place.'

'I should have thought,' replied Drinkwater, walking with Gilbert to the cabin door, 'that this was almost lotus-eating.'

'Almost,' Gilbert said with a laugh, 'but a man can choke, even on lotuses.'

When he had seen Gilbert's boat off, Drinkwater returned to the cabin and stood for a moment looking out through the stern windows. The atmosphere aboard the two French ships must be wretched in the extreme with half of Hyde's marines doing duty as guards, just as disarmed French *grognards* did duty as donkeys aboard *Andromeda,* assisting with the business of re-rigging and labouring under duress. Matters can have been no happier aboard the *Gremyashchi.* Rakov had studiously avoided personal contact with Drinkwater and conducted all intercourse through the medium of his son, a lieutenant who spoke better English than his father. Drinkwater turned and his eye was caught by Gilbert's abandoned, half-full glass. He recalled the consul's offer of some 'tolerable wine'.

His own was obviously intolerable. Well, so be it; lotus-eating clearly had its drawbacks. Drinkwater eased himself into his chair, reached for pen, ink and paper and called his servant.

'Frampton, pass word for a midshipman to report in a quarter of an hour. I shall be entertaining at six bells in the afternoon watch. Dinner for,' he paused and made a quick calculation, 'for seventeen. Yes, I know, we shall have to borrow some of the wardroom silver and their table. A pig and some vegetables will be sent off this morning from the shore.'

'Aye, aye, sir.' Frampton's tone bore the dull acquiescent tone of the hopeless servitor. He began his shuffling retreat to his pantry with a sigh when Drinkwater, who had already bent to his writing, looked up.

'Oh and, Frampton, the consul will also be sending off a quantity of tolerable wine.'

'Very good, sir.'

The unusual nature of the gathering aboard HMS *Andromeda* that sunlit afternoon precluded any real sociability. Two thirds of those present had recently been, as the colloquialism had it, at hammer and tongs with each other, while the motives of the other third were highly suspect. A jolly, convivial dinner being out of the question, Drinkwater had decided that the proceedings would be formal and the serving of the meal incidental to the real business in hand. To this end, Drinkwater instructed Hyde to parade those of his marines left aboard *Andromeda,* and two files lined the quarterdeck as a guard of honour, commanded by Hyde, resplendent in scarlet, with his gorget glittering at his throat and a drawn sword in his white-gloved hand. The turnout of the marines owed much to the assiduous training of the late and lamented Sergeant McCann who lay, with over a score of his ship-mates, buried off the western cape of the island of Graciosa.

Drinkwater had also turned out in full dress, as had his three lieutenants, the master and the surgeon, though Drinkwater suspected the latter resented the flummery of the occasion. All the British officers wore their hangers and, in accordance with Drinkwater's instructions, each had his assigned group of foreign officers to look after. In his written invitations, Drinkwater had stated *Andromeda*'s boats would pick up the French officers, and his midshipmen had been given explicit orders to allow the barge from the *Gremyashchi* to arrive alongside ahead of them. Gilbert and the Portuguese customs officer, however, came off first.

'Captain Drinkwater, may I introduce Senhor Bensaude,' Gilbert said, smiling.

'Welcome aboard, sir, I understand you have a good command of English and will translate the news for us.'

340

'It will be my pleasure, Captain.'

'I have acquainted Senhor Bensaude with the delicacies of the situation,' Gilbert added.

'Indeed, I understand quite perfectly,' Bensaude added, his accent curiously muted.

'Your English is flawless, Senhor,' Drinkwater replied, impressed.

'I formerly worked in a Lisbon house exporting wine to England. It was run by an English family by the name of Co'burn.'

'Ah, that explains matters.' Drinkwater turned to Gilbert. 'And thank you for your pigs; as you can smell, they will be ready shortly.'

Marlowe approached with the news that the *Gremyashchi*'s boat was coming alongside, and a few moments later Captain Count Vladimir Ivanovich Rakov and his son were engaged in conversation with Gilbert and Lieutenants Ashton and Frey, while Drinkwater welcomed the party from the French ships.

He recognized their leader immediately. The thin, ascetic, sunburnt features with the dependent moustaches, the pigtails and queue were that of the hussar officer Drinkwater had cut down and he had last seen slumped against a carronade slide. Beneath the burnished complexion, the hussar's skin bore a ghastly pallor. Like Drinkwater, he wore a sling, but he concealed this beneath his brown, silverfrogged pelisse which he wore, contrary to common practice, over his sword-arm. A large sabretache dangled from his hip, vying for the attention of any onlookers with his sky-blue overalls, but he wore no sword.

The hussar officer carried an extravagantly plumed busby under his left arm. His hessian boots were of

341

scarlet leather and bore gold tassels. Apart from regimental differences, he reminded Drinkwater, in his dress, of Lieutenant Dieudonné, whom he had fought on the ice at the edge of the Elbe.*

'I am Colonel Marbet,' the hussar officer said in halting English, inclining his head in a curt bow. Then, having established his precedence, he stood back and a naval officer came forward.

'I am Capitaine de Frégate Duhesme.' Drinkwater had a vague recollection of seeing this man before, after he had suffered the ministrations of debridement and bone-setting by Kennedy, when he accepted the formal surrender of *L'Aigle* and relinquished the details to Marlowe and Frey, with the sole instruction to return her commander's sword to him.

'Welcome aboard, Capitaine. I understand Capitaine Friant of the *Arbeille* is too indisposed to join us.'

'He is badly wounded,' answered Duhesme in good English. 'Colonel Marbet of the Second Hussars is the senior of us, but this is Capitaine Duroc of the Imperial Horse Grenadiers . . .'

The big man in the blue and white coat held a huge bearskin under the crook of his left arm and wore ungainly jack-boots and spurs. These had been buffed for the occasion, and judging by the gleam in his eyes, there was fight still left in Duroc.

Drinkwater coughed to gain their collective attention. 'Gentlemen, there is much to discuss and it would be the better done over dinner. Please be so kind as to follow me into the cabin.' And without further preamble he led the way below.

* See *Under False Colours*

As soon as the company was seated and their glasses filled, and while the lieutenants each carved a joint of pork, Drinkwater rose and addressed them all.

'Gentlemen, welcome aboard His Britannic Majesty's frigate *Andromeda*. For those of you who do not already know it, I am Nathaniel Drinkwater, a post-captain in the Royal Navy of Great Britain.' He spoke slowly, allowing Duhesme to translate for Marbet and Duroc. 'The unfortunate circumstances that led to the actions between our several vessels,' Drinkwater paused a moment, laying emphasis on the point and staring at Rakov, 'have been overtaken by events. Mr Gilbert here, the British consul at Angra do Heroismo, has informed me that news has arrived from Lisbon which affects us all, one way or another.

'Capitaine Duhesme, would you be kind enough to translate what I have said for the benefit of Count Rakov . . .'

'Not necessary,' Rakov said. 'I understand . . .'

'I beg your pardon, Count, I did not know you spoke English very well.'

'I serve with Admiral Hanikov's squadron in North Sea. You not know . . .'

'On the contrary, Count, I am perfectly acquainted with Admiral Hanikov's movements in the North Sea. Now I shall proceed . . .'

Drinkwater ignored Rakov's glare and continued while the plates were passed and vegetables served. Frampton and the wardroom messmen fussed about the fringes of the tables and Drinkwater noted Gilbert's wine was tolerable enough to be swallowed in considerable quantities.

'Mr Gilbert has solicitously brought off Senhor

Bensaude, an officer of the Portuguese customs service, to impartially translate this news to us.' Drinkwater turned to Bensaude. 'Senhor, if you would be so kind . . .'

Bensaude rose and the crackle of the newspaper filled the expectant cabin as he held it up to read. He was not a tall man, but the broadsheet's top touched the deck-beams above his head.

'The despatch is dated Paris, 2nd May, and the date of this newspaper is Lisbon, 14th May. The despatch states that: "It is reported from Frejus that Napoleon Bonaparte arrived at that place and embarked in the British Frigate *Undaunted*, Captain Ussher commanding, on the evening of 28th April. Bonaparte landed at Portoferraio on the morning of 4th May and assumed the title of King of Elba . . .'

But Bensaude got no further, the succulent pork and its steaming accompaniment of cabbage and aubergines went ignored for three full minutes, while the assembly digested the fact of an Elban exile and its implications for them all. Drinkwater's attempt to break the parties by interspersing his own officers among his guests only added to the babel, for Rakov leaned across Frey and Duroc to speak to his son, at first in French and then in Russian, while Duroc, his face dark with anger, almost bellowed at Marbet across Hyde, Marlowe and the interval between the two tables. For Drinkwater himself, the thought that a mere four days difference would have saved them all the necessity of the tragic adventure that now drew to its conclusion, ate like acid into his soul. He thought again of the urgency of Hortense's news, of the awful consequences should the thing come to pass, and of

344

the needless dead who had been sacrificed to prevent something that would, as matters turned out, never have happened anyway.

Thought of the dead made him look at Marbet. The hussar was trying to listen to Duroc, who boomed at him passionately, but the fight with pain and sickness was obvious to a fellow sufferer. Drinkwater felt a sudden presentiment that Marbet would not see France again. The guilty certainty diverted him and he wondered if the French conspirators knew Hortense Santhonax, then dismissed from his mind any intention to ask. If they agreed to what he was about to propose, he did not want another, vengeful death laid to his account. Let Hortense prosper, even though he must himself support her. The thought of this brought Drinkwater to himself. He waited a moment for things to quieten down and when there seemed no prospect of this, he thumped on the table until the cutlery and the glasses rang, simultaneously calling them all to order with a commanding, 'Gentlemen! Gentlemen! Please do not neglect your victuals!'

He paused just long enough for those translating to effect a silence. Like guilty schoolboys they picked up knife and fork. He took advantage of their awkwardness and resumed his speech. 'I appreciate this news excites us all. Colonel Marbet and Capitaine Duhesme, I trust that you will return to a French port. If I may suggest it, flying the Bourbon lilies to ease matters. I am sure Count Rakov would join me in signing a document saying that you were lately on a cruise and learned about the fate of the Emperor from us . . .' Drinkwater smiled as Marbet looked at Duhesme and Duroc, exchanging quick, low remarks with both officers. While this public, if muted conference took place, Drinkwater caught Rakov's eye.

'As for you and the *Gremyashchi*, Count Rakov, I consider the unfortunate matter of our exchange of fire should be regarded as accidental.' Drinkwater watched Rakov's expression, ramming his point home: 'Unless of course you wish me to report your opening fire upon the British flag . . . It was doubtless an error, probably attributable to one of your officers . . .' Drinkwater picked up his glass and smiled over it. 'Well, then, it seems a pity that the French national cruisers *L'Aigle* and *Arbeille* had not heard of the abdication of the Emperor Napoleon and the restoration of King Louis, and engaged this ship before Capitaine Duhesme could be acquainted with the facts . . .'

Drinkwater looked round the table. The French were disconsolate; not only had they suffered defeat, they now knew the fate of their Emperor was no glorious resurrection in Canada, but that of a petty king, on an arid and near worthless island off the Italian coast. Count Rakov seemed sunk in gloom, alternating deep draughts of wine with short bursts of conversation with his son who seemed to be arguing some point of cogency.

Drinkwater raised an eyebrow at Gilbert who gave an almost imperceptible nod of satisfaction, before addressing a remark to Bensaude. Drinkwater decided to avail himself of the pork before him, which had been carved in small slices for him to eat one-handed. It was almost cold, but the flavour remained delicious, and with Gilbert's wine to wash it down Drinkwater began to relax.

'Capitaine Drinkwater . . .'

Drinkwater looked up. Duhesme was addressing him from the far table. 'Colonel Marbet . . .' Duhesme looked at Marbet who nodded with an exhausted resignation, then at Duroc whose face looked more drawn than ever. Duhesme began again. 'We agree with your idea and accept your proposal.'

'That is good news, Colonel.' Drinkwater turned to Rakov. 'Count, it remains for you to agree . . .'

Rakov coughed and put his wine glass down with a heavy nod. 'Ver' well. I agree.'

Drinkwater looked round the table and raised his own glass high. 'Gentlemen, we have all lived our lives under the shadow of the eagle and the eagle is now caged. Let us drink to peace, gentlemen.' He looked round the table. Duroc's face was full of the rage of humiliation and mutilated pride and Drinkwater added, 'At least for the time being.'

A full belly dimmed the pain of his arm and Drinkwater felt the burden of responsibility lifted from his shoulders. It was the first time he had felt relief since his fateful meeting with Hortense Santhonax. He spoke to several of his departing guests as they went over the side.

'I hope you recover fully from your wound, Colonel,' he said to Marbet as the French officer prepared to be helped over the side into Midshipman Paine's cutter. 'And I am sorry that I was the means by which you suffered it.'

Duhesme was at Marbet's elbow, assisting him and acting as interpreter. The hussar looked at Drinkwater, shrugged and muttered something which Duhesme translated as, 'Per'aps the war is not yet over, Capitaine,

347

and peace may be short. The eagle, as you call the Emperor, is not caged, but perched upon a little rock. If he raises himself, he can see France.'

'I fear you are right. This may be *au revoir* then.'

Duhesme translated and Marbet, fixing his eyes upon Drinkwater, muttered a comment which Duhesme duly interpreted.

'For me, Capitaine, the Colonel says, it is good-bye . . .' And Drinkwater saw death quite clearly in Marbet's deep-set eyes.

'He is a brave man, Capitaine,' Duhesme added.

'That is the tragedy of war, M'sieur,' Drinkwater replied. 'Tell him I honour his courage and that his Emperor was gallantly served.'

Moved by the incongruous sight of the curiously attired hussars as they somehow descended to the boat despite their tasselled boots, pelisses and wounds, Drinkwater turned aside.

Rakov's barge left after *Andromeda*'s cutter had swept the French away. Saying his farewells, Drinkwater asked, 'What does the name *Gremyashchi* signify, Count Rakov?'

The Russian officer consulted his son and replied, 'It means "thunderer".'

'Well I'm damned! I was appointed to command a British ship of that name. Well Count, it seems we have always been allies. May I say that I hope we part friends.' Drinkwater held out his hand and, after a moment's hesitation, Rakov took it.

Gilbert and Bensaude were the last to leave and both shook Drinkwater's hand warmly. 'I am obliged to you both,' Drinkwater said, 'and can only express my sincere thanks.'

'It has been a pleasure Captain,' said Gilbert, 'and I consider you have rendered these islands a signal service. Bonaparte's presence here would have been disastrous for us; his presence elsewhere beyond these islands would have been far worse. You have moreover buried hatchets with commendable diplomacy.'

'I agree absolutely with Mr Gilbert,' Bensaude said, and then they were gone and Drinkwater swept his officers back into the cabin, refilled their glasses and addressed them as they stood there in an untidy, expectant knot.

'There will be several unanswered questions occurring to you, gentlemen, not least among them what the events of recent days have been about. Perhaps I can best explain them by saying that it is more important to remember what they have not been about. They have not been about the prolongation of the war in Europe; more importantly, they have not been about the triumph of the Americans, of Canadian rebels and perhaps the establishment of a second Napoleonic empire in the North Americas.

'I have offered the French a means by which they may return to France with honour, allowing them to go back to their homes and families. I have also offered the Russians a means by which they too can return to the Baltic without discredit.

'In these conclusions I believe we have done our duty and upheld the dignity of the British crown. Now I wish only to drink to your healths.'

Drinkwater swallowed his wine and put the glass on the nearest table. A moment's silence filled the cabin and then Marlowe raised his own glass and looked round.

'I give you Captain Drinkwater, gentlemen!'

And they raised their glasses to him, men who seemed still to be no more than mere boys, but with whom he had gone through the testing time, and who had not let him down. As they filed out, he turned away and surreptitiously wiped the tears from his eyes.

'Any orders sir?' Marlowe asked from the door. He was the last to leave.

'Let me know when the ship is ready for sea, Mr Marlowe.'

'Aye, aye, sir.'

After they had all gone and Frampton had cleared away, Drinkwater sat at the table and, spreading a sheet of paper, began to write his report of proceedings. He penned the superscription, thinking of John Barrow, the Second Secretary, who would read his words to the assembled Board of Admiralty. He had much to say and began with the well-rehearsed formula: *Sir, I have the honour to report* . . . Then he paused in thought and laid down his pen. A moment later he had fallen asleep, smudging the wet ink.

'Well, Ashton, it's homeward bound as soon as we're ready for sea,' Marlowe announced, and Hyde, who was disrobing himself from the tight constraints of his sash, reappeared in the doorway of his cabin.

'That's damned good news,' he said.

'I'm not certain I relish existing on half-pay,' Ashton grumbled, throwing himself into a chair.

'I shouldn't think you'll have to,' remarked Frey acidly.

Hyde chuckled, then added soberly, 'Well at least you

ain't dead, like poor McCann. I still don't understand why he ran out of cover like that. It was so unlike McCann, who was always so strict and disciplined in everything he did.' No one offered an opinion and Hyde yawned and stretched. 'A full belly always makes me sleepy,' he observed, yawning.

'Most things make you sleepy,' Ashton jibed.

'Aren't you supposed to be on deck, Josiah?' Marlowe asked.

'When I have changed into undress garb,' Ashton mumbled, sighing and half rising.

'You have a sleep too,' Frey said, emerging from his cabin in the plain coat of working rig, 'I'll tend the deck.'

'Damned lick-spittle,' Ashton said.

'Don't be so bloody offensive, Ashton,' Hyde called from his cabin, and Marlowe looked pointedly at the third lieutenant.

'Hyde's right, Josiah . . .'

'Oh, damn the lot of you,' Ashton said, and getting up he retired to his cabin, slamming the door so that the whole flimsy bulkhead shook and Hyde reappeared in the doorway of his hutch.

'You know,' he remarked conversationally to Marlowe, 'when I first met him, I rather liked him. It's remarkable how a sea-passage can change things, ain't it?'

'Yes,' replied Marlowe, 'it is.'

'It was a moonlit night when we engaged the *Sybille*, d'you remember?'*

* See *The Flying Squadron*

'I was in the gun-deck, sir,' Frey replied. 'It is invariably near dark there . . .'

Drinkwater chuckled; 'I'm sorry, I had forgot. I sometimes think I have been too long upon a quarterdeck. In fact,' he said with a sigh, 'I fear I am fit for precious little else.'

So bright was the moonlight that it cast the shadow of the ship on the heaving black sea beyond them and the undulating movement of the water made the shadow run ahead of *Andromeda*, adding an illusory component to the frigate's apparent speed as she ran to the north and east, bound for the chops of the Channel. Above their heads the ensign cracked in the wind which lumped the sea up on the starboard quarter, and *Andromeda* scended with alternating rushes forward on the advancing crests, and a slowing as she fell back into the following crests.

The two officers stood for a moment at the windward hance and watched the sea.

''Tis beautiful though,' Drinkwater observed wistfully.

'You are thinking you will not long be able to stand here and admire it.' Frey made it a statement, not a question and Drinkwater took their conjoint thoughts forward.

'Could you paint such a scene?'

'I could try. I should like to attempt it in oils.'

'I commissioned Nick Pocock to paint the moonlit action with the *Sybille*. The canvas hung in my miserable office in the Admiralty. If you could do it, I should like a painting of *Andromeda* coming home . . .'

'At the end of it all,' said Frey.

'D'you think so?' asked Drinkwater. 'While I certainly

hope so, I doubt Napoleon will sit on his Tuscan rock and sulk for ever.'

'I suppose we must put our trust in God, then,' Frey said wryly.

'I have to confess, I do not believe in God,' said Drinkwater, staring astern where a faint phosphorescence in the sea drew the line of the wake on the vastness of the ocean. 'But I believe in Providence,' he added, 'by which I mean that power that argues for order and harmony in the universe and which, I am certain, guides and chastises us.'

He turned to the younger man by his side whose face was a pale oval in the gloom of the night and sighed. 'You only have to look at the stars,' he said, and both officers glanced up at the mighty arch of the cloudless sky. The myriad stars sparkled brilliantly in the depths of the heavens; several they knew by name, especially those by which they had traced their path across the Atlantic, but there were many, many more beyond their knowledge. The light, following breeze ruffled their hair as they stared upwards, then abruptly Drinkwater turned and began to walk forward, along the length of *Andromeda*'s quarterdeck. The planking gleamed faintly in the starlight.

'Have you noticed,' Drinkwater remarked as they fell into step beside each other, 'there is always a little light to see by.'

'Yes,' agreed his companion.

After a pause, Drinkwater asked, 'Who is the midshipman of the watch?'

'Paine.'

'Pass word for him, will you.'

Paine reported to the two officers, apprehensive in

353

the darkness. 'Mr Paine,' said Drinkwater, 'I wished to say how well you acquitted yourself in the action.'

'Thank you, sir.'

'Now cut along.'

'Aye, aye, sir.'

'Well,' Drinkwater yawned and stretched as the midshipman ran off, 'it's time I turned in.' He gave a final glance at the binnacle and the illuminated compass card within. 'You have the ship, sir,' he said formally, adding 'Keep her heading for home, Mr Frey.'

And even in the gloom, Frey saw Drinkwater smiling to himself as he finally went below.

A Laying of Keels

The wedding party emerged from St James's in Piccadilly and turned west, bound for Lothian's Hotel and the wedding breakfast. It was a perfect summer's day and Drinkwater felt the sun hot on his back after the cool of the church. He creaked in the heavy blue cloth and gilt lace of full-dress and his sword tapped his thigh as he walked. His left sleeve was pinned across his breast and within it his arm was still bound in a splint while the bone knitted, but beyond a dull ache, he hardly noticed it. Drinkwater cast a look sideways at Elizabeth and marvelled at how beautiful she looked, handsomer now, he thought gallantly, than in the bloom of youth when he had first laid eyes upon her gathering apples in her apron. She felt his glance and turned her head, her wide mouth smiling affectionately.

Thinking of her protestations that she was unacquainted with either the bride or groom when Drinkwater had written from Chatham that she should come up to town and meet him at their London house, he asked, 'Are you glad to be here, Bess?'

'I am glad that you are here,' she said, 'and almost in one piece.'

He drew her closer and lowered his voice, 'And I am glad you brought Catriona.'

James Quilhampton's widow walked behind them on the arm of Lieutenant Frey, who looked, to Drinkwater's surprise, as sunny as the morning.

'Do you think we shall hear more wedding bells?' he began, when Elizabeth silenced him with a sharp elbow in his ribs.

'You shout, sir,' she teased, her voice low. 'You are not upon your quarterdeck now.'

Drinkwater smiled ruefully. No, he was not, nor likely to be again . . .

'I should have liked *you* to have brought your surgeon, so that I might thank him for saving your arm.' Elizabeth had been uncharacteristically angry when she had learned of her husband's wound, remonstrating with him that he had doubtless exposed himself unnecessarily, just as the war was over and she might reasonably expect to have him home permanently. Drinkwater had not argued; in essence she was quite right and he understood her fear of widowhood.

'Oh,' chuckled Drinkwater, 'Mr Kennedy is not a man for this sort of social occasion.'

'I shall write to him, nevertheless.'

'He would appreciate that very much.'

Ahead of them the bride and groom, now Lieutenant and Mrs Frederic Marlowe, turned into Albemarle Street, followed by the best man and brother-in-law to the groom, Lieutenant Josiah Ashton. Only a very sharp-eyed and uncharitable observer would have remarked the bride's condition as expectant,

356

or her white silk dress as a trifle reprehensible in the circumstances.

Sarah looked round and smiled at the little column behind her and her husband. A gallant, pausing on the corner, raised his beaver as a compliment.

'Damned pretty girl,' Drinkwater remarked.

'And I don't mean you to turn into a country squire with an eye to every comely young woman,' Elizabeth chid him.

'I doubt that I shall turn into anything other than what you wish, my dear,' Drinkwater said smoothly, then watched apprehensively as a small dog ran up and down the party, yapping with excitement.

They had just turned into and crossed Albemarle Street when a man stepped out of a doorway in the act of putting on his hat. He almost bumped into Drinkwater and recoiled with an apology.

'I do beg your pardon sir.' The gleam of recognition kindled in his eye. 'Ah, it is Captain Drinkwater, is it not? Good morning to you.'

Drinkwater recognized him at once and stopped. Behind them Frey and Catriona Quilhampton were forced to follow suit.

'Why Mr Barrow!' He turned to his wife. 'Elizabeth, may I present Mr Barrow, Second Secretary to their Lordships at the Admiralty. Mr Barrow, my wife . . .'

Barrow removed his hat and bent over Elizabeth's extended hand.

'I am delighted to make your acquaintance, Mrs Drinkwater. I have long esteemed your husband.'

'Thank you, sir. So have I.'

'Mr Barrow,' Drinkwater said hurriedly, 'may I present Lieutenant Frey, a most able officer and an accomplished artist and surveyor, and Mrs Catriona Quilhampton, widow of the late Lieutenant James Quilhampton, a most deserving officer . . .'

'Madam, my sympathies. I recall your husband died in the Vikkenfiord.' Barrow displayed his prodigious memory with a courtly smile and turned to Frey. 'I have just called on Murray the publisher, Mr Frey, perhaps you should offer some of your watercolours for engraving; I presume you do watercolours . . .'

'Indeed, sir, yes, often at sea of conspicuous features, islands and the like.' Frey was conscious of being put on the spot.

'Well perhaps Mr Murray might consider them for publication; could you supply some text? The observations and jottings of a naval officer during the late war, perhaps? Now I should think the public might take a great liking to that, such is their thirst for glory at the moment.'

'I, er, I am not certain, sir . . .'

'Well,' said Barrow briskly, 'nothing ventured, nothing gained. I must get on and you have fallen far behind your party.'

They drew apart and then Barrow swung back. 'Oh, Captain, I almost forgot, I have a letter for you from Bushey Park. Are you staying in Lord North Street?'

'Indeed.'

'Very well, I shall have it sent round; it will be there by the time you have concluded your present business . . .' Barrow looked up the street at the retreating wedding party. 'The Marlowe wedding I presume.'

'Yes.'

'Well, I wish them joy. Mesdames, gentlemen, good day.' And raising his hat again, Barrow was gone.

'What an extraordinary man,' observed Elizabeth.

'Yes, he is, and a remarkable one as well. Frey, I hope you did not mind my mentioning your talent.'

'You flattered me over much, sir.'

'Not at all, Frey, not at all. Mr Barrow is an influential body and not one you can afford to ignore.' Drinkwater nodded at the brass plate on the door from which Barrow had just emerged, adding, 'And he is a man of diverse parts. He contributes to *The Quarterly Review* for Mr Murray, I understand. Now we must step out, or be lost to our hosts.'

'What is the significance of a letter from Bushey Park, Nathaniel?' Elizabeth asked as they hurried on.

'It is the residence of Prince William Henry, my dear.'

'The Duke of Clarence?'

'The same. And admiral-of-the-fleet to boot.'

'Lord, lord,' remarked Elizabeth smiling mockingly, 'I wonder what so august a prince has to say to my husband?'

'I haven't the remotest idea,' Drinkwater replied, but the news cast a shadow over the proceedings, ending the period of carefree irresponsibility Drinkwater had enjoyed since leaving Angra and replacing it with a niggle of worry.

'One would think,' he muttered to himself, 'that a cracked arm would be sufficient to trouble a man.'

'I did not quite catch you,' Elizabeth said as they reached Lothian's Hotel.

'Nothing, m'dear, nothing at all.'

*   *   *

'Congratulations, Frederic; she is a most beautiful young woman and you are a fortunate man.' Drinkwater raised his glass.

'I owe you a great deal, sir,' said Marlowe, looking round at the glittering assembly.

'Think nothing of it, my dear fellow.'

'There was a time when the prospect of this day seemed as remote as meeting the Great Chan.'

'Or Napoleon himself!' Drinkwater jested.

'Indeed, sir.'

'It is a curious fact about the sea-officer's life,' Drinkwater expanded, warmed by the wine and the cordiality of the occasion, 'that it is almost impossible to imagine yourself in a situation you knew yourself to have been in a sennight past.'

'I know exactly what you mean, sir.'

'The past is often meaningless; enjoy the present, it is all we have.' Drinkwater ignored the insidious promptings of ghosts and smiled.

'That is very true.' Marlowe sipped at his wine.

'How is Ashton?' Drinkwater asked, looking at the young officer across the room where he was in polite conversation with an elderly couple.

'As decent a fellow as can be imagined. Shall I forgive him the past too?'

'If you have a mind to. It is sometimes best; though I should keep him at arm's length and not be eager to confide over much in him.'

'No, no, of course not.' Marlowe paused and smiled at a passing guest.

'I am keeping you from your duties.'

'Not at all, sir. I should consider it an honour to meet your wife, sir.'

'Oh, good heavens, forgive me . . .'

They walked over to where Elizabeth was in conversation with Lieutenant Hyde and a young woman whose name Drinkwater did not know but who seemed much attached to the handsome marine officer.

'Excuse me,' he interjected, 'Elizabeth, may I present Frederic Marlowe . . .'

Marlowe bowed over Elizabeth's hand. 'I wished to meet you properly, ma'am. Receiving guests at the door is scarcely decent . . .'

'I'm honoured, Mr Marlowe. You are to be congratulated upon your bride's loveliness.'

'Thank you ma'am. I should like to say . . .' Marlowe shot an imploring glance at Drinkwater who tactfully turned to Hyde and his young belle.

'You have the advantage of me, Mr Hyde . . .'

'I have indeed, sir. May I present Miss Cassandra Wilcox . . .'

Drinkwater looked into a pair of fine blue eyes which were surrounded by long lashes and topped by an intricate pile of blonde hair. 'I fear I am out of practice for such becoming company, Miss Wilcox, you will have to forgive an old man.'

'Tush, Captain, you are not old . . .'

'Oh, old enough for Mr Hyde and his fellows to refer to me as Our Father,' said Drinkwater laughing and catching Hyde's eye.

'How the devil did you know, sir?' queried Hyde, eyebrows raised in unaffected surprise.

'Oh, the wisdom of the omnipotent, Mr Hyde. It was my business to know.' Drinkwater smiled at Miss Wilcox. 'Have you known Mr Hyde long, Miss Wilcox?'

'No sir, we met at Sir Quentin's two nights ago.'

'We sang a duet, sir . . . at Marlowe's father's,' Hyde added, seeing Drinkwater's puzzlement.

'Ah yes, of course, he is the gentleman in plum velvet.'

'The rather *large* gentleman in plum velvet,' added Miss Wilcox mischievously, leaning forward confidentially and treating Drinkwater to a view of her ample bosom. She seemed an ideal companion for the flashy Hyde.

'Would you oblige me by introducing me, Hyde?'

'Of course, sir.'

'Miss Wilcox, it has been a pleasure. I shall detain Hyde but a moment.' Drinkwater bowed and Cassandra Wilcox curtseyed.

'Is Frey about to strangle himself in the noose of matrimony, sir?' Hyde asked as they crossed the carpet to where Sir Quentin, a large, florid man as unlike his heir as could be imagined, guffawed contentedly amid a trio of admiring ladies.

'It very much looks like it, don't it.' Drinkwater looked askance at Hyde. 'You do not approve?'

'She is his senior, I'd say,' Hyde said with a shrug, 'by a margin.'

'But a deserving soul and Frey is a man of great compassion. What about yourself and Miss Wilcox?'

'A man must have a reason for staying in town, sir, or at this season for visiting in the country . . . Excuse me, ladies; Sir Quentin, may I introduce Captain Nathaniel Drinkwater?'

It was a pleasant stroll across St James's Park towards the abbey. They walked in silence for a while and then Elizabeth, casting a quick look over her shoulder at Frey and Catriona Quilhampton who lingered behind them, remarked, 'You seem to have made an impression on young Frederic Marlowe, my dear.'

Drinkwater grunted. 'What did he have to say?'

'Rather a lot. He said you saved him from a fate worse than death.'

'I'd say that was rather overstating matters. He was simply in some distress, both personally and professionally. He was concerned at the unexpected delay in our return to London . . .'

'Ah,' observed Elizabeth perceptively, 'then the lady *was* expecting.'

'Good heavens, Bess, do you miss nothing!'

'And professionally?' Elizabeth prompted.

'Oh he had had some experience that had not passed off well. He was unsure of himself.'

'A bit like Humpty-Dumpty? Only in this case the king's men did put him back together again?'

'Yes,' laughed Drinkwater, looking at his wife. 'Damn it, Elizabeth, but you are a lovely woman.'

The letter from Bushey was waiting for them when they arrived at the house in Lord North Street. Williams handed it to Drinkwater on a salver and, after he had struggled for a moment one-handed, Elizabeth rescued him from his embarrassment just as Catriona and Frey entered the room.

'Some tea, Williams, I think,' Elizabeth ordered as the company sat.

'How is the arm. sir?' Frey asked.

'Oh, pretty well. Not for the first time Kennedy saved me, though I suspect he rather wished I had got my just deserts.'

'Nathaniel! That's an ungrateful thing to say!' Elizabeth was profoundly shocked.

'Oh, you don't know Kennedy, m'dear.' Drinkwater flicked open the letter, read it while the company waited – all by now aware of the writer – expectantly watching Drinkwater's face.

'Well?' Elizabeth asked, as, expressionless, Drinkwater laid the letter in his lap.

'Well what?'

'What news? What does His Royal Highness write to you about? Or is it more secrets?'

'No, no.' Drinkwater took a deep breath. 'He has promised Birkbeck, who was my especial concern, a dockyard post.'

'That is good news, sir,' commented Frey approvingly.

'Yes.'

'And . . .?' Elizabeth prompted and then, when Drinkwater sat silently, fisted her hands and beat them into her lap. 'Oh, Nathaniel, why do you have to be so tiresome? Either tell us, or say you cannot!'

Drinkwater looked up with a familiar, wry smile upon his face. 'Well, my dear, His Royal Highness,' he said the words with sonorous and deferential dignity, 'has been so impressed with the actions of *Andromeda* and, though modesty prevents me from laying undue emphasis upon the point, with my services . . .'

'Oh, Nathaniel, please go on, you are submitting us to the most excruciating torture.'

'Please do tell us,' put in Frey.

'Catriona, m'dear,' Drinkwater appealed to his red-haired guest, 'surely you don't want to hear this nonsense?'

'Oh, but I surely do,' Catriona replied in her soft Scots burr.

'Very well,' Drinkwater sighed. 'His Royal Highness has been graciously pleased to suggest I am made a knight-commander of the Bath . . .'

'Why, sir,' exclaimed Frey leaping up from his chair, 'that is wonderful news!'

Drinkwater looked at his wife. She had gone quite pale and held both hands in front of her face while Catriona looked concernedly at her friend.

'You had better hear me out,' Drinkwater went on. 'His Royal Highness also says that since hauling down his flag, he is not presently in a position to recommend me, but that he,' Drinkwater unscrewed the letter and read aloud, '"will ever be completely sensible of the great service rendered to the nation by His Majesty's frigate *Andromeda* in the late action off the Azores and, should His Royal Highness be in a future position to honour Captain Drinkwater, His Royal Highness will be the first to acknowledge that debt in the aforementioned manner . . ."'

Drinkwater crushed the letter with a rueful laugh amid a perfect silence.

'I think it is time for bed. It has been a long and eventful day.' Drinkwater stretched and Frey tossed off his glass of *oporto*.

'Sir, before we retire I should like to acquaint you of my, of our, decision.'

'Of course, Frey. Pray go on.'

'You will have guessed,' Frey said, smiling, 'my proposal has been accepted.'

Drinkwater stood and held out his hand. 'Congratulations, my dear fellow.' They shook hands and Drinkwater said, 'I am glad you don't share Hyde's opinion of marriage.'

'What was that?'

'That it was a noose.'

'Doubtless Hyde would find it so.' Frey paused, adding, 'I know the lady to be . . .'

'Please say no more, my dear fellow. The lady has much to commend her and James would be pleased to know you care for Catriona, for her existence has not been easy. I am delighted; we shall be neighbours. Come, a last glass to drink to all our futures now that the war is at an end.'

'If not to your knighthood.'

'Ah, that . . .' Drinkwater shrugged. 'There is many a slip 'twixt the cup and the lip.'

Both men smiled across their glasses, then Drinkwater said, 'You know, in all the years I have been married, I have never been at home longer than a few months. Perhaps my permanent presence may not be an unalloyed joy to my wife.'

'That does not constitute a noose.'

'No, but I would not want it to be even a lanyard . . .' Drinkwater paused reflectively and Frey waited, knowing the sign of a germinating idea from the sudden abstraction. 'You will live at Woodbridge when you have spliced yourself with Catriona?' he asked at last.

'That is our intention, yes. I shall have only my half-pay and intend trying my hand at painting. Portraits perhaps.'

'That is a capital idea; portraits will be all the vogue now the war is over, but I too have an idea which might prevent any talk of nooses or the like.'

'I guessed you were hatching something.'

'What I am hatching is a little cutter. It occurs to me that the coming of peace and the decision of Their Lordships to break up the *Andromeda* leaves us without a ship. We could have a little cutter built at Woodbridge and I daresay for fifty pounds one could get a tolerable yacht knocked up . . .'

'*We*, sir?' Frey frowned.

'I daresay you'd ship occasionally as first luff with me, wouldn't you?'

'Oh,' said Frey grinning hugely, 'I daresay I might.'

Drinkwater nodded with satisfaction. 'Then the matter's settled.'

Author's Note

At the time of Napoleon's abdication, negotiations between Talleyrand and Tsar Alexander, who was then resident at the château of Bondy, were conducted by Caulaincourt and Count Mikhail Orlov. Among the subjects discussed was the most suitable place to exile Napoleon. St Helena and the Azores were suggested. In the event Elba was chosen, with the inevitable consequence that discontent at the resumption of Bourbon rule allowed Napoleon to return and seize power again, only to suffer final defeat at Waterloo in June 1815. Although it was to be Alexander who approved Elba in the teeth of opposition from the British and the Austrians, Alexander's complex but essentially vacillating, capricious and quixotic nature was such that so clement and generous a decision may easily have contradicted an earlier, harsh and extreme one. As the most charismatic sovereign among the crowned heads, the role of allied leader fell to Alexander almost by default. He had been captivated by the spell of Napoleon's personality and suborned by the insidious influence of Talleyrand. Alexander nevertheless saw himself as the implacable enemy of Napoleon, the usurper, who challenged the concept of legitimate monarchy with a new, unorthodox and dangerous creed.

From Alexander's meeting with Talleyrand at Erfurt in 1808, the wily Frenchman had begun manipulating the Tsar, insisting the peace of Europe rested with him, not to mention the future of France. Alexander's own position rested almost entirely upon two props; the weight of his armies, with their patient, peasant soldiery, and the British gold which kept them in the field. And along with the implicit expectations of Britain, he had to balance the demands of Austria. Both countries were represented by brilliant statesmen, Castlereagh and Metternich, whose intellects far surpassed Alexander's own. Among them all, however, Talleyrand must be regarded as the most able. He was careful to distance himself from the more disreputable goings-on, but we know he was distantly party to a number of stratagems which he doubtless encouraged as a means of distracting attention from his own plans. There was, for instance, a group who wished to assassinate Napoleon, so the humbling of Britain in the wake of the humiliation of Napoleon is a not improbable option considered during the negotiations between Bondy and Paris in the uncertain spring of 1814.

The atmosphere was thus ripe for plots by officers loyal to Napoleon, and there existed a number of these groups pledged to restore the Emperor. A growing Bonapartist faction laboured under the impositions of the first Bourbon restoration, increased the discontent among the middle classes and ensured Napoleon received a rapturous reception when he finally returned from his Elban exile. Most significant was the loyalty of the French army in its entirety. It is said that when the former Imperial Guard paraded for Louis XVIII, they had murder in their eyes.

As for Louis, I have taken few liberties with the sparse accounts of his Channel crossing. Prince William Henry had formerly commanded the frigate *Andromeda* and while accounts vary as to whether he was aboard the *Royal Sovereign*, the *Impregnable* or the *Jason* at the time of the return of the Bourbon king, I have followed Admiral Byam Martin's recollections, which seemed the most credible, as he knew the Prince well and had a low opinion of him. In a letter to his son, George FitzClarence, Prince William Henry himself boasted he commanded 'our fleet' off Calais. The squadron under his flag did, however, include French and Russian warships as well as the principal Trinity House yacht. A painting of the event was exhibited by Nicholas Pocock at the Royal Academy in 1815. HMS *Impregnable* was commanded by Henry Blackwood who had been captain of the *Euryalus* at Trafalgar. Blackwood had been created a baronet and hoisted his flag as an admiral before the end of 1814. Sir Peter Parker of the *Menelaus* was less fortunate; he was killed later that year in the United States near Baltimore, where he had landed to create a diversion during operations against the Americans.

During the period of Napoleon's exile on Elba, the allied plenipotentiaries assembled at Vienna to determine the future shape of Europe after the fall of Napoleon and break-up of the First French Empire. The congress was characterized by its dances more than its debates and the former allies nearly came to a renewed war, with Britain and Russia leading opposite factions. Napoleon's father-in-law, the Emperor Francis of Austria, was vigorously opposed to the deposed Emperor's presence so close to his own possessions in northern Italy, as well as against any further intimacy between Napoleon and his daughter, Marie-Louise. To effect the latter policy he appointed Count Neipperg to her entourage with instructions to seduce the Archduchess. Neipperg's successful debauchery ensured the intellectually dull Marie-Louise forgot her husband and, after Napoleon's death, married the one-eyed, but dashing count.

During the tortuous negotiations in Vienna and Napoleon's occupation of the Elban throne, his ultimate fate continued to be discussed, and both the Azores and St Helena were again suggested as possible final solutions to the problem of what to do with the quondam Emperor. At one point the purchase of an Azorean island from the Portuguese was considered. In the event, the dilatory nature of the debates, the increasing discontent in France and the refusal of Louis XVIII to pay Napoleon his pension, guaranteed a brief, heady success for Napoleon as he returned to France for what history knows as 'The Hundred Days'. The action however, immediately united the congress, which unanimously declared Napoleon an outlaw with the consequence of ultimate defeat for his cause at Waterloo, and his final exile on St Helena.

Taking advantage of the wranglings and intrigues at Vienna, Talleyrand skilfully rehabilitated France among the first rank of European powers. Indeed at one point when a new war seemed inevitable, the idea was mooted that Napoleon himself be brought home from exile in order to command French armies in the field against the Russian faction!

Thus was the eagle finally caged, though Captain Nathaniel Drinkwater was to play one last part in the drama during the Hundred Days.

Other bestselling Warner titles available by mail: